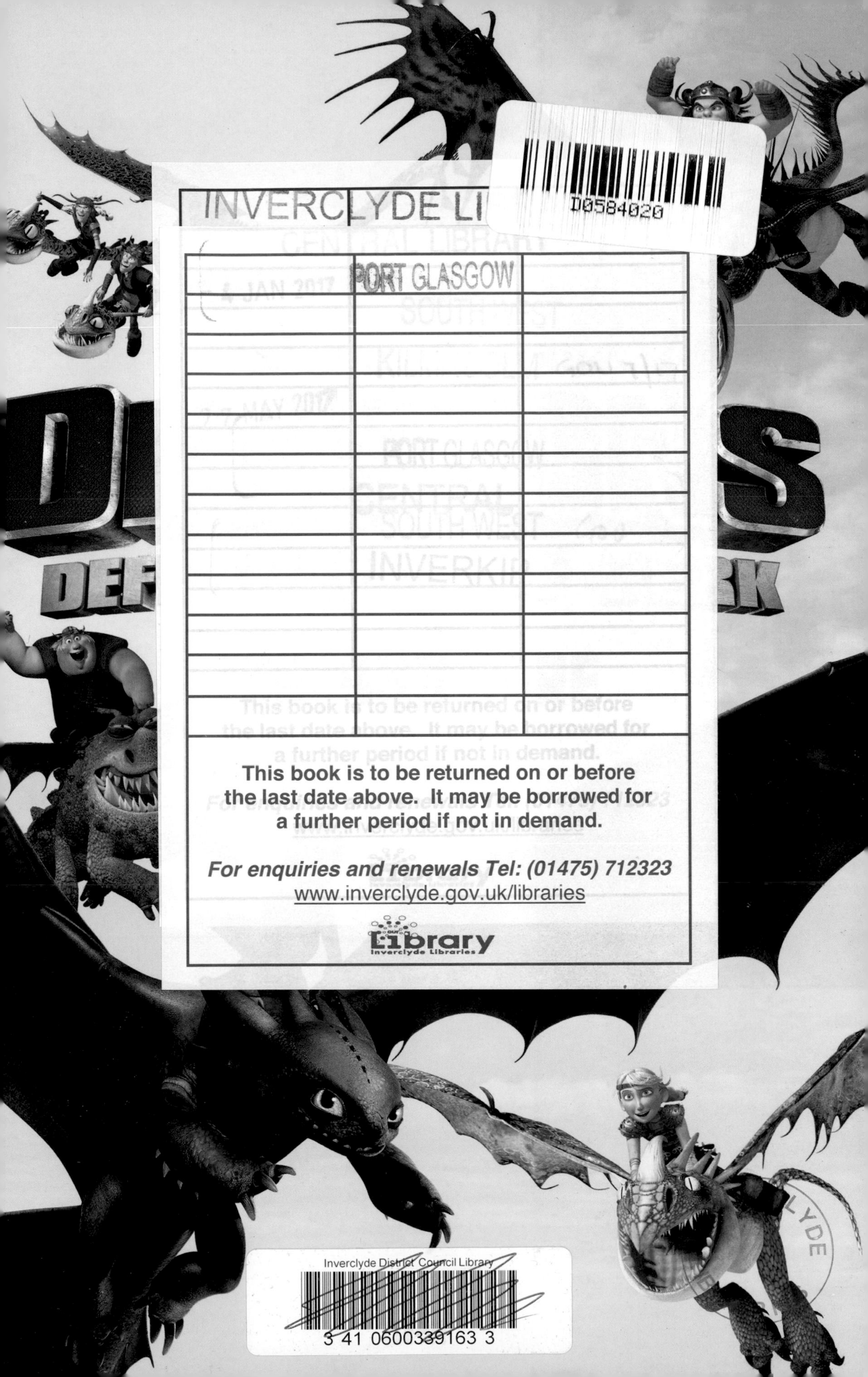

INVERCLYDE LIBRARIES

D0584020

	PORT GLASGOW	
4 JAN 2017		
2 7 MAY 2017		

**This book is to be returned on or before
the last date above. It may be borrowed for
a further period if not in demand.**

For enquiries and renewals Tel: (01475) 712323
www.inverclyde.gov.uk/libraries

Library
Inverclyde Libraries

Inverclyde District Council Library

3 41 0600339163 3

TITAN COMICS

Senior Editor
MARTIN EDEN

Production Manager
OBI ONUORA

Production Supervisors
JACKIE FLOOK,
MARIA PEARSON

Production Assistant
PETER JAMES

Senior Sales Manager
STEVE TOTHILL

**Direct Sales &
Marketing Manager**
RICKY CLAYDON

Publishing Manager
DARRYL TOTHILL

Publishing Director
CHRIS TEATHER

Operations Director
LEIGH BAULCH

Executive Director
VIVIAN CHEUNG

Publisher
NICK LANDAU

DreamWorks Dragons Defenders
of Berk: Ice and Fire
ISBN: 9781785856785

Published by Titan Comics,
a division of Titan Publishing Group Ltd.
144 Southwark St. London, SE1 0UP

DreamWorks Dragons: Defenders of Berk © 2016 DreamWorks Animation LLC. All Rights Reserved. No part of this publication may be reproduced, stored in a retrieval system, or transmitted, in any form or by any means, without the prior written permission of the publisher. Names, characters, places and incidents featured in this publication are either the product of the author's imagination or used fictitiously. Any resemblance to actual persons, living or dead (except for satirical purposes), is entirely coincidental.

10 9 8 7 6 5 4 3 2 1
First printed in China in October 2016.

A CIP catalogue record for this title is available from the British Library.

Titan Comics. TC1917

Special thanks to Corinne Combs, Barbara Layman, Lawrence Hamashima, Mike Sund, and all at DreamWorks. Thanks to Andre Siregar.

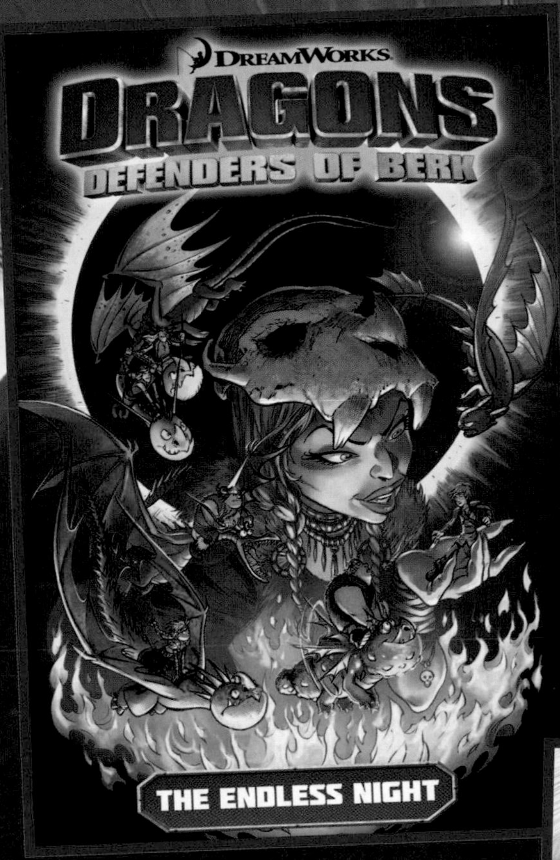
DreamWorks
DRAGONS
DEFENDERS OF BERK
THE ENDLESS NIGHT

THE ENDLESS NIGHT

A witch named Skuld the Sorceress threatens Berk with destruction… and she starts displaying her powers by making the skies turn black! What can the Dragon Defenders do to save their town?

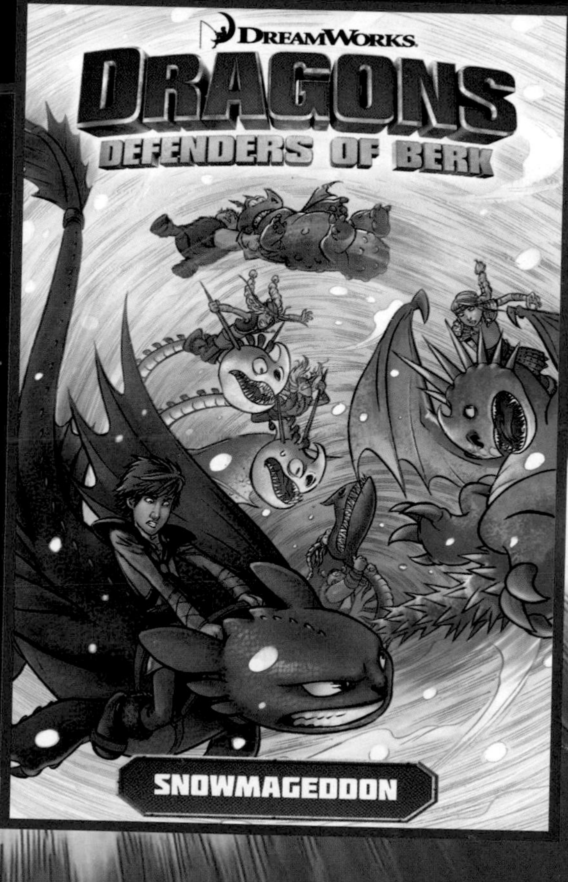
DreamWorks
DRAGONS
DEFENDERS OF BERK
SNOWMAGEDDON

SNOWMAGEDDON

Hiccup and his friends investigate the mystery of a nearby town that has gone quiet – and what they discover can only be described as… 'Snowmageddon!'

PLUS BONUS STORIES:

CRUEL TO BE KIND & THAW FLEET

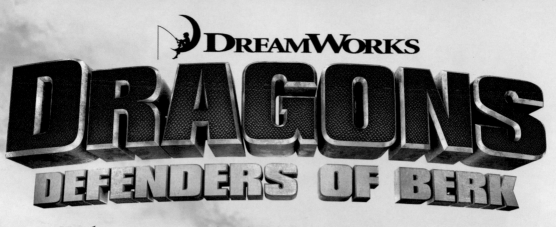

DreamWorks

DRAGONS
DEFENDERS OF BERK

Welcome to Berk, the home of Hiccup and his dragon, Toothless, plus Hiccup's friends who train at the Dragon Training Academy!

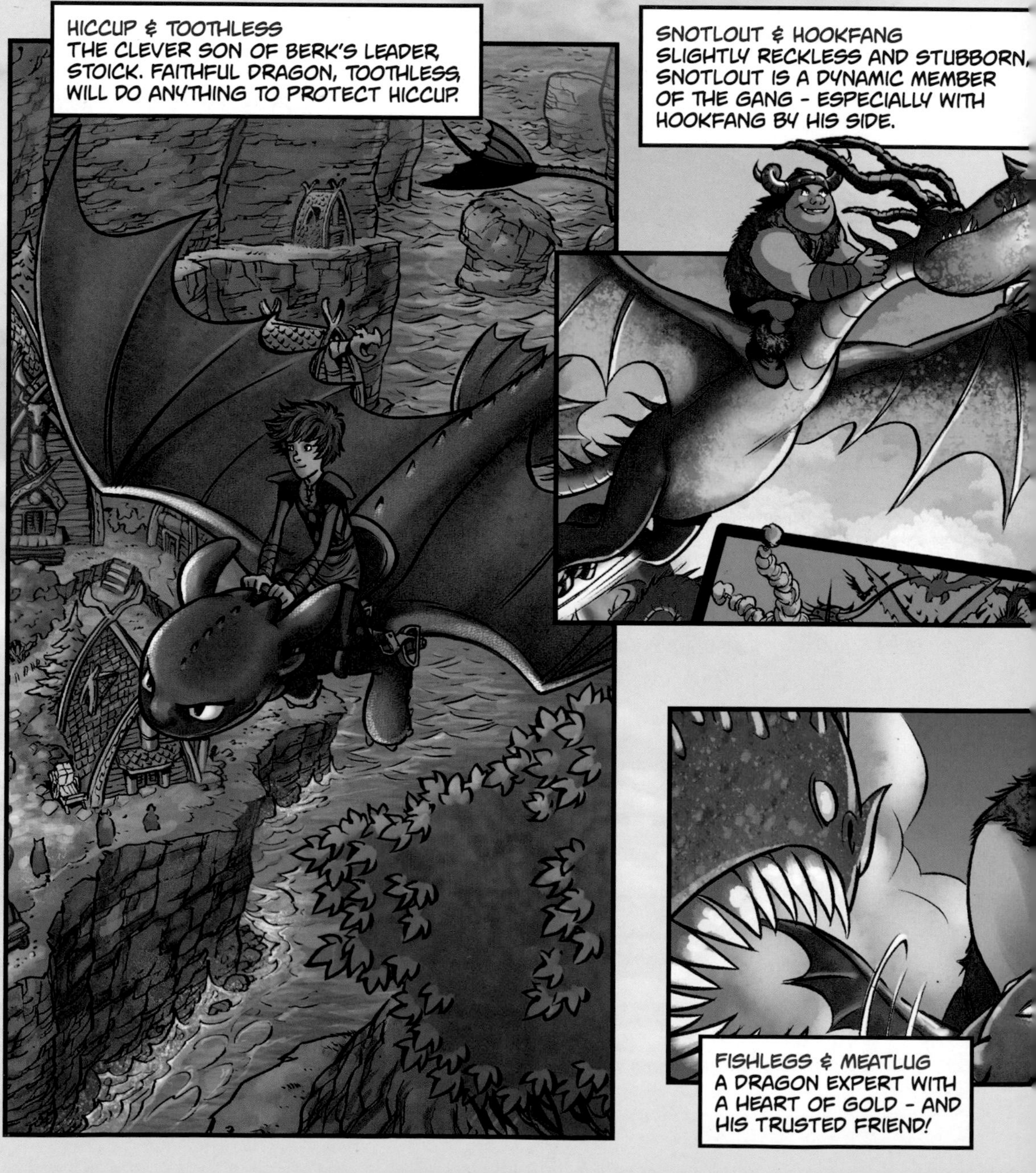
HICCUP & TOOTHLESS
THE CLEVER SON OF BERK'S LEADER, STOICK. FAITHFUL DRAGON, TOOTHLESS, WILL DO ANYTHING TO PROTECT HICCUP.
SNOTLOUT & HOOKFANG
SLIGHTLY RECKLESS AND STUBBORN, SNOTLOUT IS A DYNAMIC MEMBER OF THE GANG - ESPECIALLY WITH HOOKFANG BY HIS SIDE.
FISHLEGS & MEATLUG
A DRAGON EXPERT WITH A HEART OF GOLD - AND HIS TRUSTED FRIEND!

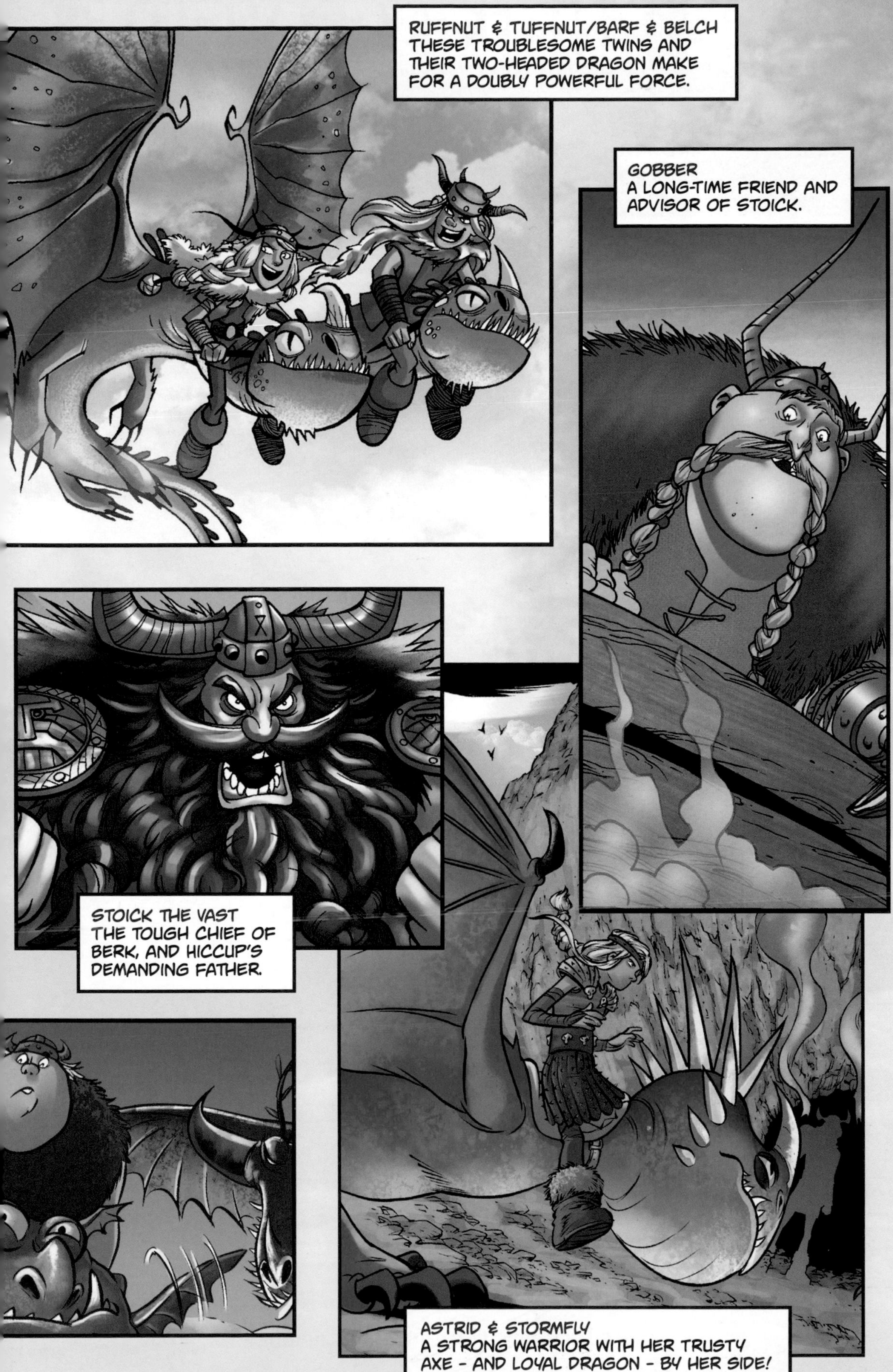

RUFFNUT & TUFFNUT/BARF & BELCH
THESE TROUBLESOME TWINS AND THEIR TWO-HEADED DRAGON MAKE FOR A DOUBLY POWERFUL FORCE.
GOBBER
A LONG-TIME FRIEND AND ADVISOR OF STOICK.
STOICK THE VAST
THE TOUGH CHIEF OF BERK, AND HICCUP'S DEMANDING FATHER.
ASTRID & STORMFLY
A STRONG WARRIOR WITH HER TRUSTY AXE - AND LOYAL DRAGON - BY HER SIDE!

THE ENDLESS NIGHT

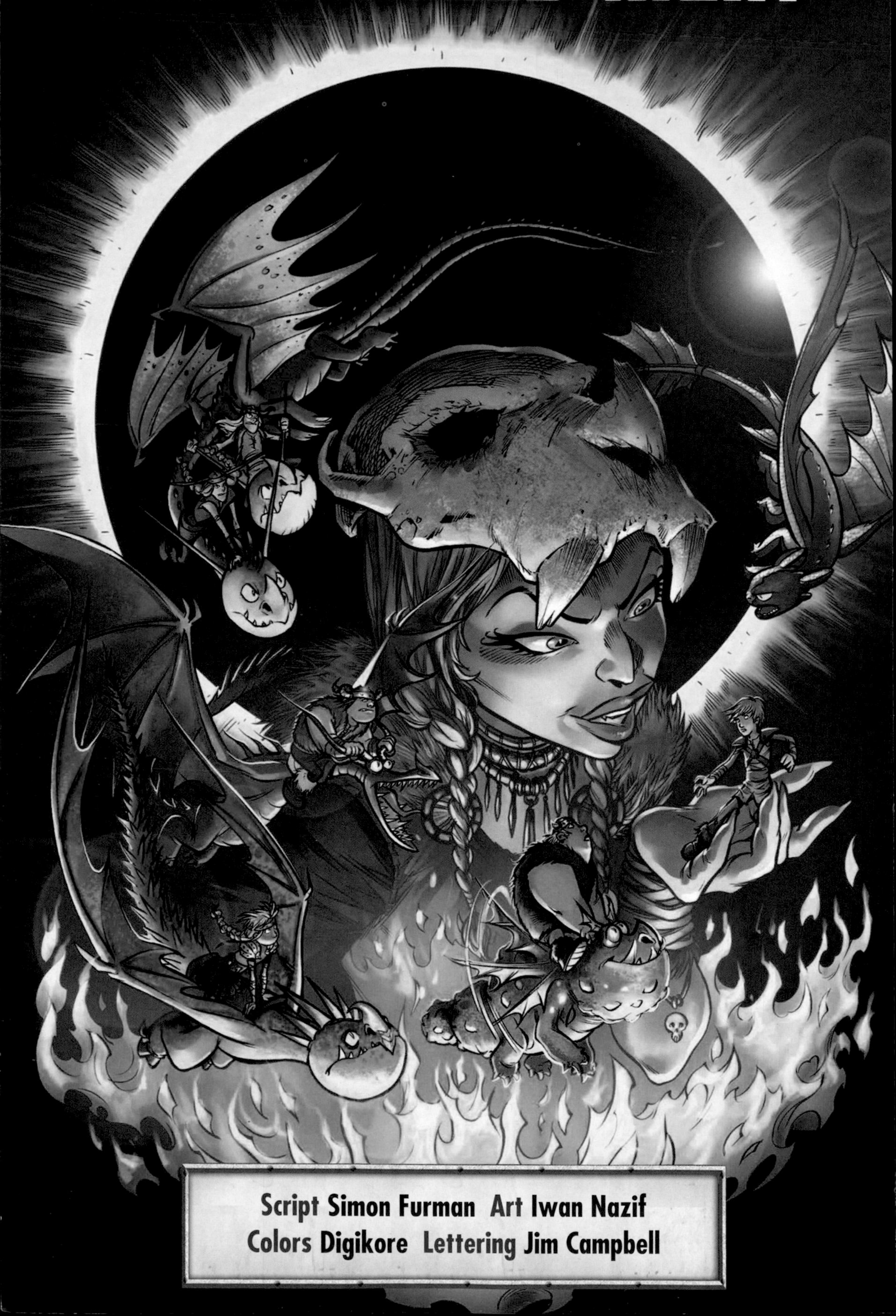
Script Simon Furman Art Iwan Nazif
Colors Digikore Lettering Jim Campbell

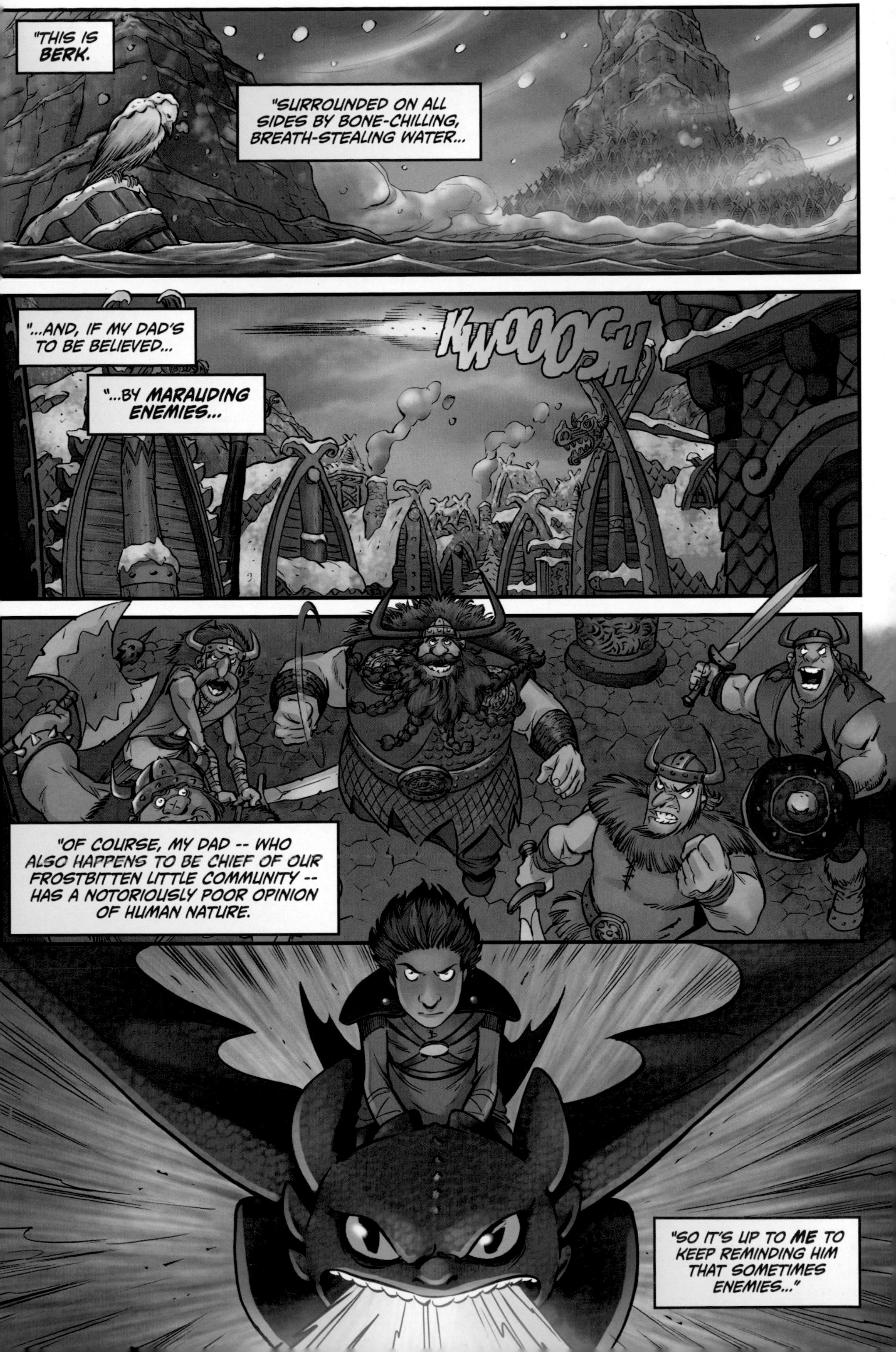
"THIS IS BERK.
"SURROUNDED ON ALL SIDES BY BONE-CHILLING, BREATH-STEALING WATER...
"...AND, IF MY DAD'S TO BE BELIEVED...
"...BY MARAUDING ENEMIES...
KWOOOSH
"OF COURSE, MY DAD -- WHO ALSO HAPPENS TO BE CHIEF OF OUR FROSTBITTEN LITTLE COMMUNITY -- HAS A NOTORIOUSLY POOR OPINION OF HUMAN NATURE.
"SO IT'S UP TO ME TO KEEP REMINDING HIM THAT SOMETIMES ENEMIES..."

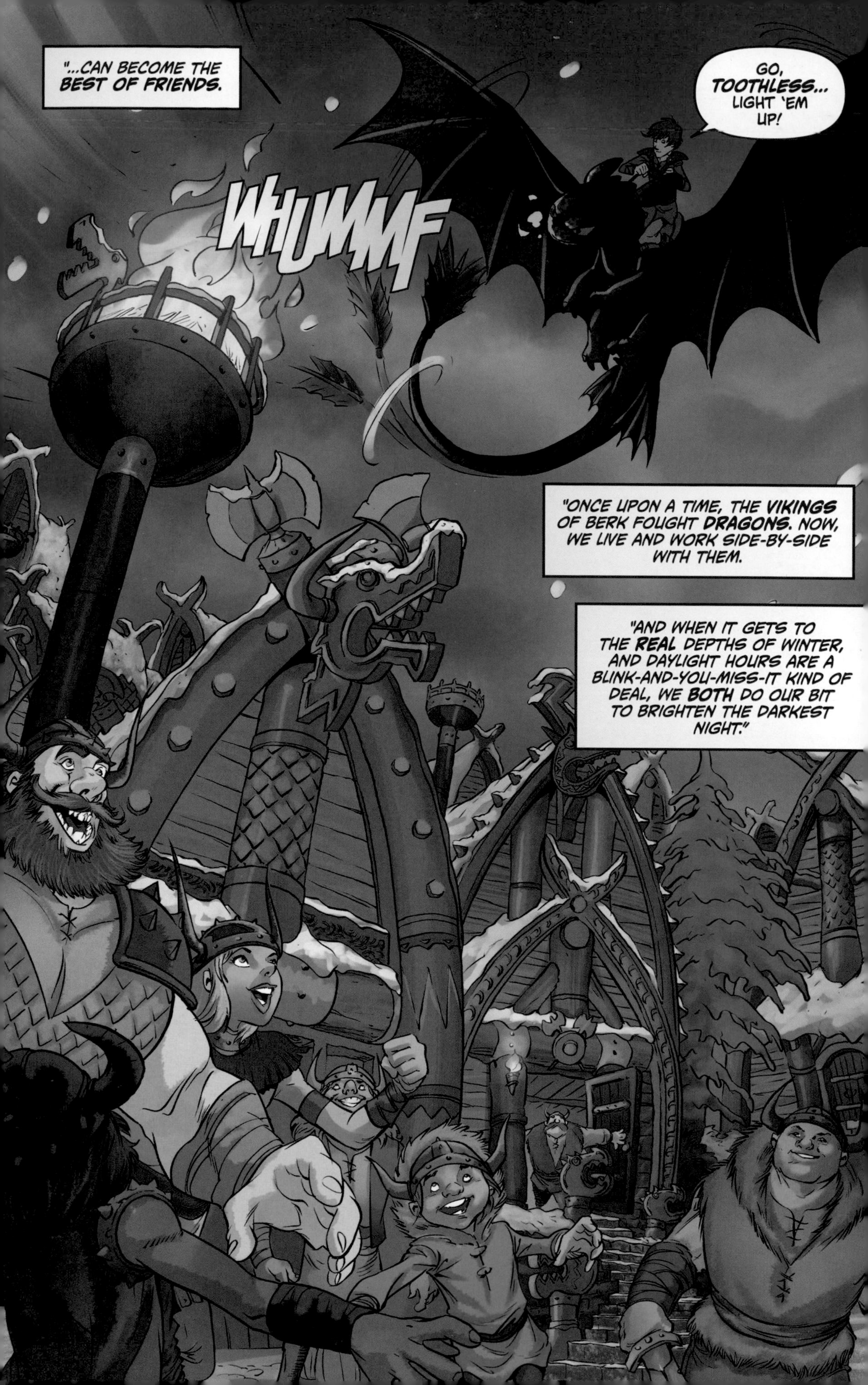
"...CAN BECOME THE BEST OF FRIENDS.
GO, TOOTHLESS... LIGHT 'EM UP!
WHUMMF
"ONCE UPON A TIME, THE VIKINGS OF BERK FOUGHT DRAGONS. NOW, WE LIVE AND WORK SIDE-BY-SIDE WITH THEM.
"AND WHEN IT GETS TO THE REAL DEPTHS OF WINTER, AND DAYLIGHT HOURS ARE A BLINK-AND-YOU-MISS-IT KIND OF DEAL, WE BOTH DO OUR BIT TO BRIGHTEN THE DARKEST NIGHT."

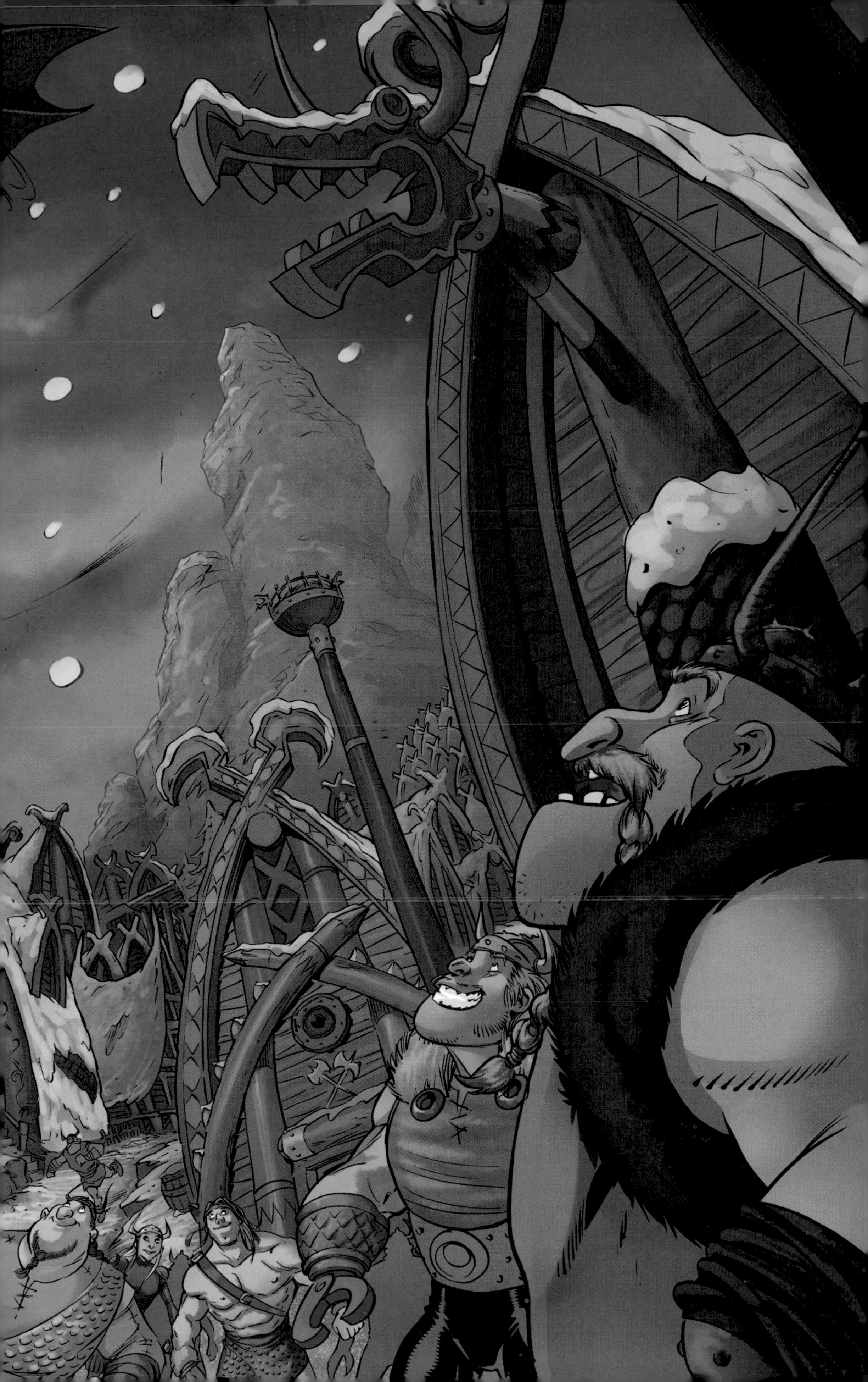

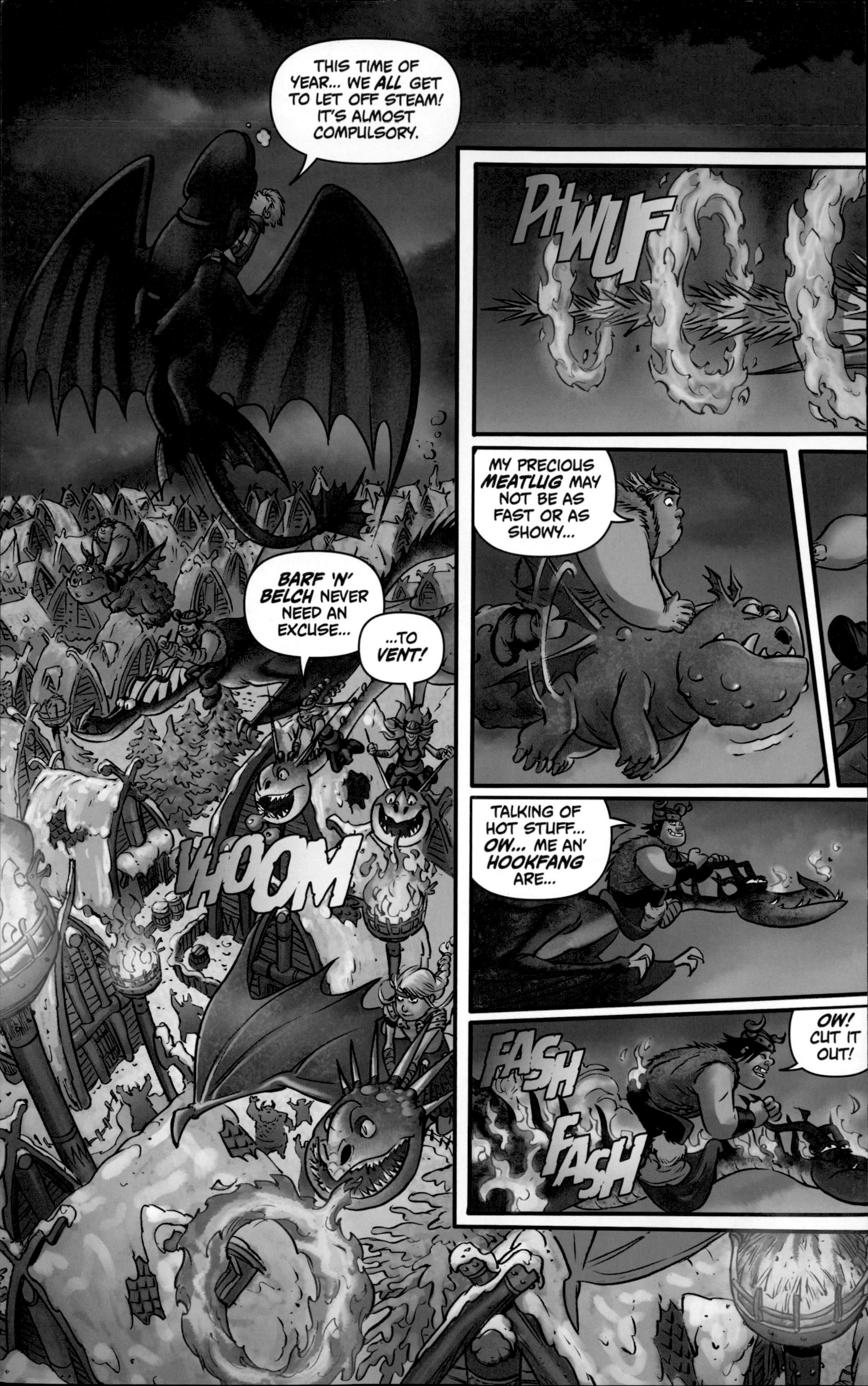
THIS TIME OF YEAR... WE ALL GET TO LET OFF STEAM! IT'S ALMOST COMPULSORY.
BARF 'N' BELCH NEVER NEED AN EXCUSE...
...TO VENT!
VHOOM
PHWUF
MY PRECIOUS MEATLUG MAY NOT BE AS FAST OR AS SHOWY...
TALKING OF HOT STUFF... OW... ME AN' HOOKFANG ARE...
FASH
FASH
OW! CUT IT OUT!

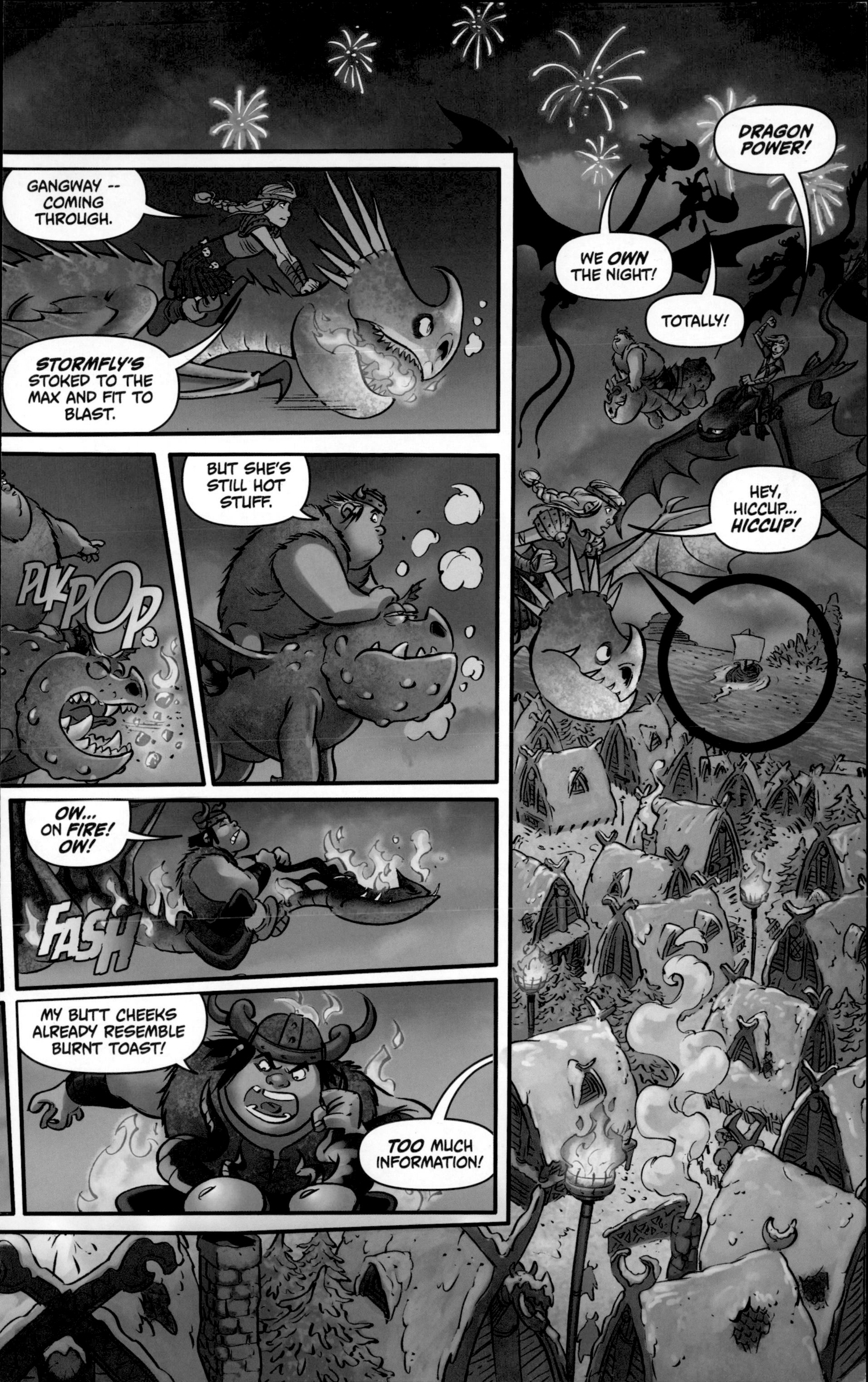
GANGWAY -- COMING THROUGH.
STORMFLY'S STOKED TO THE MAX AND FIT TO BLAST.
PUKPOP
BUT SHE'S STILL HOT STUFF.
OW... ON FIRE! OW!
FASH
MY BUTT CHEEKS ALREADY RESEMBLE BURNT TOAST!
TOO MUCH INFORMATION!
DRAGON POWER!
WE OWN THE NIGHT!
TOTALLY!
HEY, HICCUP... HICCUP!

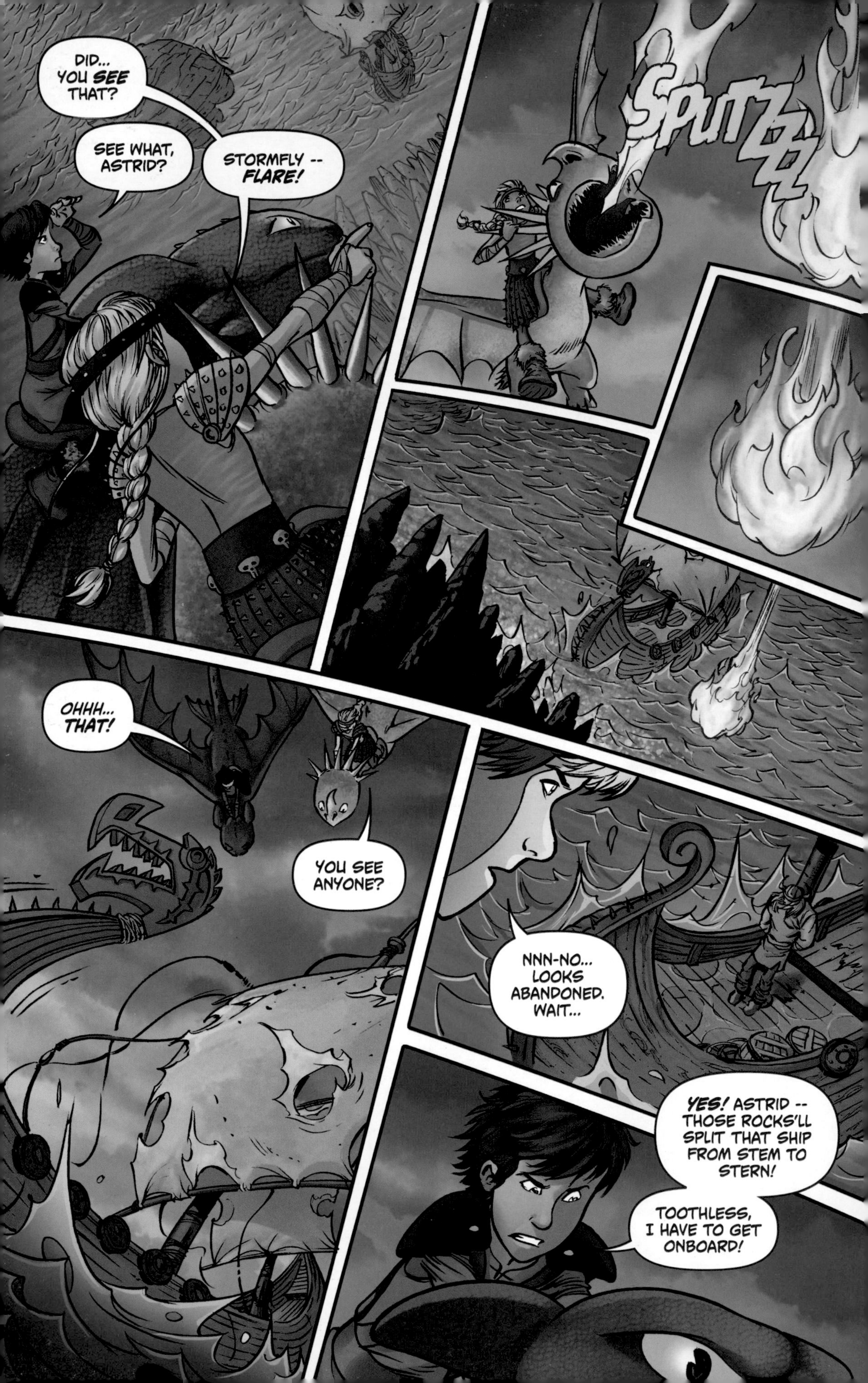
DID... YOU SEE THAT?
SEE WHAT, ASTRID?
STORMFLY -- FLARE!
SPUTZZZ
OHHH... THAT!
YOU SEE ANYONE?
NNN-NO... LOOKS ABANDONED. WAIT...
YES! ASTRID -- THOSE ROCKS'LL SPLIT THAT SHIP FROM STEM TO STERN!
TOOTHLESS, I HAVE TO GET ONBOARD!

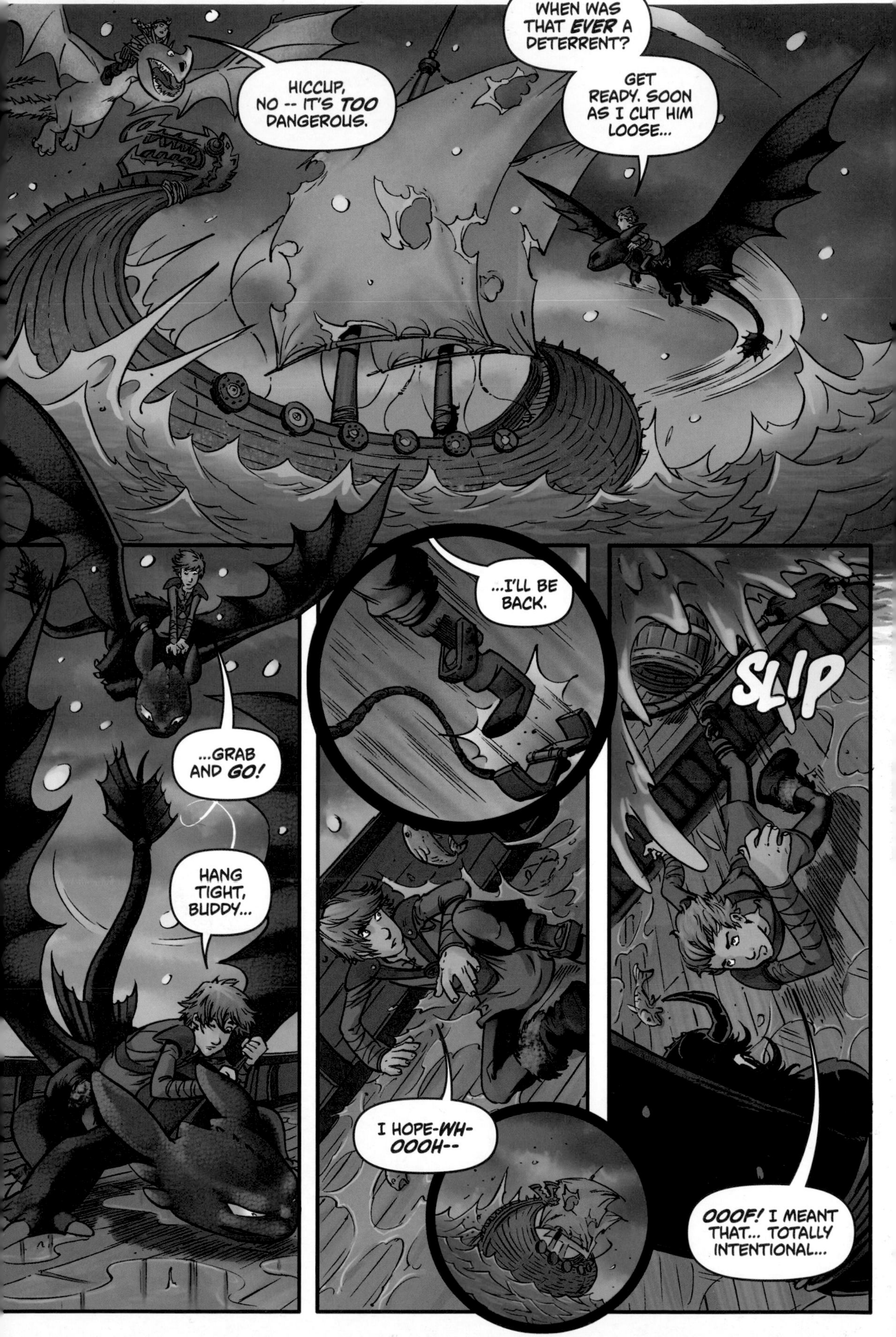
HICCUP, NO -- IT'S TOO DANGEROUS.
WHEN WAS THAT EVER A DETERRENT?
GET READY. SOON AS I CUT HIM LOOSE...
...GRAB AND GO!
HANG TIGHT, BUDDY...
...I'LL BE BACK.
I HOPE-WH-OOOH--
SLIP
OOOF! I MEANT THAT... TOTALLY INTENTIONAL...

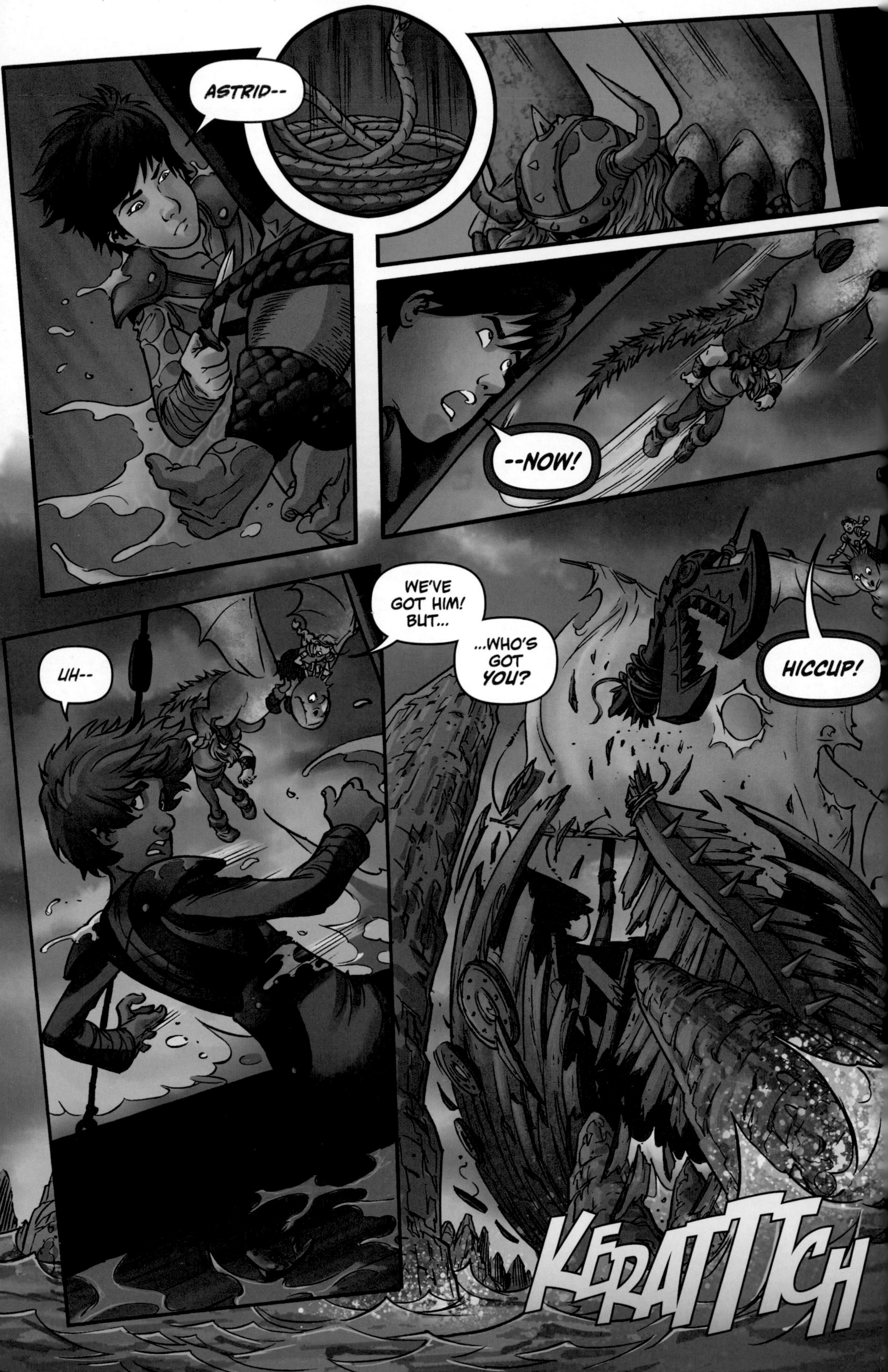
ASTRID--
--NOW!
UH--
WE'VE GOT HIM! BUT...
...WHO'S GOT YOU?
HICCUP!
KERATTTCH

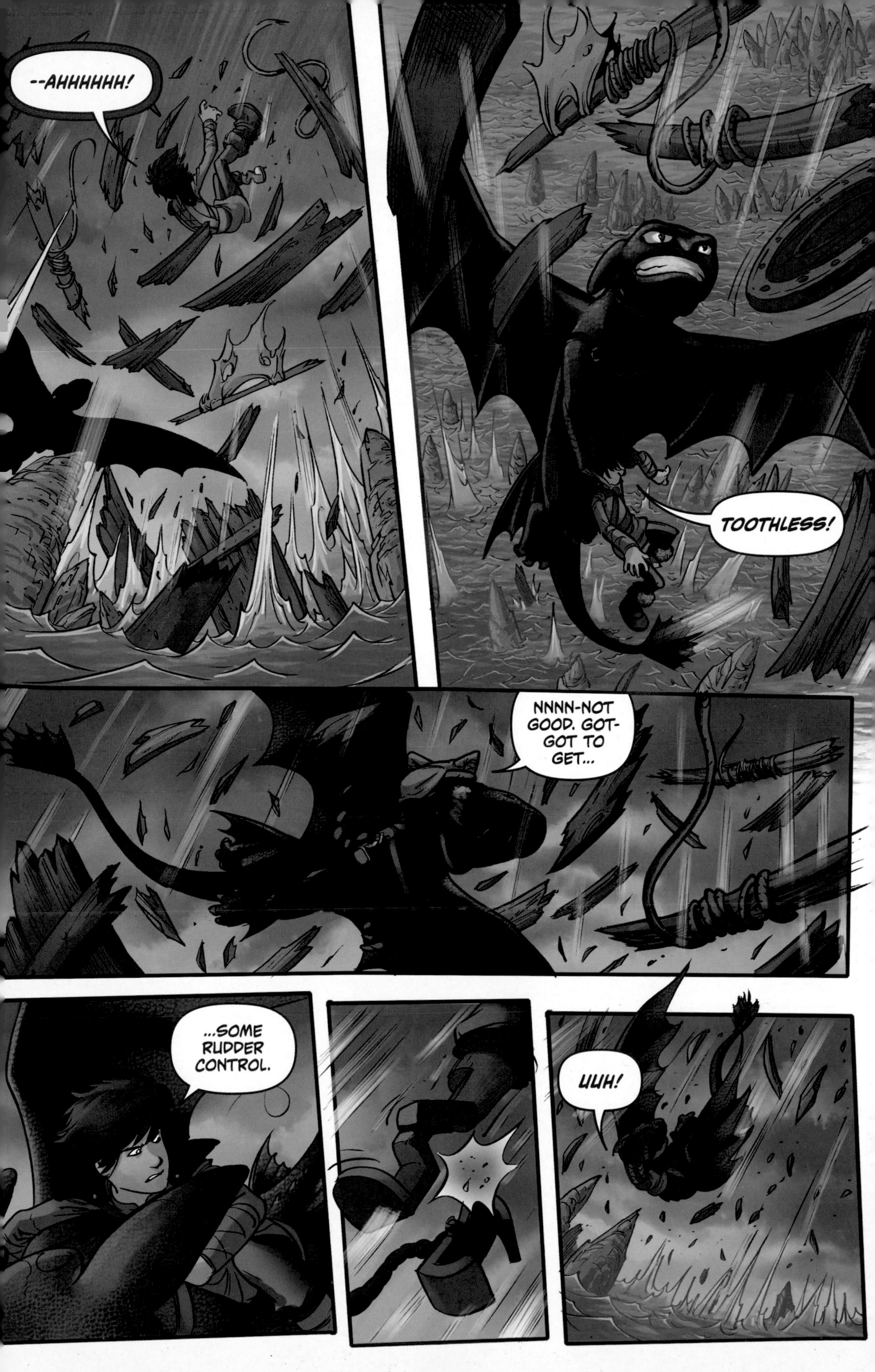
--AHHHHHH!
TOOTHLESS!
NNNN-NOT GOOD. GOT-GOT TO GET...
...SOME RUDDER CONTROL.
UUH!

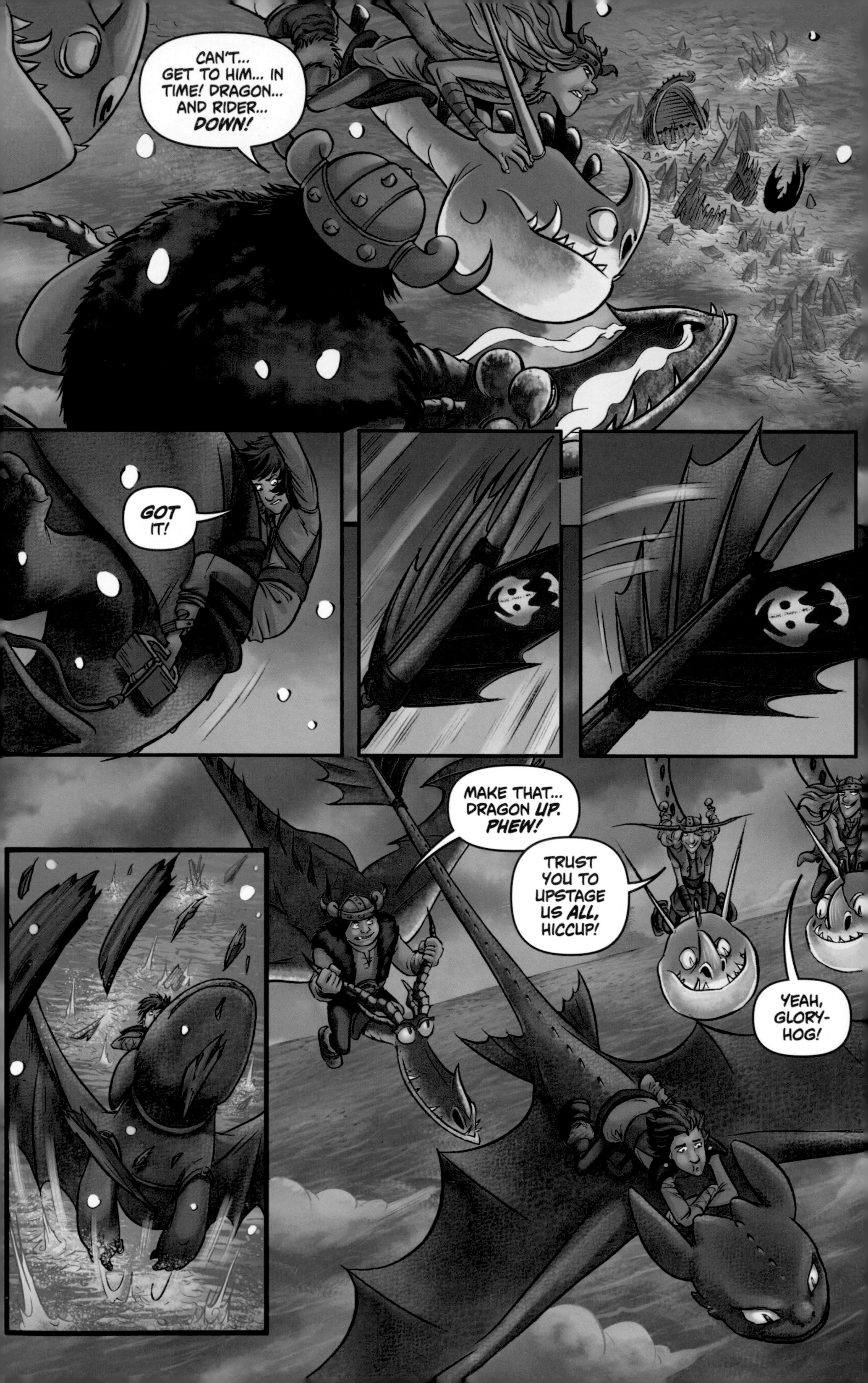
CAN'T... GET TO HIM... IN TIME! DRAGON... AND RIDER... DOWN!
GOT IT!
MAKE THAT... DRAGON UP. PHEW!
TRUST YOU TO UPSTAGE US ALL, HICCUP!
YEAH, GLORY-HOG!

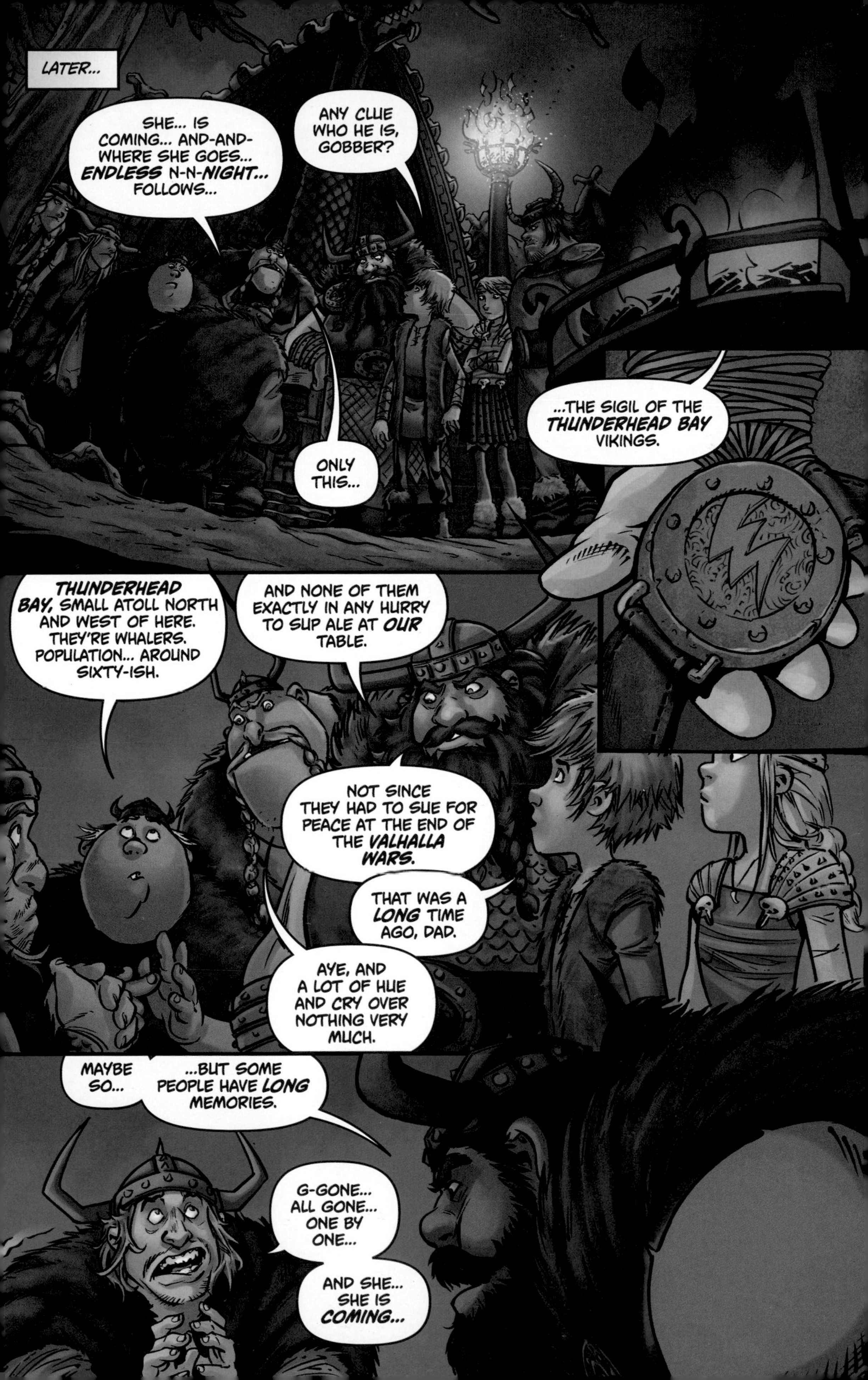
LATER...
SHE... IS COMING... AND-AND- WHERE SHE GOES... ENDLESS N-N-NIGHT... FOLLOWS...
ANY CLUE WHO HE IS, GOBBER?
ONLY THIS...
...THE SIGIL OF THE THUNDERHEAD BAY VIKINGS.
THUNDERHEAD BAY, SMALL ATOLL NORTH AND WEST OF HERE. THEY'RE WHALERS. POPULATION... AROUND SIXTY-ISH.
AND NONE OF THEM EXACTLY IN ANY HURRY TO SUP ALE AT OUR TABLE.
NOT SINCE THEY HAD TO SUE FOR PEACE AT THE END OF THE VALHALLA WARS.
THAT WAS A LONG TIME AGO, DAD.
AYE, AND A LOT OF HUE AND CRY OVER NOTHING VERY MUCH.
MAYBE SO...
...BUT SOME PEOPLE HAVE LONG MEMORIES.
G-GONE... ALL GONE... ONE BY ONE...
AND SHE... SHE IS COMING...

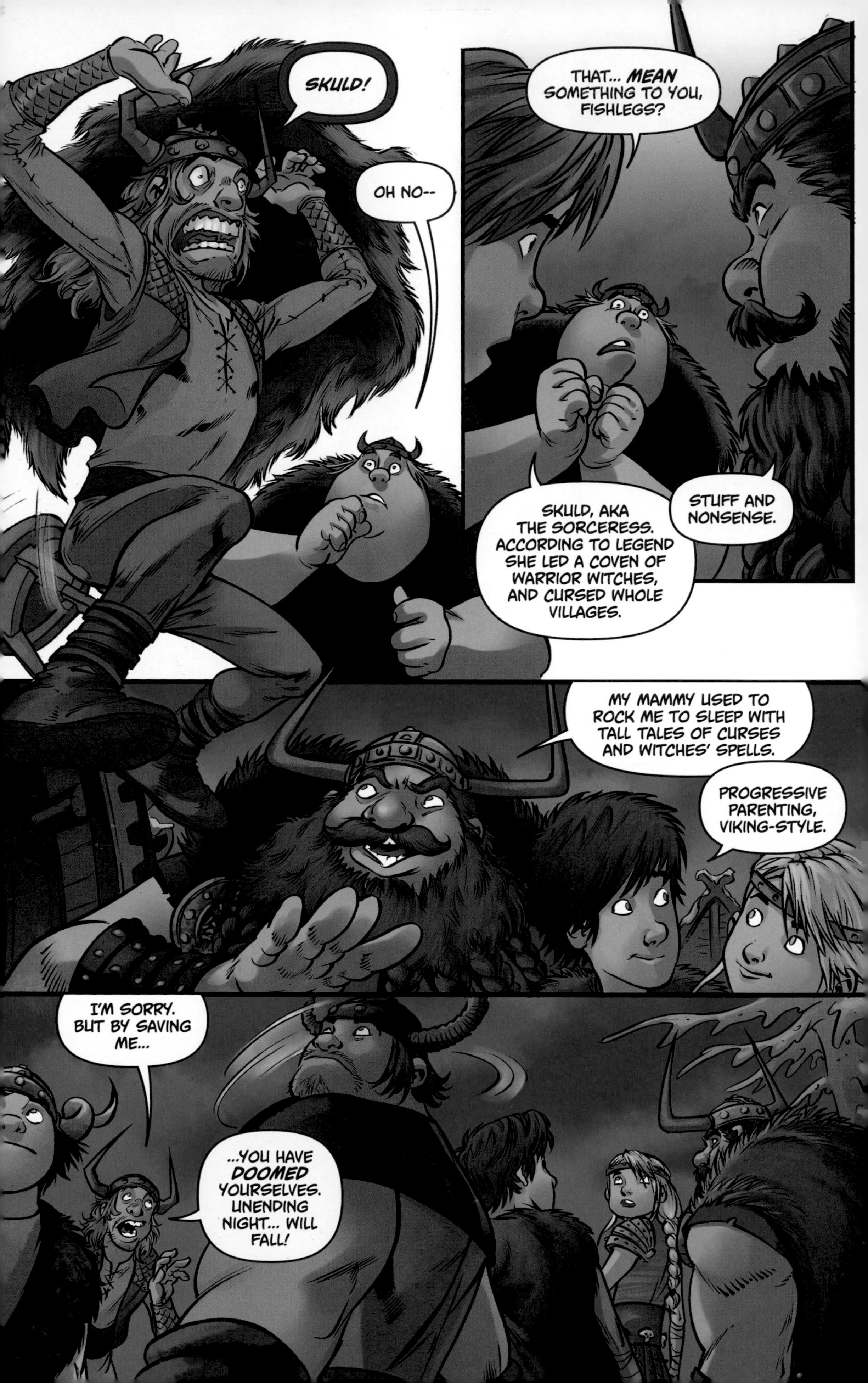
SKULD!
OH NO--
THAT... MEAN SOMETHING TO YOU, FISHLEGS?
SKULD, AKA THE SORCERESS. ACCORDING TO LEGEND SHE LED A COVEN OF WARRIOR WITCHES, AND CURSED WHOLE VILLAGES.
STUFF AND NONSENSE.
MY MAMMY USED TO ROCK ME TO SLEEP WITH TALL TALES OF CURSES AND WITCHES' SPELLS.
PROGRESSIVE PARENTING, VIKING-STYLE.
I'M SORRY. BUT BY SAVING ME...
...YOU HAVE DOOMED YOURSELVES. UNENDING NIGHT... WILL FALL!

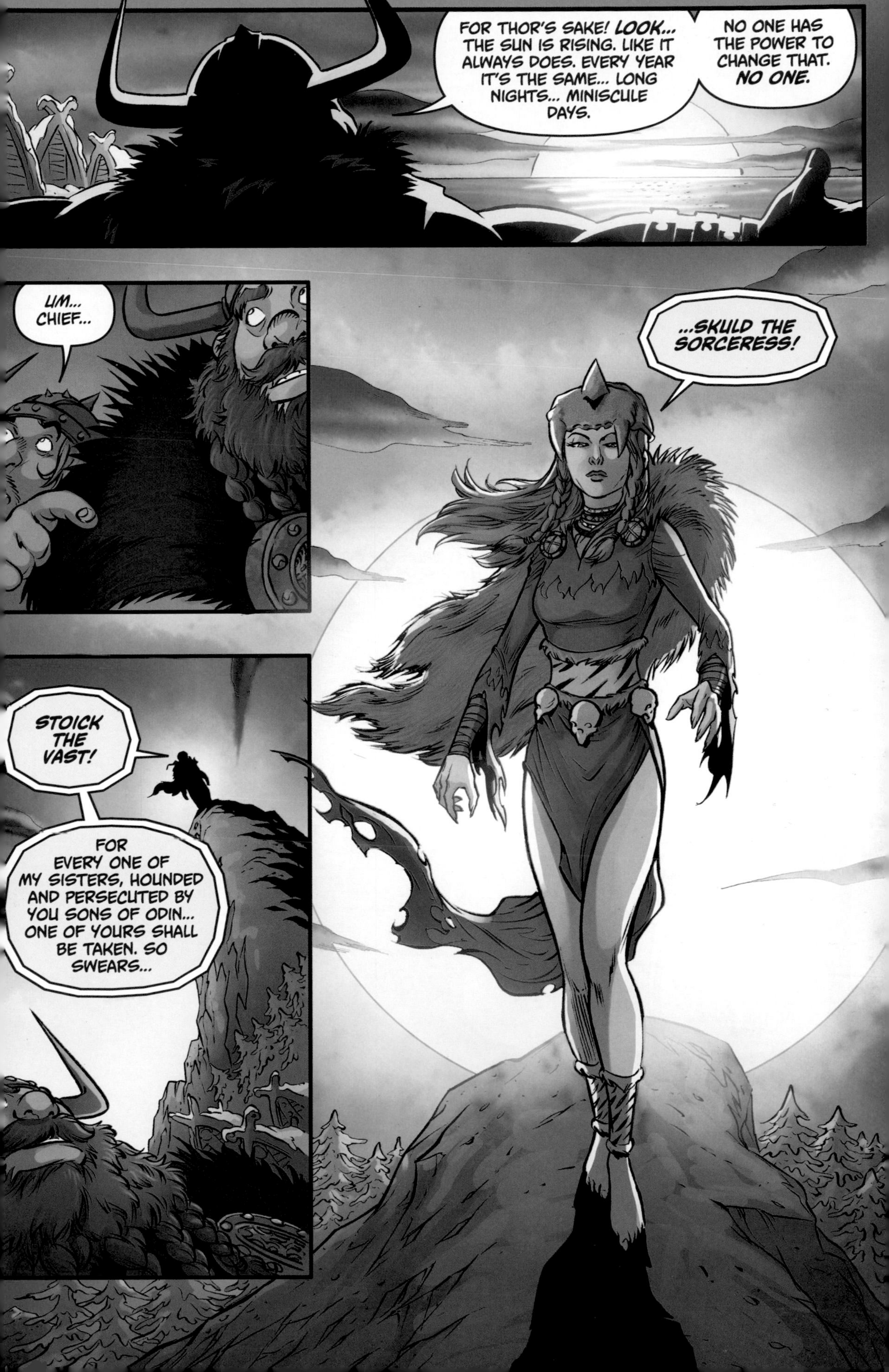
FOR THOR'S SAKE! LOOK... THE SUN IS RISING. LIKE IT ALWAYS DOES. EVERY YEAR IT'S THE SAME... LONG NIGHTS... MINISCULE DAYS.
NO ONE HAS THE POWER TO CHANGE THAT. NO ONE.
UM... CHIEF...
STOICK THE VAST!
FOR EVERY ONE OF MY SISTERS, HOUNDED AND PERSECUTED BY YOU SONS OF ODIN... ONE OF YOURS SHALL BE TAKEN. SO SWEARS...
...SKULD THE SORCERESS!

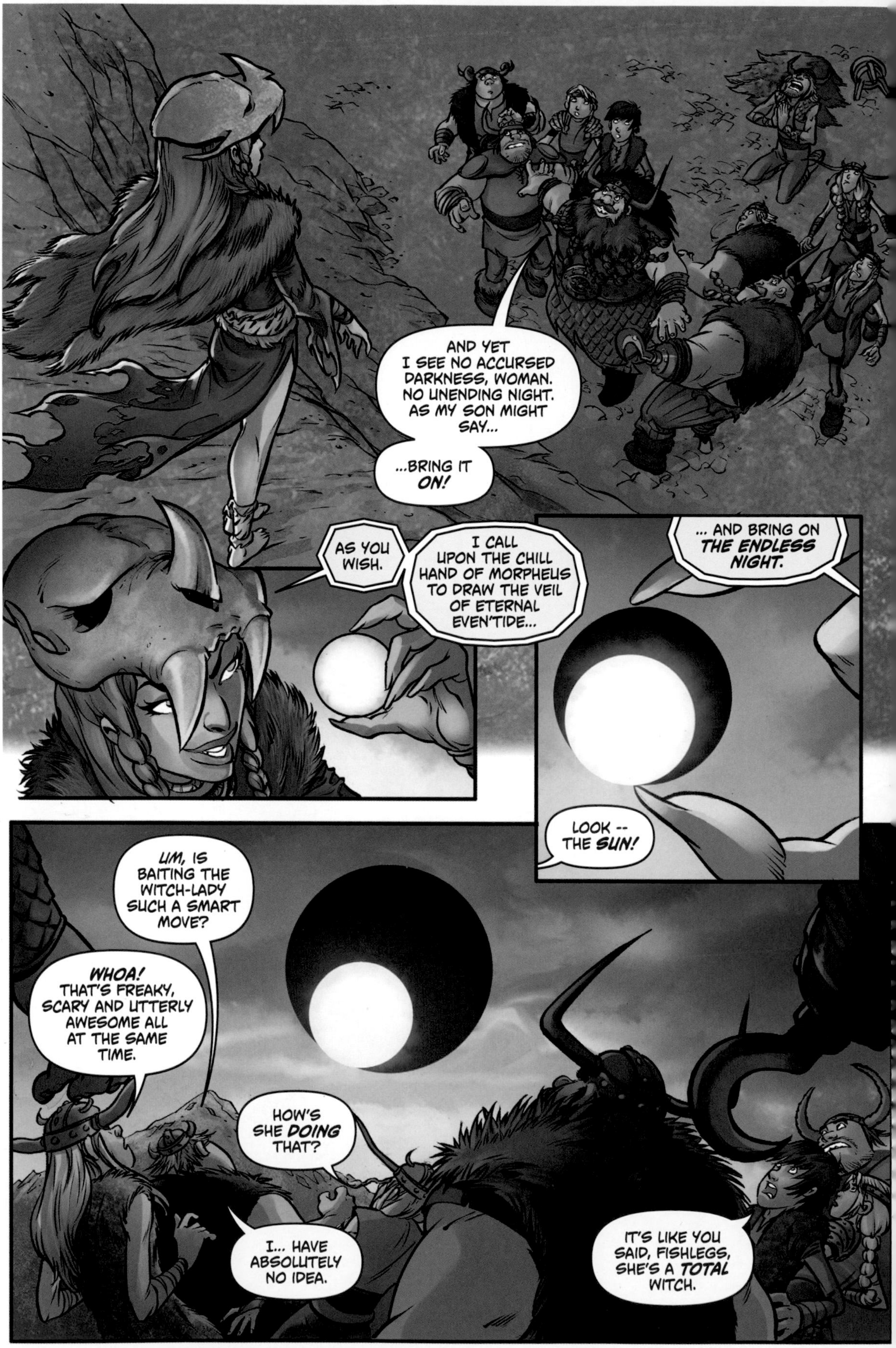
AND YET I SEE NO ACCURSED DARKNESS, WOMAN. NO UNENDING NIGHT. AS MY SON MIGHT SAY...
...BRING IT ON!
AS YOU WISH.
I CALL UPON THE CHILL HAND OF MORPHEUS TO DRAW THE VEIL OF ETERNAL EVEN'TIDE...
... AND BRING ON THE ENDLESS NIGHT.
LOOK -- THE SUN!
UM, IS BAITING THE WITCH-LADY SUCH A SMART MOVE?
WHOA! THAT'S FREAKY, SCARY AND UTTERLY AWESOME ALL AT THE SAME TIME.
HOW'S SHE DOING THAT?
I... HAVE ABSOLUTELY NO IDEA.
IT'S LIKE YOU SAID, FISHLEGS, SHE'S A TOTAL WITCH.

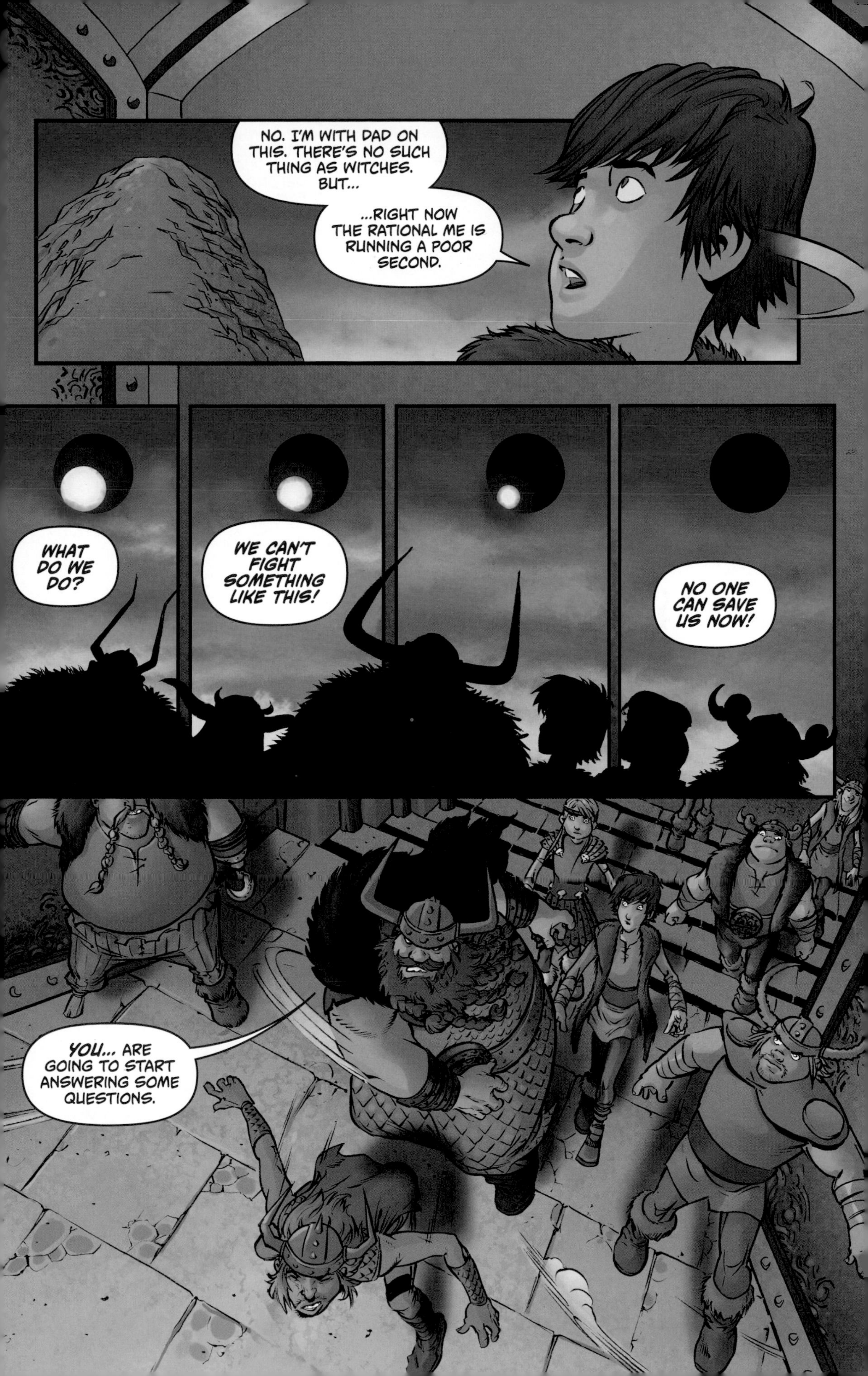
NO. I'M WITH DAD ON THIS. THERE'S NO SUCH THING AS WITCHES. BUT...
...RIGHT NOW THE RATIONAL ME IS RUNNING A POOR SECOND.
WHAT DO WE DO?
WE CAN'T FIGHT SOMETHING LIKE THIS!
NO ONE CAN SAVE US NOW!
YOU... ARE GOING TO START ANSWERING SOME QUESTIONS.

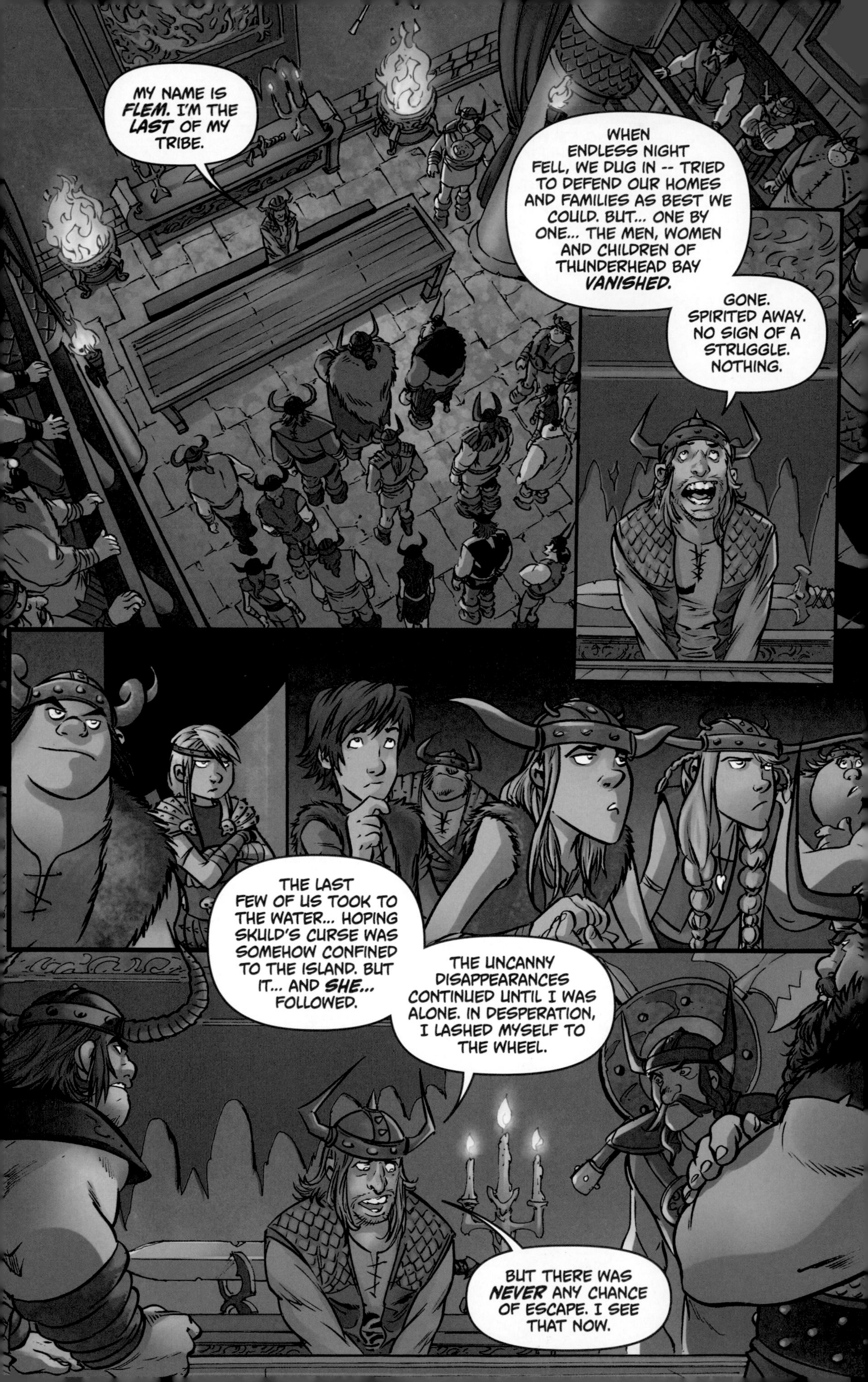
MY NAME IS FLEM. I'M THE LAST OF MY TRIBE.
WHEN ENDLESS NIGHT FELL, WE DUG IN -- TRIED TO DEFEND OUR HOMES AND FAMILIES AS BEST WE COULD. BUT... ONE BY ONE... THE MEN, WOMEN AND CHILDREN OF THUNDERHEAD BAY VANISHED.
GONE. SPIRITED AWAY. NO SIGN OF A STRUGGLE. NOTHING.
THE LAST FEW OF US TOOK TO THE WATER... HOPING SKULD'S CURSE WAS SOMEHOW CONFINED TO THE ISLAND. BUT IT... AND SHE... FOLLOWED.
THE UNCANNY DISAPPEARANCES CONTINUED UNTIL I WAS ALONE. IN DESPERATION, I LASHED MYSELF TO THE WHEEL.
BUT THERE WAS NEVER ANY CHANCE OF ESCAPE. I SEE THAT NOW.

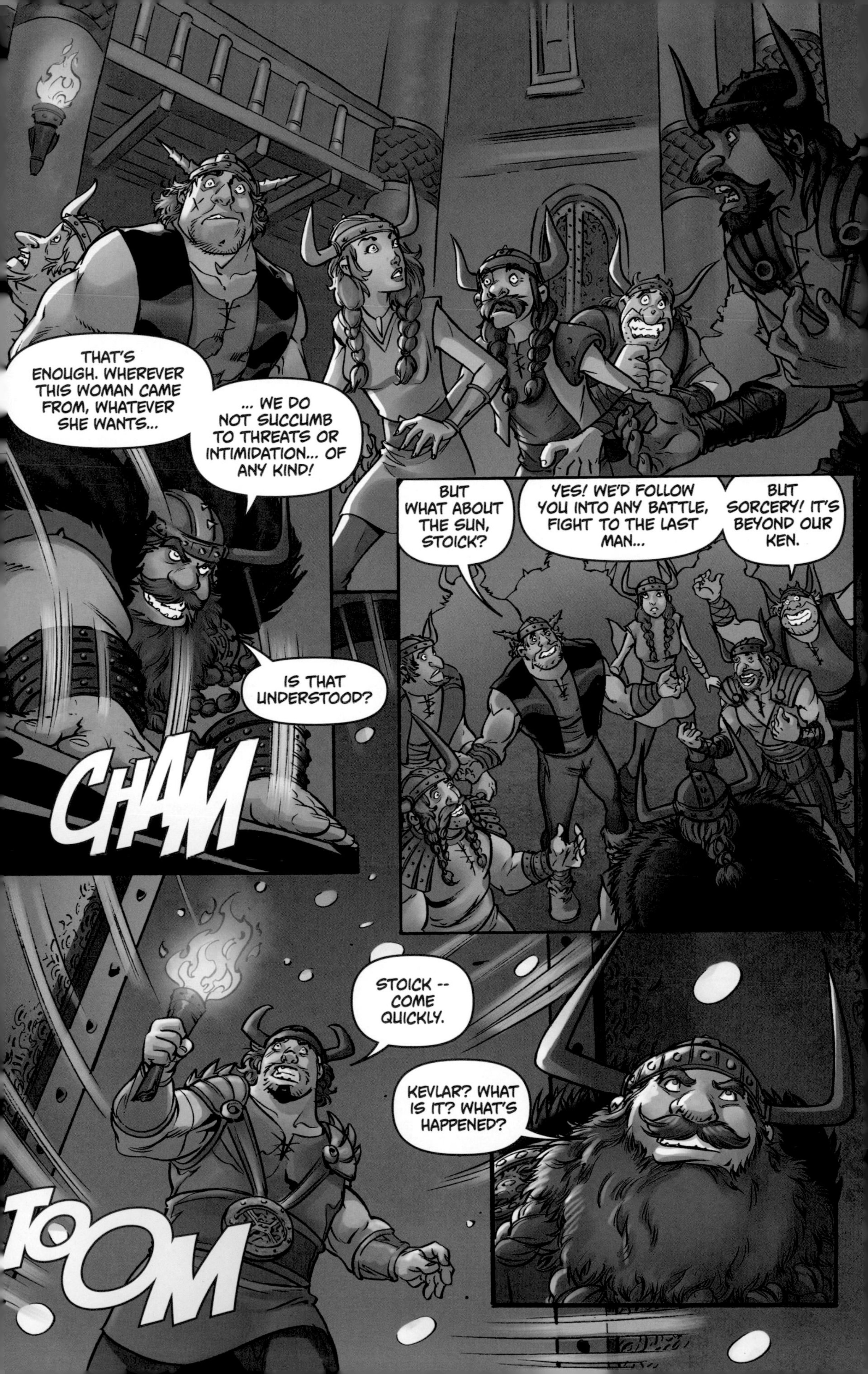
THAT'S ENOUGH. WHEREVER THIS WOMAN CAME FROM, WHATEVER SHE WANTS...
... WE DO NOT SUCCUMB TO THREATS OR INTIMIDATION... OF ANY KIND!
IS THAT UNDERSTOOD?
CHAM
BUT WHAT ABOUT THE SUN, STOICK?
YES! WE'D FOLLOW YOU INTO ANY BATTLE, FIGHT TO THE LAST MAN...
BUT SORCERY! IT'S BEYOND OUR KEN.
STOICK -- COME QUICKLY.
KEVLAR? WHAT IS IT? WHAT'S HAPPENED?
TOOM

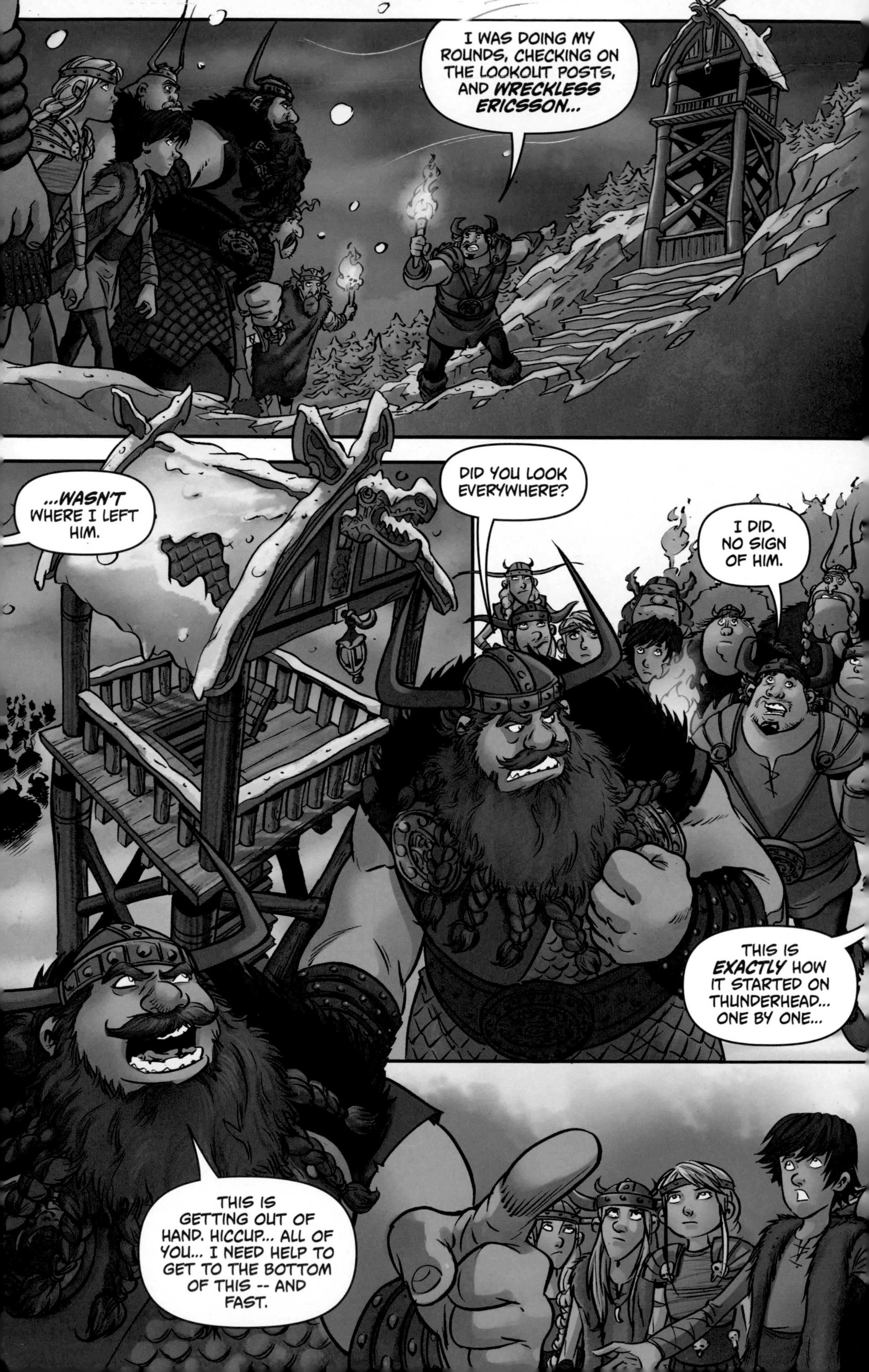
I WAS DOING MY ROUNDS, CHECKING ON THE LOOKOUT POSTS, AND *WRECKLESS ERICSSON*...
...*WASN'T* WHERE I LEFT HIM.
DID YOU LOOK EVERYWHERE?
I DID. NO SIGN OF HIM.
THIS IS *EXACTLY* HOW IT STARTED ON THUNDERHEAD... ONE BY ONE...
THIS IS GETTING OUT OF HAND. HICCUP... ALL OF YOU... I NEED HELP TO GET TO THE BOTTOM OF THIS -- AND FAST.

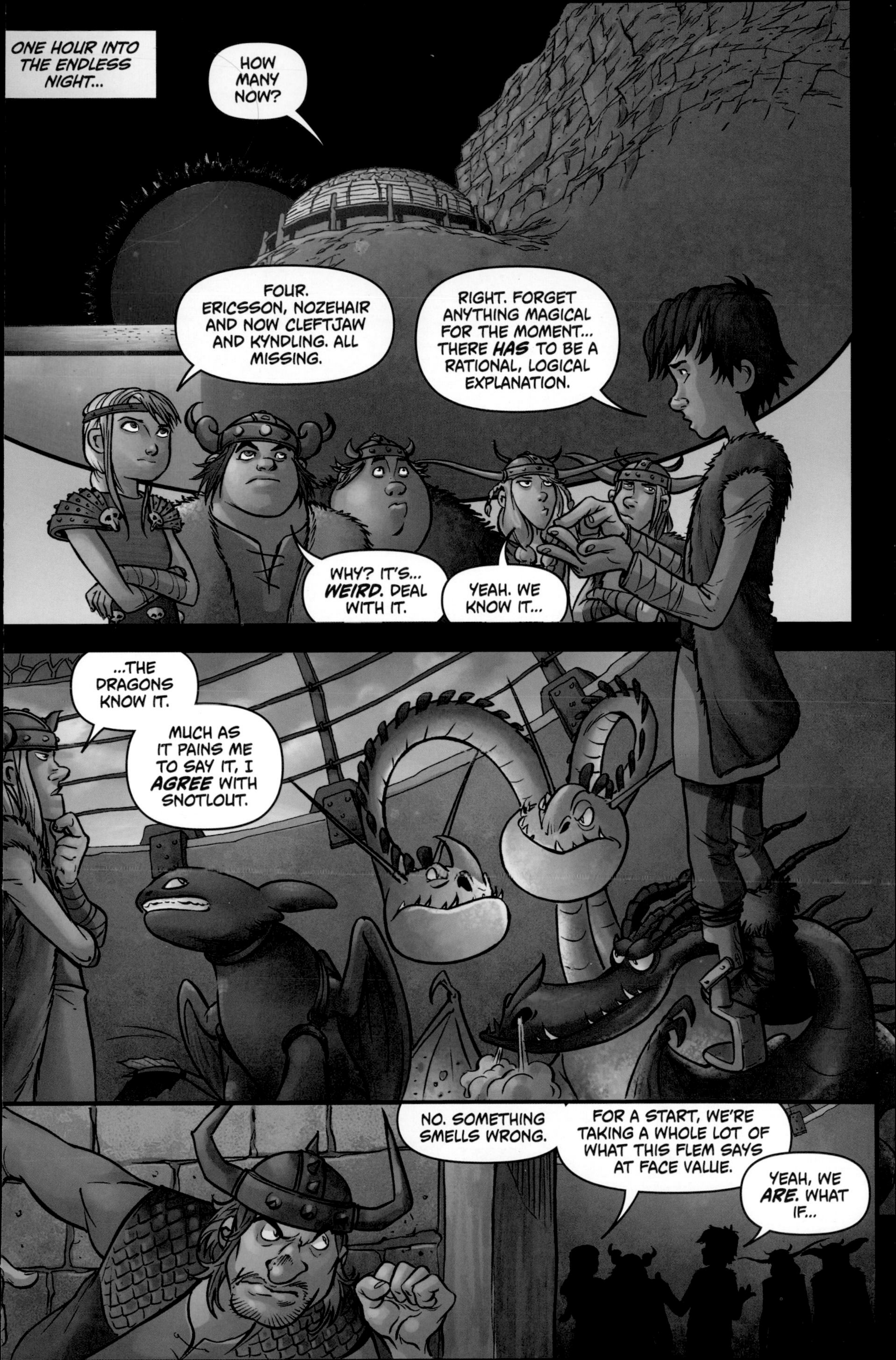
ONE HOUR INTO THE ENDLESS NIGHT...
HOW MANY NOW?
FOUR. ERICSSON, NOZEHAIR AND NOW CLEFTJAW AND KYNDLING. ALL MISSING.
RIGHT. FORGET ANYTHING MAGICAL FOR THE MOMENT... THERE HAS TO BE A RATIONAL, LOGICAL EXPLANATION.
WHY? IT'S... WEIRD. DEAL WITH IT.
YEAH. WE KNOW IT...
...THE DRAGONS KNOW IT.
MUCH AS IT PAINS ME TO SAY IT, I AGREE WITH SNOTLOUT.
NO. SOMETHING SMELLS WRONG.
FOR A START, WE'RE TAKING A WHOLE LOT OF WHAT THIS FLEM SAYS AT FACE VALUE.
YEAH, WE ARE. WHAT IF...

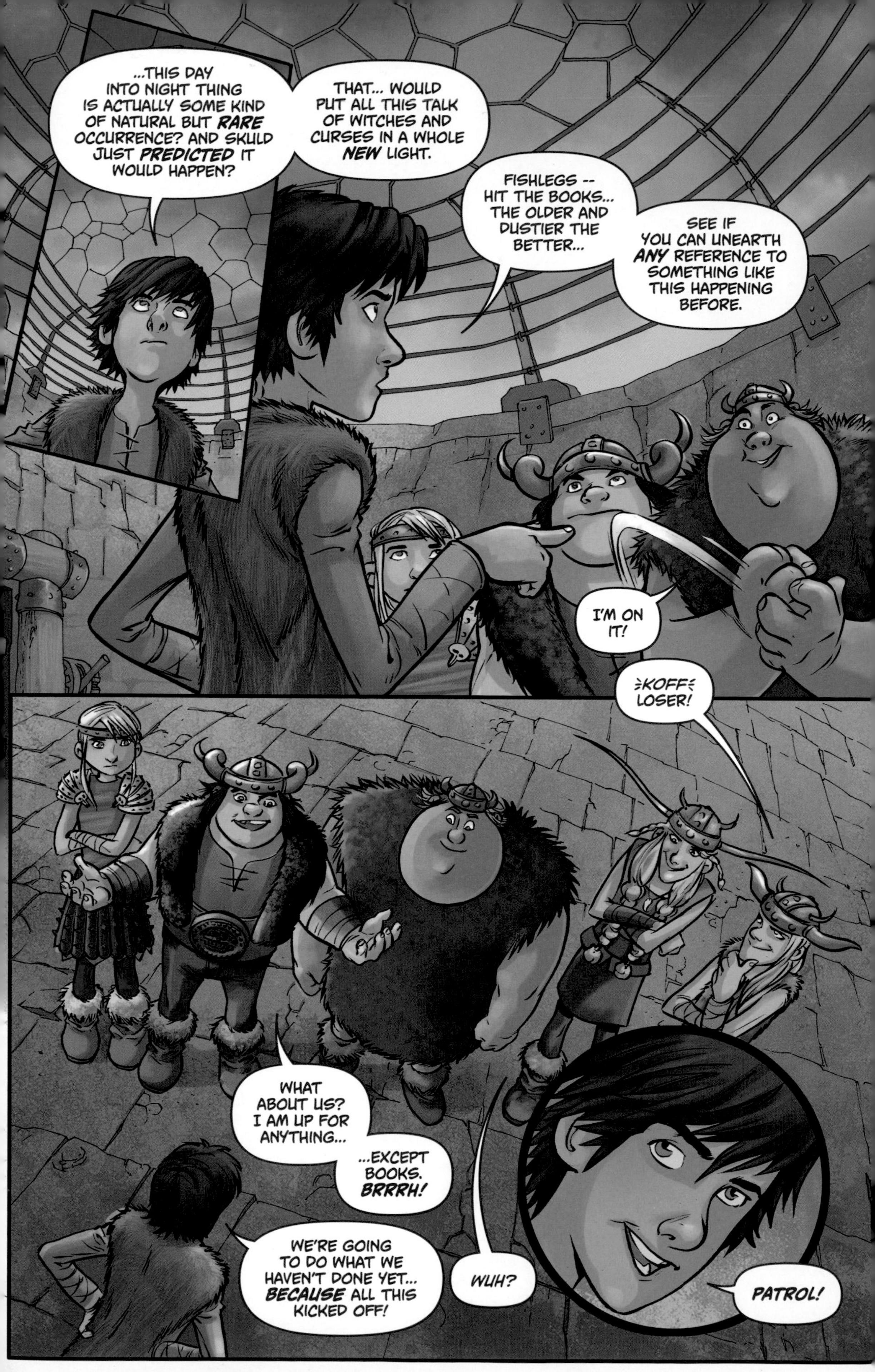
...THIS DAY INTO NIGHT THING IS ACTUALLY SOME KIND OF NATURAL BUT RARE OCCURRENCE? AND SKULD JUST PREDICTED IT WOULD HAPPEN?
THAT... WOULD PUT ALL THIS TALK OF WITCHES AND CURSES IN A WHOLE NEW LIGHT.
FISHLEGS -- HIT THE BOOKS... THE OLDER AND DUSTIER THE BETTER...
SEE IF YOU CAN UNEARTH ANY REFERENCE TO SOMETHING LIKE THIS HAPPENING BEFORE.
I'M ON IT!
KOFF LOSER!
WHAT ABOUT US? I AM UP FOR ANYTHING...
...EXCEPT BOOKS. BRRRH!
WE'RE GOING TO DO WHAT WE HAVEN'T DONE YET... BECAUSE ALL THIS KICKED OFF!
WUH?
PATROL!

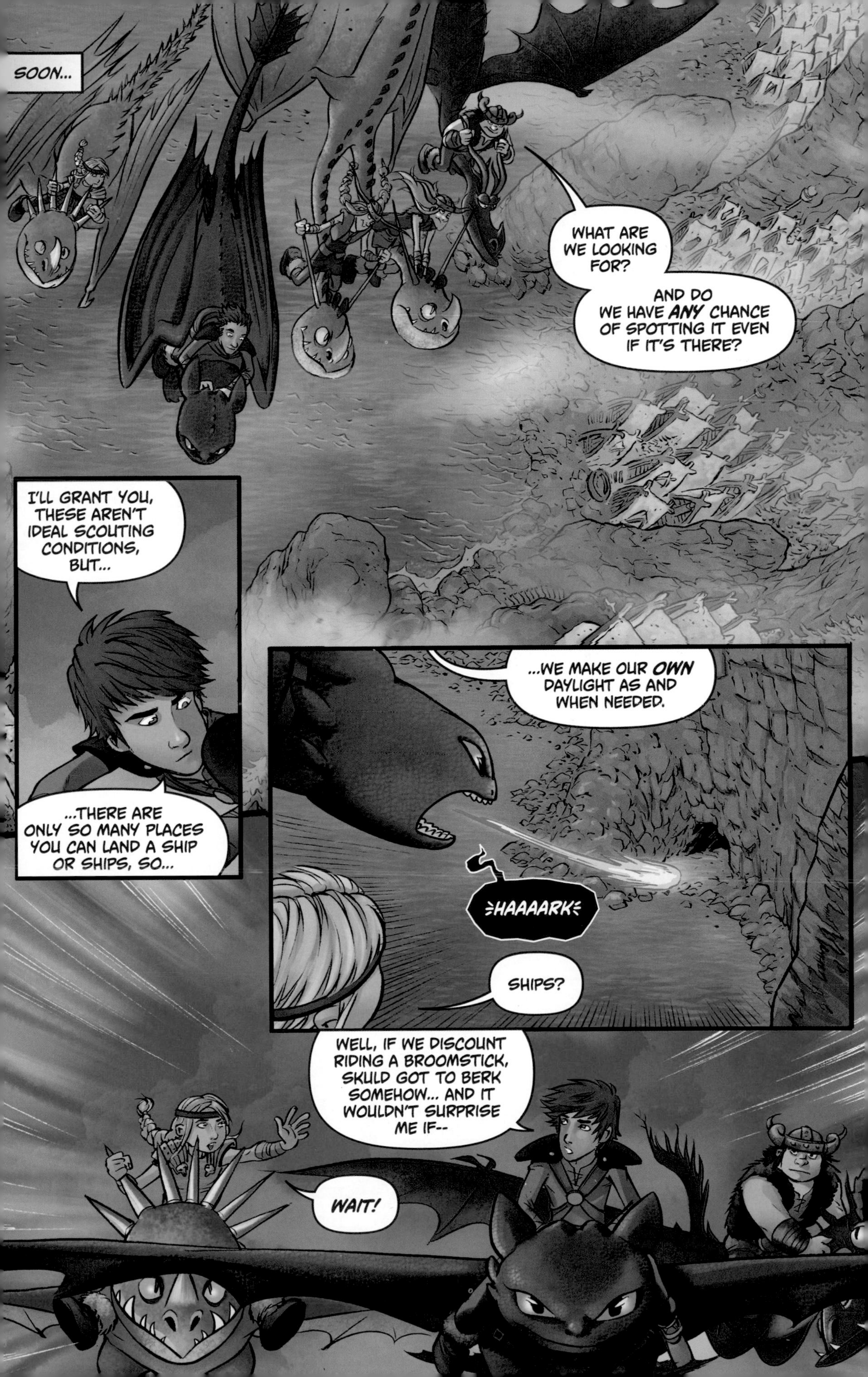
SOON...
WHAT ARE WE LOOKING FOR?
AND DO WE HAVE ANY CHANCE OF SPOTTING IT EVEN IF IT'S THERE?
I'LL GRANT YOU, THESE AREN'T IDEAL SCOUTING CONDITIONS, BUT...
...THERE ARE ONLY SO MANY PLACES YOU CAN LAND A SHIP OR SHIPS, SO...
...WE MAKE OUR OWN DAYLIGHT AS AND WHEN NEEDED.
HAAAARK
SHIPS?
WELL, IF WE DISCOUNT RIDING A BROOMSTICK, SKULD GOT TO BERK SOMEHOW... AND IT WOULDN'T SURPRISE ME IF--
WAIT!

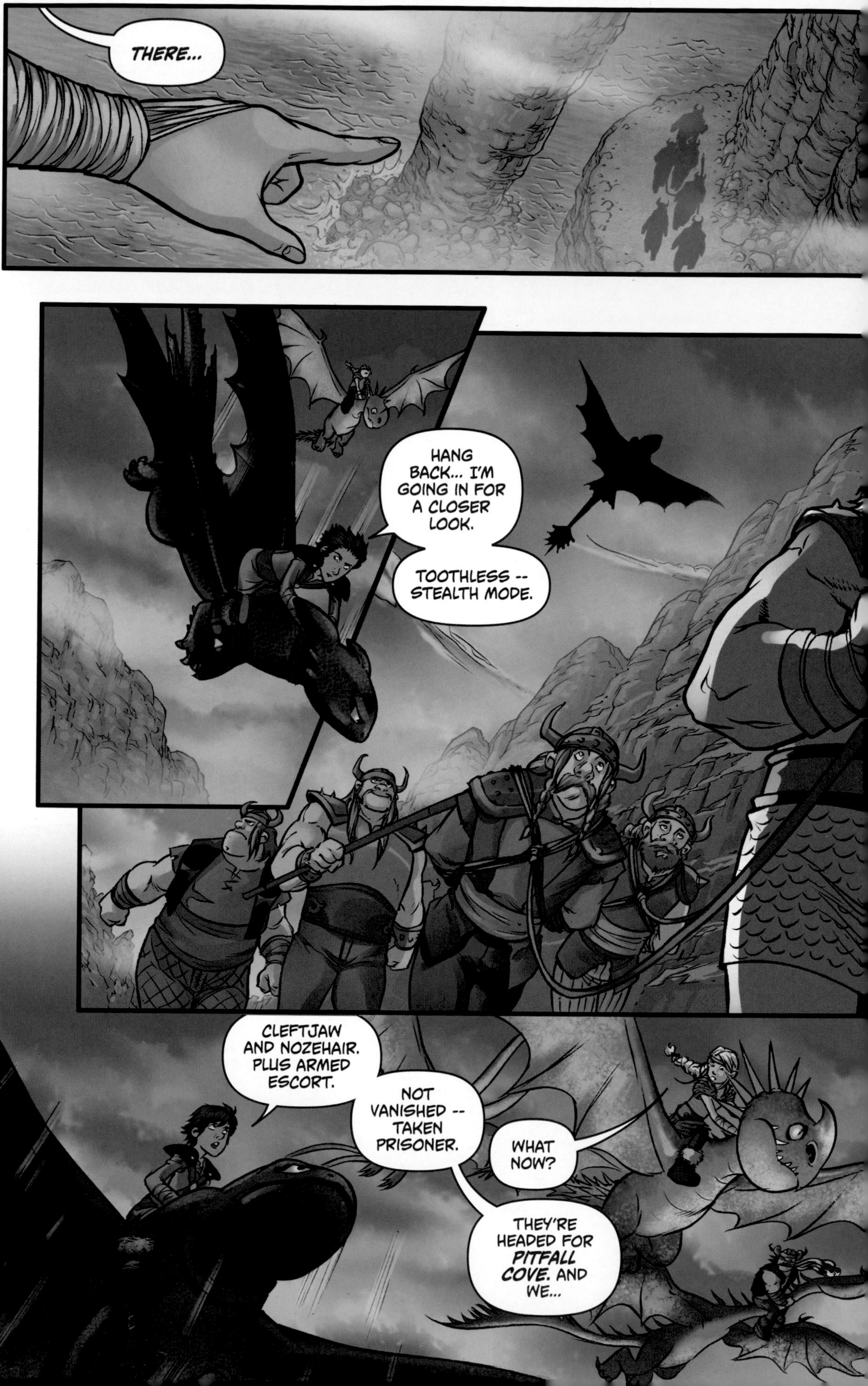
THERE...
HANG BACK... I'M GOING IN FOR A CLOSER LOOK.
TOOTHLESS -- STEALTH MODE.
CLEFTJAW AND NOZEHAIR. PLUS ARMED ESCORT.
NOT VANISHED -- TAKEN PRISONER.
WHAT NOW?
THEY'RE HEADED FOR *PITFALL COVE.* AND WE...

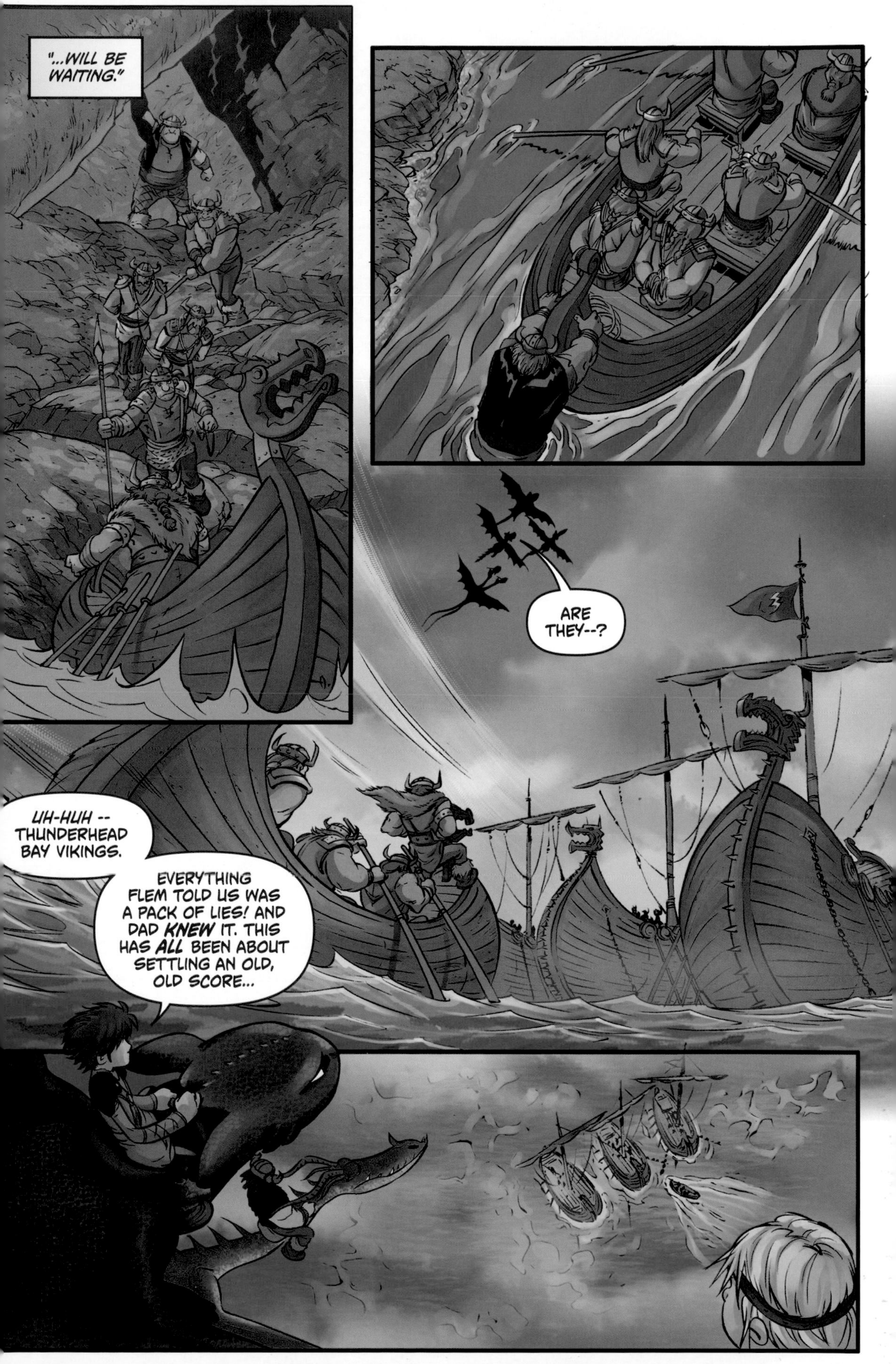
"...WILL BE WAITING."
ARE THEY--?
UH-HUH -- THUNDERHEAD BAY VIKINGS.
EVERYTHING FLEM TOLD US WAS A PACK OF LIES! AND DAD KNEW IT. THIS HAS ALL BEEN ABOUT SETTLING AN OLD, OLD SCORE...

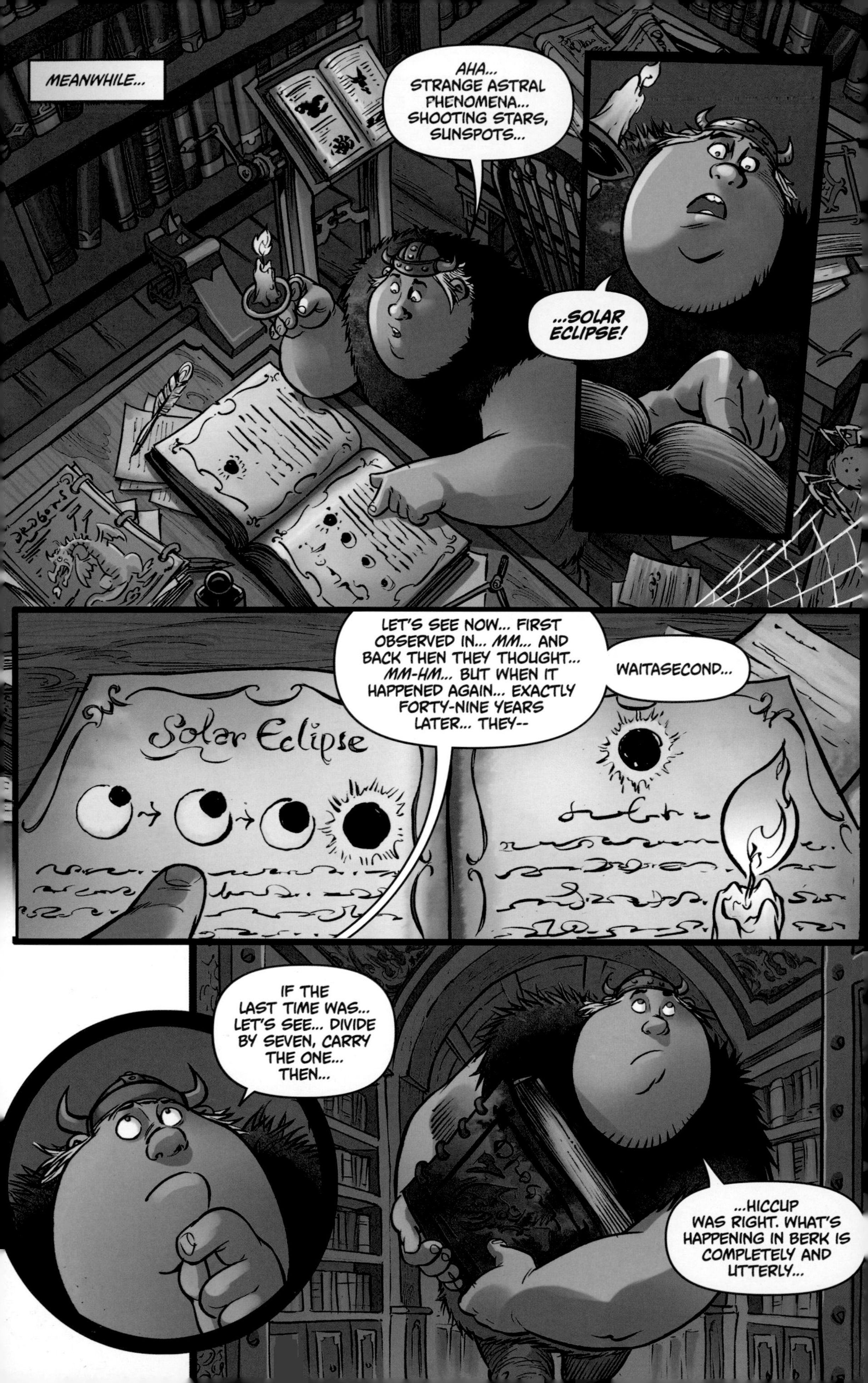
MEANWHILE...
AHA... STRANGE ASTRAL PHENOMENA... SHOOTING STARS, SUNSPOTS...
...SOLAR ECLIPSE!
LET'S SEE NOW... FIRST OBSERVED IN... *MM*... AND BACK THEN THEY THOUGHT... *MM-HM*... BUT WHEN IT HAPPENED AGAIN... EXACTLY FORTY-NINE YEARS LATER... THEY--
WAITASECOND...
Solar Eclipse
IF THE LAST TIME WAS... LET'S SEE... DIVIDE BY SEVEN, CARRY THE ONE... THEN...
...HICCUP WAS RIGHT. WHAT'S HAPPENING IN BERK IS COMPLETELY AND UTTERLY...

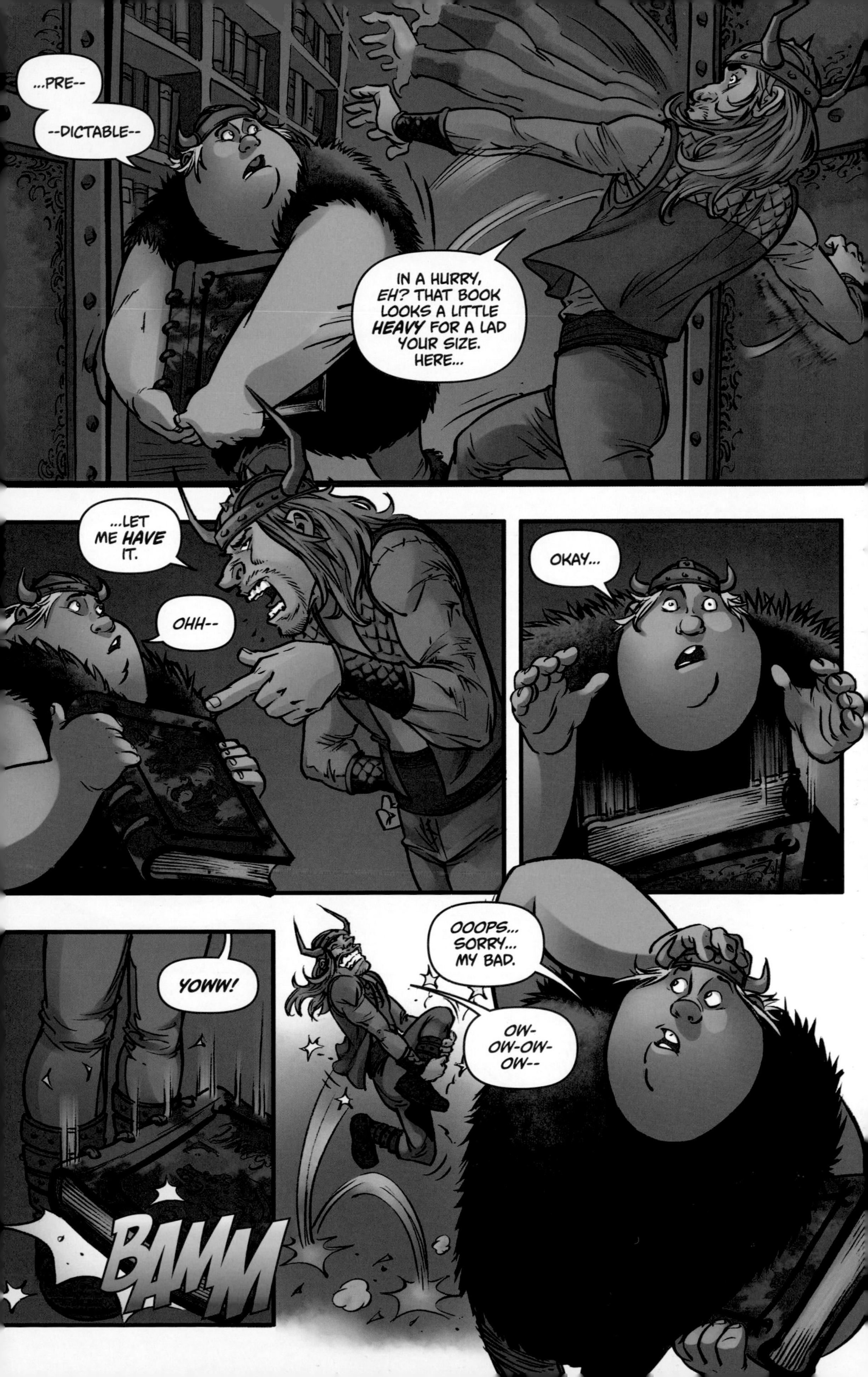
...PRE--
--DICTABLE--
IN A HURRY, EH? THAT BOOK LOOKS A LITTLE HEAVY FOR A LAD YOUR SIZE. HERE...
...LET ME HAVE IT.
OHH--
OKAY...
YOWW!
BAMM
OOOPS... SORRY... MY BAD.
OW-OW-OW-OW--

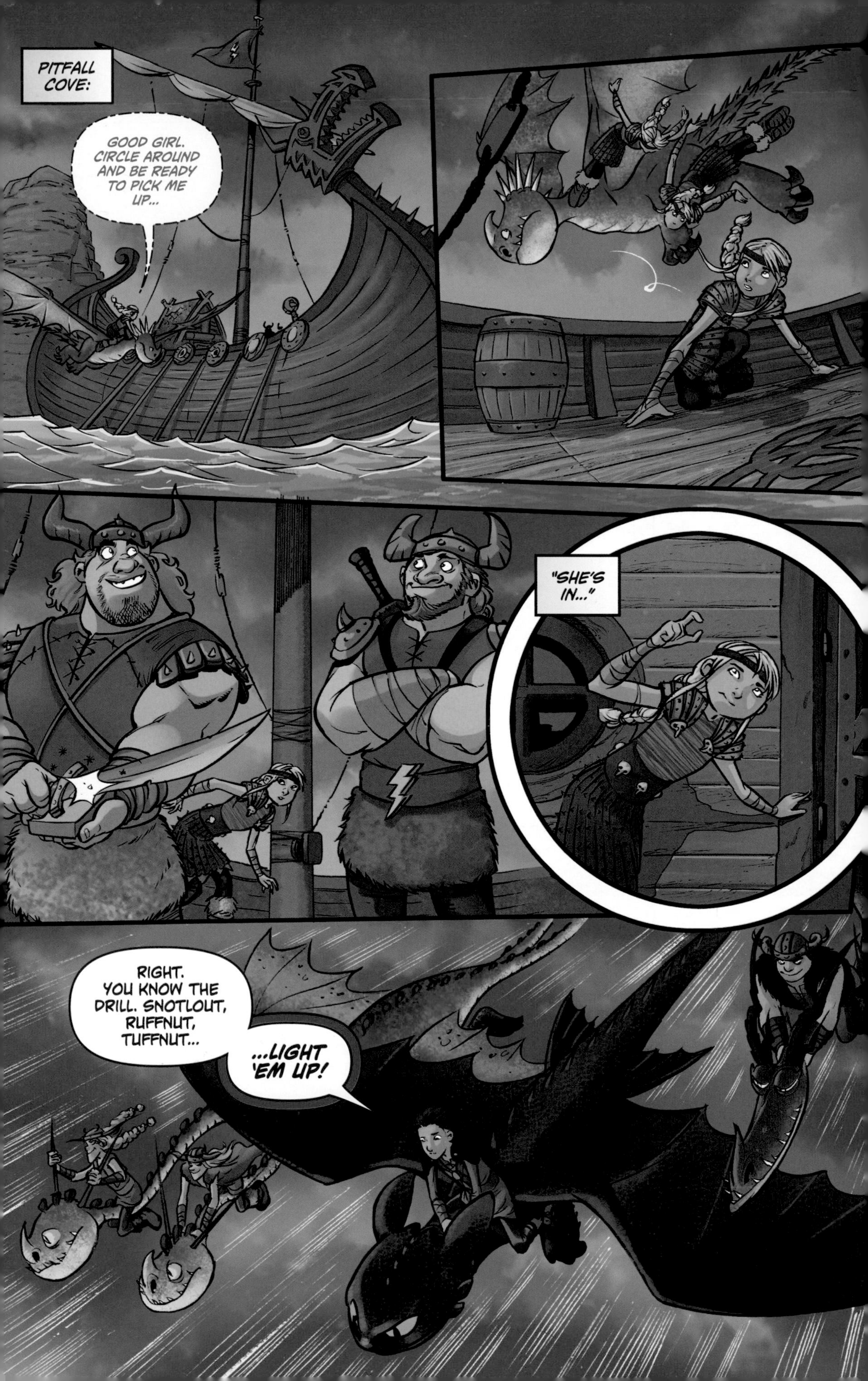
PITFALL COVE:
GOOD GIRL. CIRCLE AROUND AND BE READY TO PICK ME UP...
"SHE'S IN..."
RIGHT. YOU KNOW THE DRILL. SNOTLOUT, RUFFNUT, TUFFNUT...
...LIGHT 'EM UP!

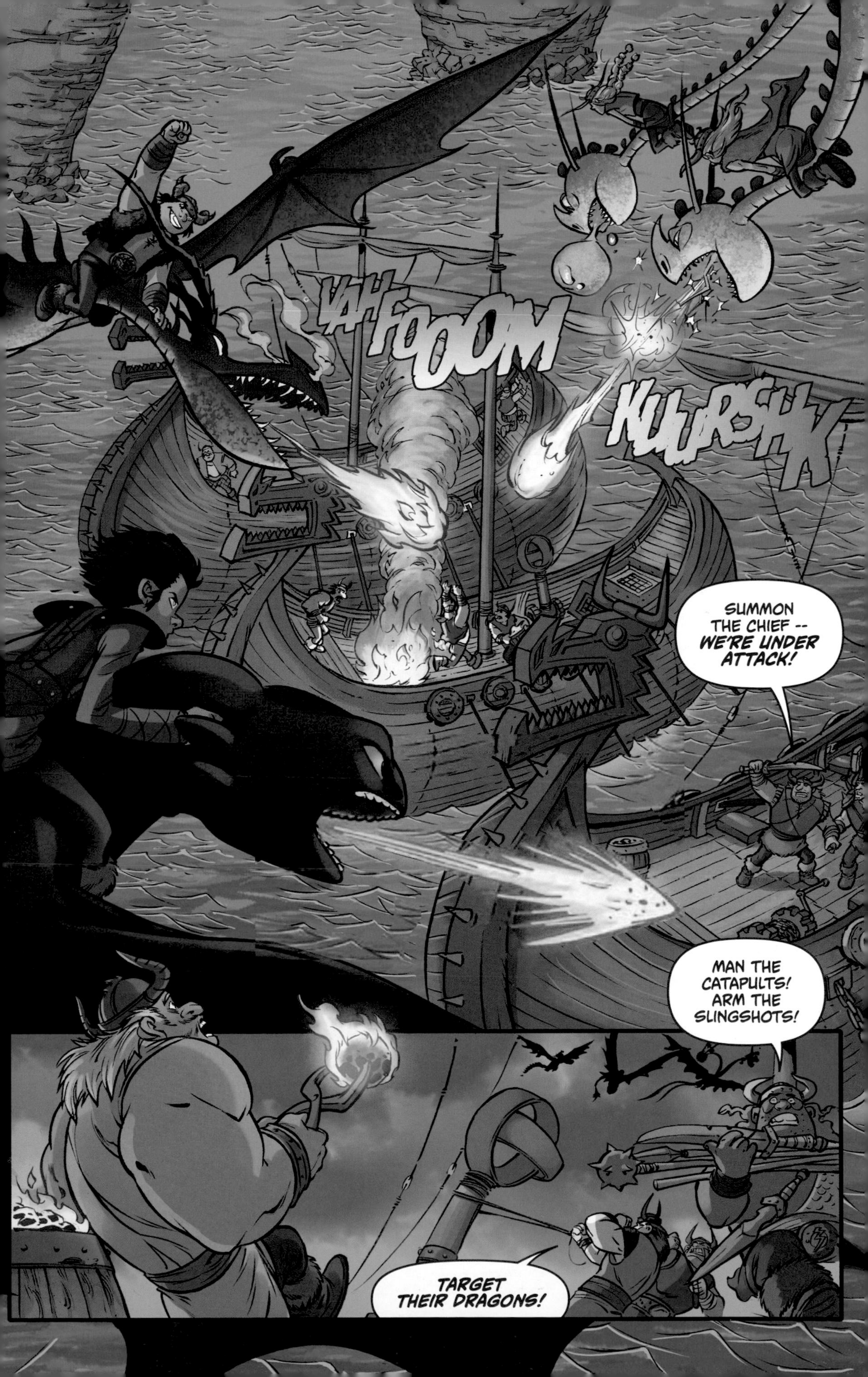

VAHFOOOM
KUURSHK
SUMMON THE CHIEF -- WE'RE UNDER ATTACK!
MAN THE CATAPULTS! ARM THE SLINGSHOTS!
TARGET THEIR DRAGONS!

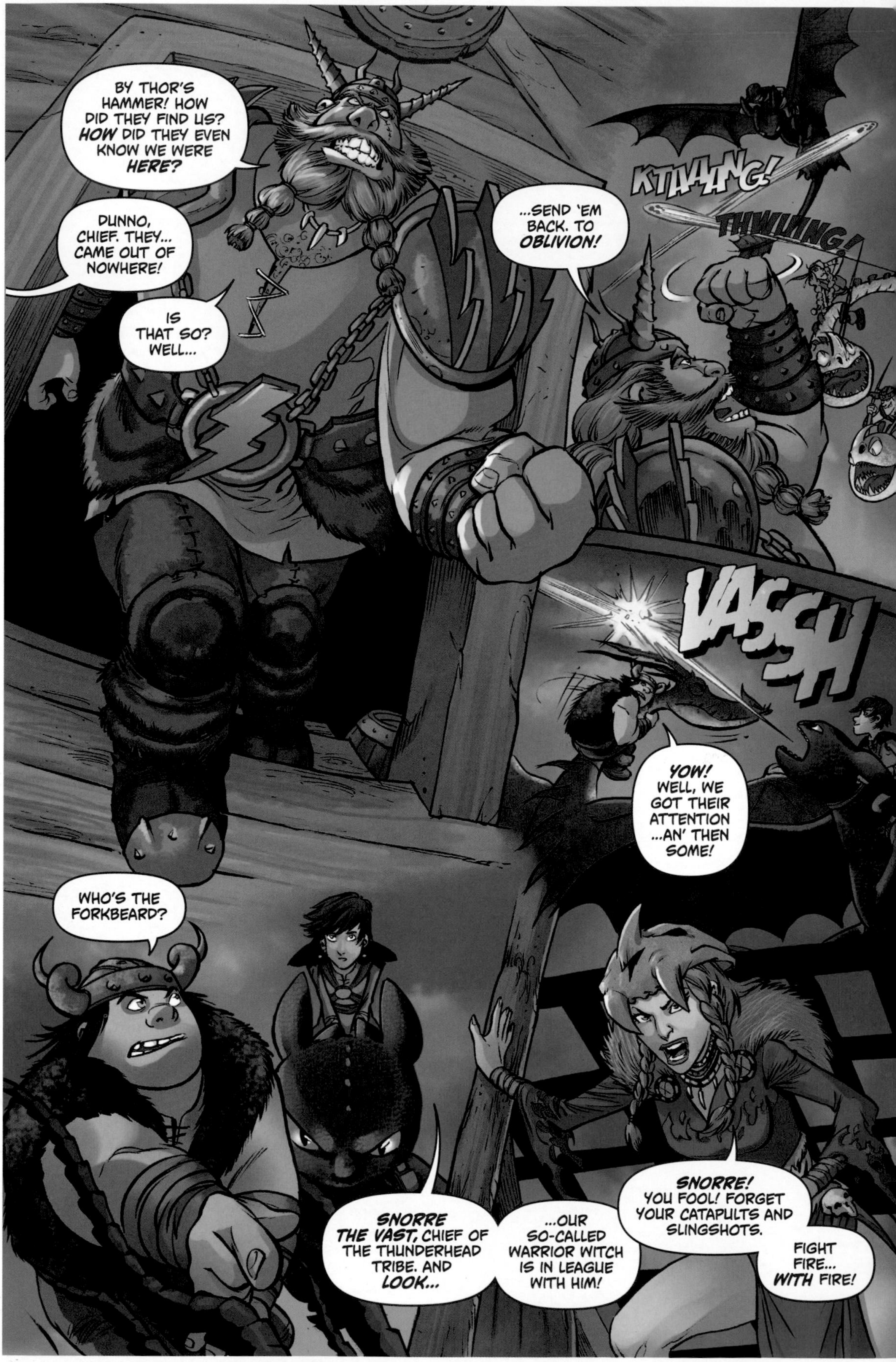
BY THOR'S HAMMER! HOW DID THEY FIND US? HOW DID THEY EVEN KNOW WE WERE HERE?
DUNNO, CHIEF. THEY... CAME OUT OF NOWHERE!
IS THAT SO? WELL...
...SEND 'EM BACK. TO OBLIVION!
KTAAAANG!
THWIIING!
VASSH
YOW! WELL, WE GOT THEIR ATTENTION ...AN' THEN SOME!
WHO'S THE FORKBEARD?
SNORRE THE VAST, CHIEF OF THE THUNDERHEAD TRIBE. AND LOOK...
...OUR SO-CALLED WARRIOR WITCH IS IN LEAGUE WITH HIM!
SNORRE! YOU FOOL! FORGET YOUR CATAPULTS AND SLINGSHOTS.
FIGHT FIRE... WITH FIRE!

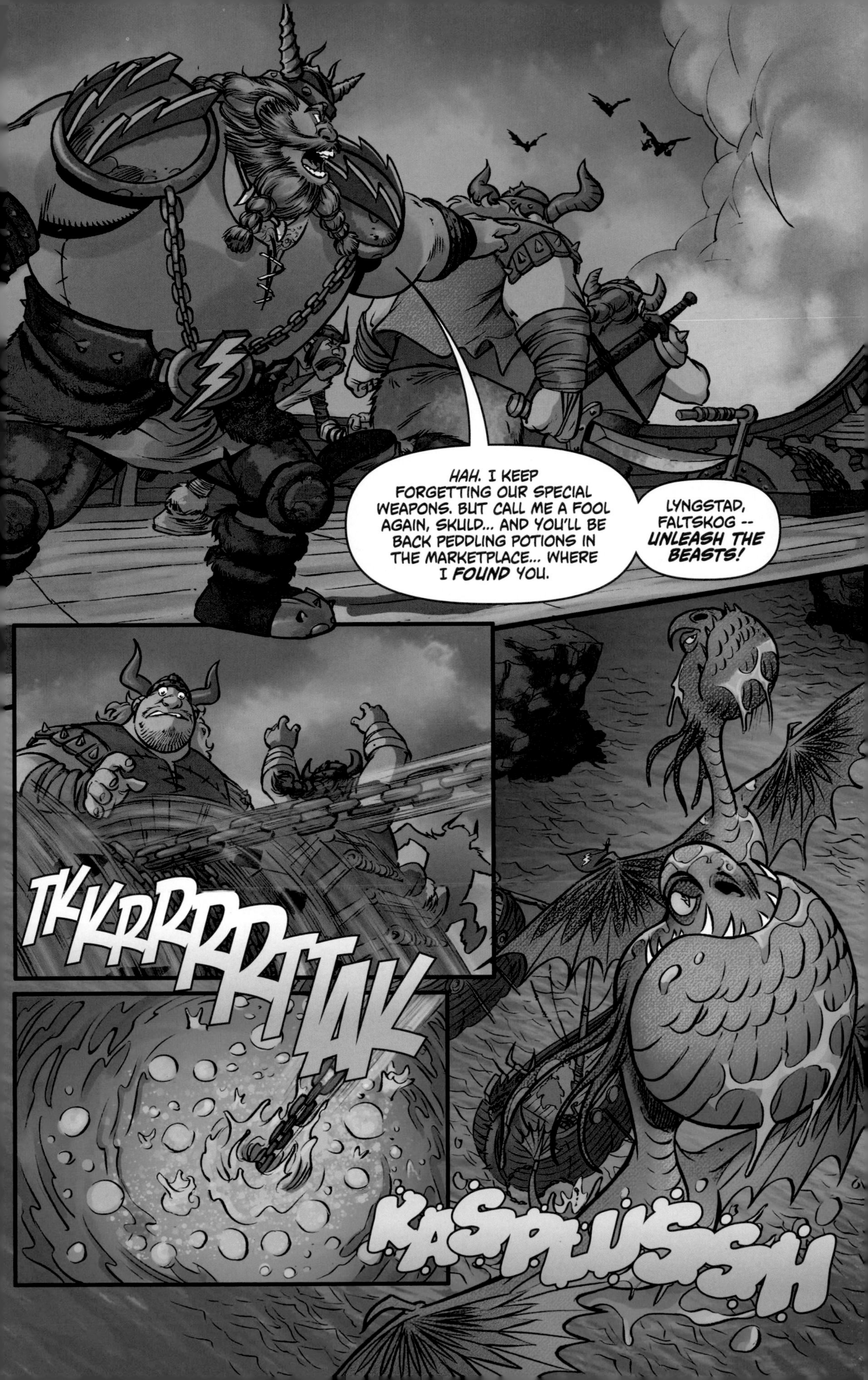
HAH. I KEEP FORGETTING OUR SPECIAL WEAPONS. BUT CALL ME A FOOL AGAIN, SKULD... AND YOU'LL BE BACK PEDDLING POTIONS IN THE MARKETPLACE... WHERE I *FOUND* YOU.
LYNGSTAD, FALTSKOG -- ***UNLEASH THE BEASTS!***
TKKRRRRTTAK
KASPLUSSSH

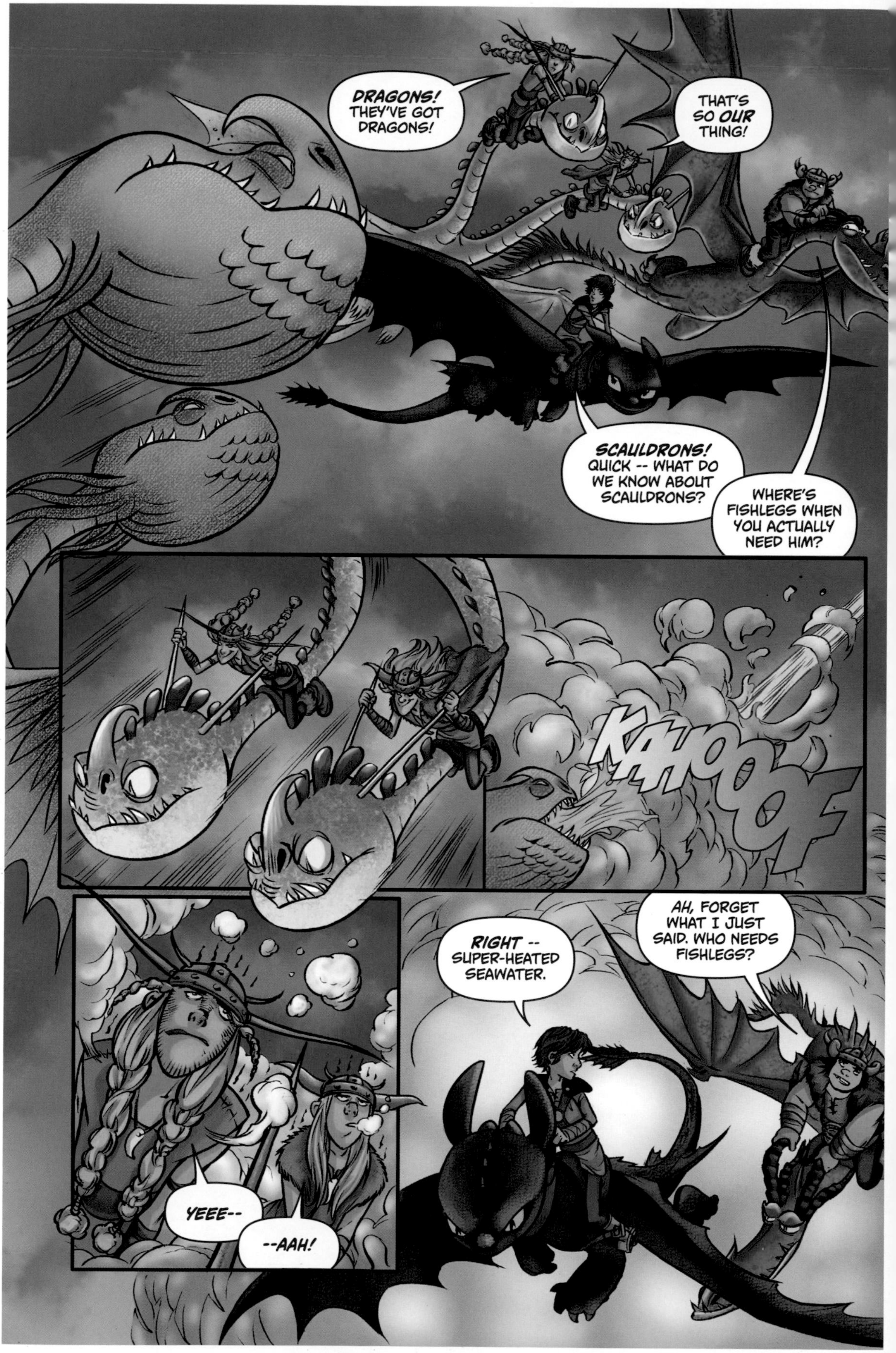
DRAGONS! THEY'VE GOT DRAGONS!
THAT'S SO OUR THING!
SCAULDRONS! QUICK -- WHAT DO WE KNOW ABOUT SCAULDRONS?
WHERE'S FISHLEGS WHEN YOU ACTUALLY NEED HIM?
KAHOOOF
YEEE--
--AAH!
RIGHT -- SUPER-HEATED SEAWATER.
AH, FORGET WHAT I JUST SAID. WHO NEEDS FISHLEGS?

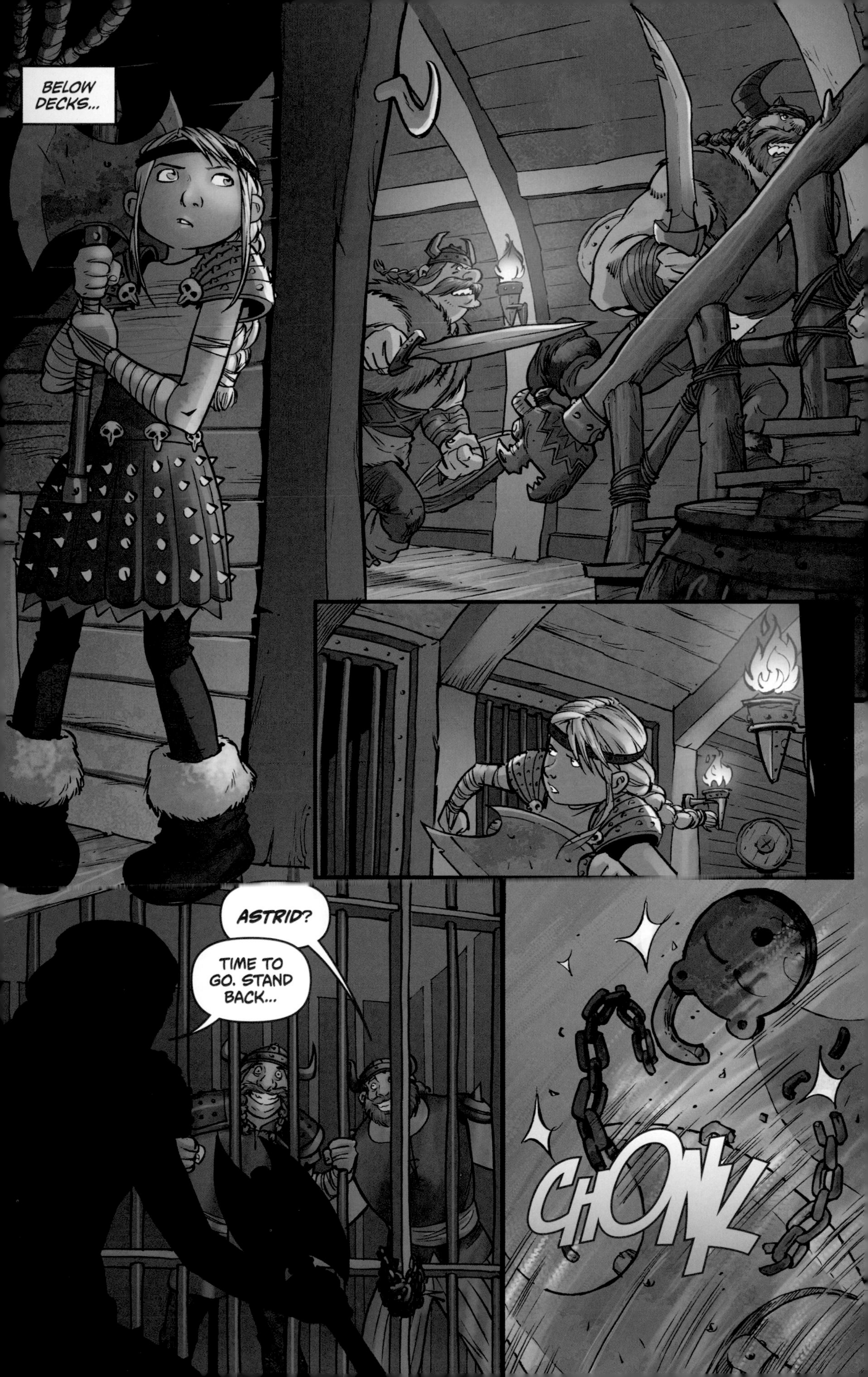
BELOW DECKS...
ASTRID?
TIME TO GO. STAND BACK...
CHONK

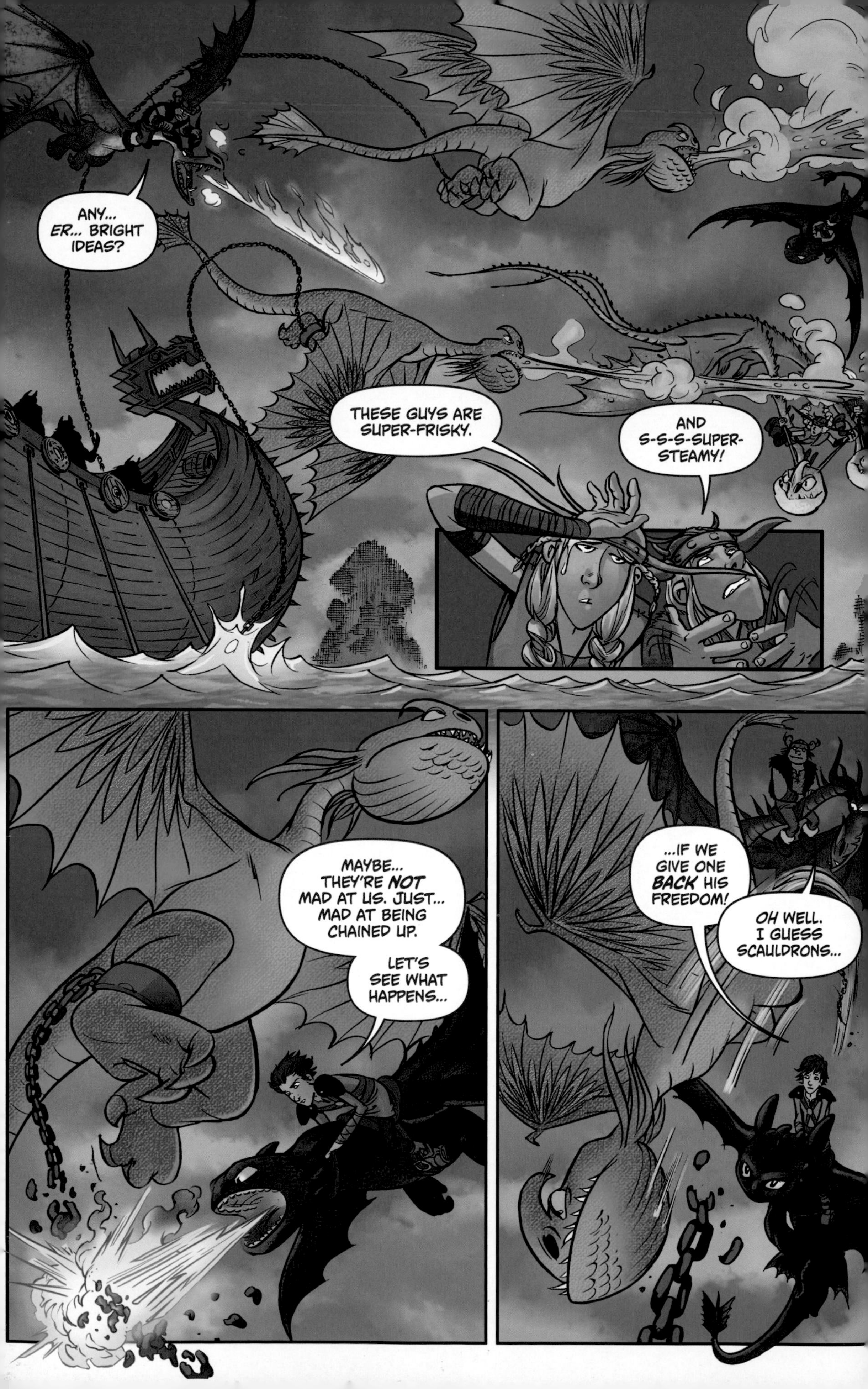
ANY... ER... BRIGHT IDEAS?
THESE GUYS ARE SUPER-FRISKY.
AND S-S-S-SUPER-STEAMY!
MAYBE... THEY'RE NOT MAD AT US. JUST... MAD AT BEING CHAINED UP.
LET'S SEE WHAT HAPPENS...
...IF WE GIVE ONE BACK HIS FREEDOM!
OH WELL. I GUESS SCAULDRONS...

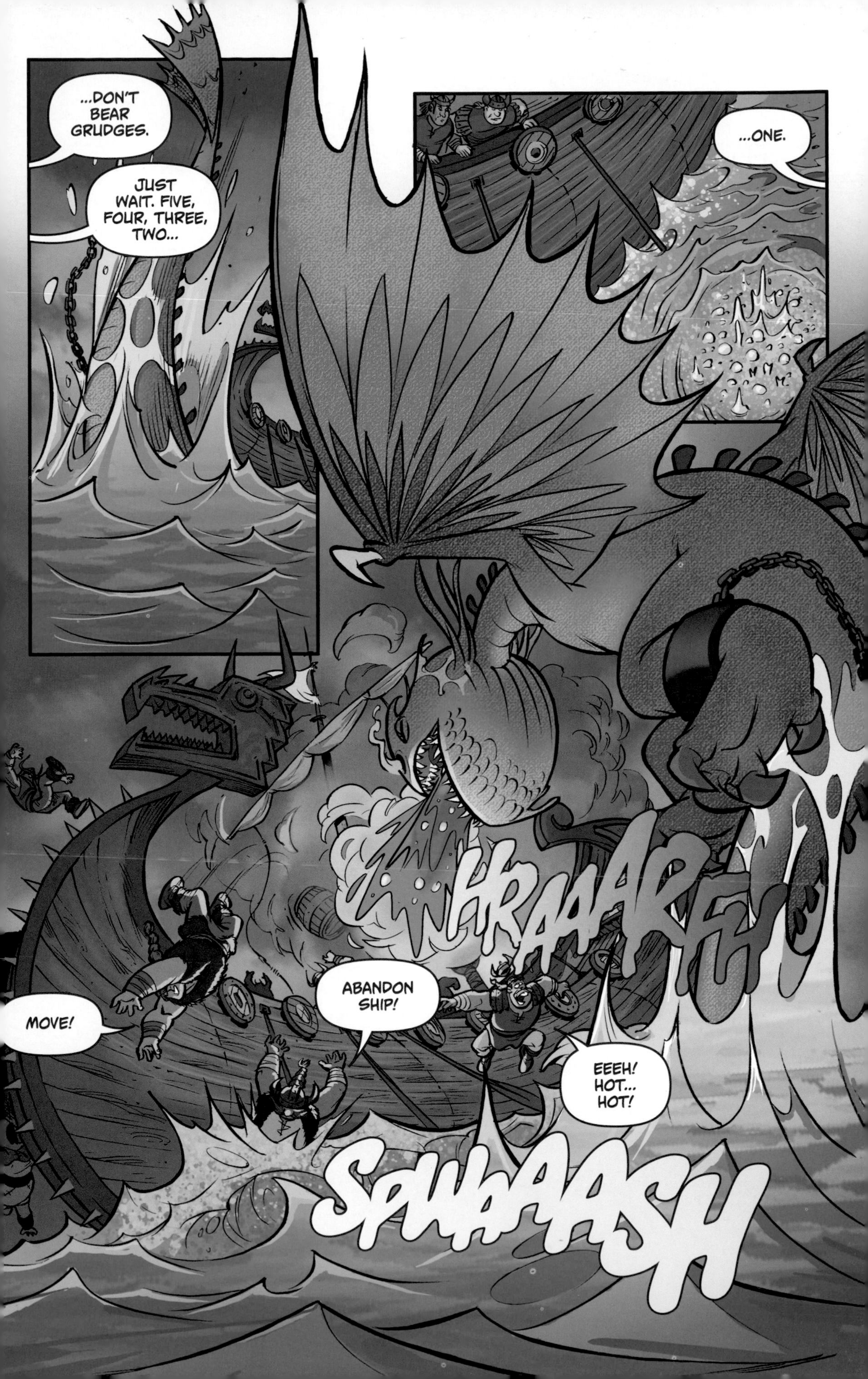
...DON'T BEAR GRUDGES.
JUST WAIT. FIVE, FOUR, THREE, TWO...
...ONE.
HRAAARGH
MOVE!
ABANDON SHIP!
EEEH! HOT... HOT!
SPLAAASH

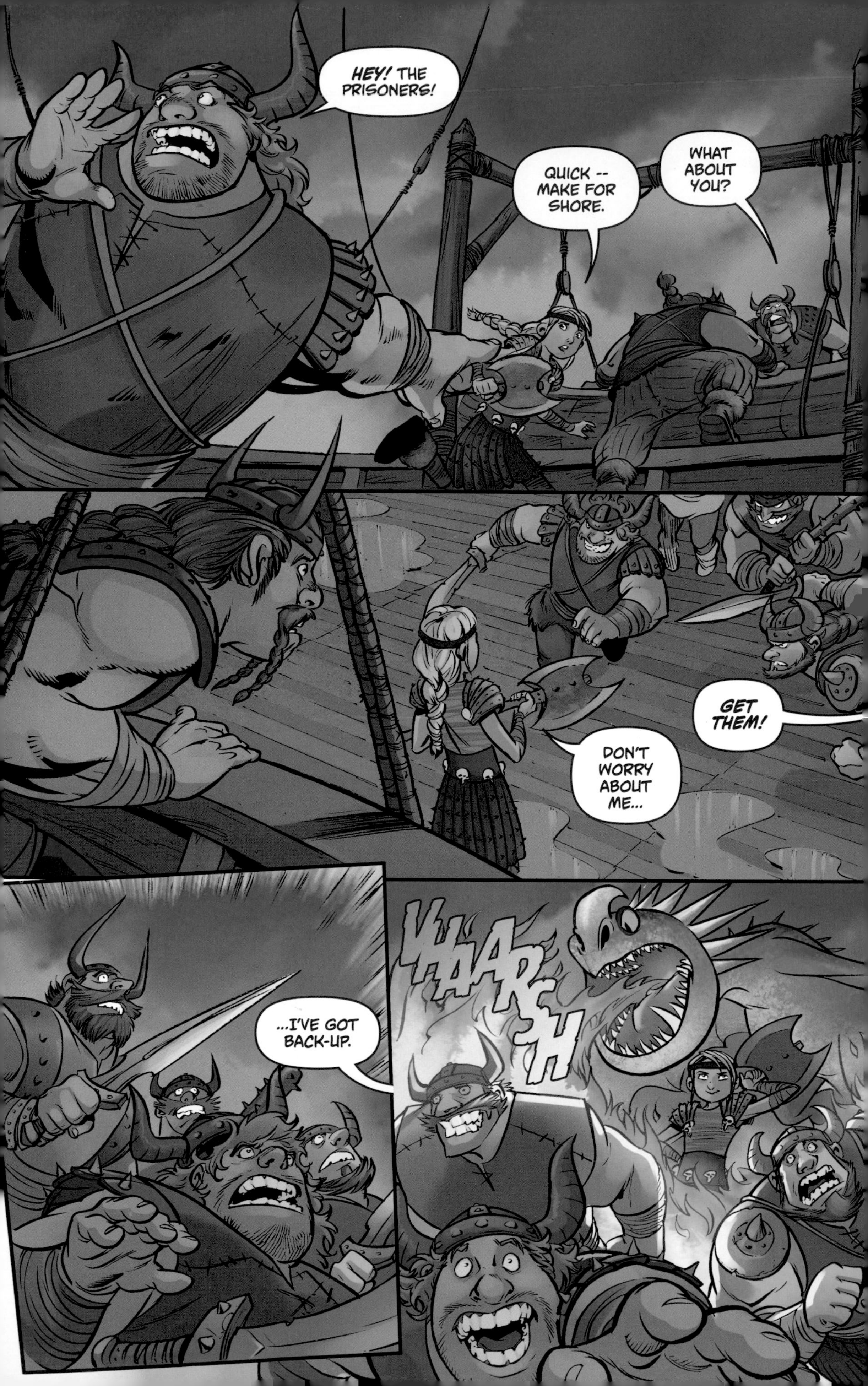
HEY! THE PRISONERS!
QUICK -- MAKE FOR SHORE.
WHAT ABOUT YOU?
GET THEM!
DON'T WORRY ABOUT ME...
...I'VE GOT BACK-UP.
VHARSH

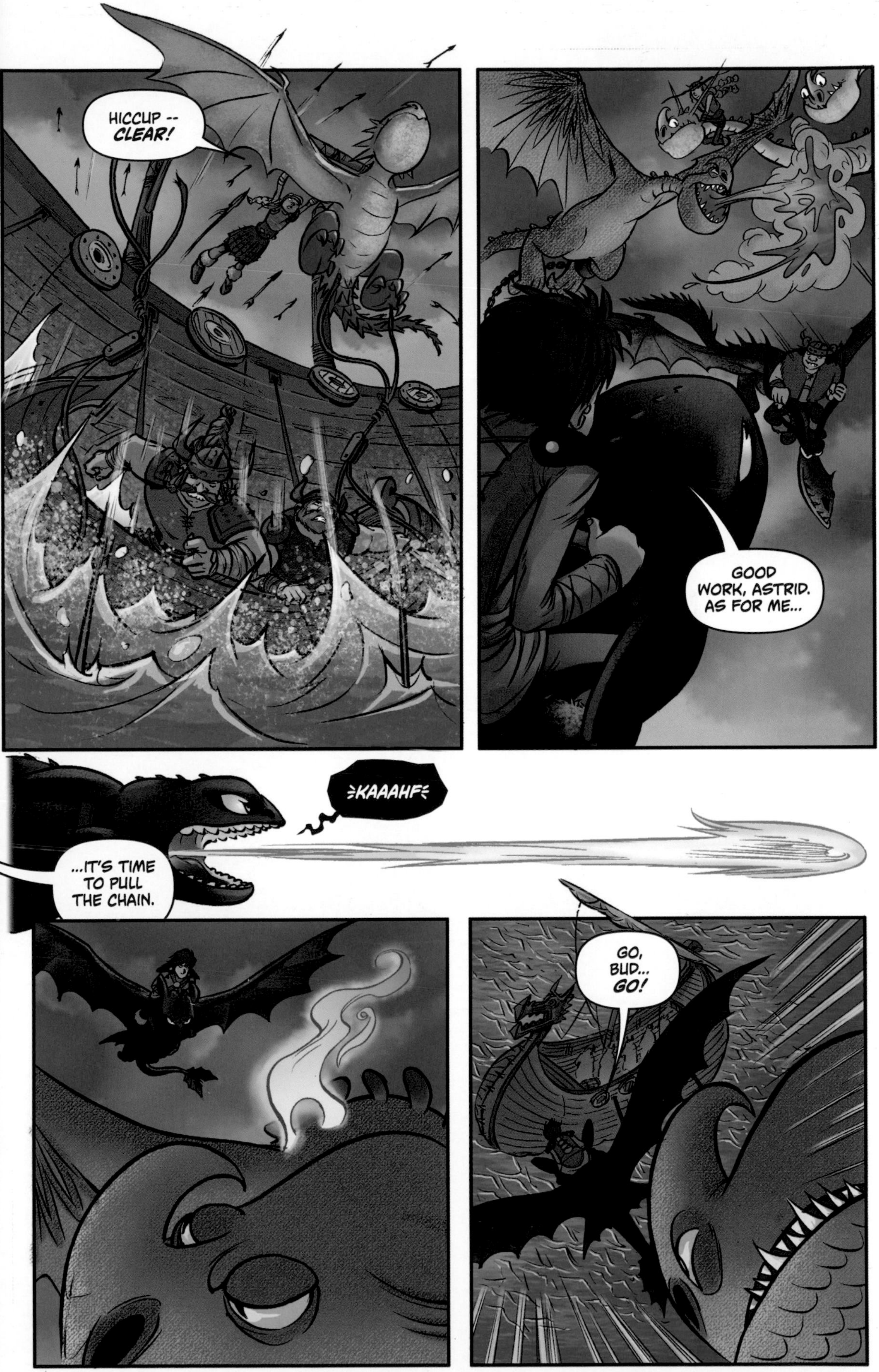
HICCUP -- CLEAR!
GOOD WORK, ASTRID. AS FOR ME...
KAAAHF
...IT'S TIME TO PULL THE CHAIN.
GO, BUD... GO!

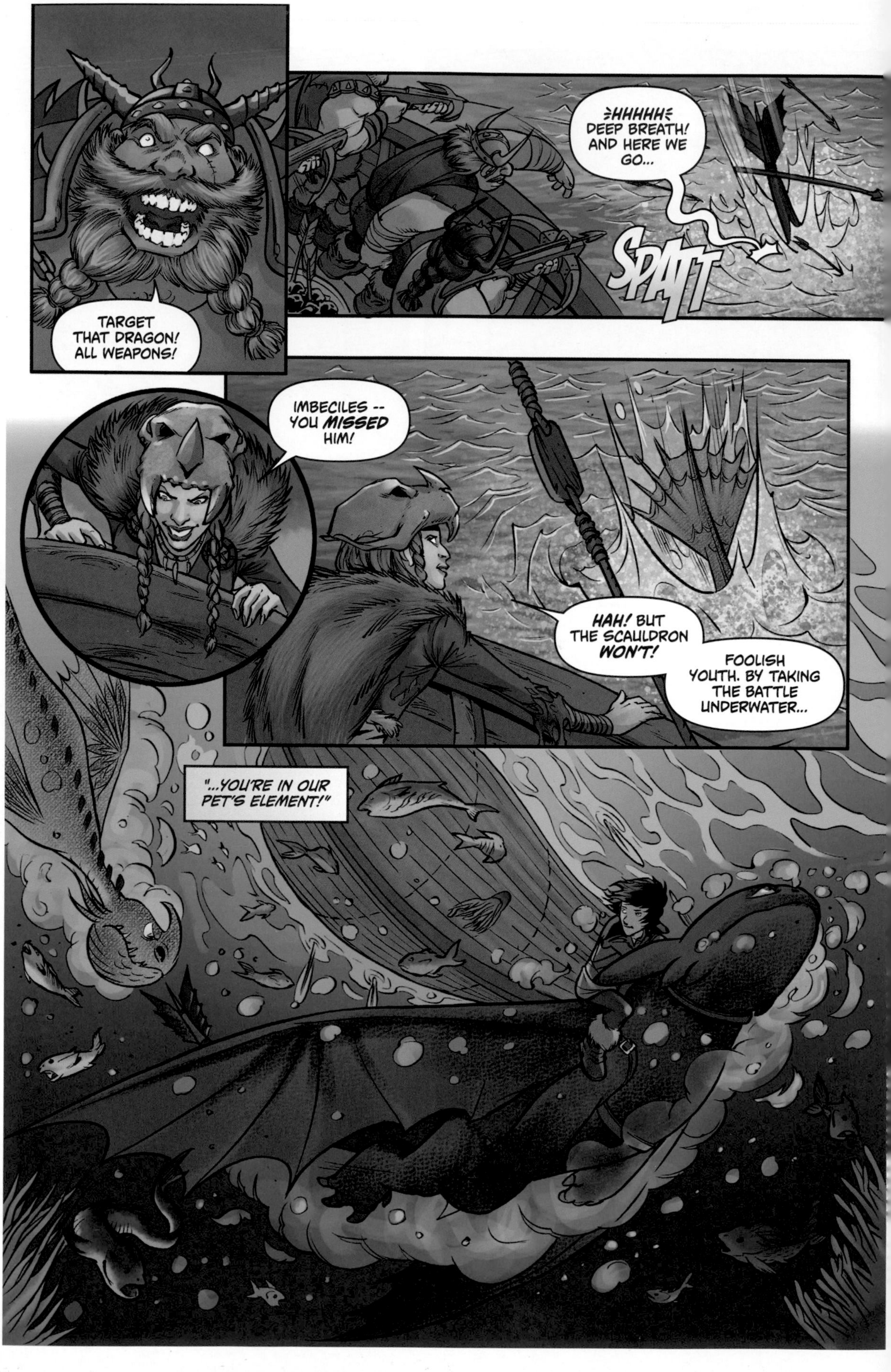
TARGET THAT DRAGON! ALL WEAPONS!
HHHHH DEEP BREATH! AND HERE WE GO...
SPATT
IMBECILES -- YOU MISSED HIM!
HAH! BUT THE SCAULDRON WON'T!
FOOLISH YOUTH. BY TAKING THE BATTLE UNDERWATER...
"...YOU'RE IN OUR PET'S ELEMENT!"

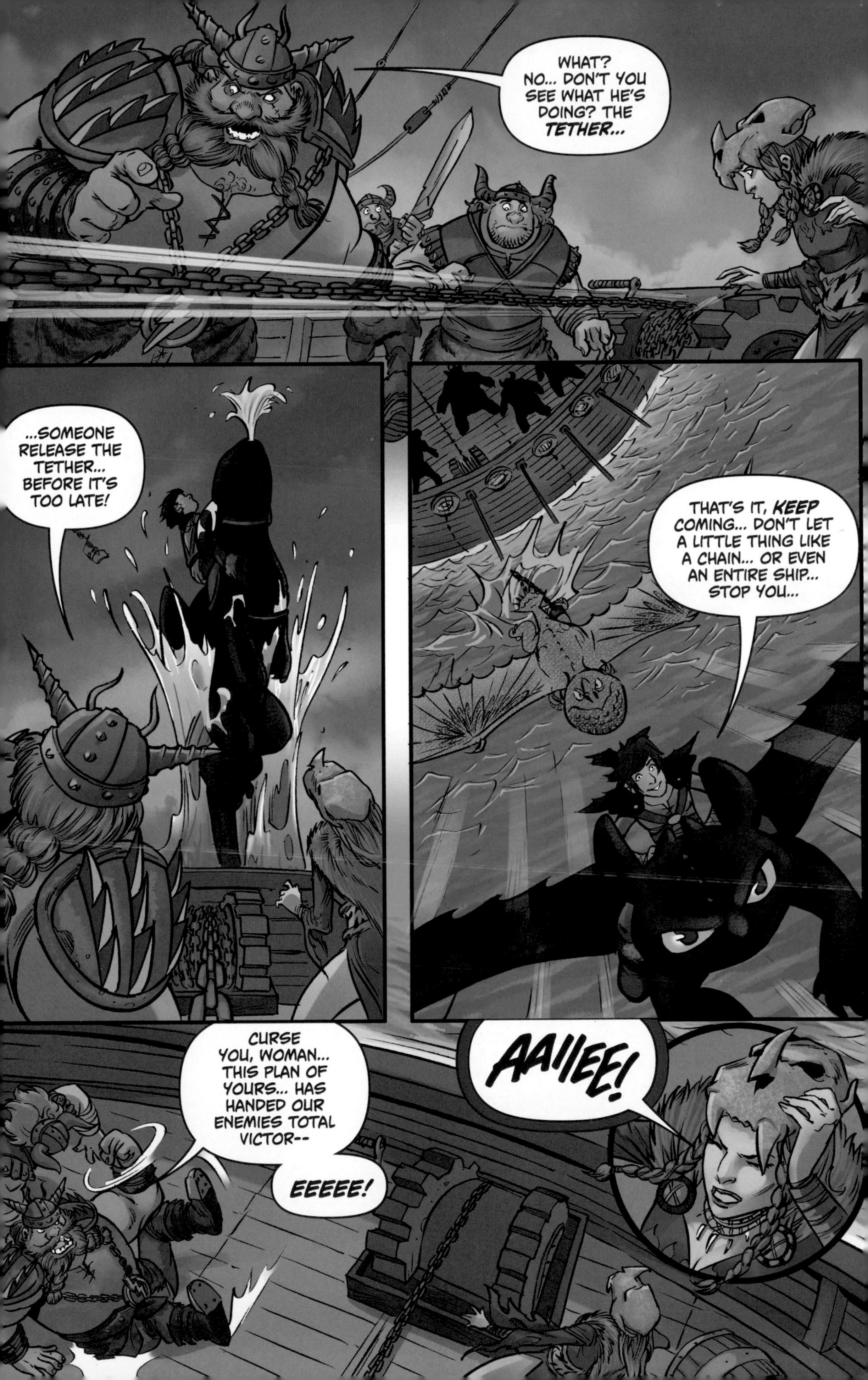

WHAT? NO... DON'T YOU SEE WHAT HE'S DOING? THE TETHER...
...SOMEONE RELEASE THE TETHER... BEFORE IT'S TOO LATE!
THAT'S IT, KEEP COMING... DON'T LET A LITTLE THING LIKE A CHAIN... OR EVEN AN ENTIRE SHIP... STOP YOU...
CURSE YOU, WOMAN... THIS PLAN OF YOURS... HAS HANDED OUR ENEMIES TOTAL VICTOR--
EEEEE!
AAIIEE!

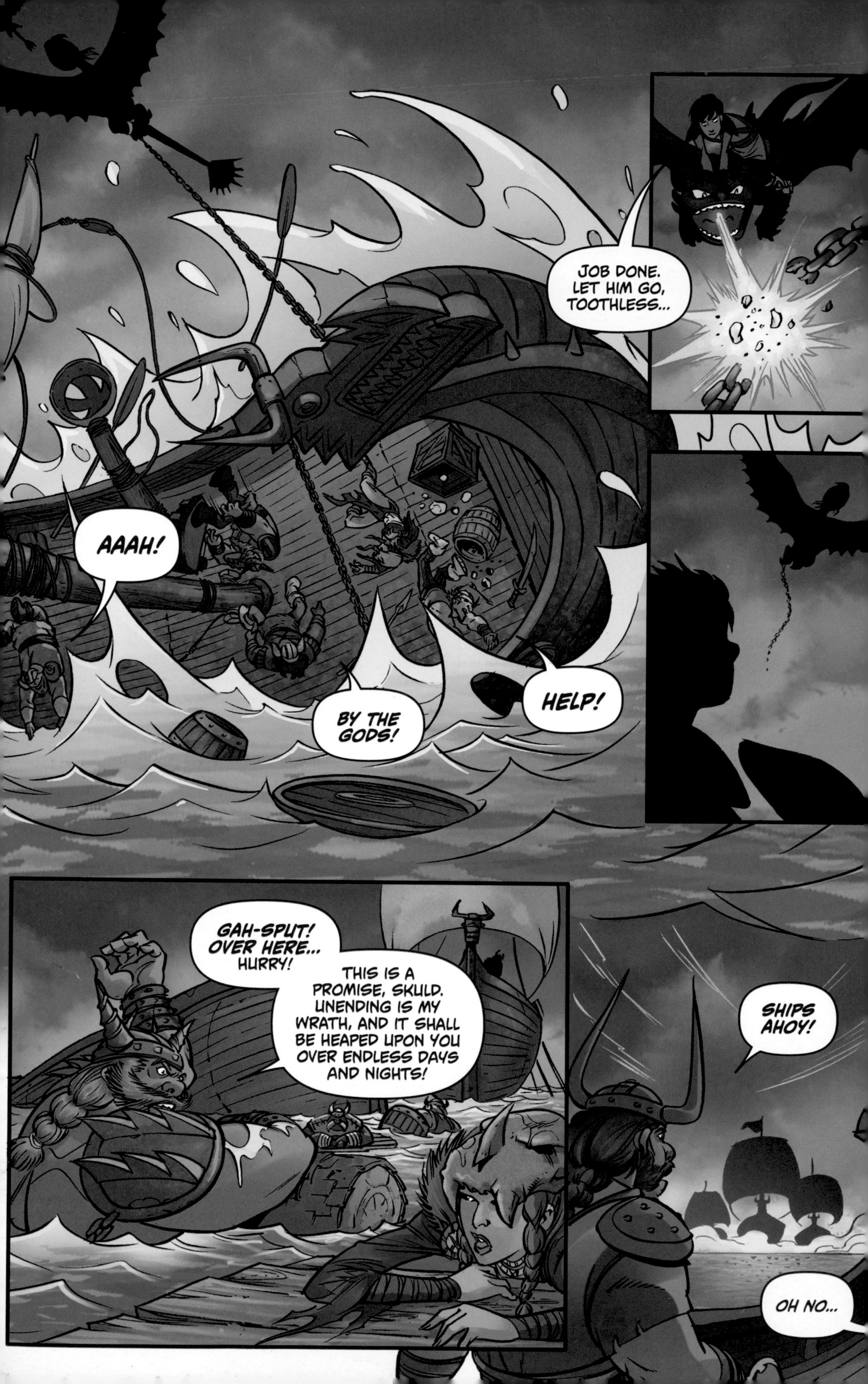
JOB DONE. LET HIM GO, TOOTHLESS...
AAAH!
BY THE GODS!
HELP!
GAH-SPUT! OVER HERE... HURRY!
THIS IS A PROMISE, SKULD. UNENDING IS MY WRATH, AND IT SHALL BE HEAPED UPON YOU OVER ENDLESS DAYS AND NIGHTS!
SHIPS AHOY!
OH NO...

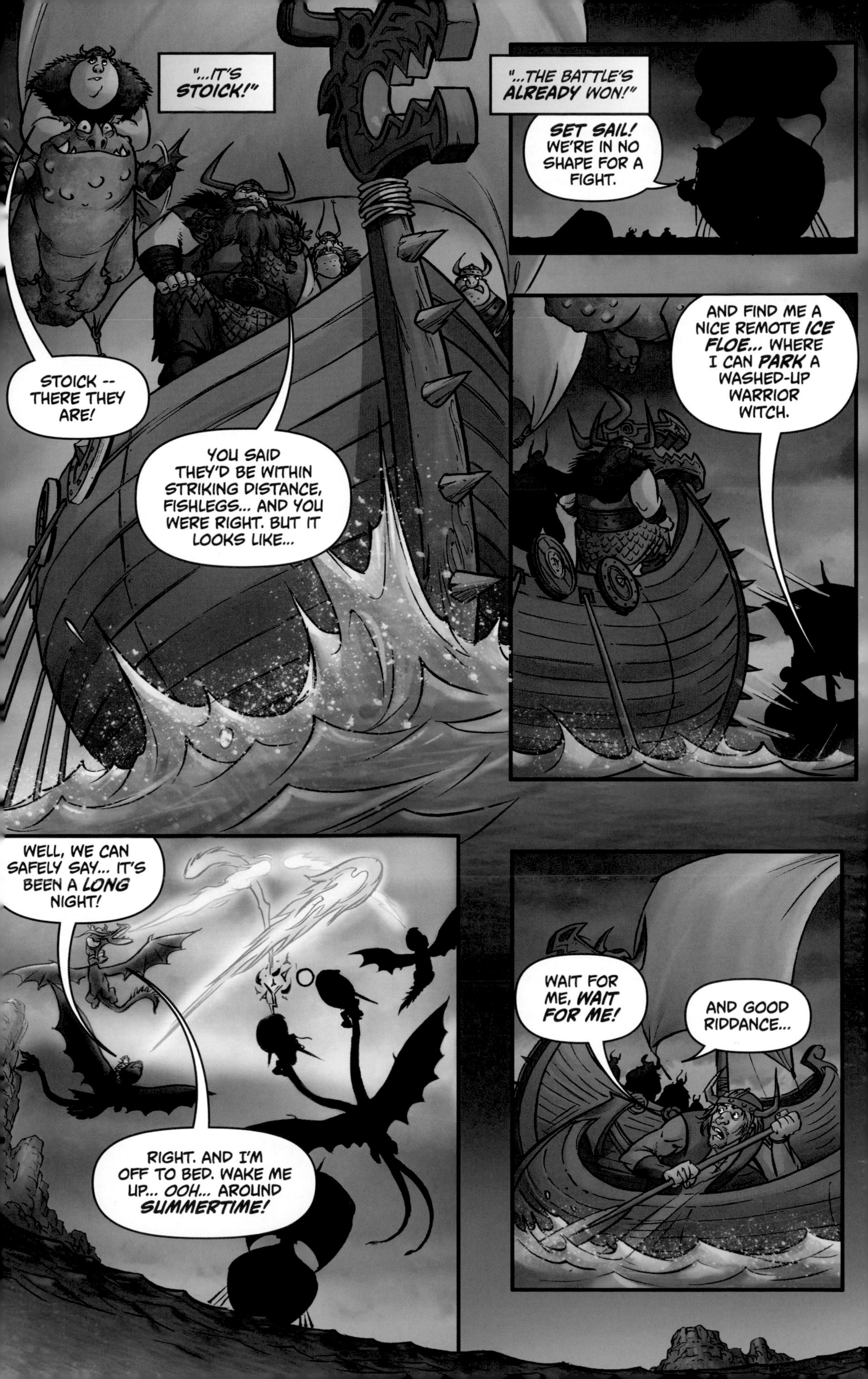
"...IT'S STOICK!"
STOICK -- THERE THEY ARE!
YOU SAID THEY'D BE WITHIN STRIKING DISTANCE, FISHLEGS... AND YOU WERE RIGHT. BUT IT LOOKS LIKE...
"...THE BATTLE'S ALREADY WON!"
SET SAIL! WE'RE IN NO SHAPE FOR A FIGHT.
AND FIND ME A NICE REMOTE ICE FLOE... WHERE I CAN PARK A WASHED-UP WARRIOR WITCH.
WELL, WE CAN SAFELY SAY... IT'S BEEN A LONG NIGHT!
RIGHT. AND I'M OFF TO BED. WAKE ME UP... OOH... AROUND SUMMERTIME!
WAIT FOR ME, WAIT FOR ME!
AND GOOD RIDDANCE...

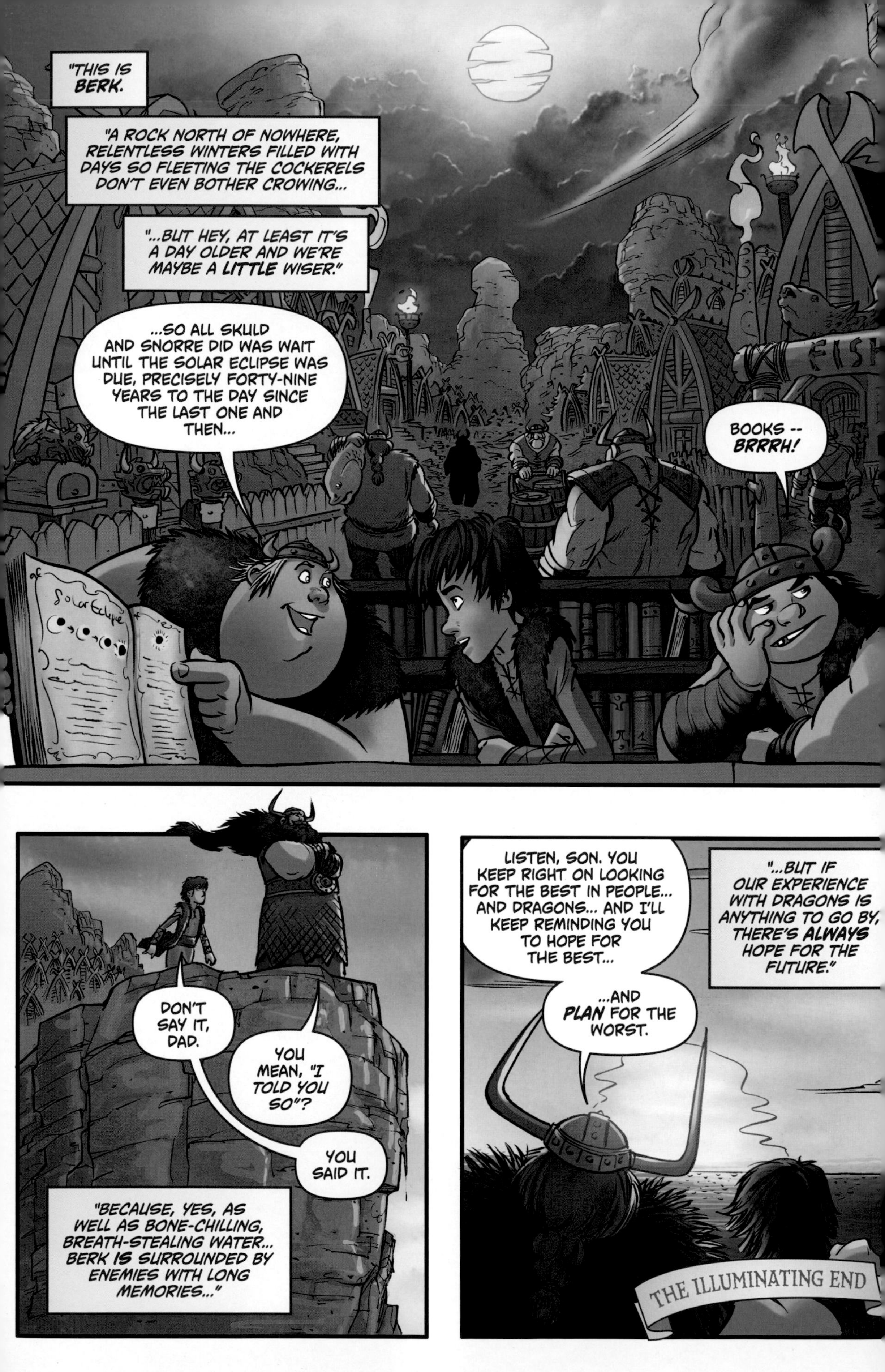
"THIS IS BERK.
"A ROCK NORTH OF NOWHERE, RELENTLESS WINTERS FILLED WITH DAYS SO FLEETING THE COCKERELS DON'T EVEN BOTHER CROWING...
"...BUT HEY, AT LEAST IT'S A DAY OLDER AND WE'RE MAYBE A LITTLE WISER."
...SO ALL SKULD AND SNORRE DID WAS WAIT UNTIL THE SOLAR ECLIPSE WAS DUE, PRECISELY FORTY-NINE YEARS TO THE DAY SINCE THE LAST ONE AND THEN...
BOOKS -- BRRRH!
Solar Eclipse
FISH
DON'T SAY IT, DAD.
YOU MEAN, "I TOLD YOU SO"?
YOU SAID IT.
"BECAUSE, YES, AS WELL AS BONE-CHILLING, BREATH-STEALING WATER... BERK IS SURROUNDED BY ENEMIES WITH LONG MEMORIES..."
LISTEN, SON. YOU KEEP RIGHT ON LOOKING FOR THE BEST IN PEOPLE... AND DRAGONS... AND I'LL KEEP REMINDING YOU TO HOPE FOR THE BEST...
...AND PLAN FOR THE WORST.
"...BUT IF OUR EXPERIENCE WITH DRAGONS IS ANYTHING TO GO BY, THERE'S ALWAYS HOPE FOR THE FUTURE."
THE ILLUMINATING END

CRUEL TO BE KIND

SCRIPT
PAUL GOODENOUGH

ART
ARIANNA FLOREAN

COLORS
CLAUDIA IANNICIELLO

LETTERING
JIM CAMPBELL

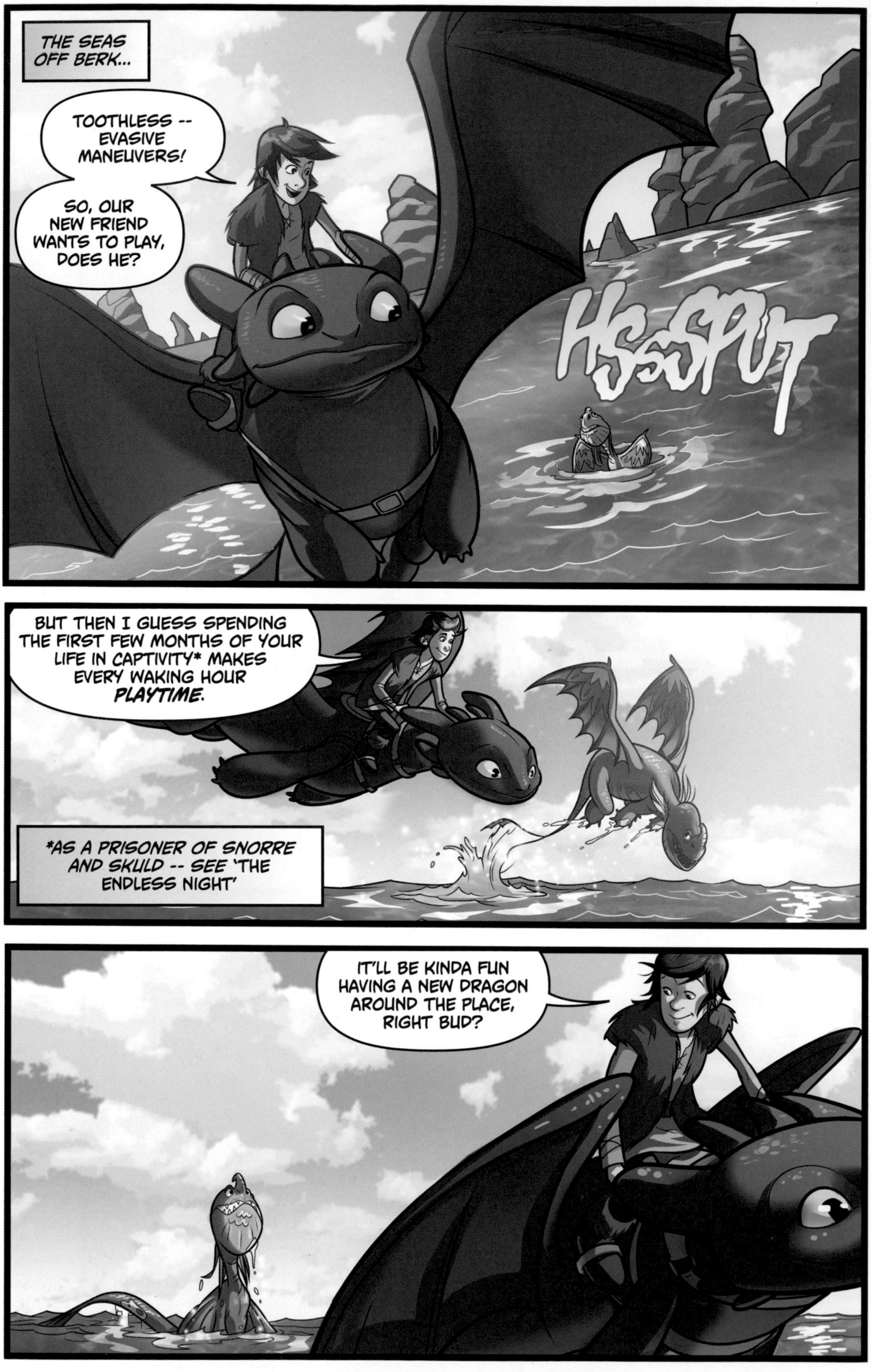
THE SEAS OFF BERK...
TOOTHLESS -- EVASIVE MANEUVERS!
SO, OUR NEW FRIEND WANTS TO PLAY, DOES HE?
HSSSPUT
BUT THEN I GUESS SPENDING THE FIRST FEW MONTHS OF YOUR LIFE IN CAPTIVITY* MAKES EVERY WAKING HOUR PLAYTIME.
*AS A PRISONER OF SNORRE AND SKULD -- SEE 'THE ENDLESS NIGHT'
IT'LL BE KINDA FUN HAVING A NEW DRAGON AROUND THE PLACE, RIGHT BUD?

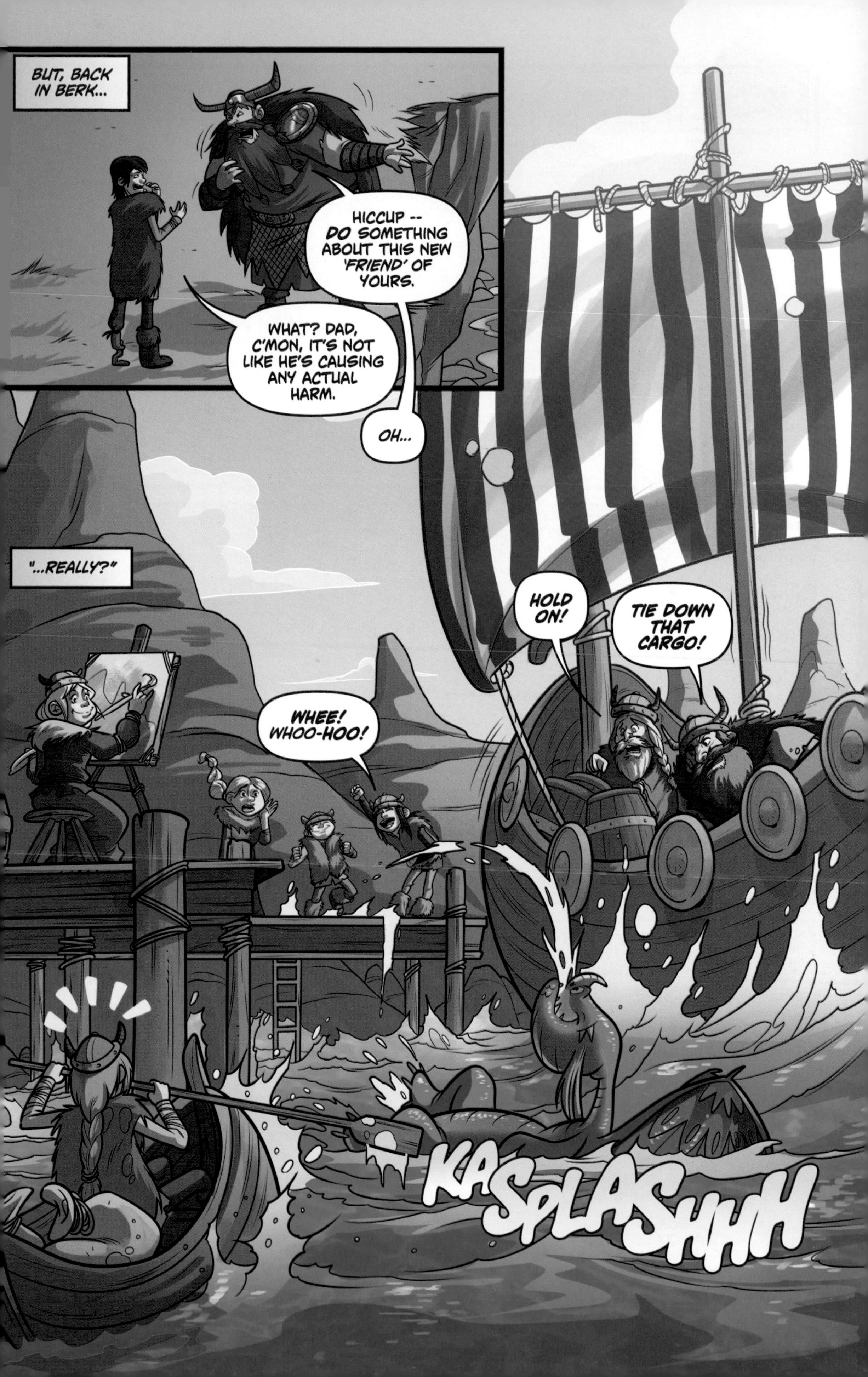
BUT, BACK IN BERK...
HICCUP -- DO SOMETHING ABOUT THIS NEW 'FRIEND' OF YOURS.
WHAT? DAD, C'MON, IT'S NOT LIKE HE'S CAUSING ANY ACTUAL HARM.
OH...
"...REALLY?"
HOLD ON!
TIE DOWN THAT CARGO!
WHEE! WHOO-HOO!
KASPLASHHH

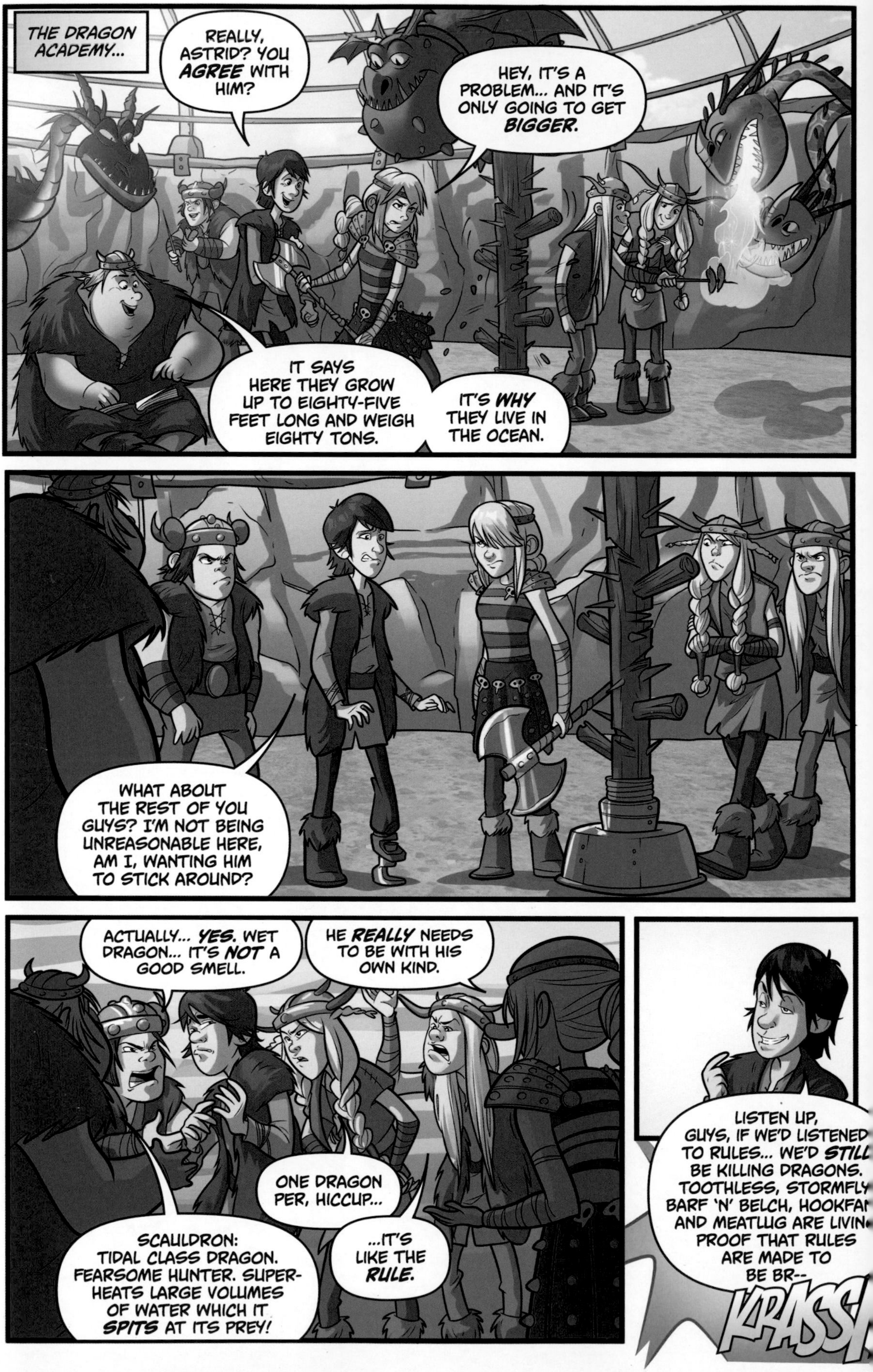

THE DRAGON ACADEMY...
REALLY, ASTRID? YOU AGREE WITH HIM?
HEY, IT'S A PROBLEM... AND IT'S ONLY GOING TO GET BIGGER.
IT SAYS HERE THEY GROW UP TO EIGHTY-FIVE FEET LONG AND WEIGH EIGHTY TONS.
IT'S WHY THEY LIVE IN THE OCEAN.
WHAT ABOUT THE REST OF YOU GUYS? I'M NOT BEING UNREASONABLE HERE, AM I, WANTING HIM TO STICK AROUND?
ACTUALLY... YES. WET DRAGON... IT'S NOT A GOOD SMELL.
HE REALLY NEEDS TO BE WITH HIS OWN KIND.
SCAULDRON: TIDAL CLASS DRAGON. FEARSOME HUNTER. SUPER-HEATS LARGE VOLUMES OF WATER WHICH IT SPITS AT ITS PREY!
ONE DRAGON PER, HICCUP...
...IT'S LIKE THE RULE.
LISTEN UP, GUYS, IF WE'D LISTENED TO RULES... WE'D STILL BE KILLING DRAGONS. TOOTHLESS, STORMFLY, BARF 'N' BELCH, HOOKFANG AND MEATLUG ARE LIVING PROOF THAT RULES ARE MADE TO BE BR--
KRASSH

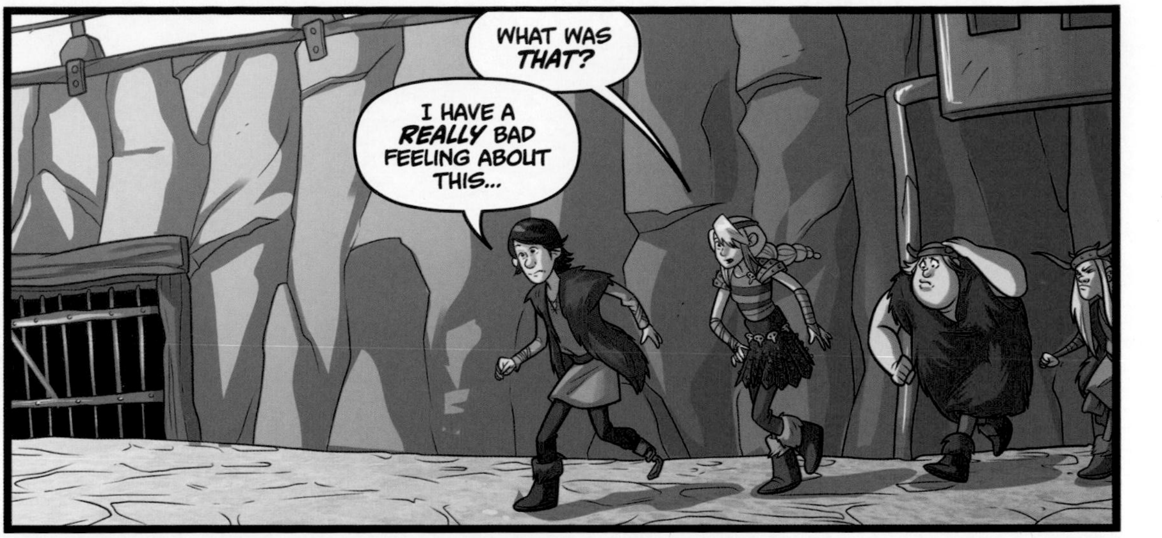
WHAT WAS THAT?
I HAVE A REALLY BAD FEELING ABOUT THIS...

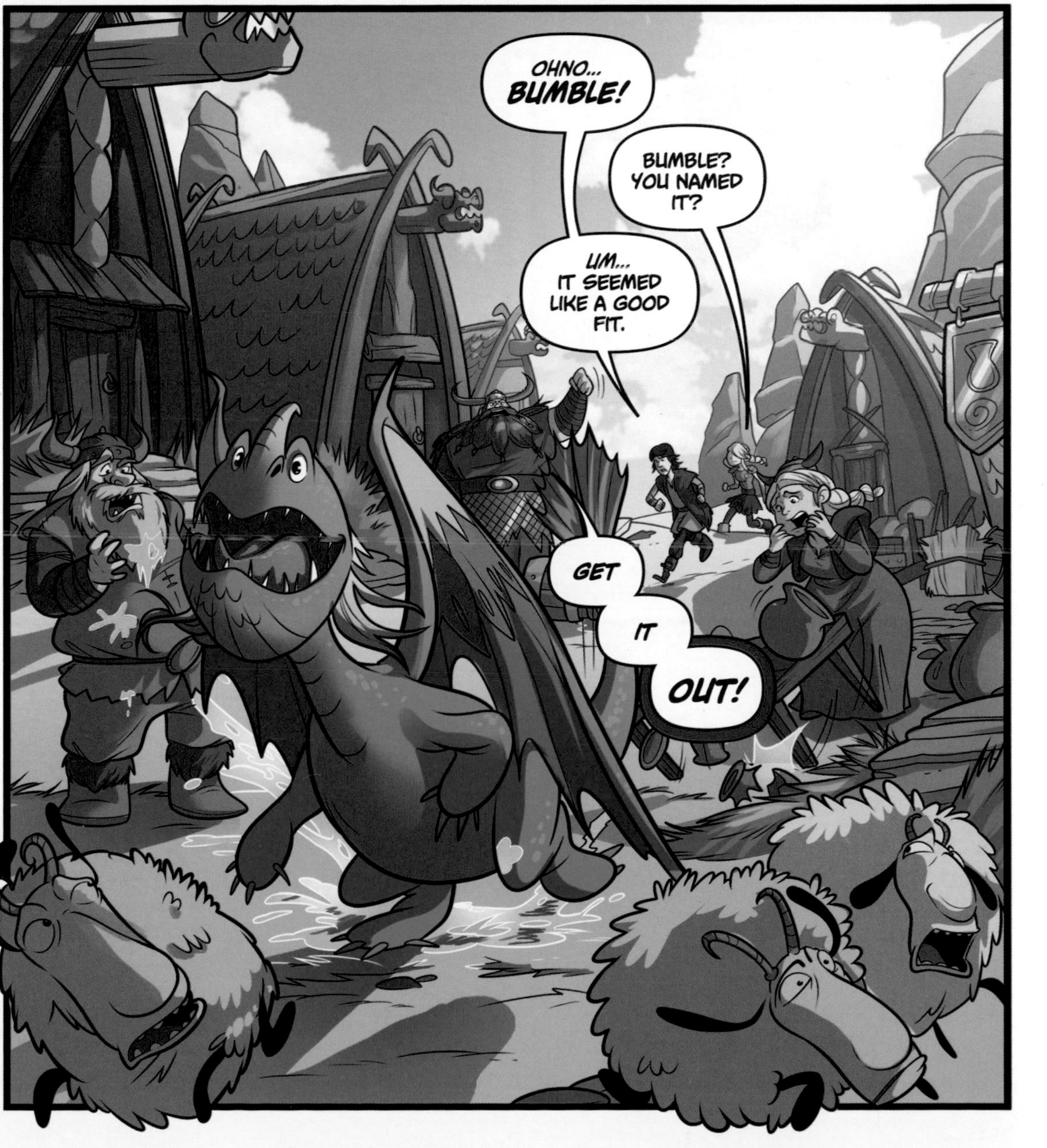
OHNO... BUMBLE!
BUMBLE? YOU NAMED IT?
UM... IT SEEMED LIKE A GOOD FIT.
GET IT OUT!

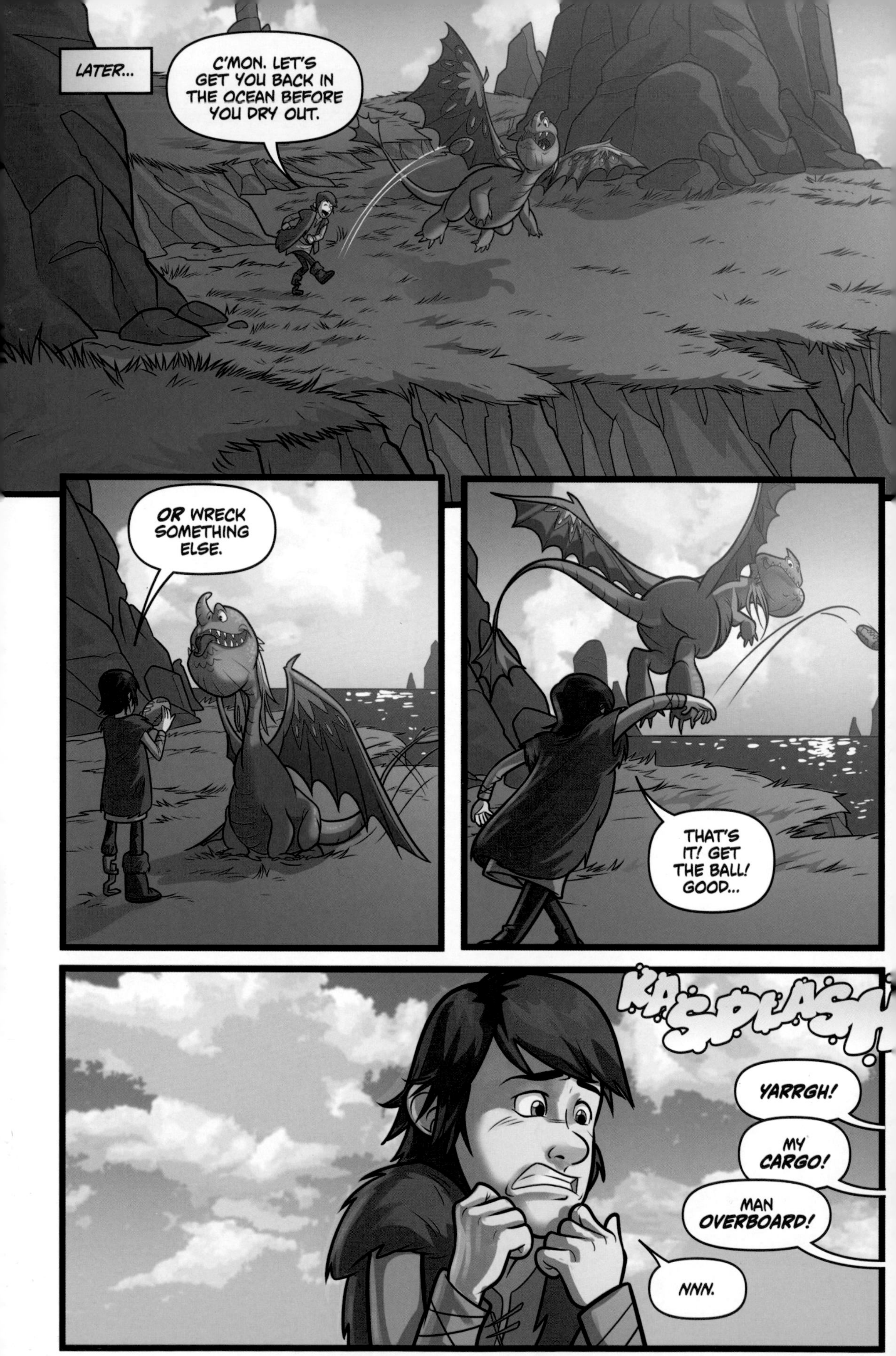
LATER...
C'MON. LET'S GET YOU BACK IN THE OCEAN BEFORE YOU DRY OUT.
OR WRECK SOMETHING ELSE.
THAT'S IT! GET THE BALL! GOOD...
KA-SPLASH!
YARRGH!
MY CARGO!
MAN OVERBOARD!
NNN.

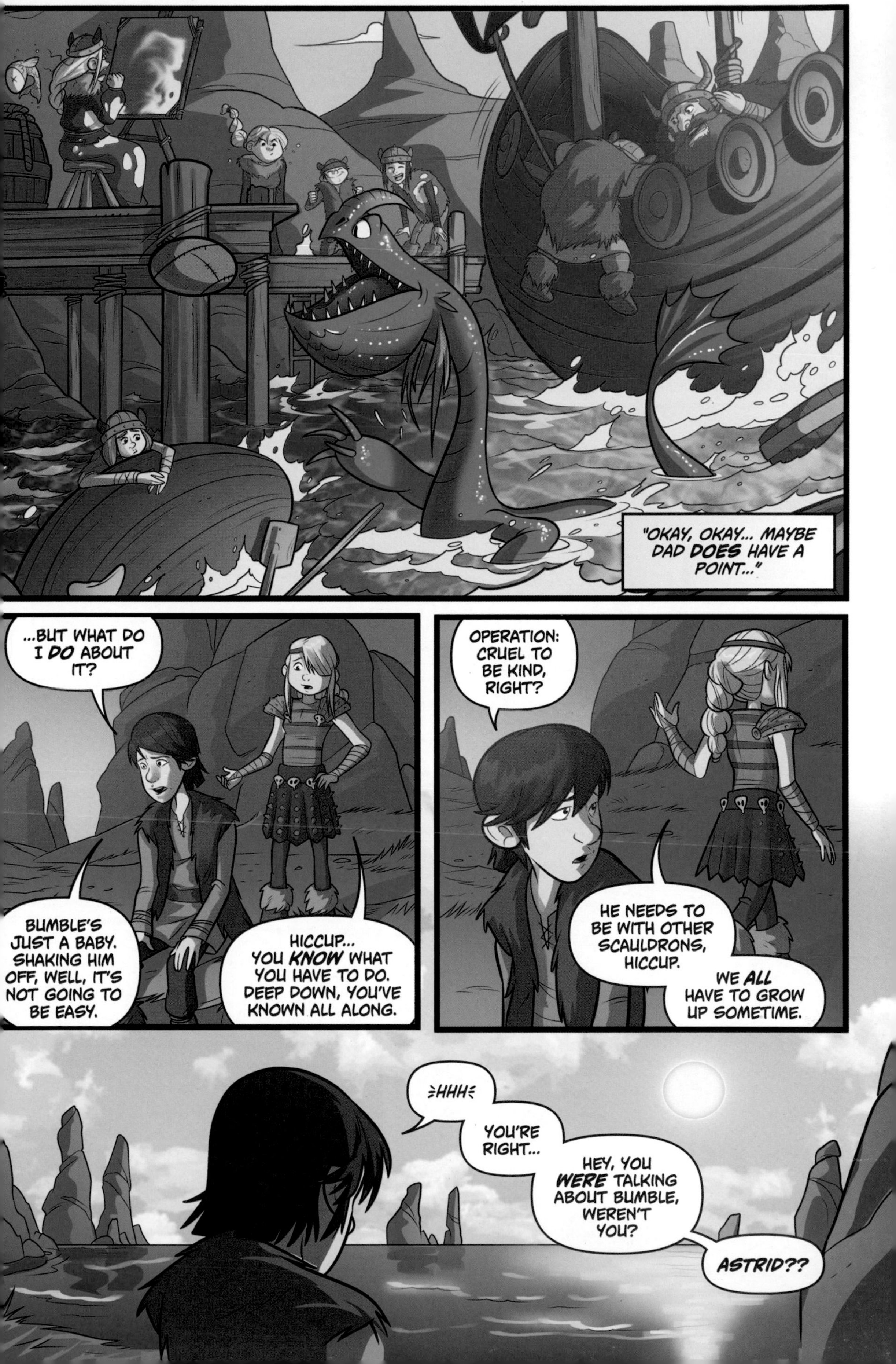
"OKAY, OKAY... MAYBE DAD DOES HAVE A POINT..."
...BUT WHAT DO I DO ABOUT IT?
BUMBLE'S JUST A BABY. SHAKING HIM OFF, WELL, IT'S NOT GOING TO BE EASY.
HICCUP... YOU KNOW WHAT YOU HAVE TO DO. DEEP DOWN, YOU'VE KNOWN ALL ALONG.
OPERATION: CRUEL TO BE KIND, RIGHT?
HE NEEDS TO BE WITH OTHER SCAULDRONS, HICCUP.
WE ALL HAVE TO GROW UP SOMETIME.
HHH
YOU'RE RIGHT...
HEY, YOU WERE TALKING ABOUT BUMBLE, WEREN'T YOU?
ASTRID??

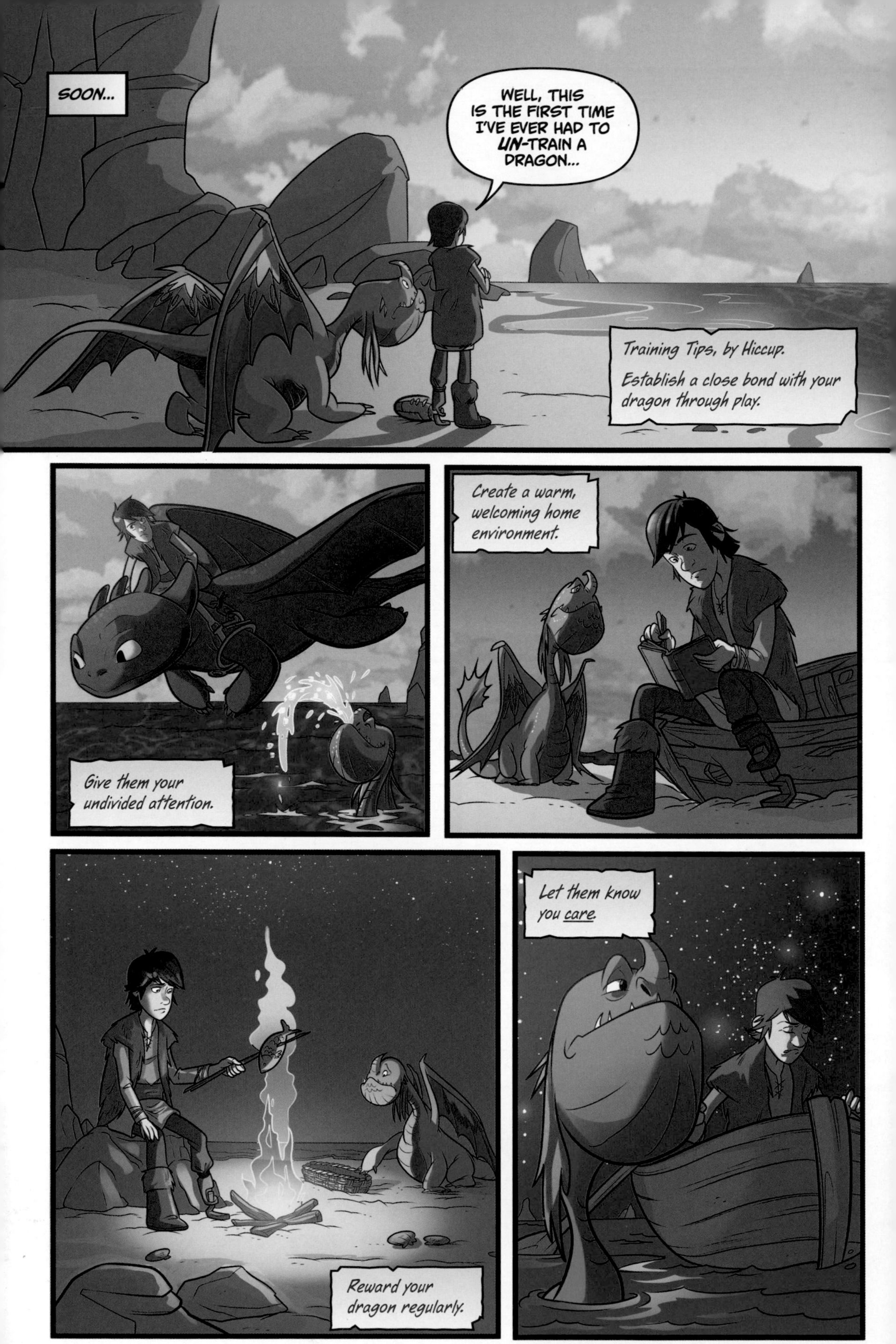
SOON...
WELL, THIS IS THE FIRST TIME I'VE EVER HAD TO UN-TRAIN A DRAGON...
Training Tips, by Hiccup.
Establish a close bond with your dragon through play.
Give them your undivided attention.
Create a warm, welcoming home environment.
Reward your dragon regularly.
Let them know you care.

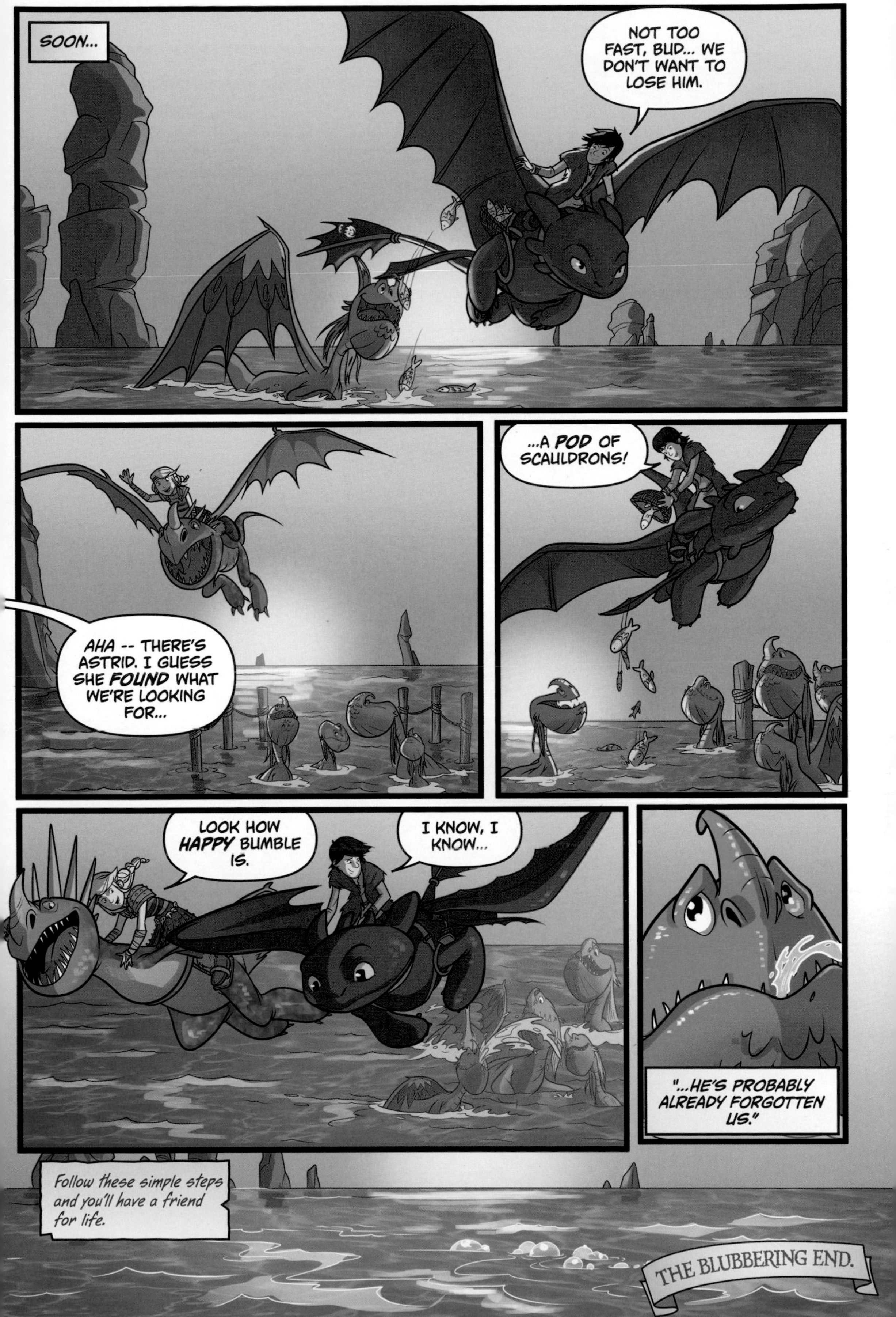
SOON...
NOT TOO FAST, BUD... WE DON'T WANT TO LOSE HIM.
AHA -- THERE'S ASTRID. I GUESS SHE *FOUND* WHAT WE'RE LOOKING FOR...
...A *POD* OF SCAULDRONS!
LOOK HOW *HAPPY* BUMBLE IS.
I KNOW, I KNOW...
"...HE'S PROBABLY ALREADY FORGOTTEN US."
Follow these simple steps and you'll have a friend for life.
THE BLUBBERING END.

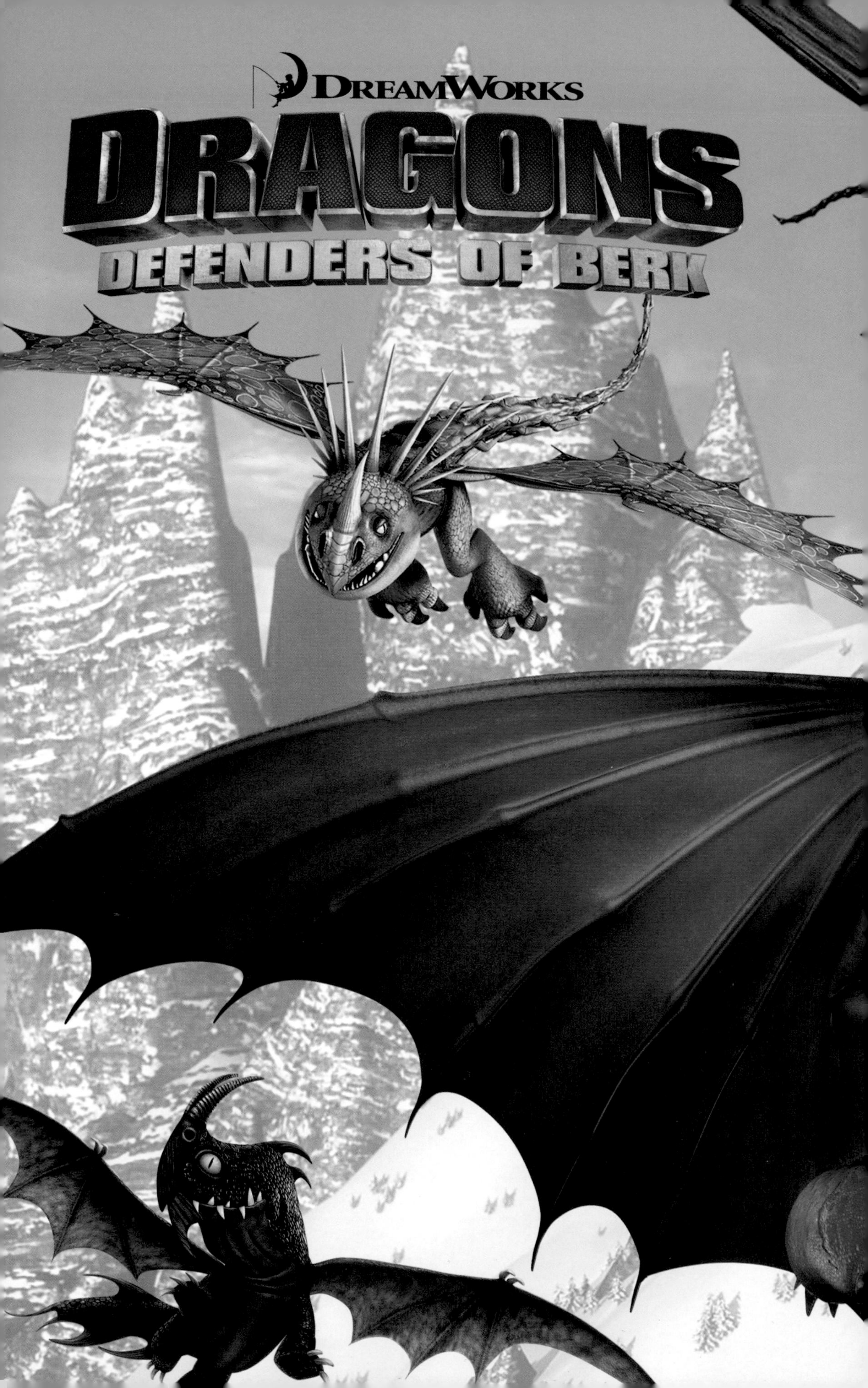
DreamWorks
DRAGONS
DEFENDERS OF BERK

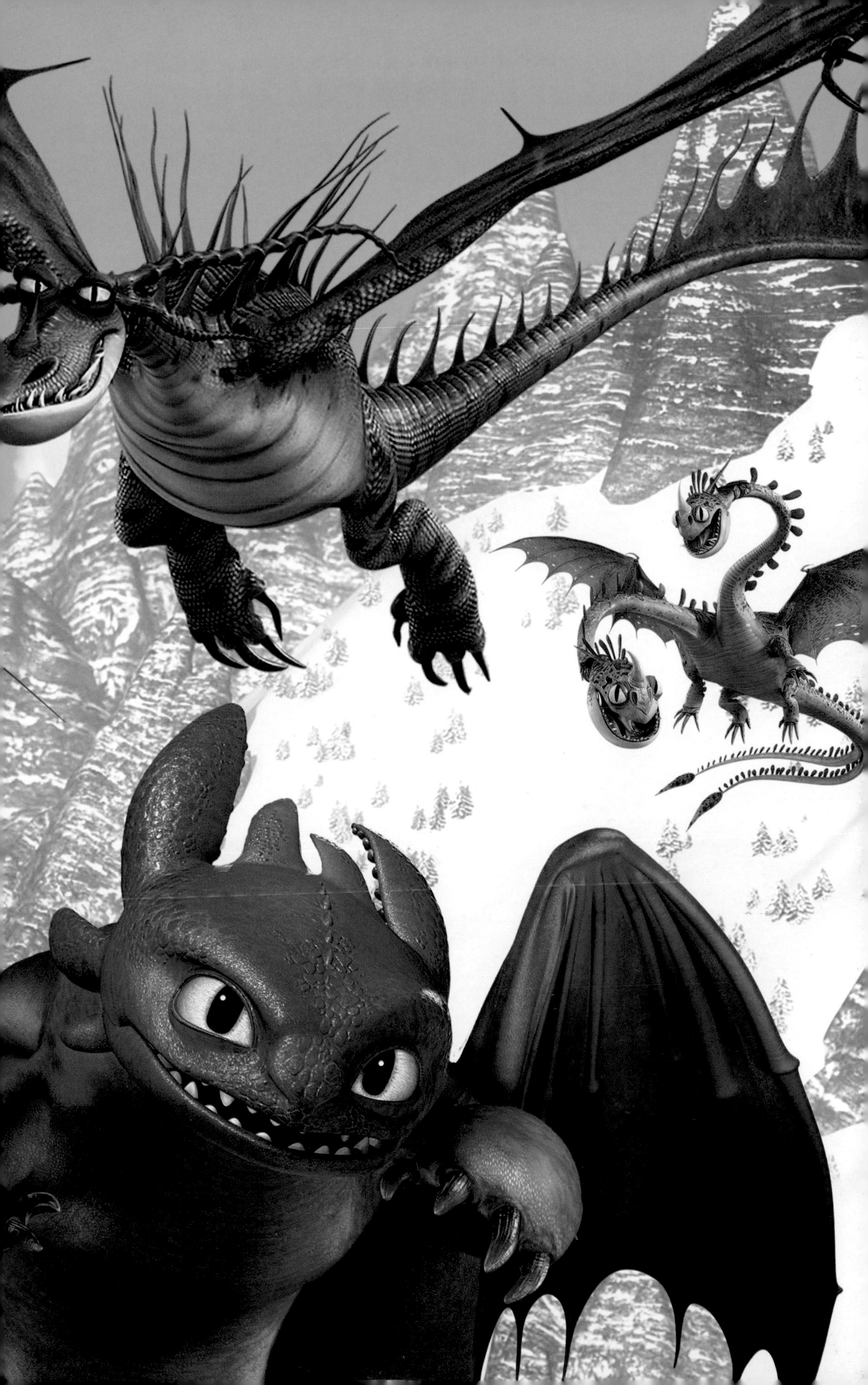

SNOWMAGEDDON

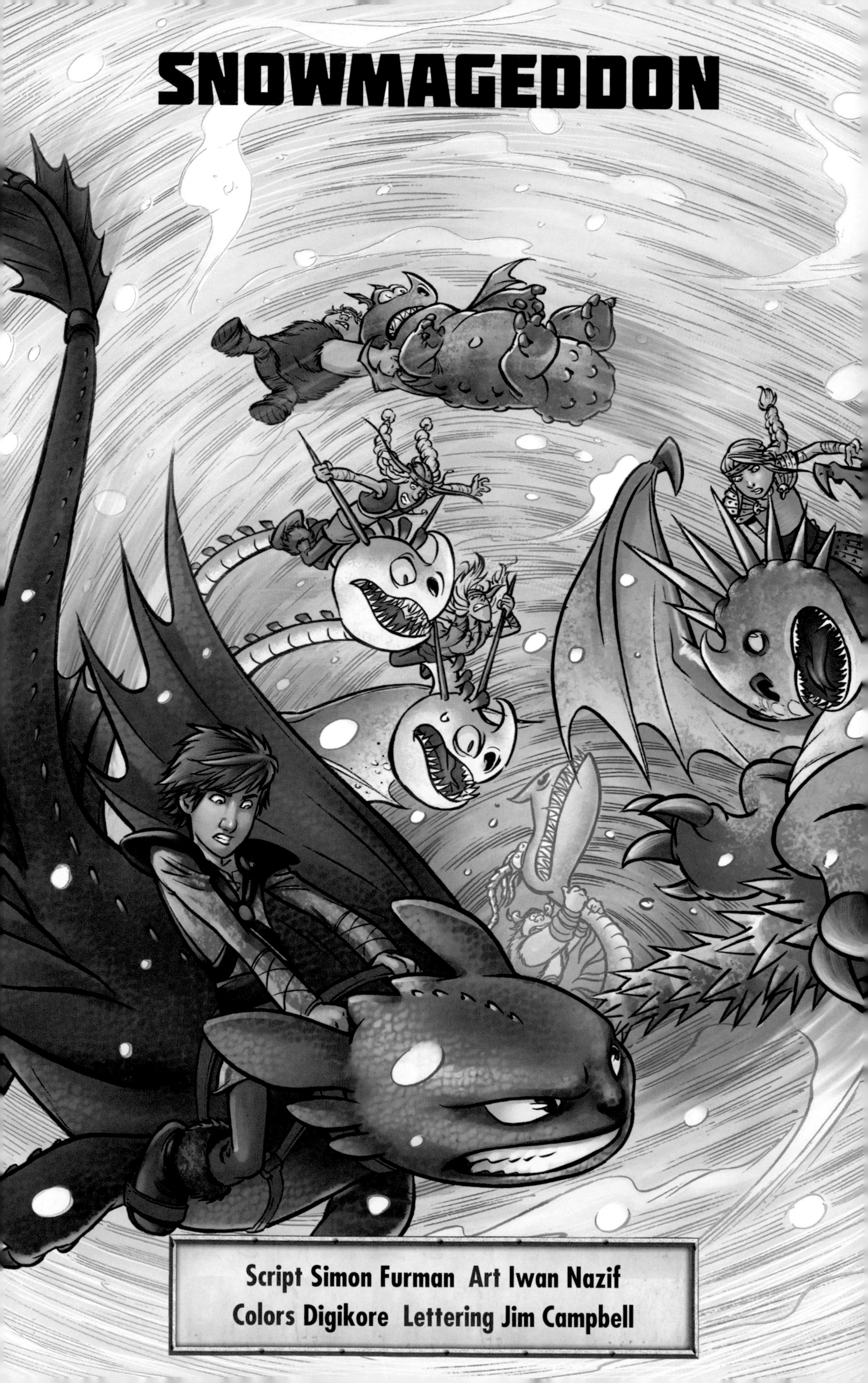
Script Simon Furman Art Iwan Nazif
Colors Digikore Lettering Jim Campbell

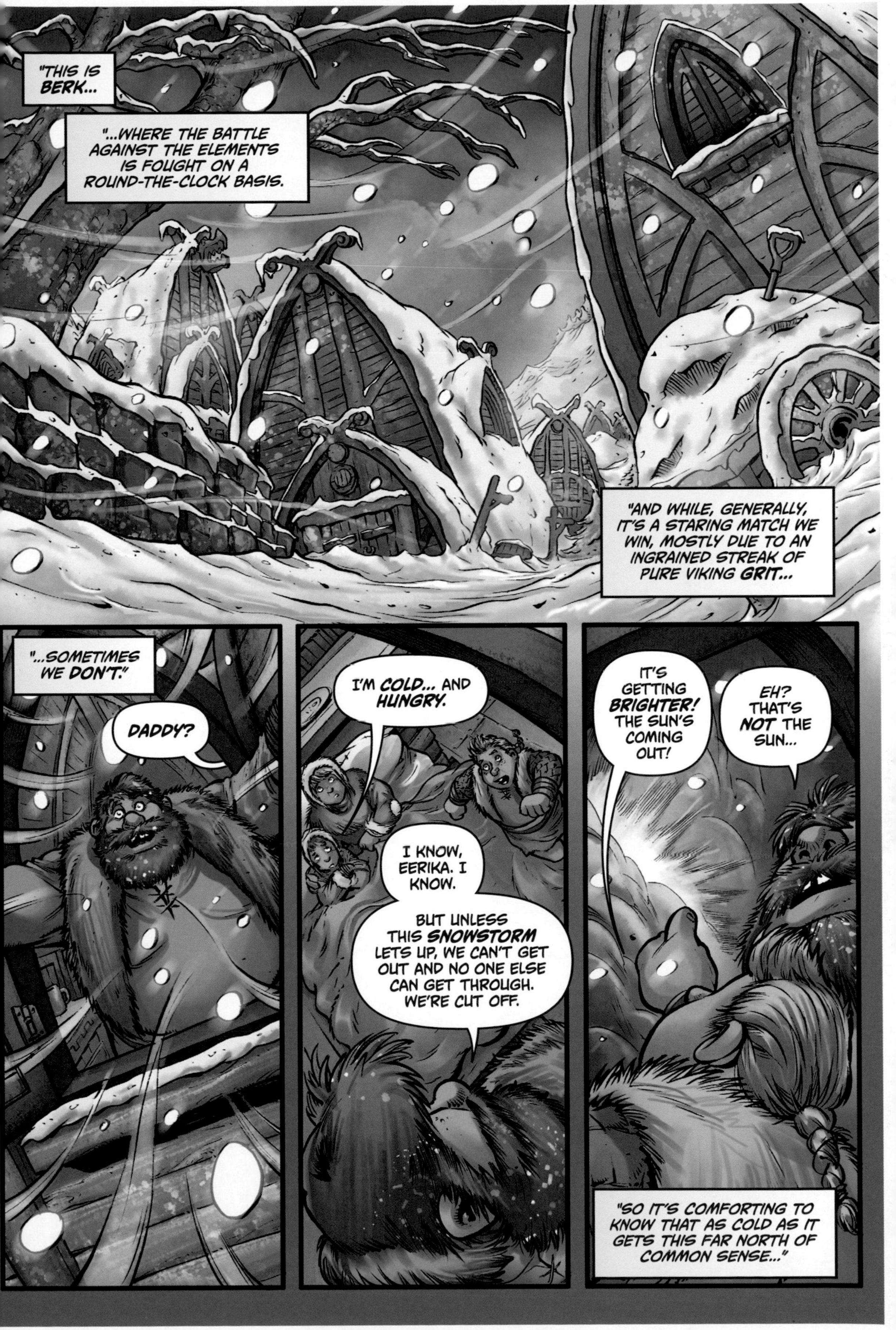
"THIS IS BERK...
"...WHERE THE BATTLE AGAINST THE ELEMENTS IS FOUGHT ON A ROUND-THE-CLOCK BASIS.
"AND WHILE, GENERALLY, IT'S A STARING MATCH WE WIN, MOSTLY DUE TO AN INGRAINED STREAK OF PURE VIKING GRIT...
"...SOMETIMES WE DON'T."
DADDY?
I'M COLD... AND HUNGRY.
I KNOW, EERIKA. I KNOW.
BUT UNLESS THIS SNOWSTORM LETS UP, WE CAN'T GET OUT AND NO ONE ELSE CAN GET THROUGH. WE'RE CUT OFF.
IT'S GETTING BRIGHTER! THE SUN'S COMING OUT!
EH? THAT'S NOT THE SUN...
"SO IT'S COMFORTING TO KNOW THAT AS COLD AS IT GETS THIS FAR NORTH OF COMMON SENSE..."

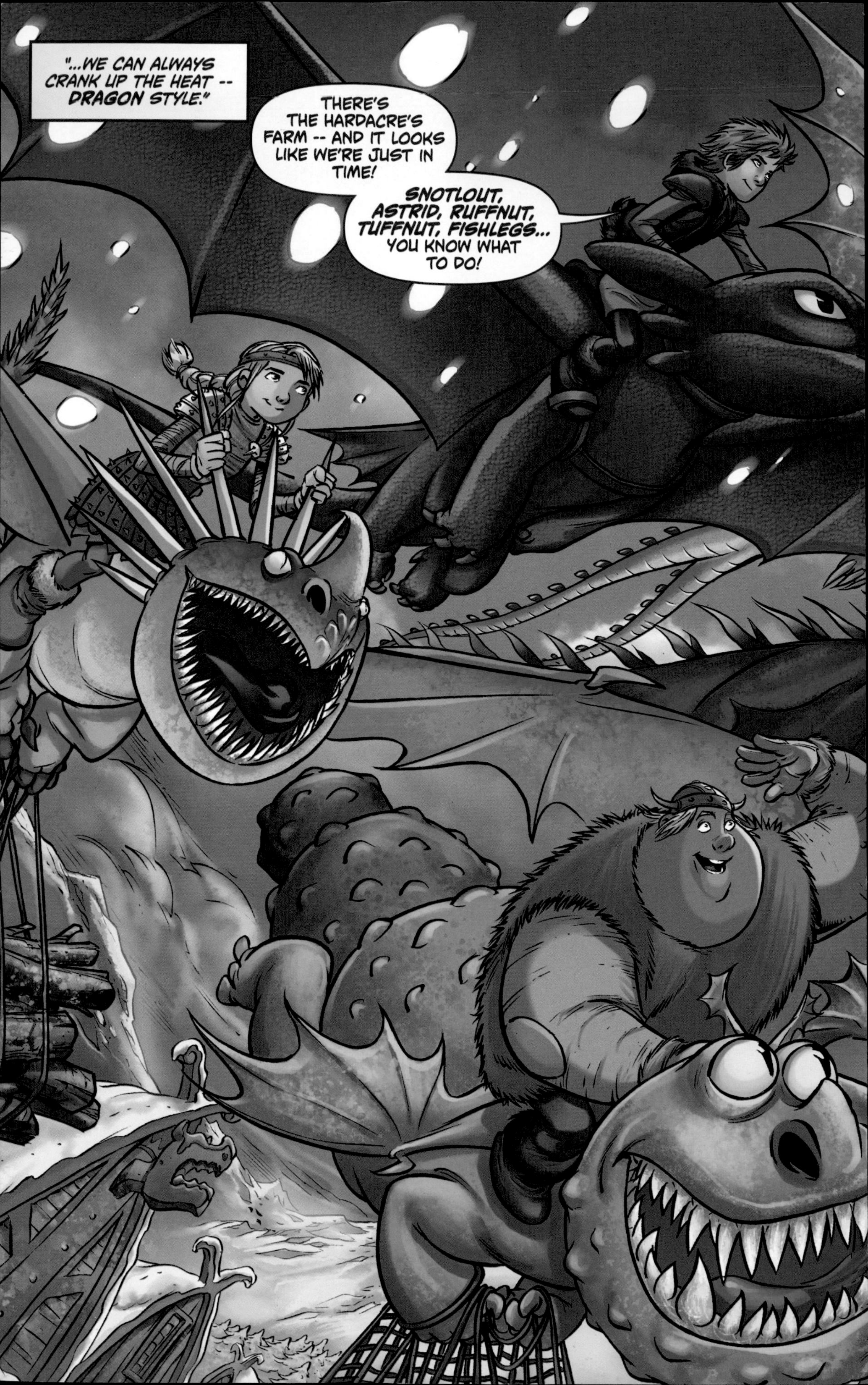
"...WE CAN ALWAYS CRANK UP THE HEAT -- DRAGON STYLE."
THERE'S THE HARDACRE'S FARM -- AND IT LOOKS LIKE WE'RE JUST IN TIME!
SNOTLOUT, ASTRID, RUFFNUT, TUFFNUT, FISHLEGS... YOU KNOW WHAT TO DO!

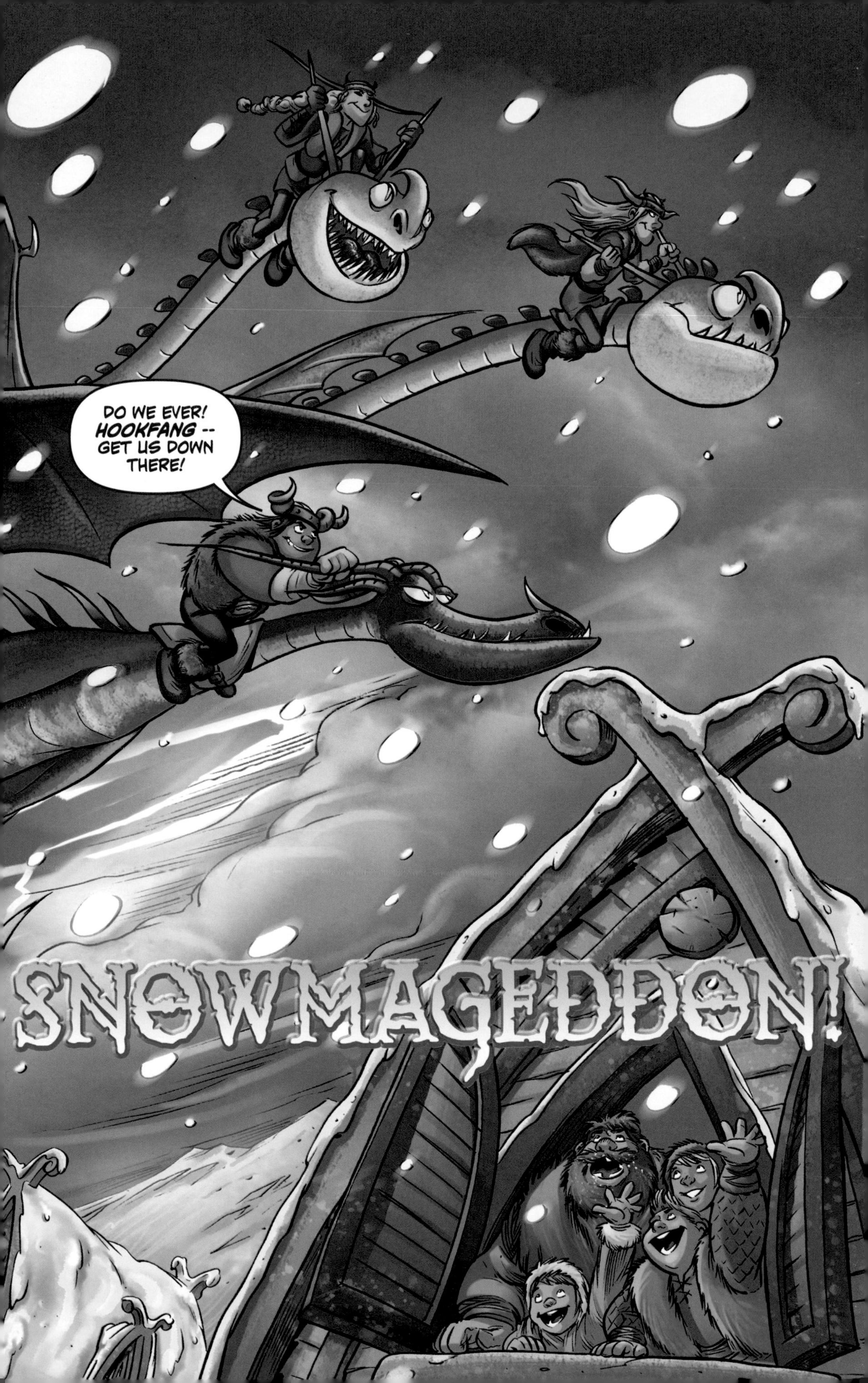
DO WE EVER! *HOOKFANG* -- GET US DOWN THERE!
SNOWMAGEDDON!

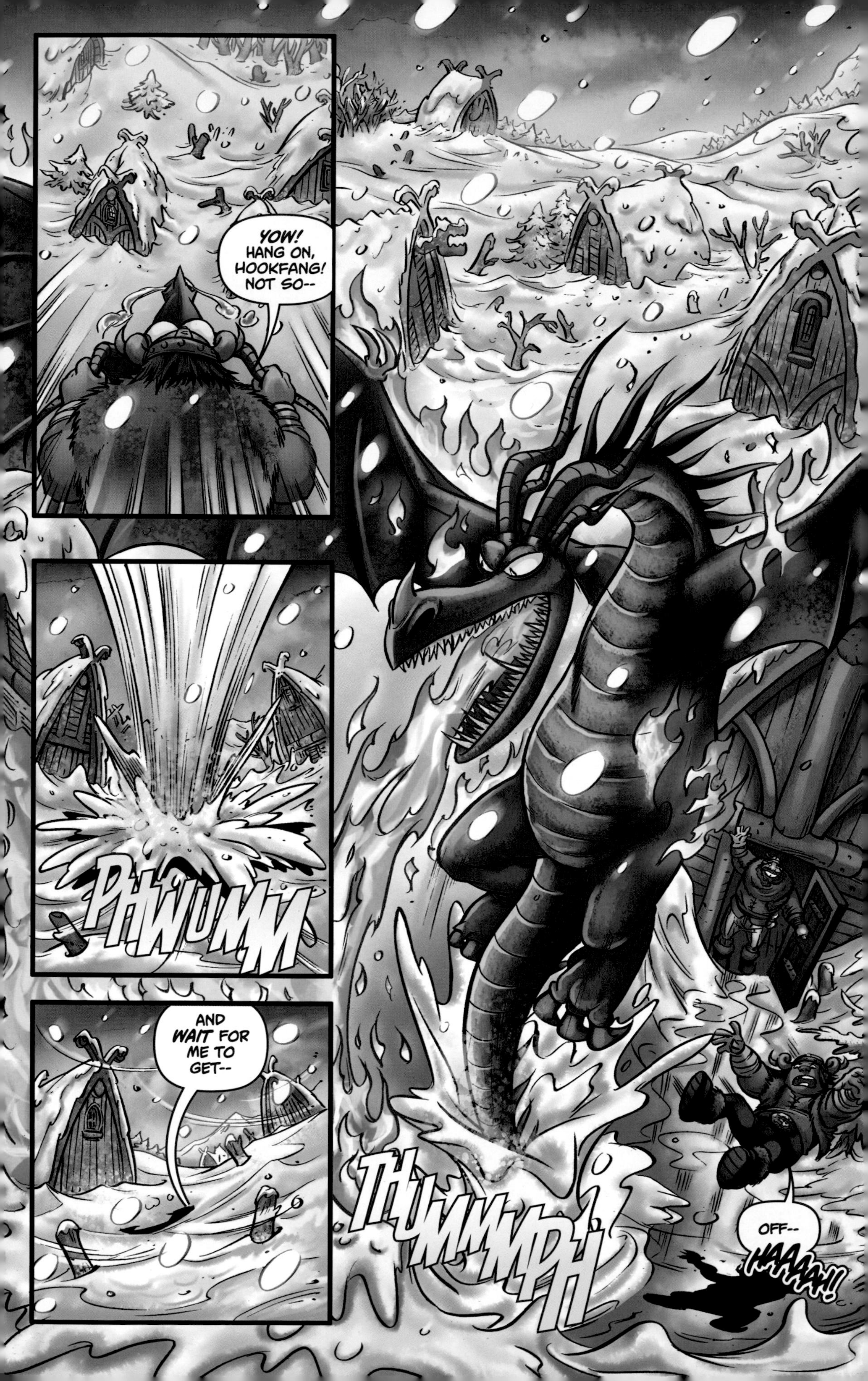
YOW! HANG ON, HOOKFANG! NOT SO--
PHWUMM
AND WAIT FOR ME TO GET--
THUMMMPH
OFF--
HAAAAH!!

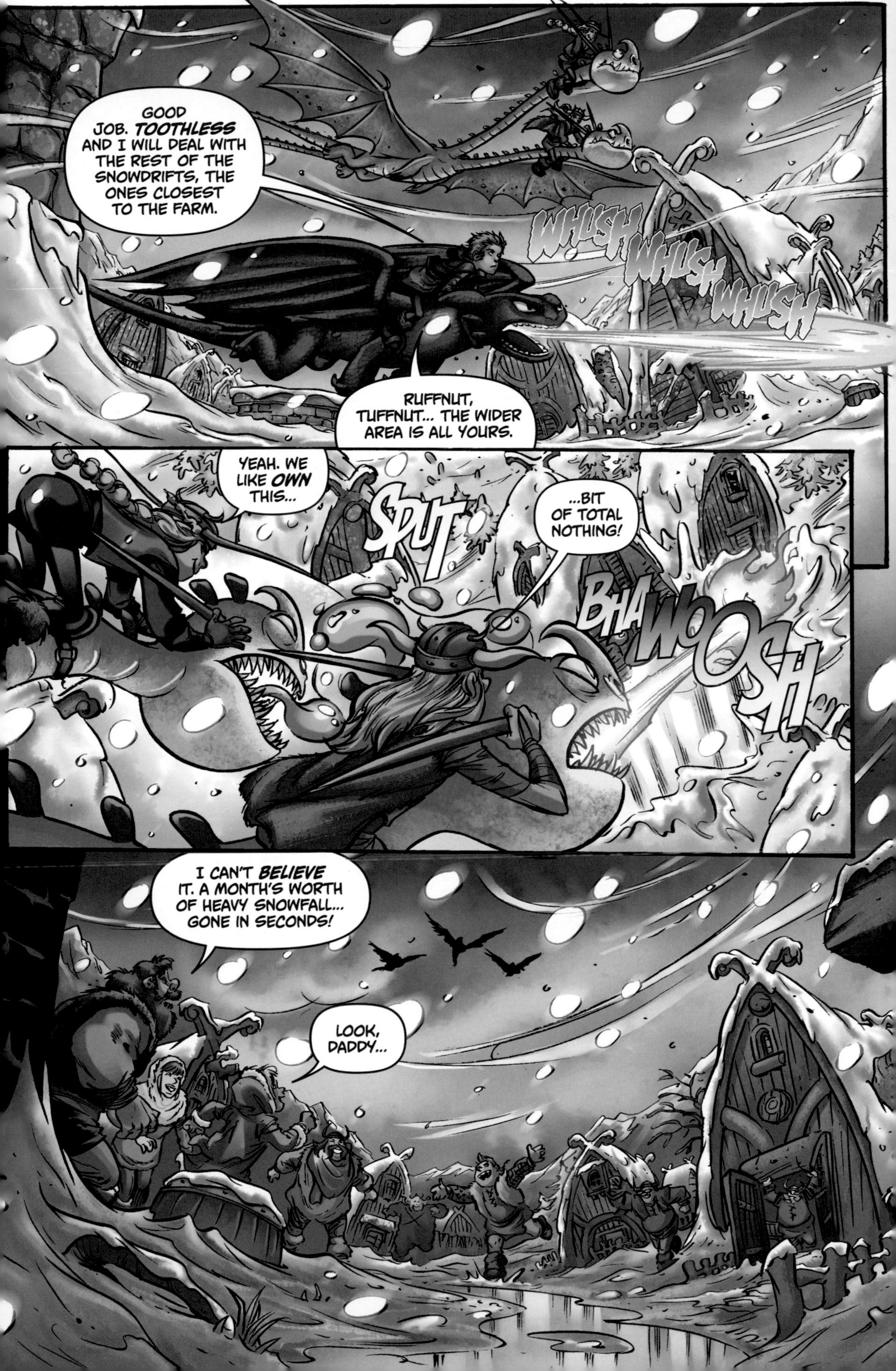
GOOD JOB. TOOTHLESS AND I WILL DEAL WITH THE REST OF THE SNOWDRIFTS, THE ONES CLOSEST TO THE FARM.
WHUSH WHUSH WHUSH
RUFFNUT, TUFFNUT... THE WIDER AREA IS ALL YOURS.
YEAH. WE LIKE OWN THIS...
SPUT
...BIT OF TOTAL NOTHING!
BHAWOOSH
I CAN'T BELIEVE IT. A MONTH'S WORTH OF HEAVY SNOWFALL... GONE IN SECONDS!
LOOK, DADDY...

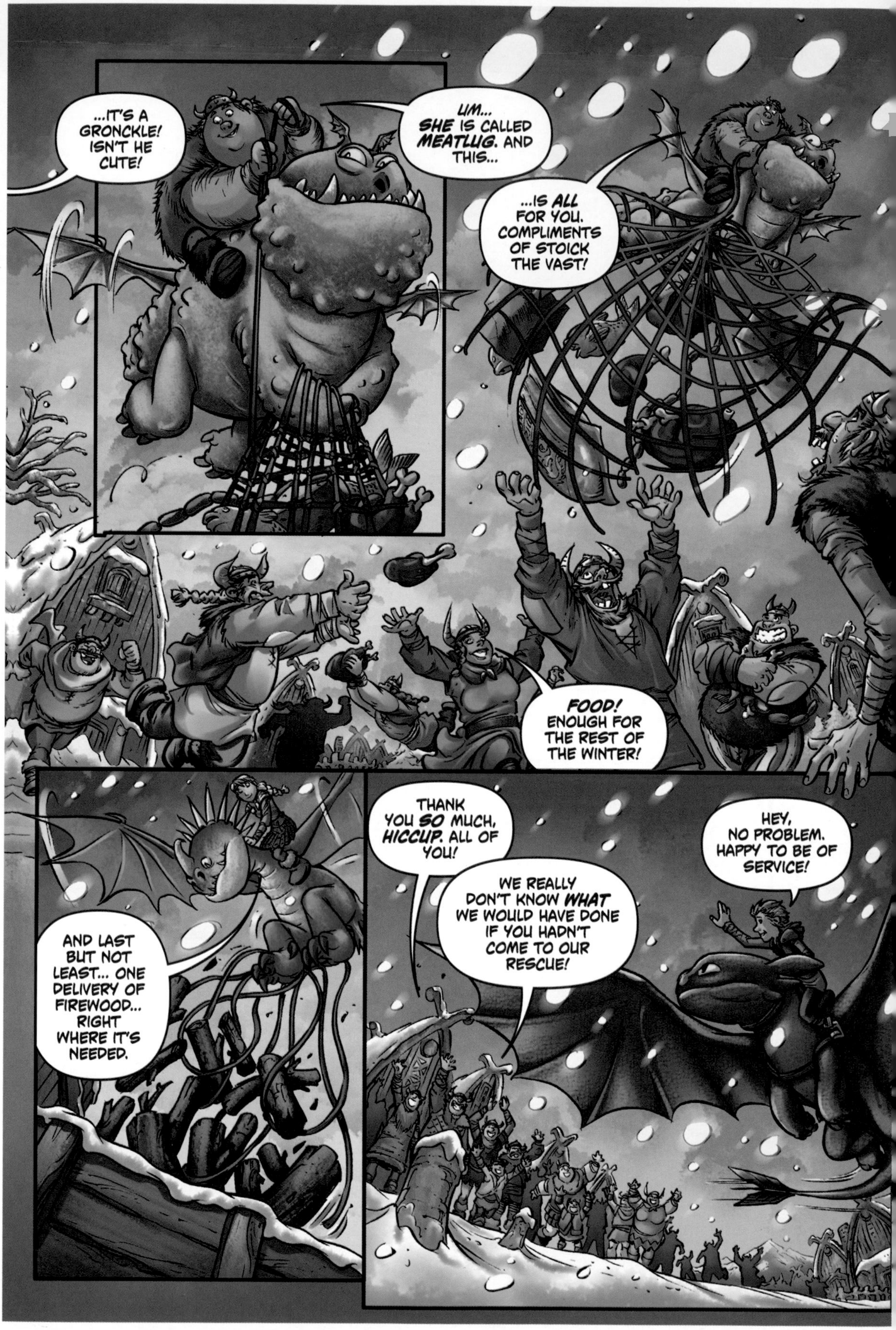
...IT'S A GRONCKLE! ISN'T HE CUTE!
UM... SHE IS CALLED MEATLUG. AND THIS...
...IS ALL FOR YOU. COMPLIMENTS OF STOICK THE VAST!
FOOD! ENOUGH FOR THE REST OF THE WINTER!
AND LAST BUT NOT LEAST... ONE DELIVERY OF FIREWOOD... RIGHT WHERE IT'S NEEDED.
THANK YOU SO MUCH, HICCUP. ALL OF YOU!
WE REALLY DON'T KNOW WHAT WE WOULD HAVE DONE IF YOU HADN'T COME TO OUR RESCUE!
HEY, NO PROBLEM. HAPPY TO BE OF SERVICE!

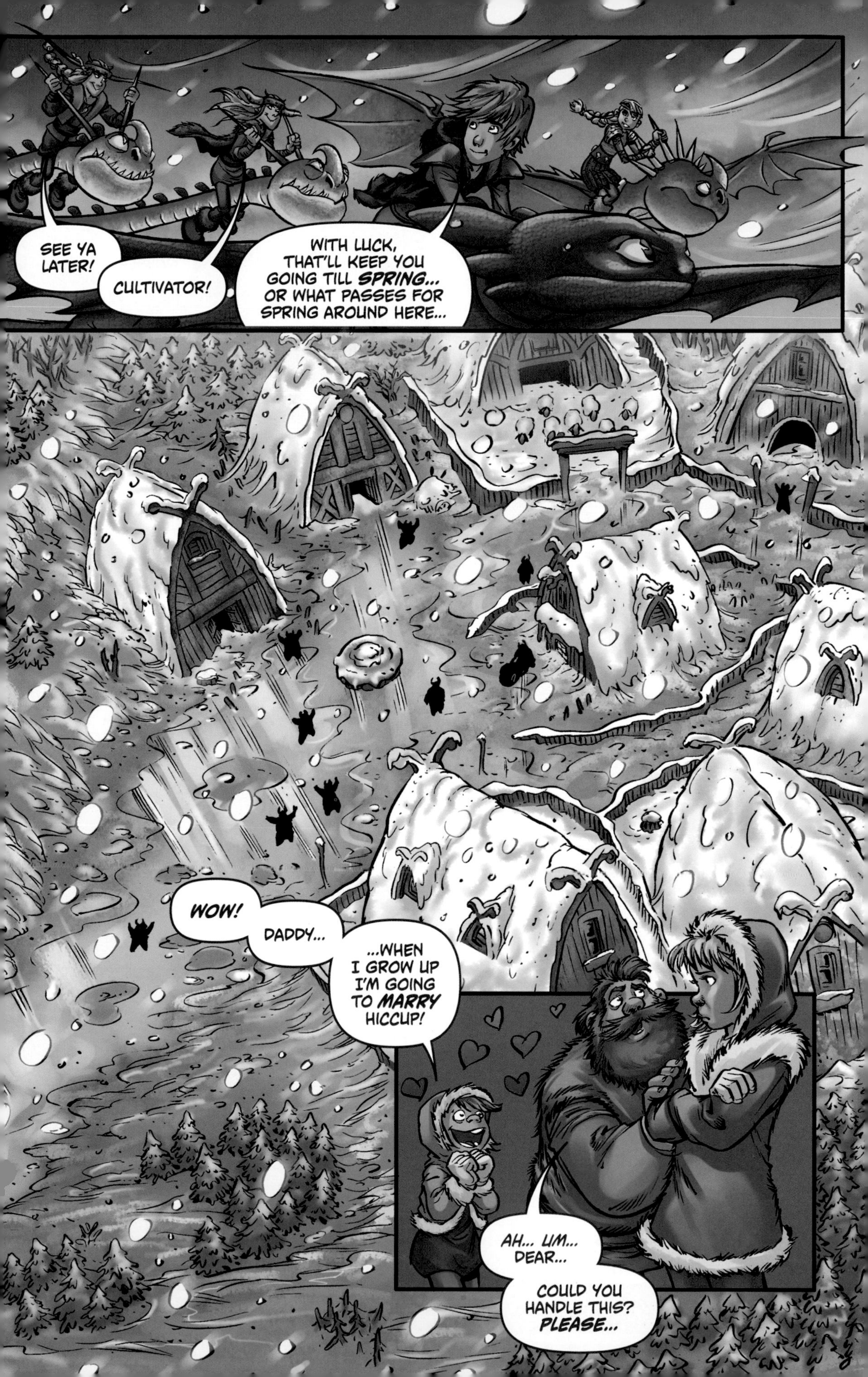
SEE YA LATER!
CULTIVATOR!
WITH LUCK, THAT'LL KEEP YOU GOING TILL SPRING... OR WHAT PASSES FOR SPRING AROUND HERE...
WOW!
DADDY...
...WHEN I GROW UP I'M GOING TO MARRY HICCUP!
AH... UM... DEAR...
COULD YOU HANDLE THIS? PLEASE...

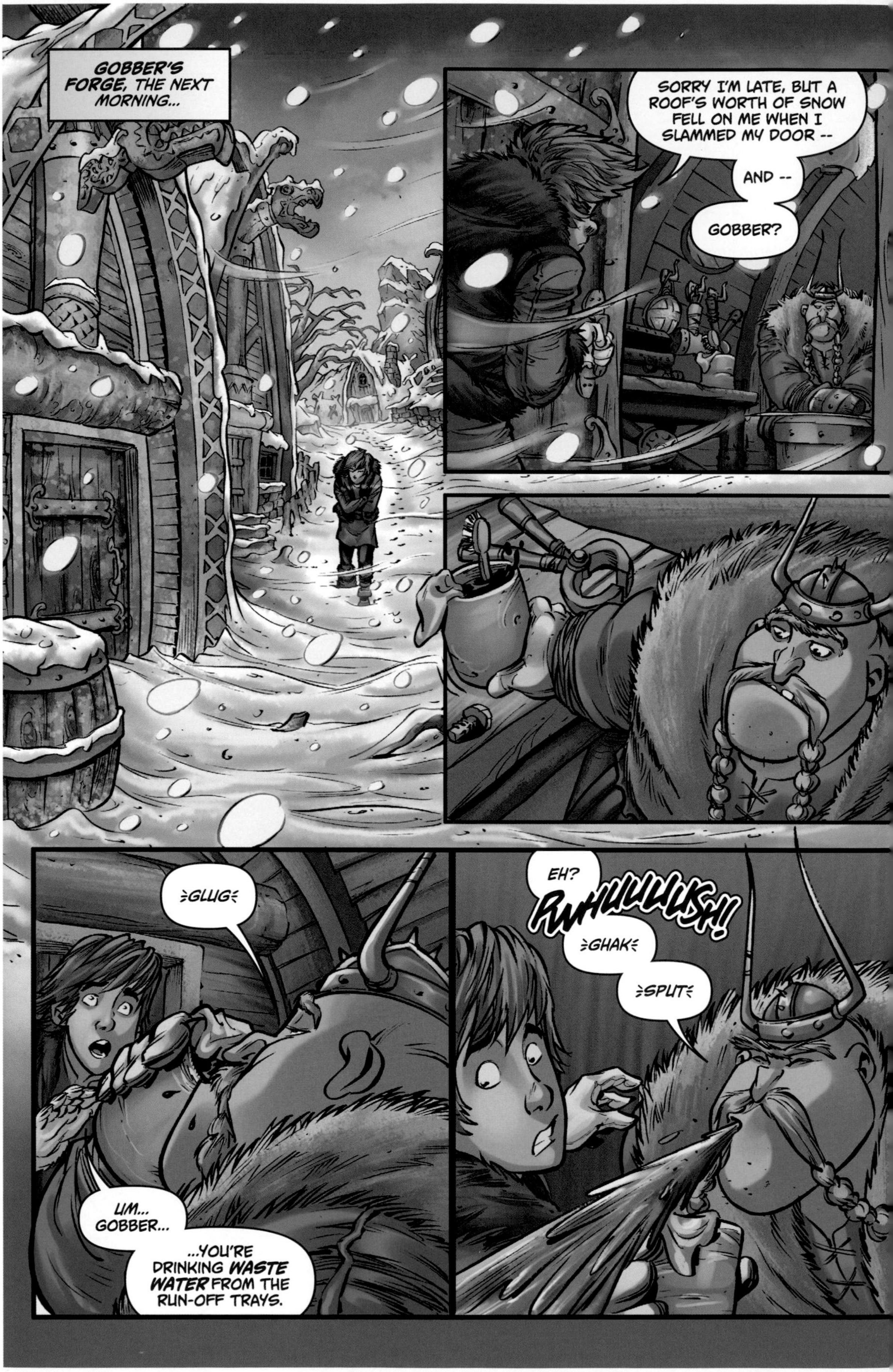
GOBBER'S FORGE, THE NEXT MORNING...
SORRY I'M LATE, BUT A ROOF'S WORTH OF SNOW FELL ON ME WHEN I SLAMMED MY DOOR --
AND --
GOBBER?
GLUG
UM... GOBBER...
...YOU'RE DRINKING WASTE WATER FROM THE RUN-OFF TRAYS.
EH?
PWHUUUUSH!!
GHAK
SPUT

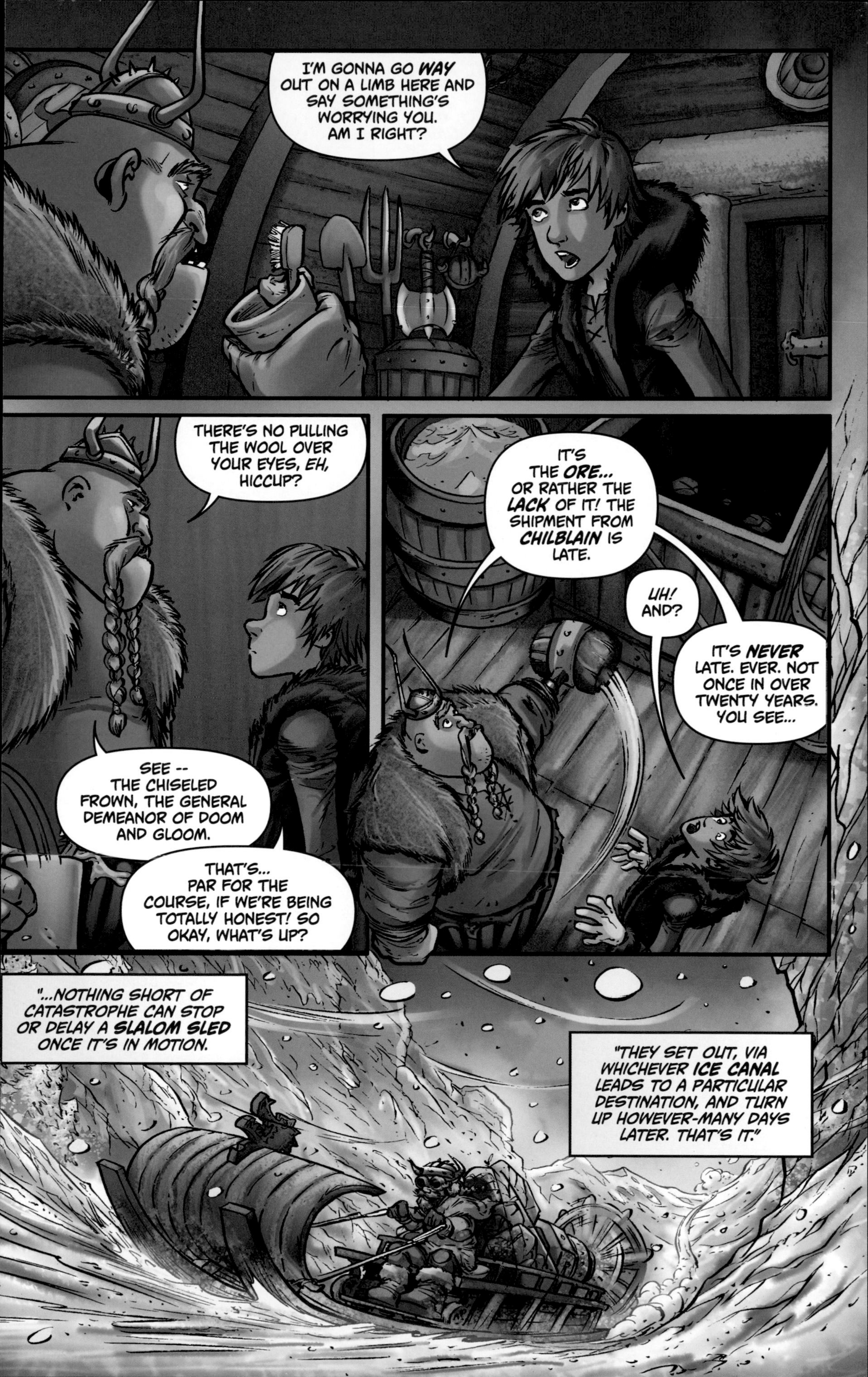
I'M GONNA GO WAY OUT ON A LIMB HERE AND SAY SOMETHING'S WORRYING YOU. AM I RIGHT?
THERE'S NO PULLING THE WOOL OVER YOUR EYES, EH, HICCUP?
SEE -- THE CHISELED FROWN, THE GENERAL DEMEANOR OF DOOM AND GLOOM.
THAT'S... PAR FOR THE COURSE, IF WE'RE BEING TOTALLY HONEST! SO OKAY, WHAT'S UP?
IT'S THE ORE... OR RATHER THE LACK OF IT! THE SHIPMENT FROM CHILBLAIN IS LATE.
UH! AND?
IT'S NEVER LATE. EVER. NOT ONCE IN OVER TWENTY YEARS. YOU SEE...
"...NOTHING SHORT OF CATASTROPHE CAN STOP OR DELAY A SLALOM SLED ONCE IT'S IN MOTION.
"THEY SET OUT, VIA WHICHEVER ICE CANAL LEADS TO A PARTICULAR DESTINATION, AND TURN UP HOWEVER-MANY DAYS LATER. THAT'S IT."

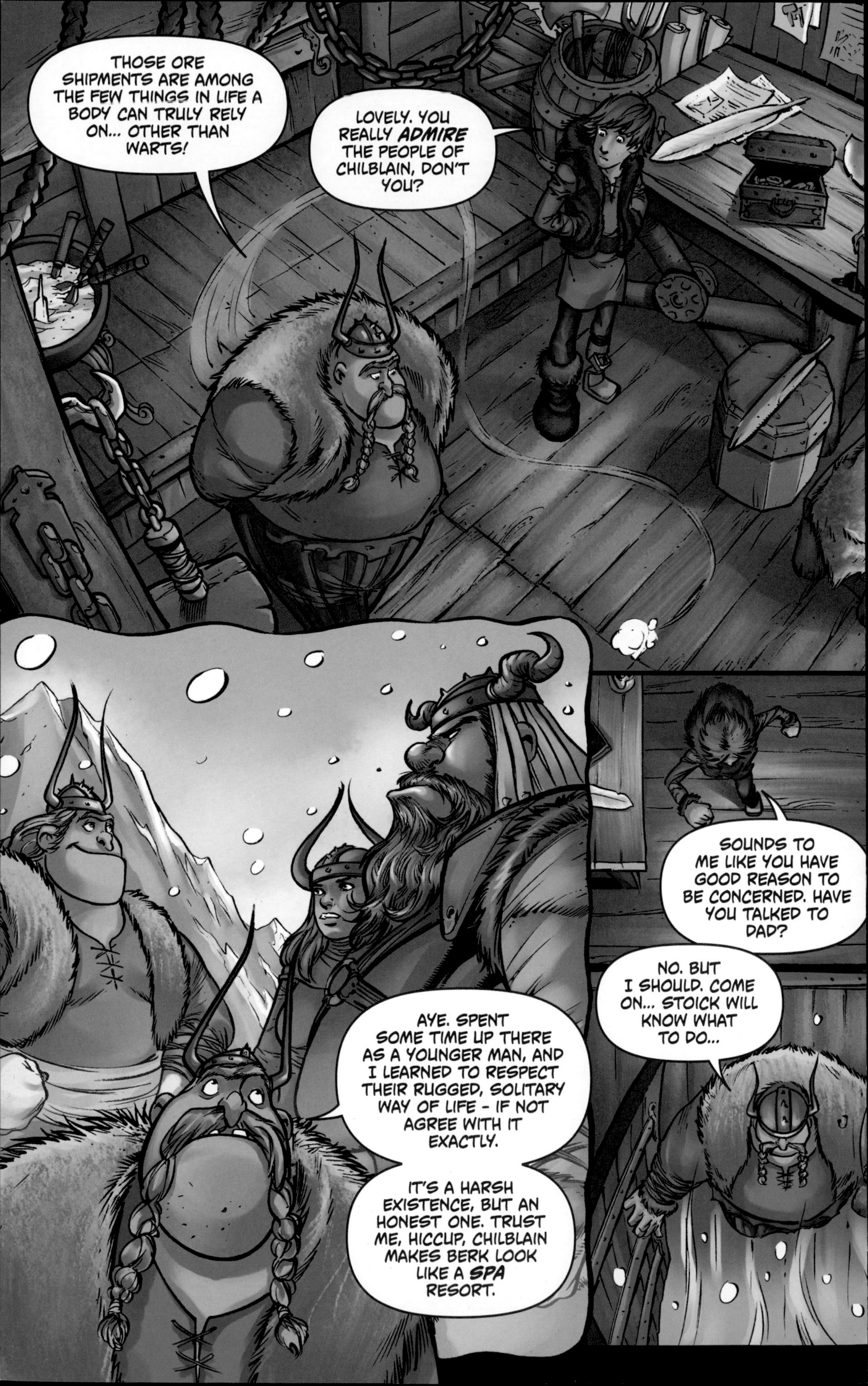
THOSE ORE SHIPMENTS ARE AMONG THE FEW THINGS IN LIFE A BODY CAN TRULY RELY ON... OTHER THAN WARTS!
LOVELY. YOU REALLY *ADMIRE* THE PEOPLE OF CHILBLAIN, DON'T YOU?
AYE. SPENT SOME TIME UP THERE AS A YOUNGER MAN, AND I LEARNED TO RESPECT THEIR RUGGED, SOLITARY WAY OF LIFE - IF NOT AGREE WITH IT EXACTLY.
IT'S A HARSH EXISTENCE, BUT AN HONEST ONE. TRUST ME, HICCUP, CHILBLAIN MAKES BERK LOOK LIKE A *SPA* RESORT.
SOUNDS TO ME LIKE YOU HAVE GOOD REASON TO BE CONCERNED. HAVE YOU TALKED TO DAD?
NO. BUT I SHOULD. COME ON... STOICK WILL KNOW WHAT TO DO...

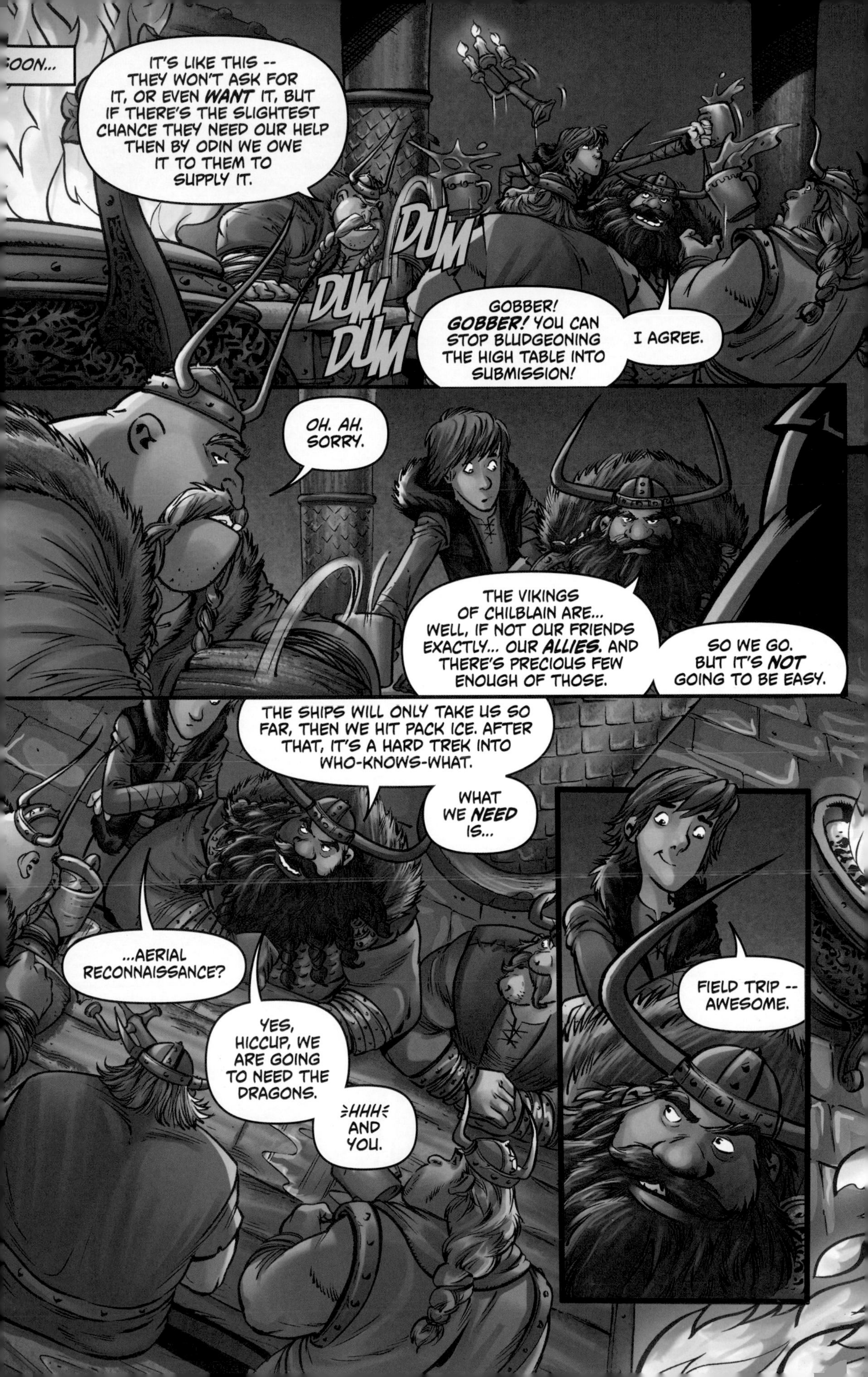
SOON...
IT'S LIKE THIS -- THEY WON'T ASK FOR IT, OR EVEN *WANT* IT, BUT IF THERE'S THE SLIGHTEST CHANCE THEY NEED OUR HELP THEN BY ODIN WE OWE IT TO THEM TO SUPPLY IT.
DUM
DUM DUM
I AGREE.
GOBBER! *GOBBER!* YOU CAN STOP BLUDGEONING THE HIGH TABLE INTO SUBMISSION!
OH. AH. SORRY.
THE VIKINGS OF CHILBLAIN ARE... WELL, IF NOT OUR FRIENDS EXACTLY... OUR *ALLIES.* AND THERE'S PRECIOUS FEW ENOUGH OF THOSE.
SO WE GO. BUT IT'S *NOT* GOING TO BE EASY.
THE SHIPS WILL ONLY TAKE US SO FAR, THEN WE HIT PACK ICE. AFTER THAT, IT'S A HARD TREK INTO WHO-KNOWS-WHAT.
WHAT WE *NEED* IS...
...AERIAL RECONNAISSANCE?
YES, HICCUP, WE ARE GOING TO NEED THE DRAGONS.
HHH AND YOU.
FIELD TRIP -- AWESOME.

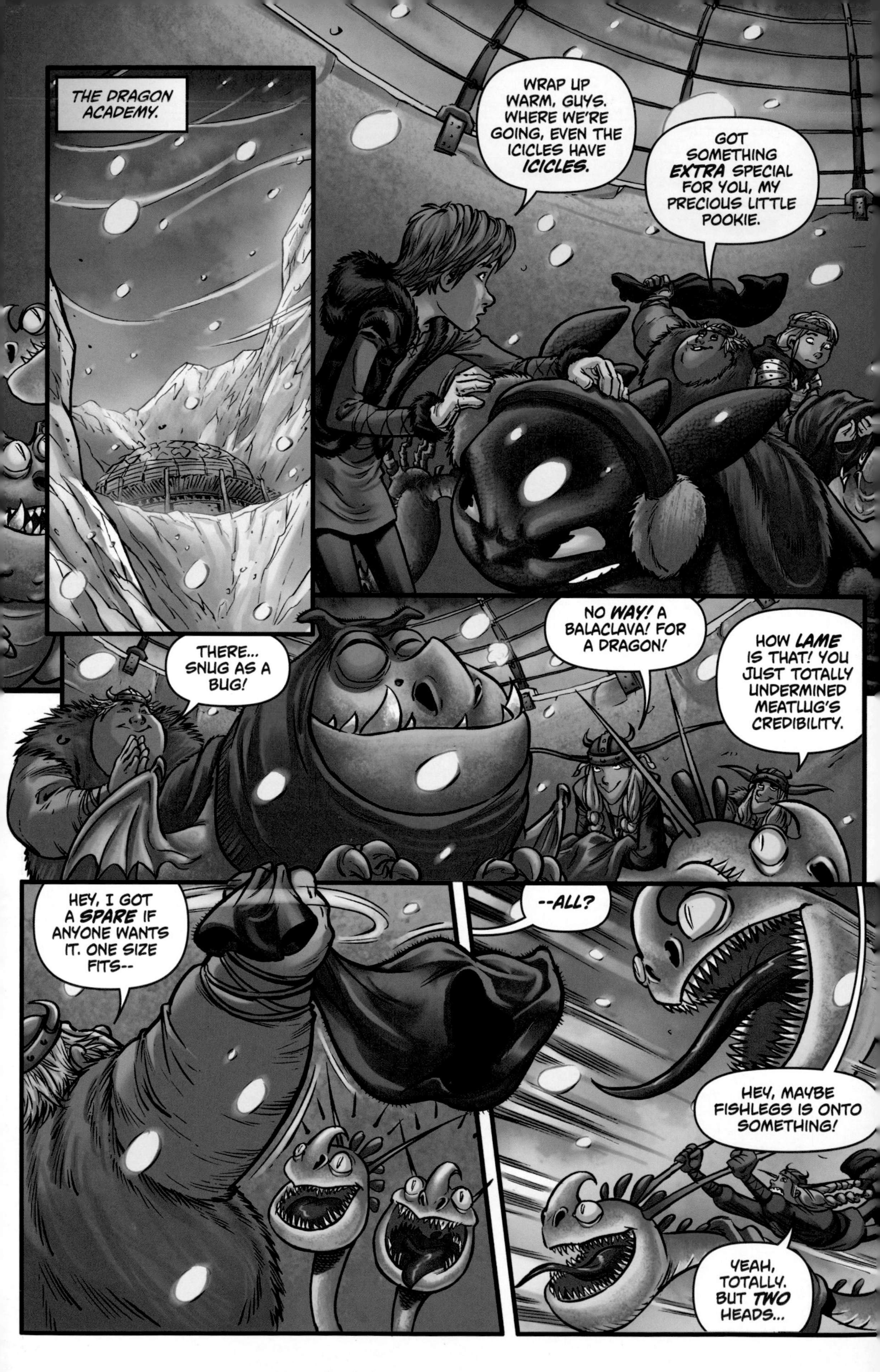
THE DRAGON ACADEMY.
WRAP UP WARM, GUYS. WHERE WE'RE GOING, EVEN THE ICICLES HAVE ICICLES.
GOT SOMETHING EXTRA SPECIAL FOR YOU, MY PRECIOUS LITTLE POOKIE.
THERE... SNUG AS A BUG!
NO WAY! A BALACLAVA! FOR A DRAGON!
HOW LAME IS THAT! YOU JUST TOTALLY UNDERMINED MEATLUG'S CREDIBILITY.
HEY, I GOT A SPARE IF ANYONE WANTS IT. ONE SIZE FITS--
--ALL?
HEY, MAYBE FISHLEGS IS ONTO SOMETHING!
YEAH, TOTALLY. BUT TWO HEADS...

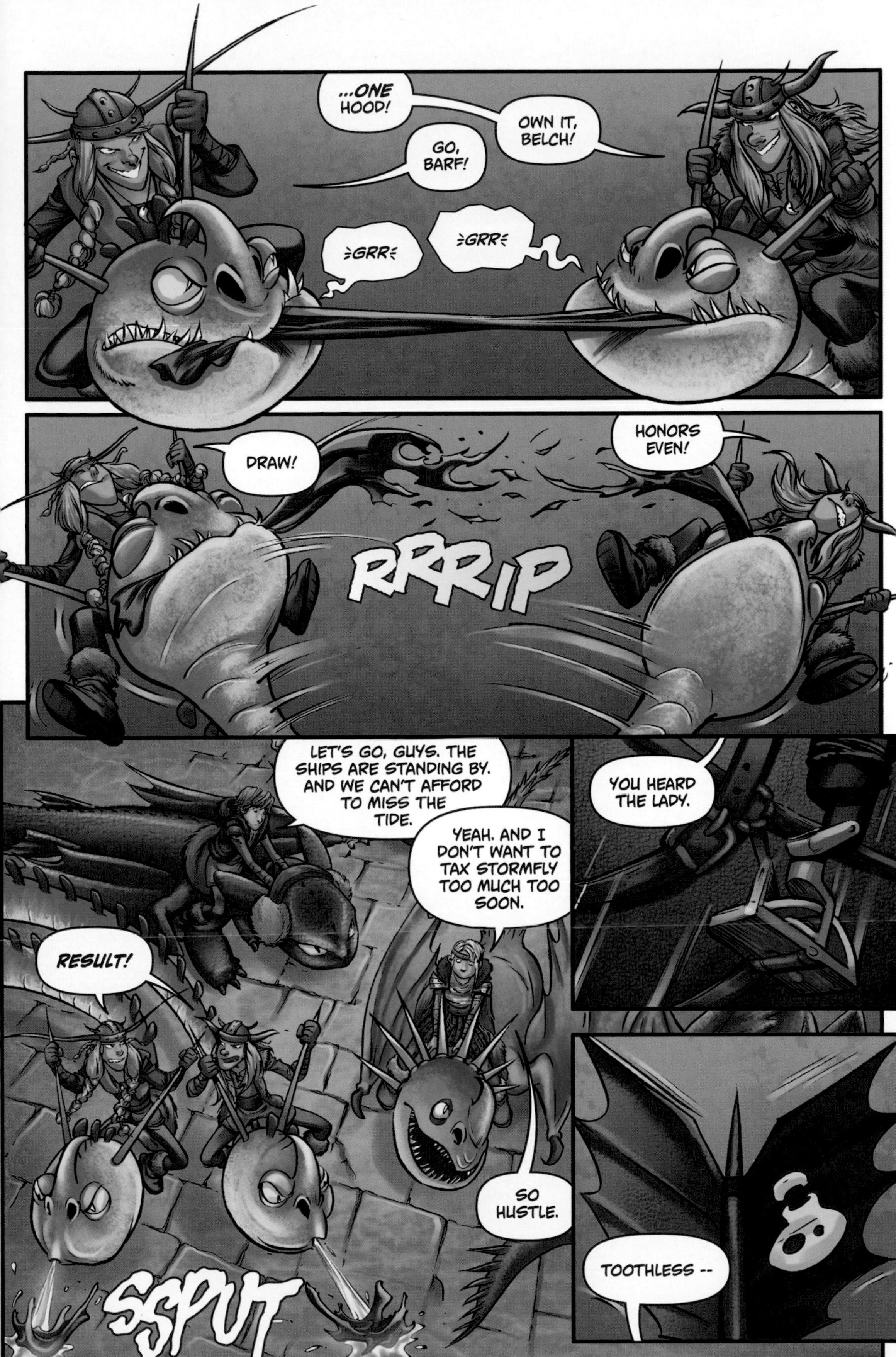
...ONE HOOD!
OWN IT, BELCH!
GO, BARF!
GRR
GRR
DRAW!
HONORS EVEN!
RRRIP
LET'S GO, GUYS. THE SHIPS ARE STANDING BY. AND WE CAN'T AFFORD TO MISS THE TIDE.
YEAH. AND I DON'T WANT TO TAX STORMFLY TOO MUCH TOO SOON.
RESULT!
SO HUSTLE.
SSPUT
YOU HEARD THE LADY.
TOOTHLESS --

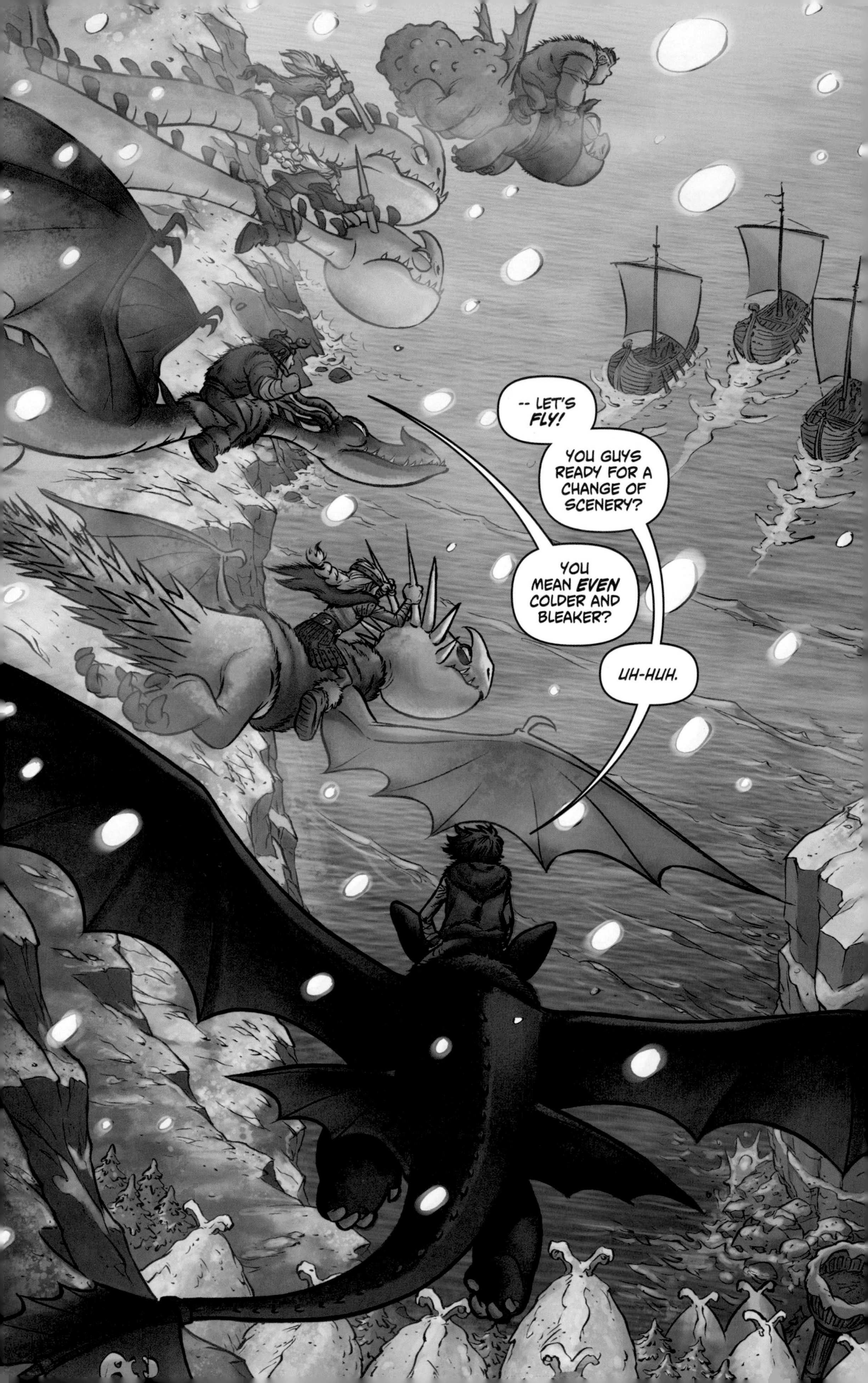
-- LET'S FLY!
YOU GUYS READY FOR A CHANGE OF SCENERY?
YOU MEAN EVEN COLDER AND BLEAKER?
UH-HUH.

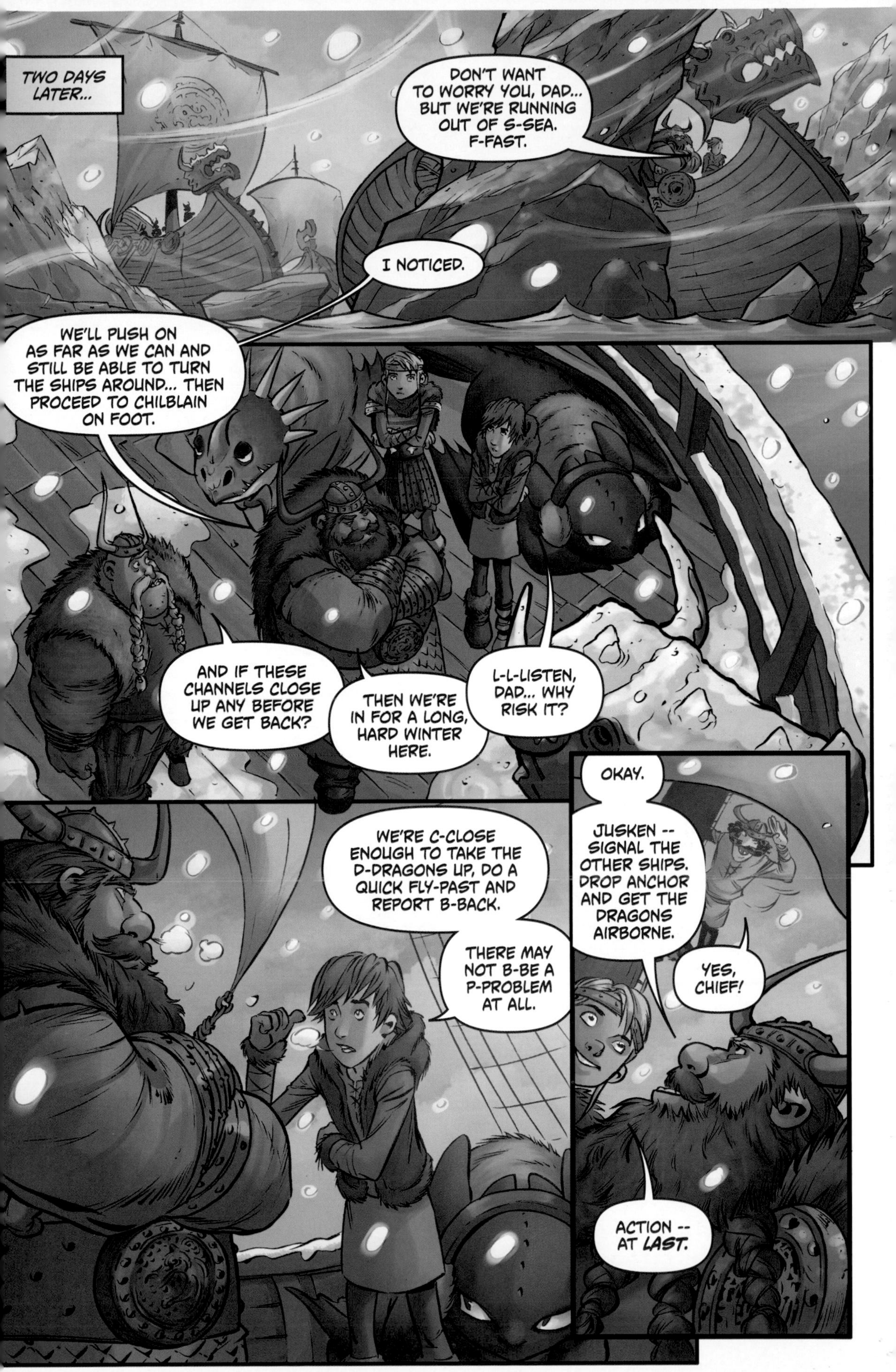
TWO DAYS LATER...
DON'T WANT TO WORRY YOU, DAD... BUT WE'RE RUNNING OUT OF S-SEA. F-FAST.
I NOTICED.
WE'LL PUSH ON AS FAR AS WE CAN AND STILL BE ABLE TO TURN THE SHIPS AROUND... THEN PROCEED TO CHILBLAIN ON FOOT.
AND IF THESE CHANNELS CLOSE UP ANY BEFORE WE GET BACK?
THEN WE'RE IN FOR A LONG, HARD WINTER HERE.
L-L-LISTEN, DAD... WHY RISK IT?
WE'RE C-CLOSE ENOUGH TO TAKE THE D-DRAGONS UP, DO A QUICK FLY-PAST AND REPORT B-BACK.
THERE MAY NOT B-BE A P-PROBLEM AT ALL.
OKAY.
JUSKEN -- SIGNAL THE OTHER SHIPS. DROP ANCHOR AND GET THE DRAGONS AIRBORNE.
YES, CHIEF!
ACTION -- AT *LAST*.

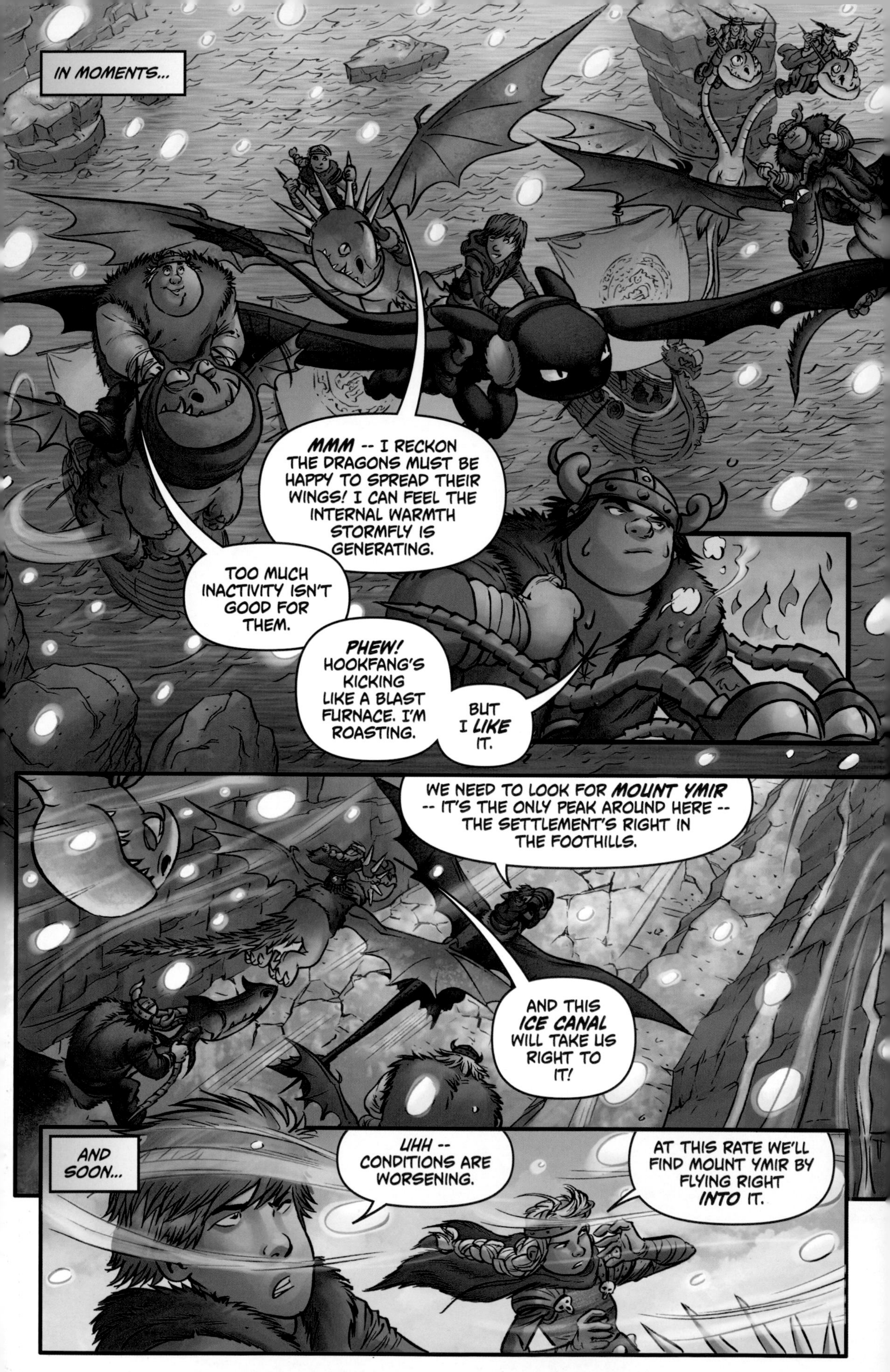
IN MOMENTS...
MMM -- I RECKON THE DRAGONS MUST BE HAPPY TO SPREAD THEIR WINGS! I CAN FEEL THE INTERNAL WARMTH STORMFLY IS GENERATING.
TOO MUCH INACTIVITY ISN'T GOOD FOR THEM.
PHEW! HOOKFANG'S KICKING LIKE A BLAST FURNACE. I'M ROASTING.
BUT I LIKE IT.
WE NEED TO LOOK FOR MOUNT YMIR -- IT'S THE ONLY PEAK AROUND HERE -- THE SETTLEMENT'S RIGHT IN THE FOOTHILLS.
AND THIS ICE CANAL WILL TAKE US RIGHT TO IT!
AND SOON...
UHH -- CONDITIONS ARE WORSENING.
AT THIS RATE WE'LL FIND MOUNT YMIR BY FLYING RIGHT INTO IT.

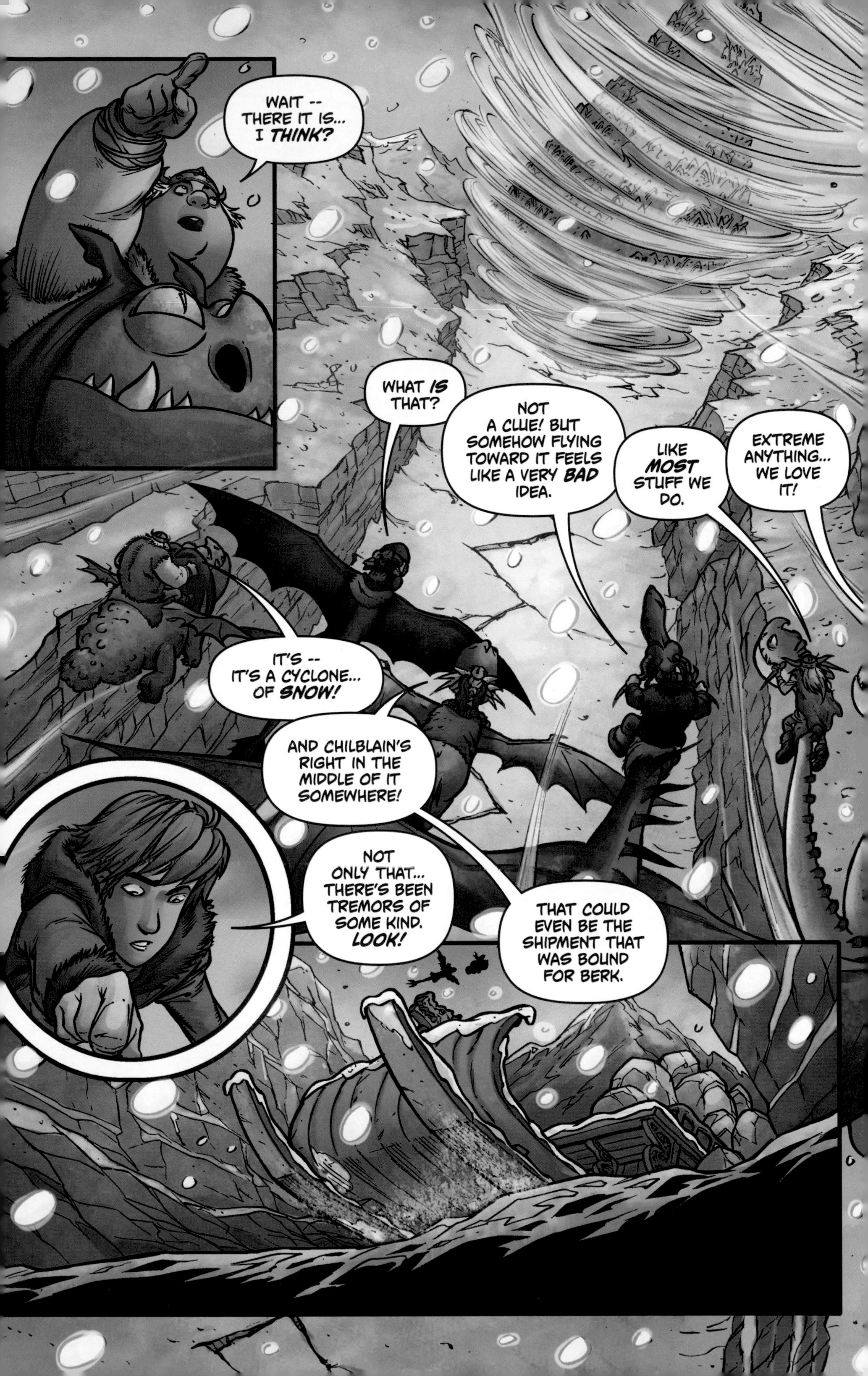
WAIT -- THERE IT IS... I *THINK?*
WHAT *IS* THAT?
NOT A CLUE! BUT SOMEHOW FLYING TOWARD IT FEELS LIKE A VERY *BAD* IDEA.
LIKE *MOST* STUFF WE DO.
EXTREME ANYTHING... WE LOVE IT!
IT'S -- IT'S A CYCLONE... OF *SNOW!*
AND CHILBLAIN'S RIGHT IN THE MIDDLE OF IT SOMEWHERE!
NOT ONLY THAT... THERE'S BEEN TREMORS OF SOME KIND. *LOOK!*
THAT COULD EVEN BE THE SHIPMENT THAT WAS BOUND FOR BERK.

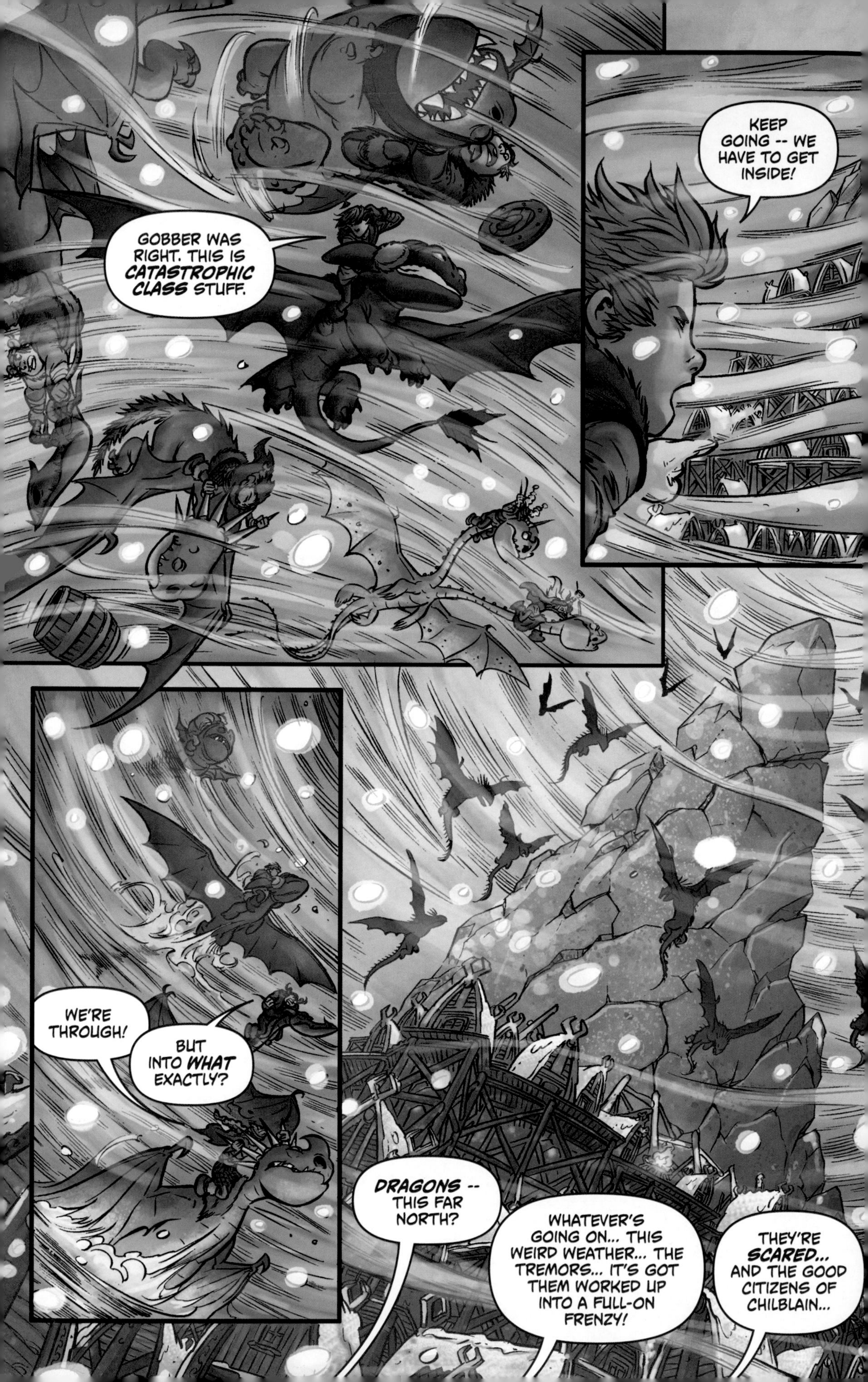
GOBBER WAS RIGHT. THIS IS ***CATASTROPHIC CLASS*** STUFF.
KEEP GOING -- WE HAVE TO GET INSIDE!
WE'RE THROUGH!
BUT INTO ***WHAT*** EXACTLY?
DRAGONS -- THIS FAR NORTH?
WHATEVER'S GOING ON... THIS WEIRD WEATHER... THE TREMORS... IT'S GOT THEM WORKED UP INTO A FULL-ON FRENZY!
THEY'RE ***SCARED...*** AND THE GOOD CITIZENS OF CHILBLAIN...

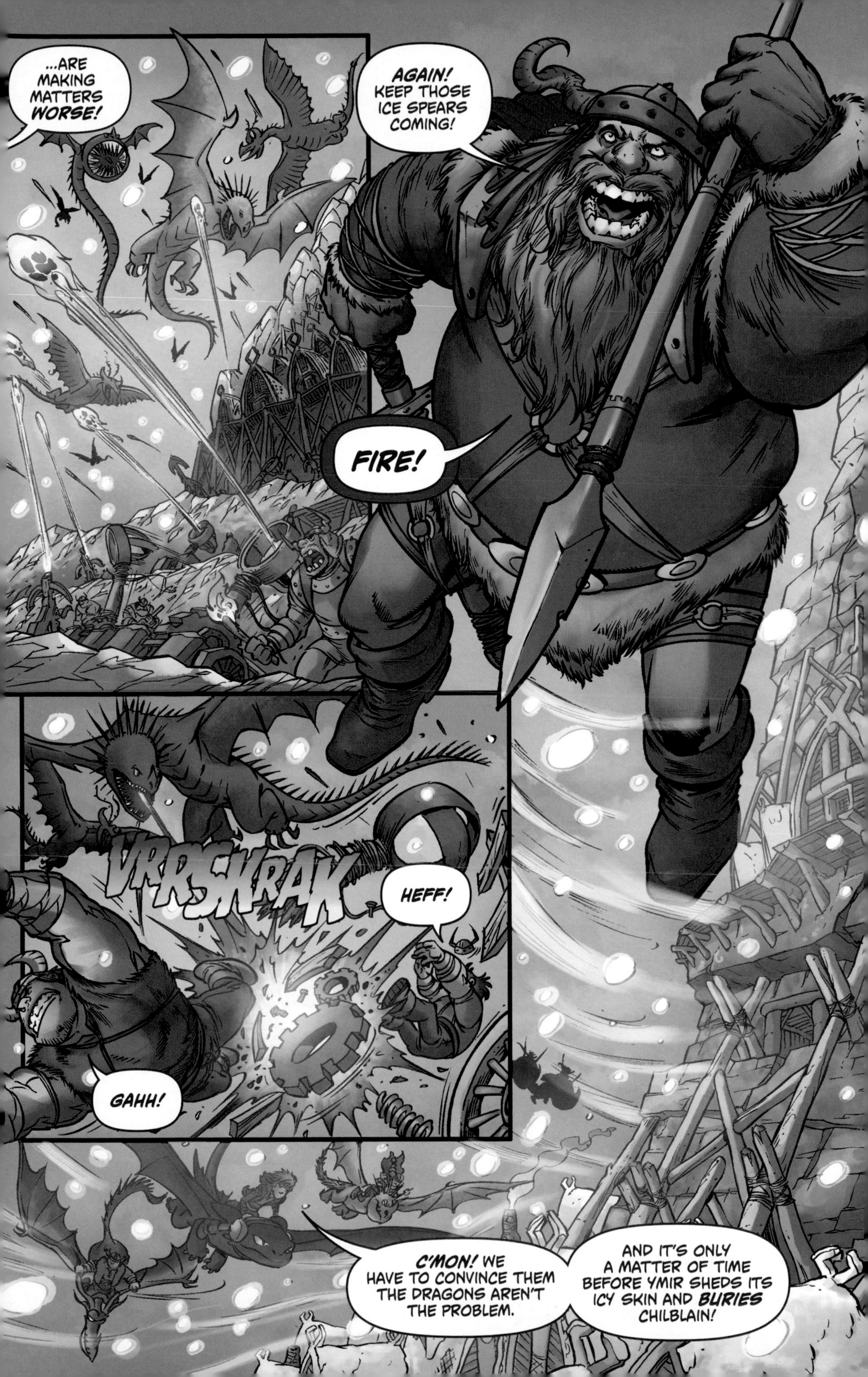
...ARE MAKING MATTERS WORSE!
AGAIN! KEEP THOSE ICE SPEARS COMING!
FIRE!
VRRSKRAK
HEFF!
GAHH!
C'MON! WE HAVE TO CONVINCE THEM THE DRAGONS AREN'T THE PROBLEM.
AND IT'S ONLY A MATTER OF TIME BEFORE YMIR SHEDS ITS ICY SKIN AND BURIES CHILBLAIN!

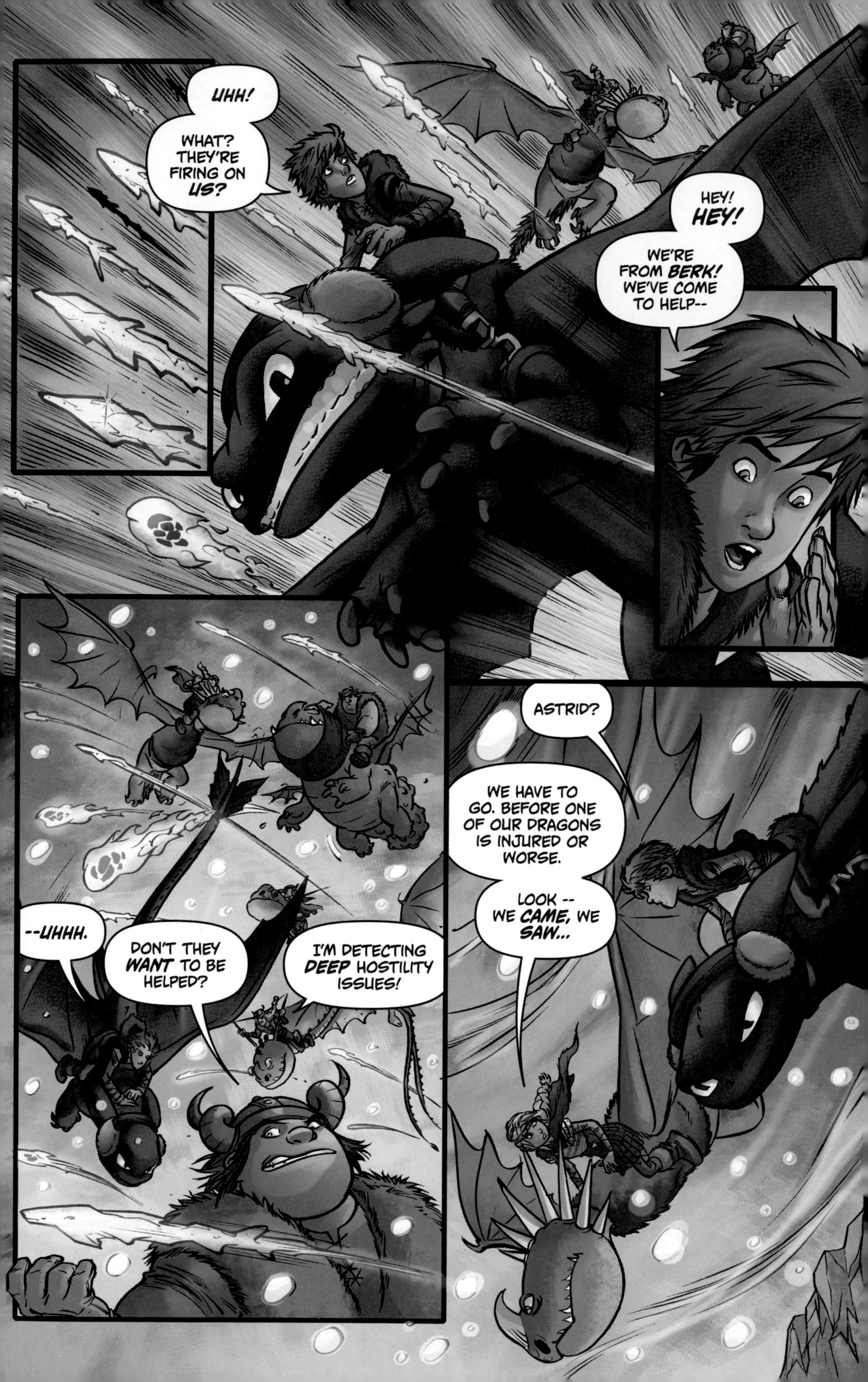
UHH!
WHAT? THEY'RE FIRING ON US?
HEY! HEY!
WE'RE FROM BERK! WE'VE COME TO HELP--
--UHHH.
DON'T THEY WANT TO BE HELPED?
I'M DETECTING DEEP HOSTILITY ISSUES!
ASTRID?
WE HAVE TO GO. BEFORE ONE OF OUR DRAGONS IS INJURED OR WORSE.
LOOK -- WE CAME, WE SAW...

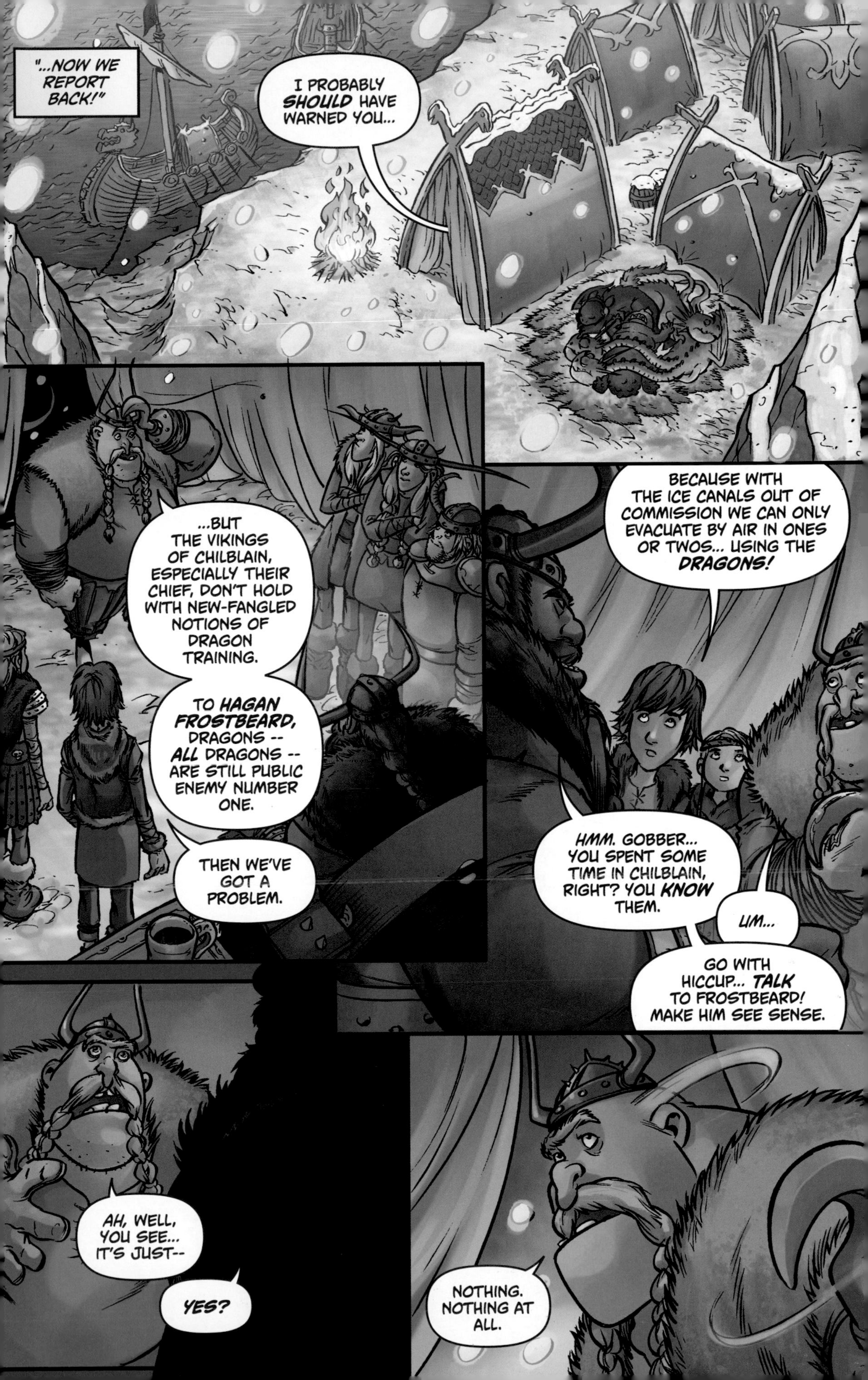

"...NOW WE REPORT BACK!"
I PROBABLY SHOULD HAVE WARNED YOU...
...BUT THE VIKINGS OF CHILBLAIN, ESPECIALLY THEIR CHIEF, DON'T HOLD WITH NEW-FANGLED NOTIONS OF DRAGON TRAINING.
TO HAGAN FROSTBEARD, DRAGONS -- ALL DRAGONS -- ARE STILL PUBLIC ENEMY NUMBER ONE.
THEN WE'VE GOT A PROBLEM.
BECAUSE WITH THE ICE CANALS OUT OF COMMISSION WE CAN ONLY EVACUATE BY AIR IN ONES OR TWOS... USING THE DRAGONS!
HMM. GOBBER... YOU SPENT SOME TIME IN CHILBLAIN, RIGHT? YOU KNOW THEM.
UM...
GO WITH HICCUP... TALK TO FROSTBEARD! MAKE HIM SEE SENSE.
AH, WELL, YOU SEE... IT'S JUST--
YES?
NOTHING. NOTHING AT ALL.

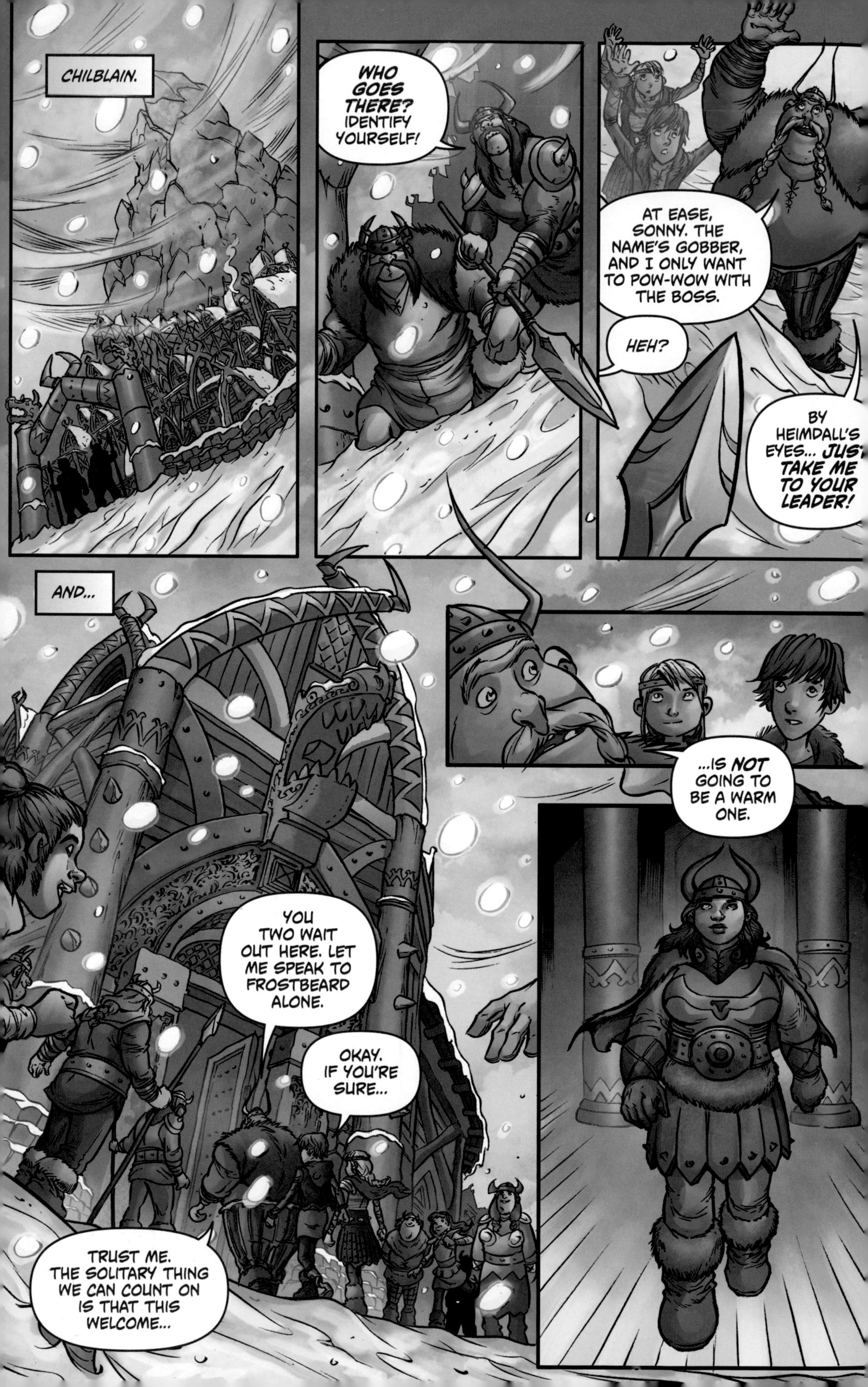
CHILBLAIN.
WHO GOES THERE? IDENTIFY YOURSELF!
AT EASE, SONNY. THE NAME'S GOBBER, AND I ONLY WANT TO POW-WOW WITH THE BOSS.
HEH?
BY HEIMDALL'S EYES... JUST TAKE ME TO YOUR LEADER!
AND...
YOU TWO WAIT OUT HERE. LET ME SPEAK TO FROSTBEARD ALONE.
OKAY. IF YOU'RE SURE...
TRUST ME. THE SOLITARY THING WE CAN COUNT ON IS THAT THIS WELCOME...
...IS NOT GOING TO BE A WARM ONE.

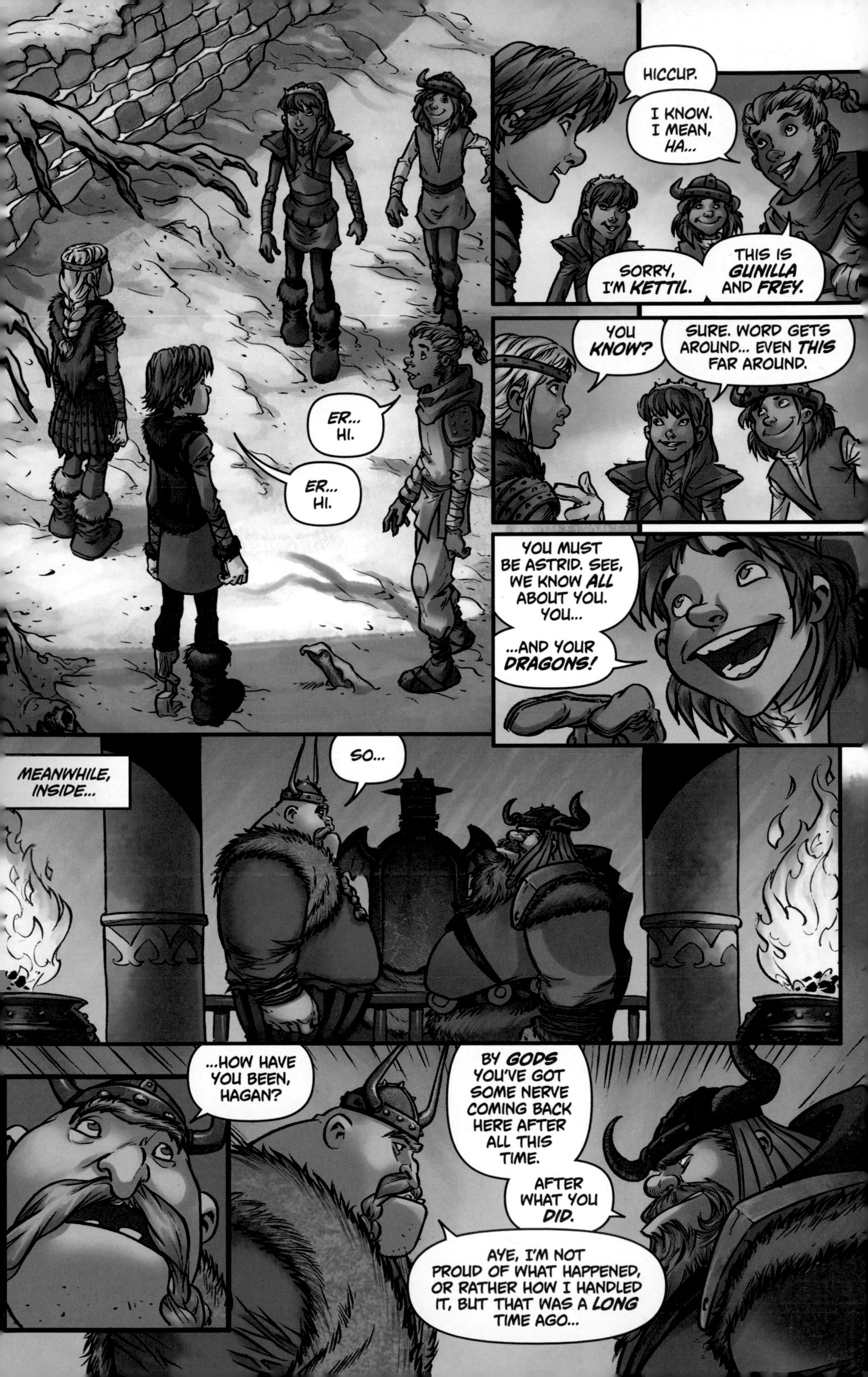
ER... HI.
ER... HI.
HICCUP.
I KNOW. I MEAN, HA...
SORRY, I'M KETTIL.
THIS IS GUNILLA AND FREY.
YOU KNOW?
SURE. WORD GETS AROUND... EVEN THIS FAR AROUND.
YOU MUST BE ASTRID. SEE, WE KNOW ALL ABOUT YOU. YOU...
...AND YOUR DRAGONS!
MEANWHILE, INSIDE...
SO...
...HOW HAVE YOU BEEN, HAGAN?
BY GODS YOU'VE GOT SOME NERVE COMING BACK HERE AFTER ALL THIS TIME.
AFTER WHAT YOU DID.
AYE, I'M NOT PROUD OF WHAT HAPPENED, OR RATHER HOW I HANDLED IT, BUT THAT WAS A LONG TIME AGO...

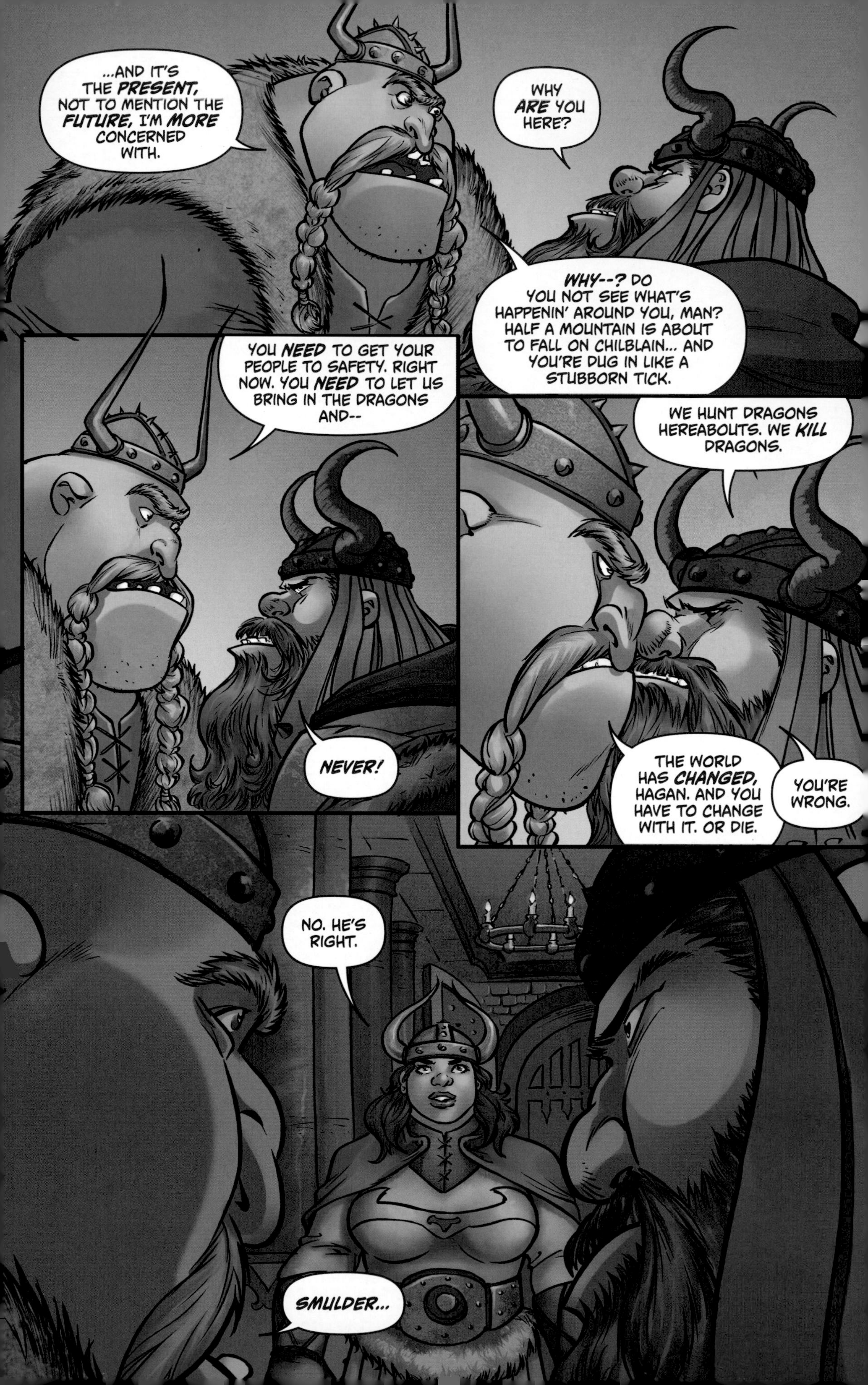
...AND IT'S THE PRESENT, NOT TO MENTION THE FUTURE, I'M MORE CONCERNED WITH.
WHY ARE YOU HERE?
WHY--? DO YOU NOT SEE WHAT'S HAPPENIN' AROUND YOU, MAN? HALF A MOUNTAIN IS ABOUT TO FALL ON CHILBLAIN... AND YOU'RE DUG IN LIKE A STUBBORN TICK.
YOU NEED TO GET YOUR PEOPLE TO SAFETY. RIGHT NOW. YOU NEED TO LET US BRING IN THE DRAGONS AND--
NEVER!
WE HUNT DRAGONS HEREABOUTS. WE KILL DRAGONS.
THE WORLD HAS CHANGED, HAGAN. AND YOU HAVE TO CHANGE WITH IT. OR DIE.
YOU'RE WRONG.
NO. HE'S RIGHT.
SMULDER...

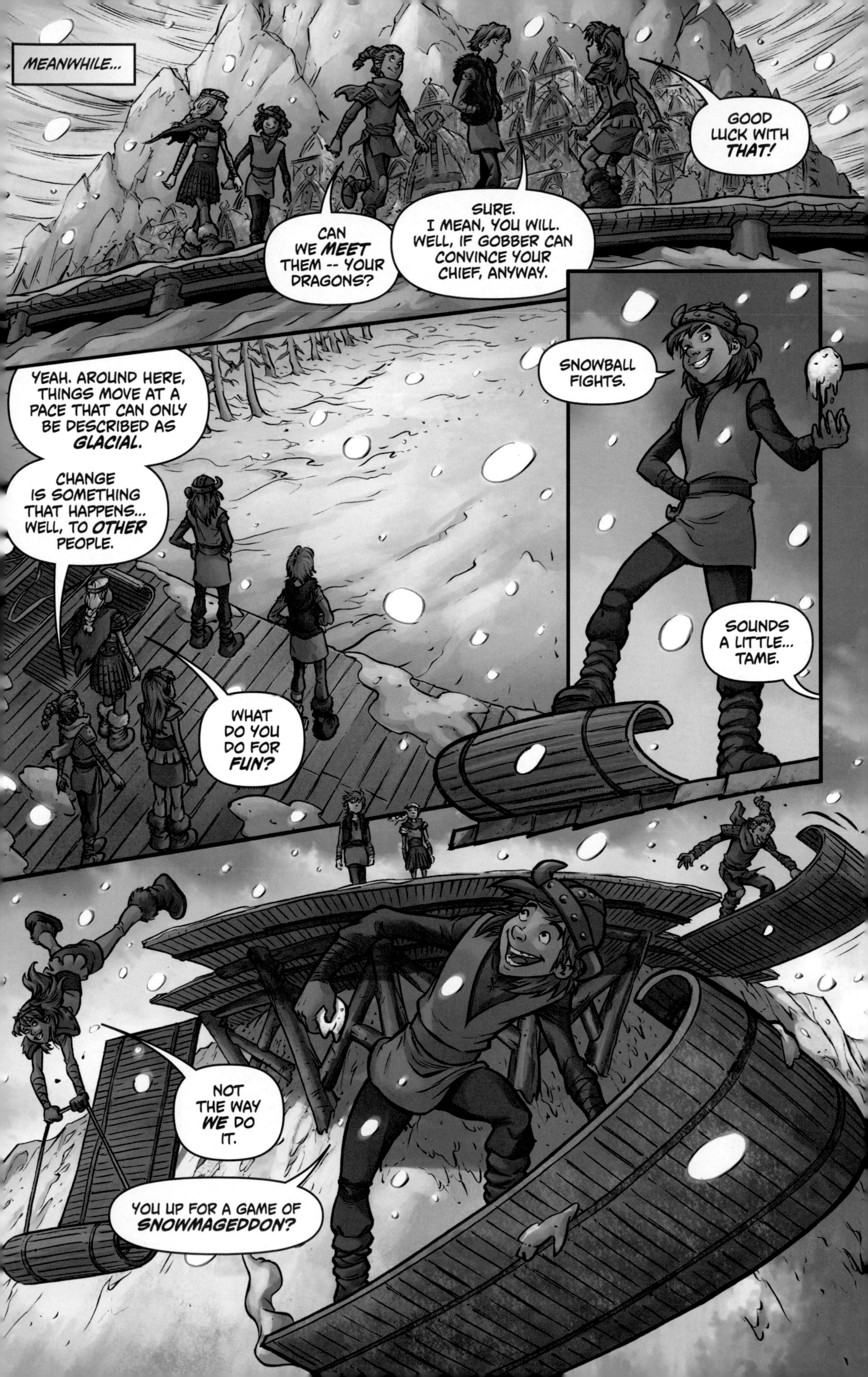
MEANWHILE...
GOOD LUCK WITH THAT!
CAN WE MEET THEM -- YOUR DRAGONS?
SURE. I MEAN, YOU WILL. WELL, IF GOBBER CAN CONVINCE YOUR CHIEF, ANYWAY.
YEAH. AROUND HERE, THINGS MOVE AT A PACE THAT CAN ONLY BE DESCRIBED AS GLACIAL.
CHANGE IS SOMETHING THAT HAPPENS... WELL, TO OTHER PEOPLE.
WHAT DO YOU DO FOR FUN?
SNOWBALL FIGHTS.
SOUNDS A LITTLE... TAME.
NOT THE WAY WE DO IT.
YOU UP FOR A GAME OF SNOWMAGEDDON?

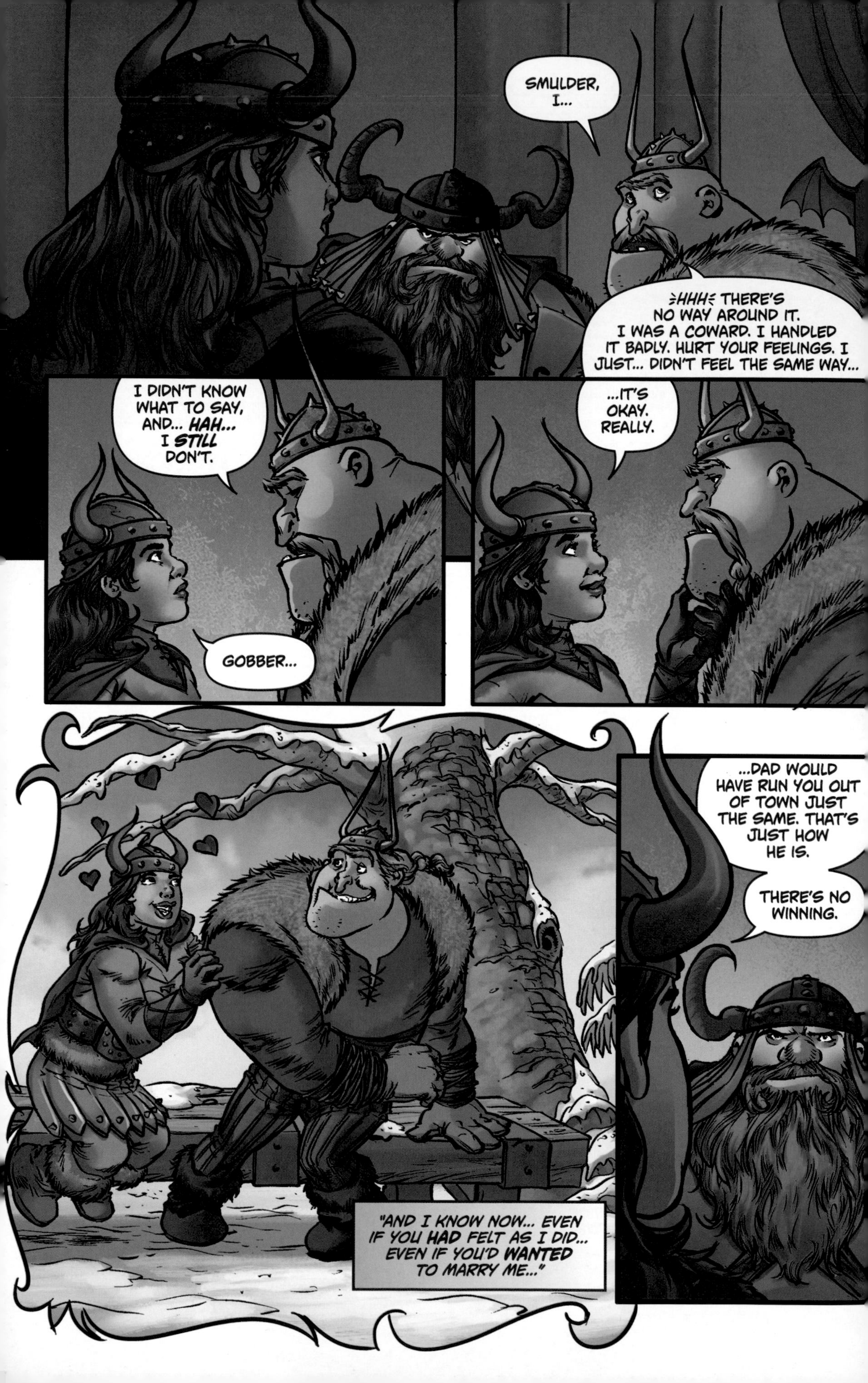
SMULDER, I...
≋HHH≋ THERE'S NO WAY AROUND IT. I WAS A COWARD. I HANDLED IT BADLY. HURT YOUR FEELINGS. I JUST... DIDN'T FEEL THE SAME WAY...
I DIDN'T KNOW WHAT TO SAY, AND... HAH... I STILL DON'T.
GOBBER...
...IT'S OKAY. REALLY.
"AND I KNOW NOW... EVEN IF YOU HAD FELT AS I DID... EVEN IF YOU'D WANTED TO MARRY ME..."
...DAD WOULD HAVE RUN YOU OUT OF TOWN JUST THE SAME. THAT'S JUST HOW HE IS.
THERE'S NO WINNING.

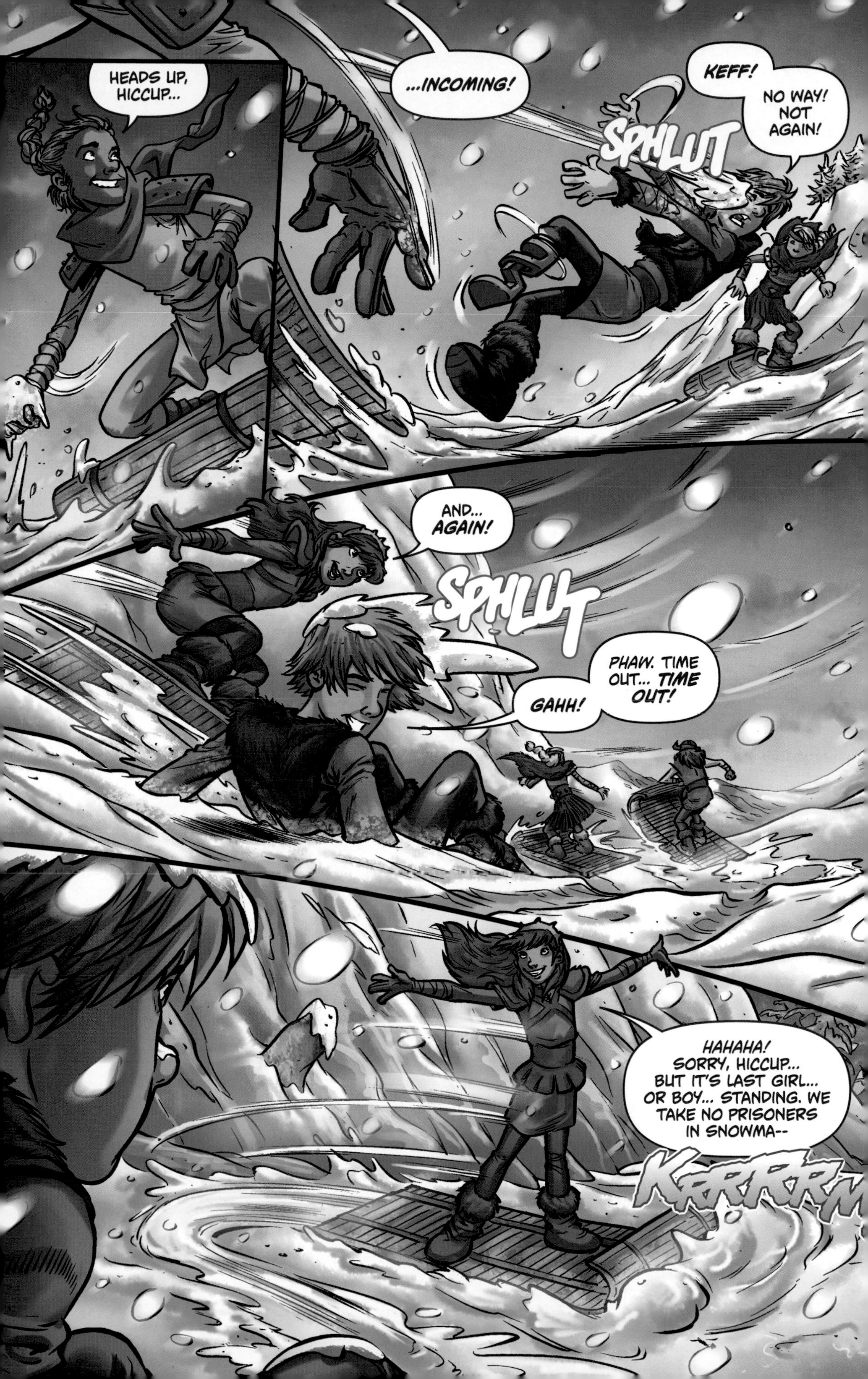
HEADS UP, HICCUP...
...INCOMING!
KEFF!
SPHLUT
NO WAY! NOT AGAIN!
AND... AGAIN!
SPHLUT
GAHH!
PHAW. TIME OUT... TIME OUT!
HAHAHA! SORRY, HICCUP... BUT IT'S LAST GIRL... OR BOY... STANDING. WE TAKE NO PRISONERS IN SNOWMA--
KRRRRM

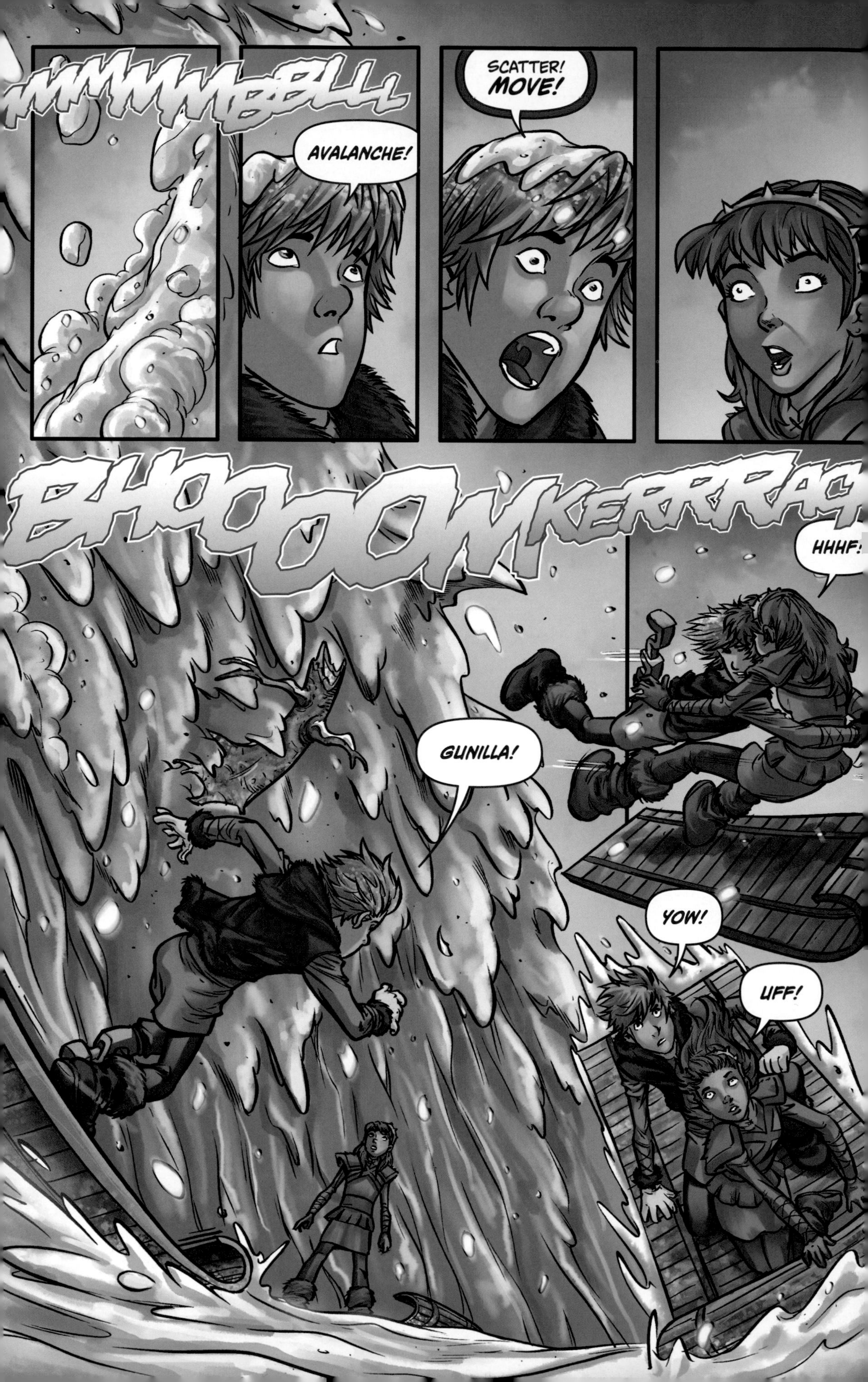
MMMMBLLL
AVALANCHE!
SCATTER! MOVE!
BHOOOOM
KERRRA
HHHF!
GUNILLA!
YOW!
UFF!

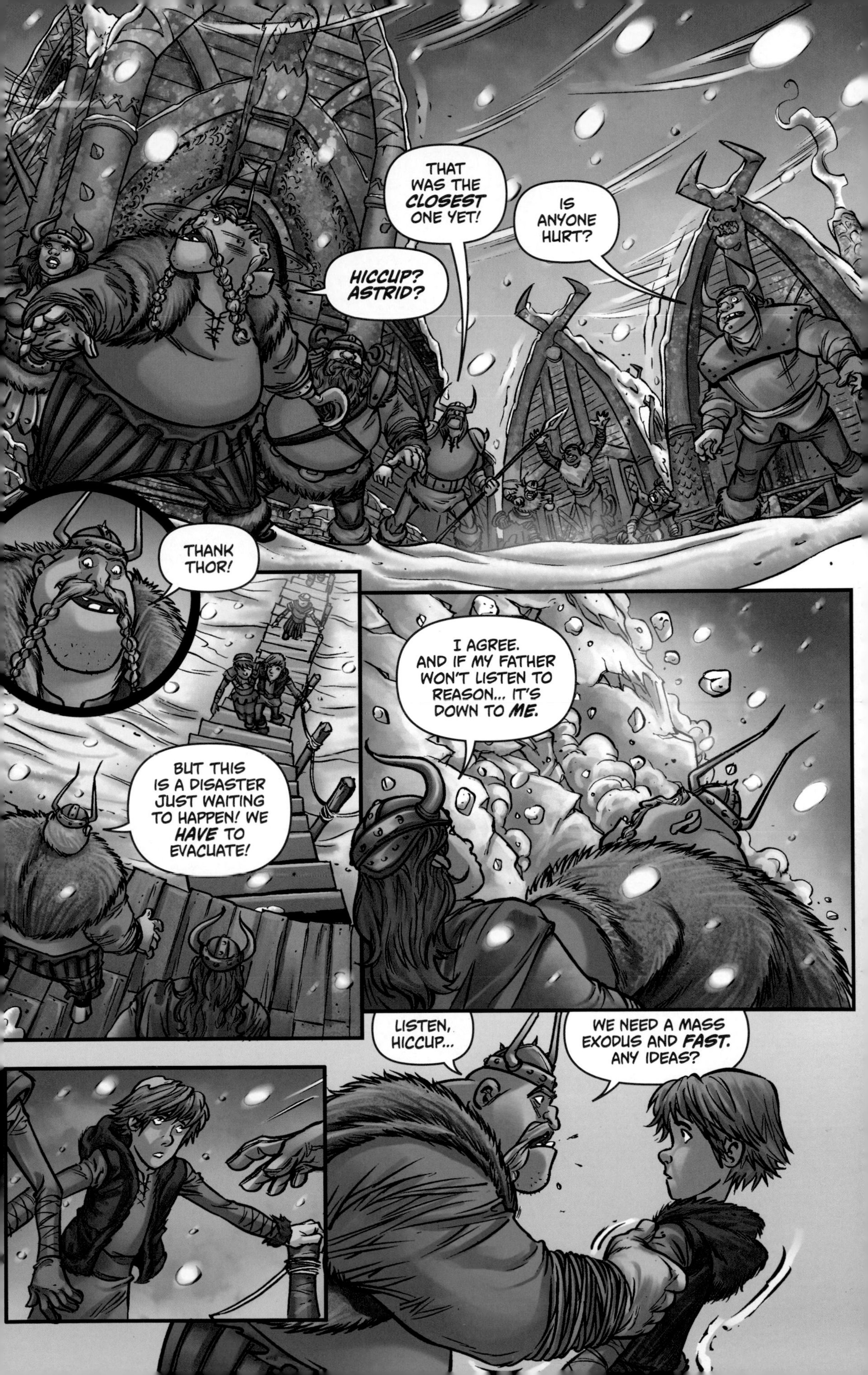
HICCUP? ASTRID?
THAT WAS THE CLOSEST ONE YET!
IS ANYONE HURT?
THANK THOR!
BUT THIS IS A DISASTER JUST WAITING TO HAPPEN! WE HAVE TO EVACUATE!
I AGREE. AND IF MY FATHER WON'T LISTEN TO REASON... IT'S DOWN TO ME.
LISTEN, HICCUP...
WE NEED A MASS EXODUS AND FAST. ANY IDEAS?

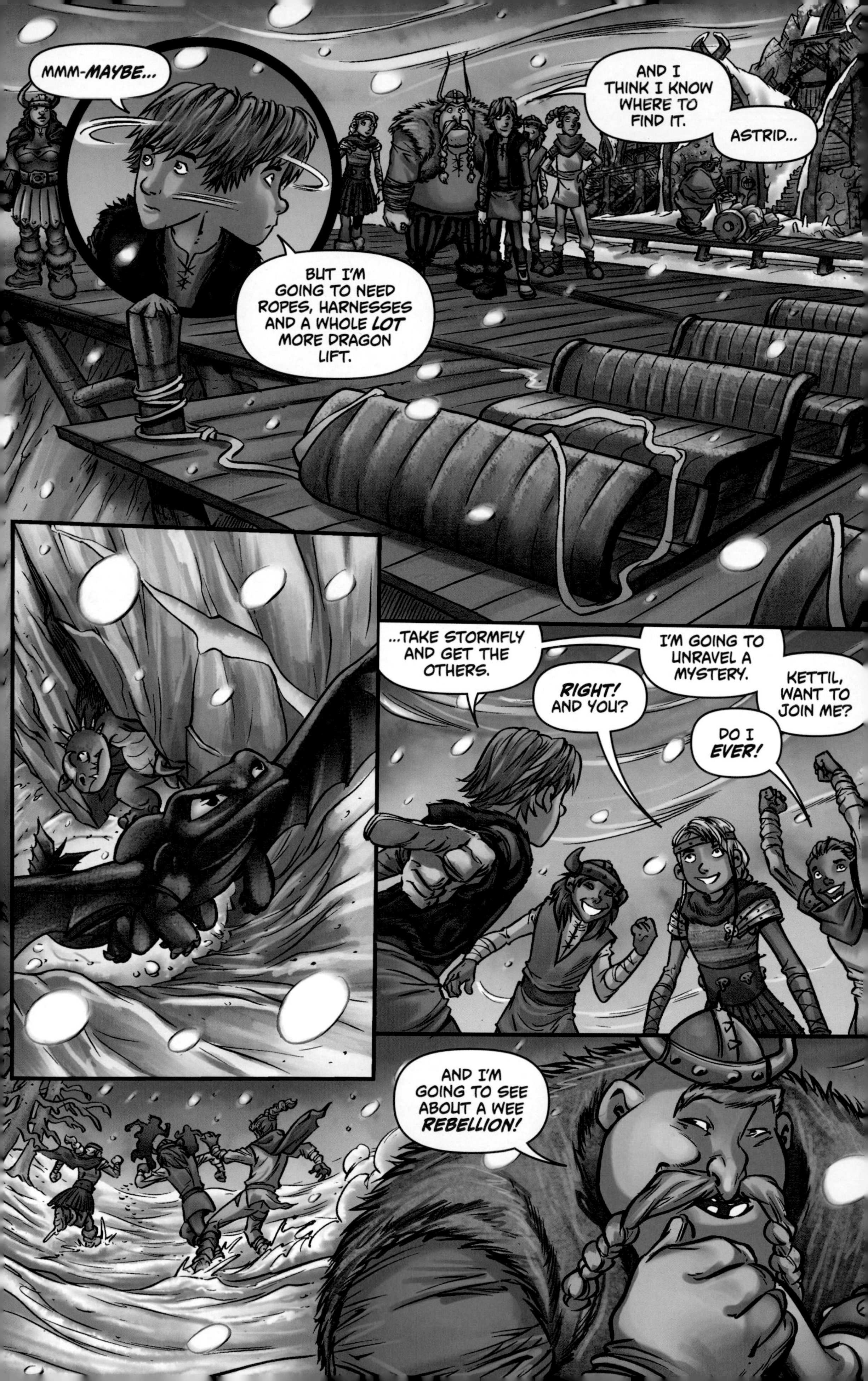
MMM-*MAYBE*...
AND I THINK I KNOW WHERE TO FIND IT.
BUT I'M GOING TO NEED ROPES, HARNESSES AND A WHOLE *LOT* MORE DRAGON LIFT.
ASTRID...
...TAKE STORMFLY AND GET THE OTHERS.
RIGHT! AND YOU?
I'M GOING TO UNRAVEL A MYSTERY.
KETTIL, WANT TO JOIN ME?
DO I *EVER!*
AND I'M GOING TO SEE ABOUT A WEE *REBELLION!*

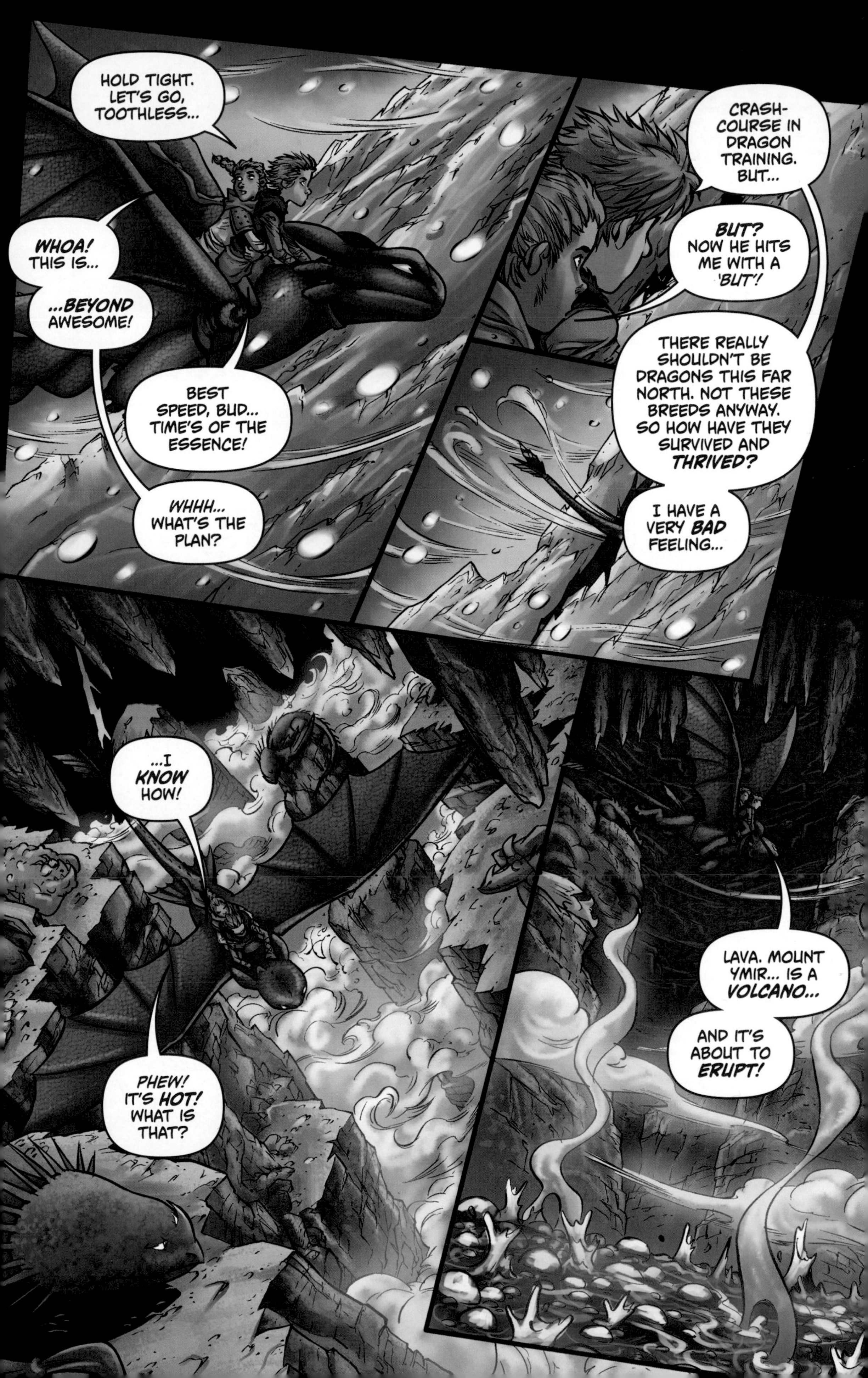
HOLD TIGHT. LET'S GO, TOOTHLESS...
WHOA! THIS IS...
...BEYOND AWESOME!
BEST SPEED, BUD... TIME'S OF THE ESSENCE!
WHHH... WHAT'S THE PLAN?
CRASH-COURSE IN DRAGON TRAINING. BUT...
BUT? NOW HE HITS ME WITH A *'BUT'!*
THERE REALLY SHOULDN'T BE DRAGONS THIS FAR NORTH. NOT THESE BREEDS ANYWAY. SO HOW HAVE THEY SURVIVED AND *THRIVED?*
I HAVE A VERY *BAD* FEELING...
...I *KNOW* HOW!
PHEW! IT'S *HOT!* WHAT IS THAT?
LAVA. MOUNT YMIR... IS A *VOLCANO...*
AND IT'S ABOUT TO *ERUPT!*

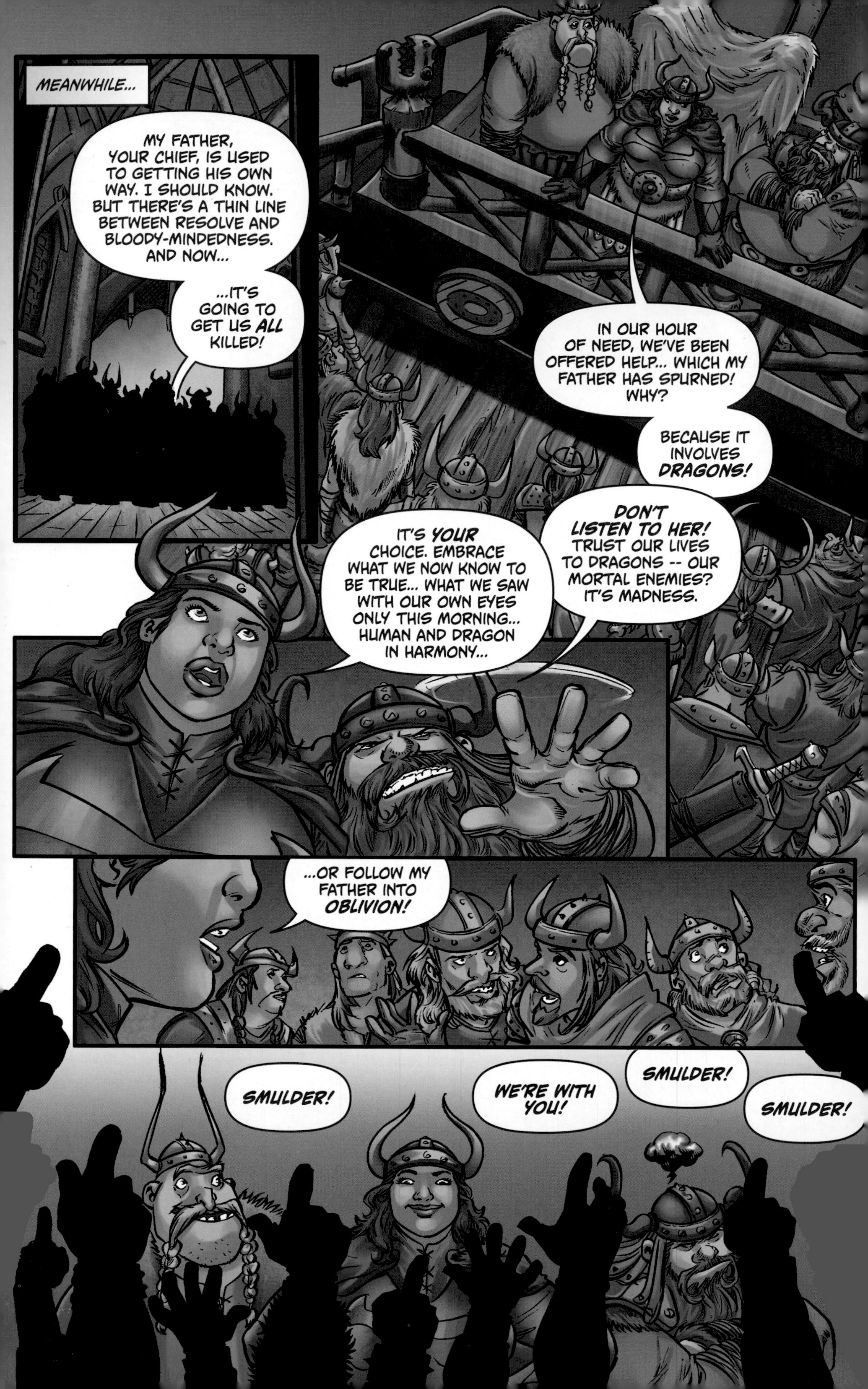
MEANWHILE...
MY FATHER, YOUR CHIEF, IS USED TO GETTING HIS OWN WAY. I SHOULD KNOW. BUT THERE'S A THIN LINE BETWEEN RESOLVE AND BLOODY-MINDEDNESS. AND NOW...
...IT'S GOING TO GET US ALL KILLED!
IN OUR HOUR OF NEED, WE'VE BEEN OFFERED HELP... WHICH MY FATHER HAS SPURNED! WHY?
BECAUSE IT INVOLVES DRAGONS!
DON'T LISTEN TO HER! TRUST OUR LIVES TO DRAGONS -- OUR MORTAL ENEMIES? IT'S MADNESS.
IT'S YOUR CHOICE. EMBRACE WHAT WE NOW KNOW TO BE TRUE... WHAT WE SAW WITH OUR OWN EYES ONLY THIS MORNING... HUMAN AND DRAGON IN HARMONY...
...OR FOLLOW MY FATHER INTO OBLIVION!
SMULDER!
WE'RE WITH YOU!
SMULDER!
SMULDER!

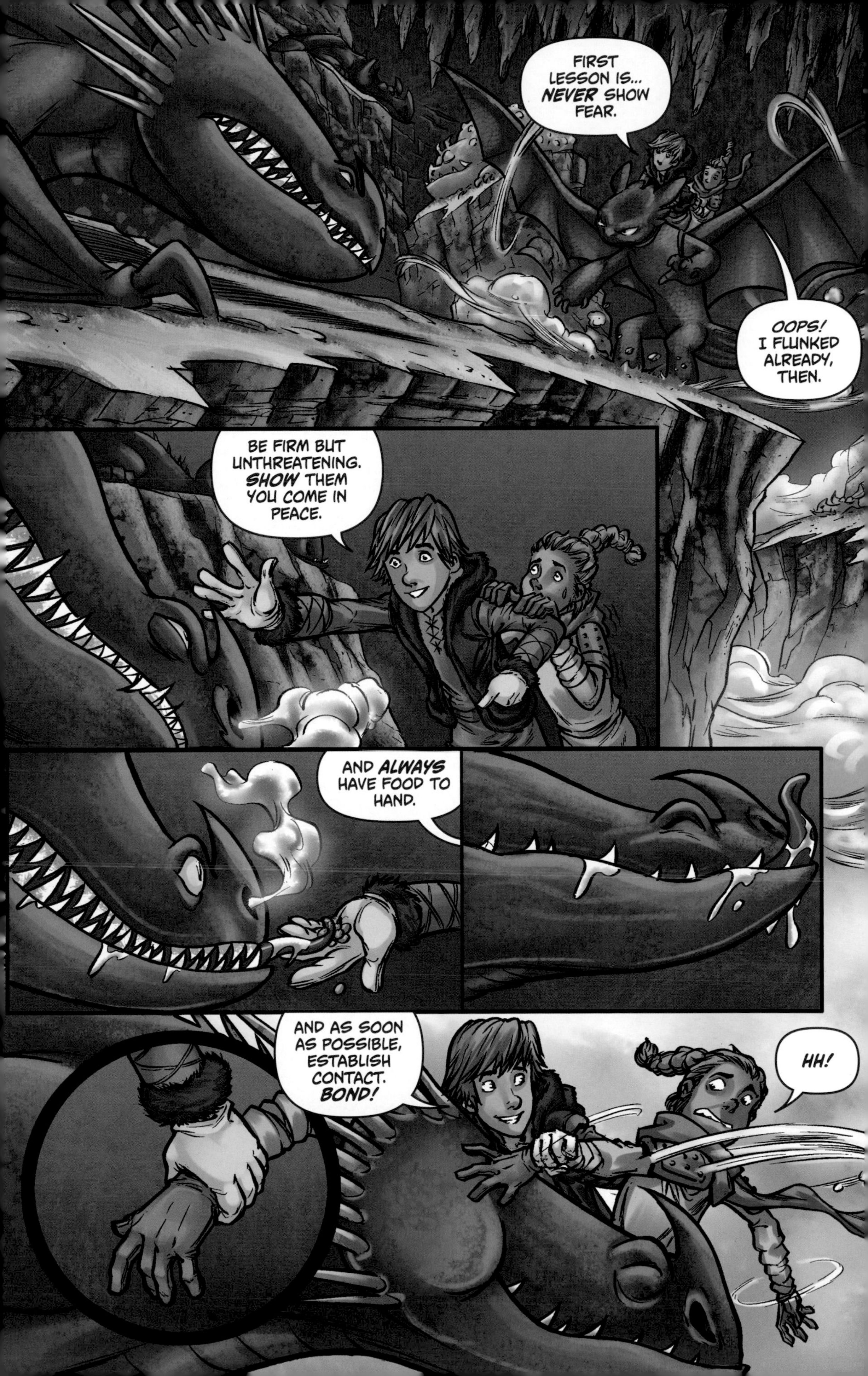
FIRST LESSON IS... NEVER SHOW FEAR.
OOPS! I FLUNKED ALREADY, THEN.
BE FIRM BUT UNTHREATENING. SHOW THEM YOU COME IN PEACE.
AND ALWAYS HAVE FOOD TO HAND.
AND AS SOON AS POSSIBLE, ESTABLISH CONTACT. BOND!
HH!

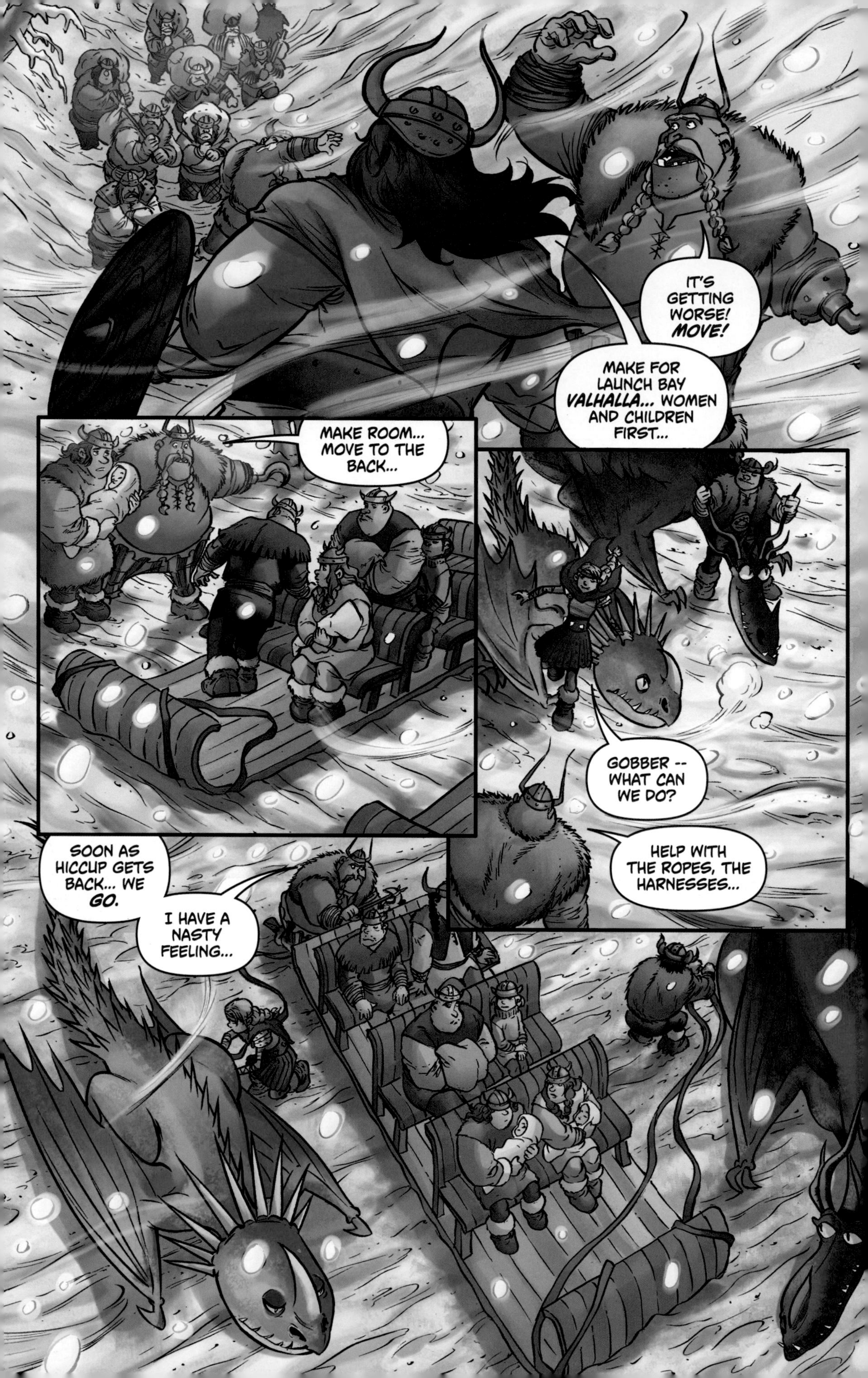

IT'S GETTING WORSE! *MOVE!*
MAKE FOR LAUNCH BAY *VALHALLA...* WOMEN AND CHILDREN FIRST...
MAKE ROOM... MOVE TO THE BACK...
GOBBER -- WHAT CAN WE DO?
HELP WITH THE ROPES, THE HARNESSES...
SOON AS HICCUP GETS BACK... WE *GO.*
I HAVE A NASTY FEELING...

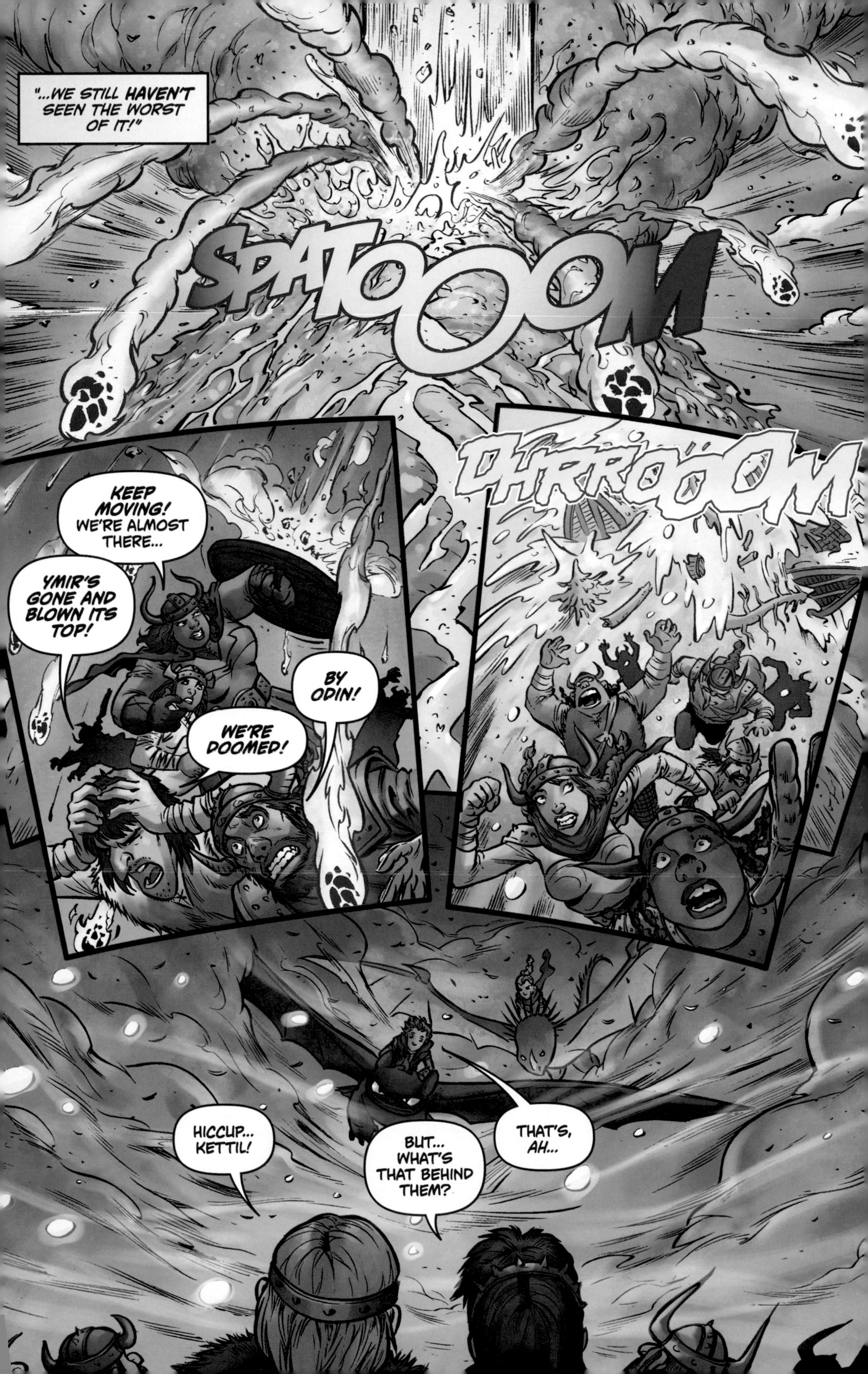
"...WE STILL HAVEN'T SEEN THE WORST OF IT!"
SPATOOOOM
KEEP MOVING! WE'RE ALMOST THERE...
YMIR'S GONE AND BLOWN ITS TOP!
WE'RE DOOMED!
BY ODIN!
DHRROOOM
HICCUP... KETTIL!
BUT... WHAT'S THAT BEHIND THEM?
THAT'S, AH...

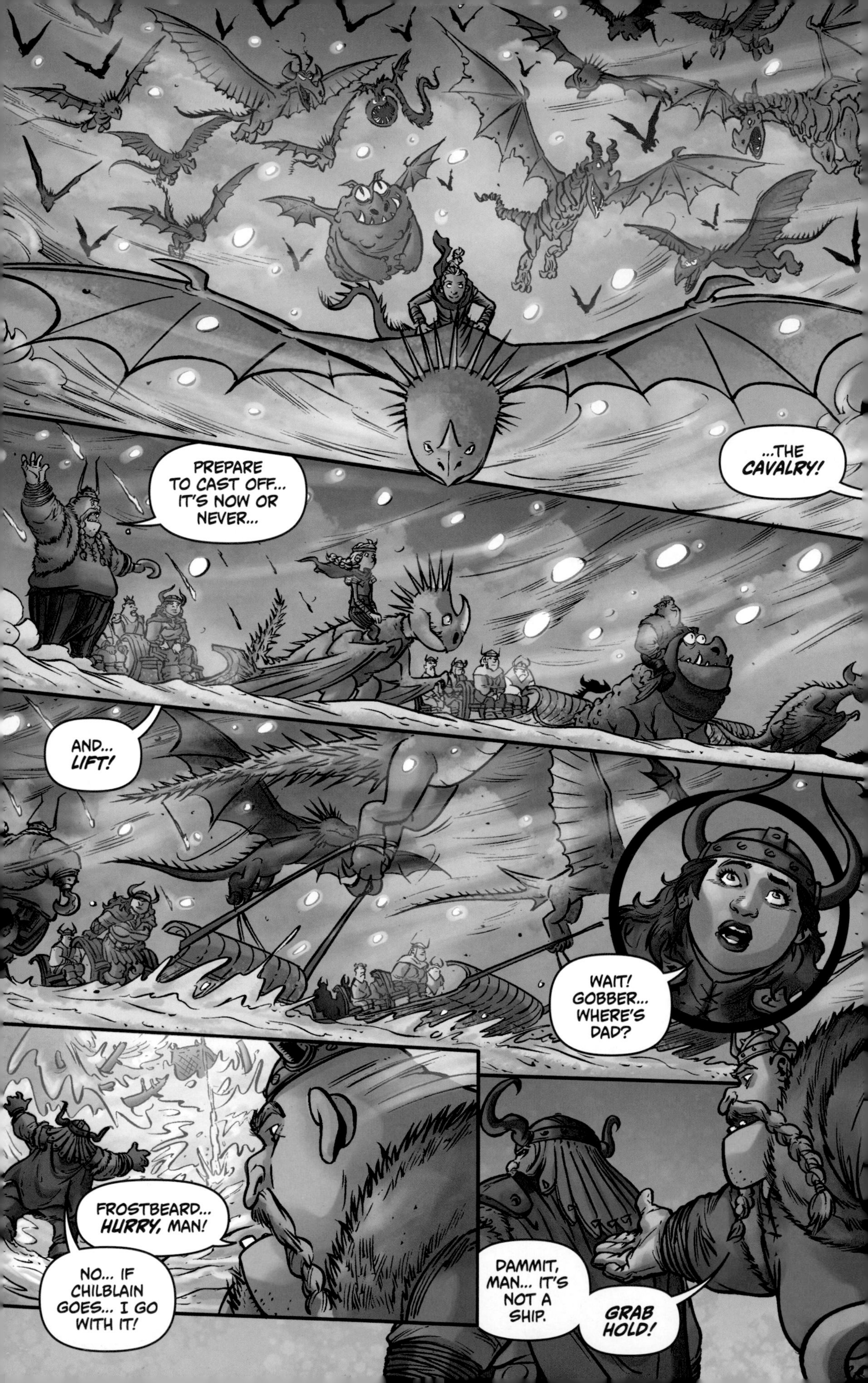

...THE CAVALRY!
PREPARE TO CAST OFF... IT'S NOW OR NEVER...
AND... LIFT!
WAIT! GOBBER... WHERE'S DAD?
FROSTBEARD... HURRY, MAN!
NO... IF CHILBLAIN GOES... I GO WITH IT!
DAMMIT, MAN... IT'S NOT A SHIP.
GRAB HOLD!

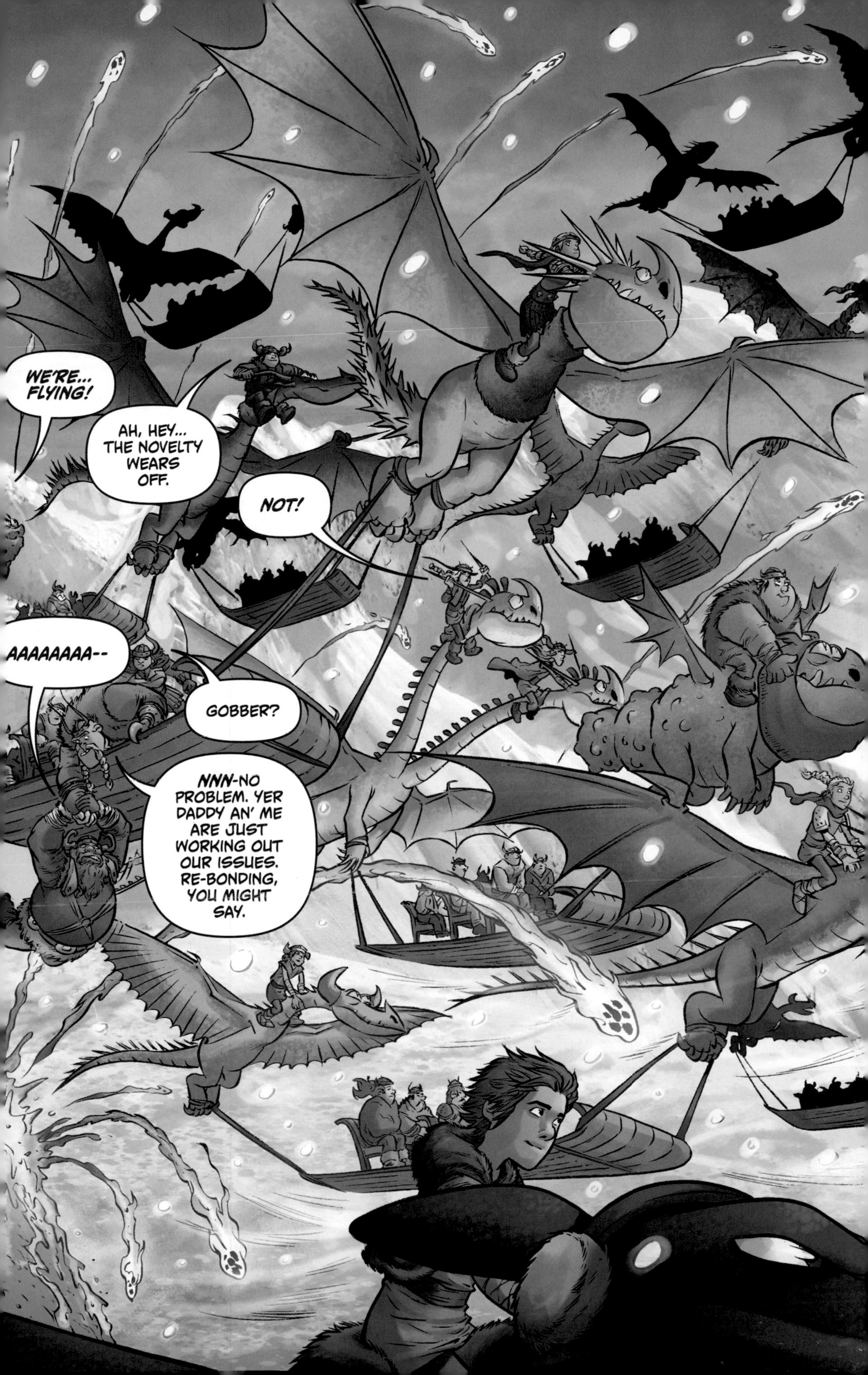
WE'RE... FLYING!
AH, HEY... THE NOVELTY WEARS OFF.
NOT!
AAAAAAAA--
GOBBER?
NNN-NO PROBLEM. YER DADDY AN' ME ARE JUST WORKING OUT OUR ISSUES. RE-BONDING, YOU MIGHT SAY.

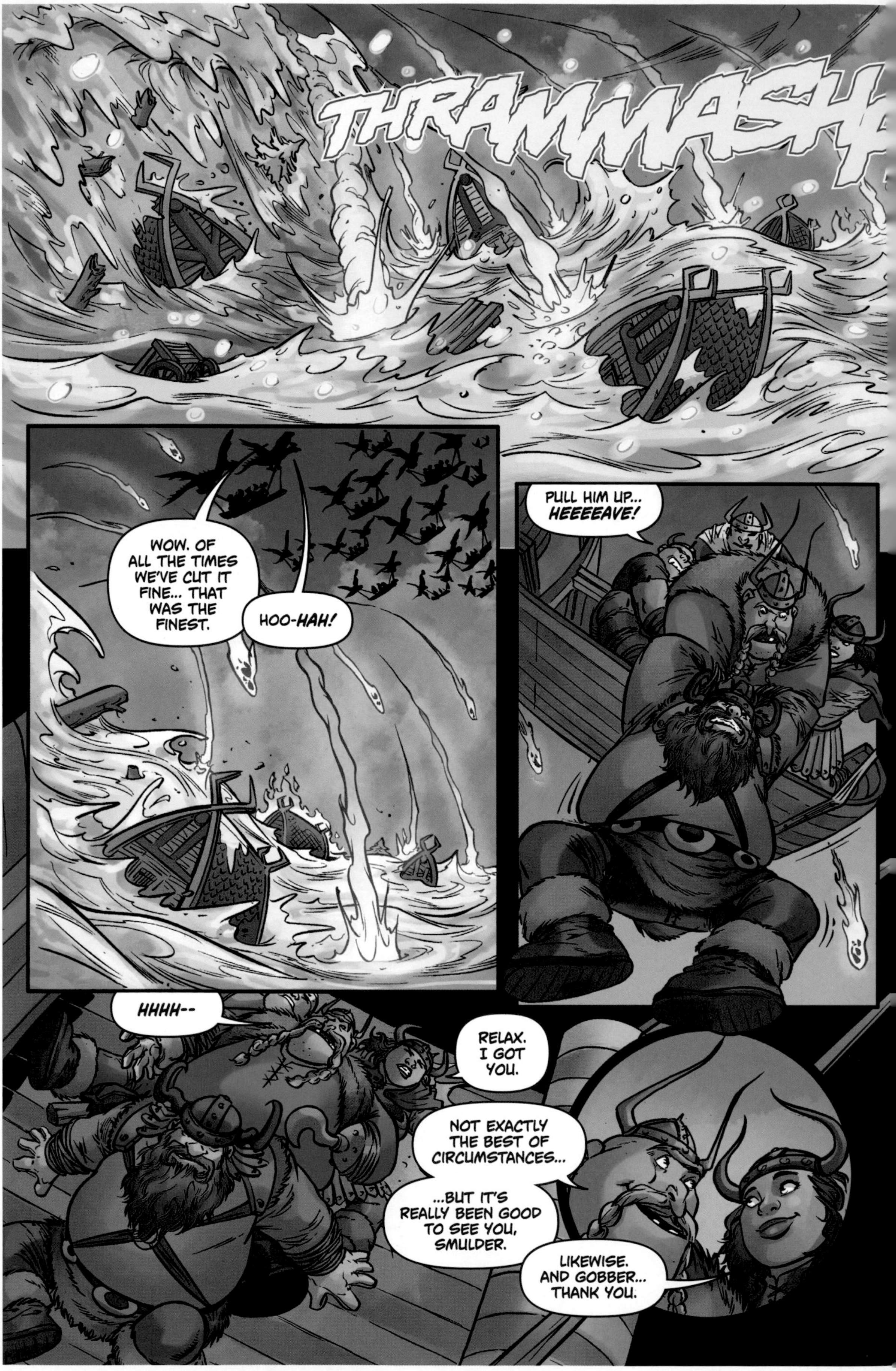
THRAMMASH
WOW. OF ALL THE TIMES WE'VE CUT IT FINE... THAT WAS THE FINEST.
HOO-HAH!
PULL HIM UP... HEEEEAVE!
HHHH--
RELAX. I GOT YOU.
NOT EXACTLY THE BEST OF CIRCUMSTANCES...
...BUT IT'S REALLY BEEN GOOD TO SEE YOU, SMULDER.
LIKEWISE. AND GOBBER... THANK YOU.

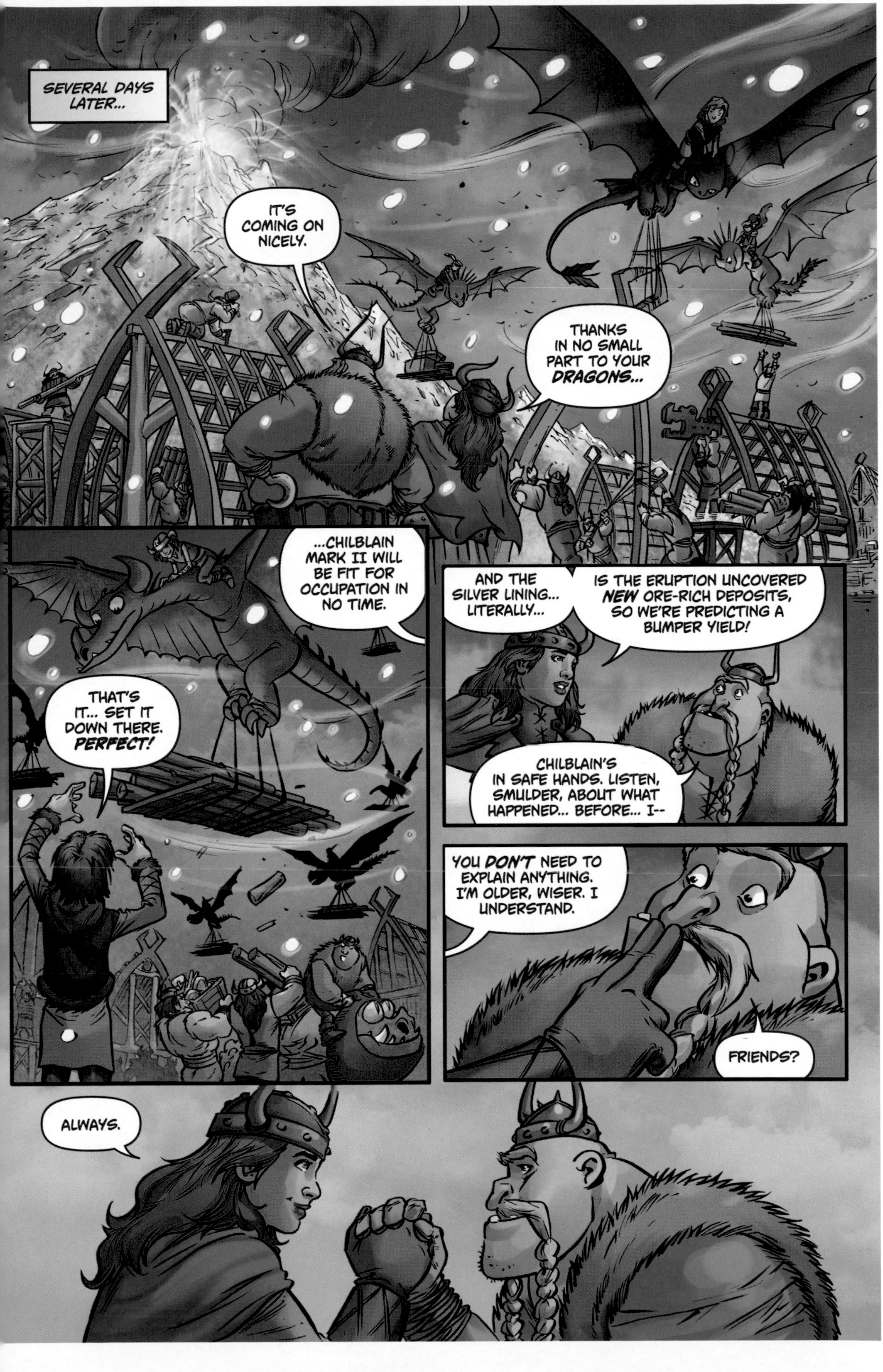
SEVERAL DAYS LATER...
IT'S COMING ON NICELY.
THANKS IN NO SMALL PART TO YOUR DRAGONS...
...CHILBLAIN MARK II WILL BE FIT FOR OCCUPATION IN NO TIME.
THAT'S IT... SET IT DOWN THERE. PERFECT!
AND THE SILVER LINING... LITERALLY...
IS THE ERUPTION UNCOVERED NEW ORE-RICH DEPOSITS, SO WE'RE PREDICTING A BUMPER YIELD!
CHILBLAIN'S IN SAFE HANDS. LISTEN, SMULDER, ABOUT WHAT HAPPENED... BEFORE... I--
YOU DON'T NEED TO EXPLAIN ANYTHING. I'M OLDER, WISER. I UNDERSTAND.
FRIENDS?
ALWAYS.

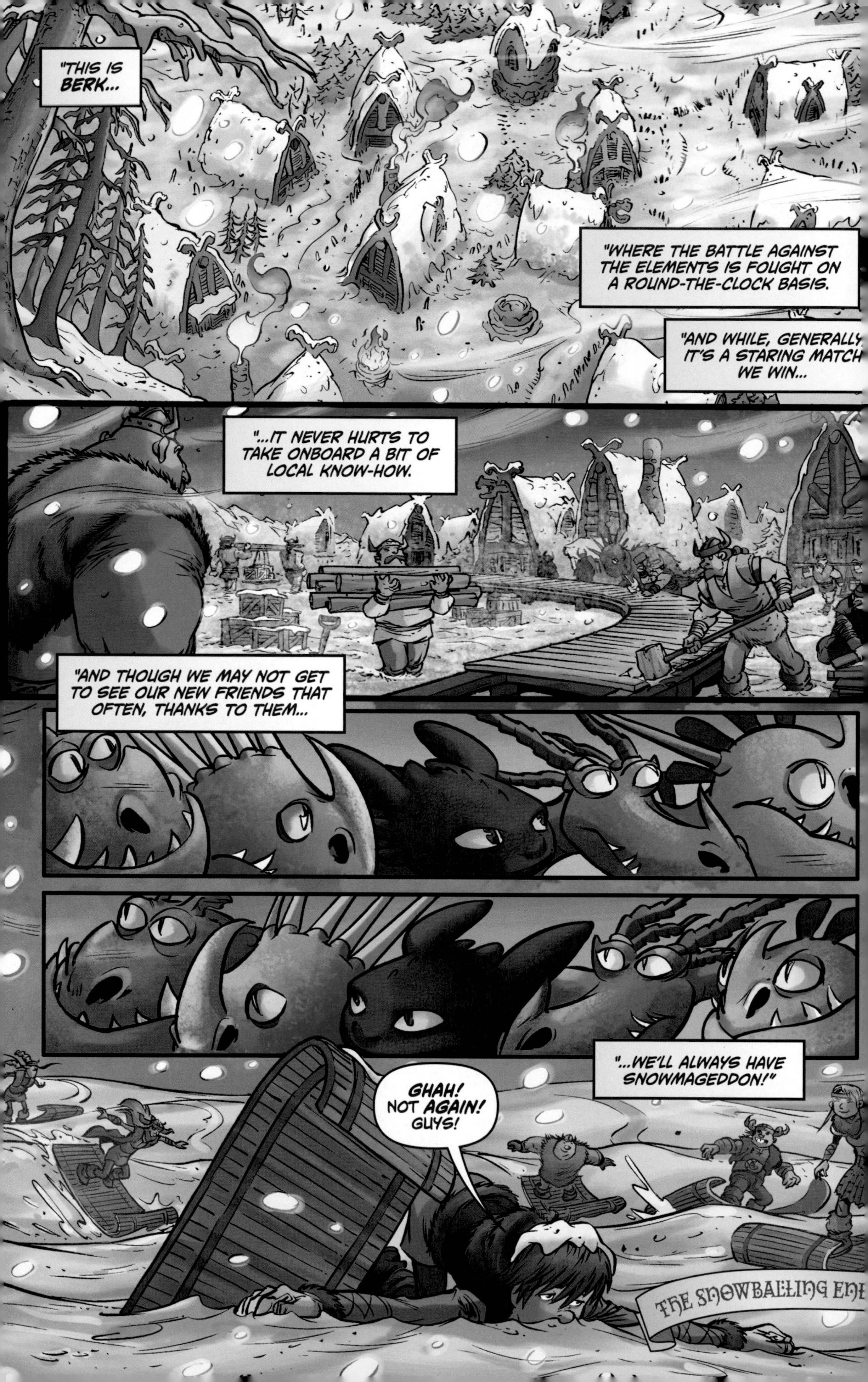
"THIS IS BERK...
"WHERE THE BATTLE AGAINST THE ELEMENTS IS FOUGHT ON A ROUND-THE-CLOCK BASIS.
"AND WHILE, GENERALLY, IT'S A STARING MATCH WE WIN...
"...IT NEVER HURTS TO TAKE ONBOARD A BIT OF LOCAL KNOW-HOW.
"AND THOUGH WE MAY NOT GET TO SEE OUR NEW FRIENDS THAT OFTEN, THANKS TO THEM...
"...WE'LL ALWAYS HAVE SNOWMAGEDDON!"
GHAH! NOT AGAIN! GUYS!
THE SNOWBALLING END

THAW FLEET

SCRIPT
SIMON FURMAN

ART
JACK LAWRENCE

COLORS
DIGIKORE

LETTERING
JIM CAMPBELL

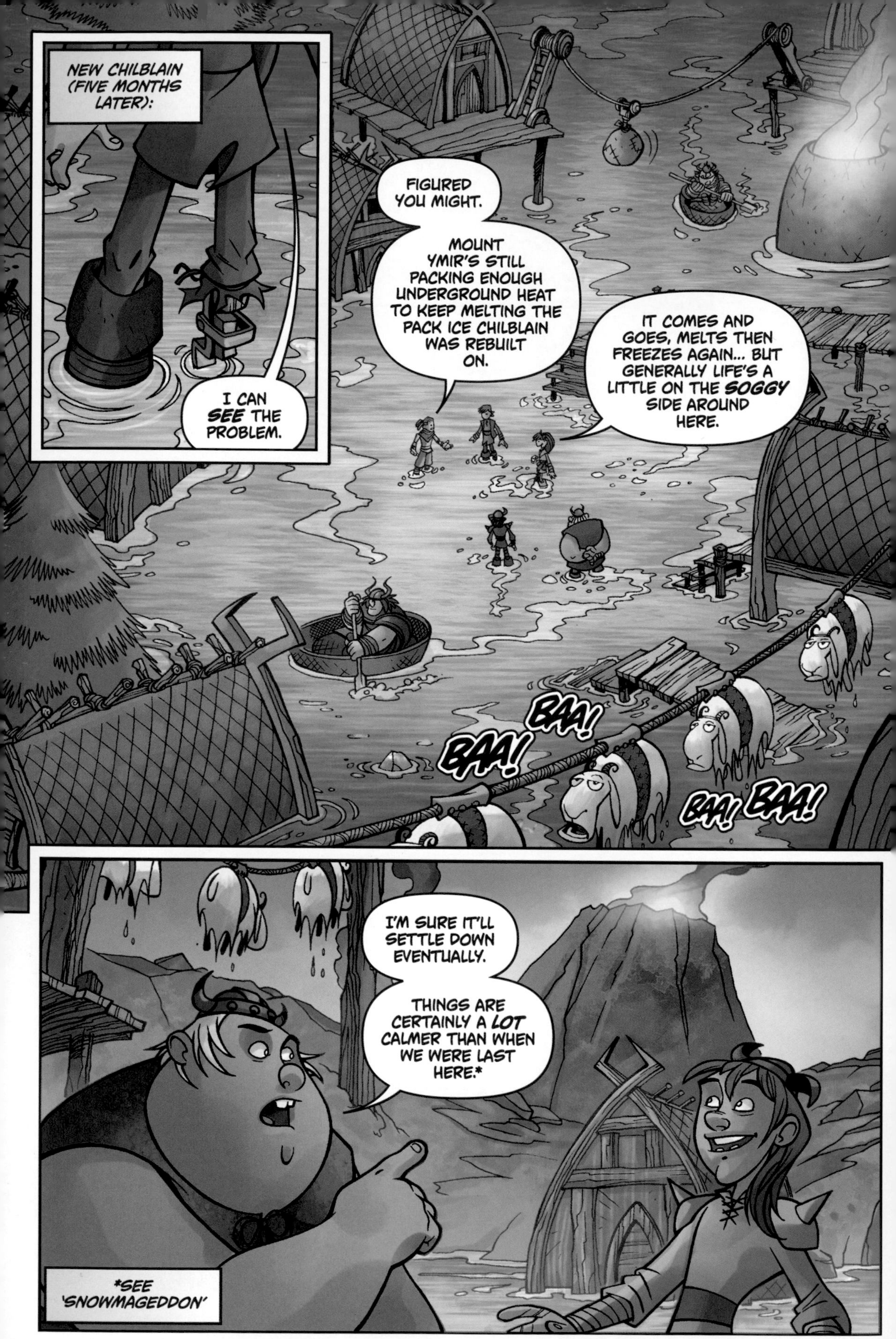
NEW CHILBLAIN (FIVE MONTHS LATER):
I CAN SEE THE PROBLEM.
FIGURED YOU MIGHT.
MOUNT YMIR'S STILL PACKING ENOUGH UNDERGROUND HEAT TO KEEP MELTING THE PACK ICE CHILBLAIN WAS REBUILT ON.
IT COMES AND GOES, MELTS THEN FREEZES AGAIN... BUT GENERALLY LIFE'S A LITTLE ON THE SOGGY SIDE AROUND HERE.
BAA!
BAA!
BAA! BAA!
I'M SURE IT'LL SETTLE DOWN EVENTUALLY.
THINGS ARE CERTAINLY A LOT CALMER THAN WHEN WE WERE LAST HERE.*
*SEE 'SNOWMAGEDDON'

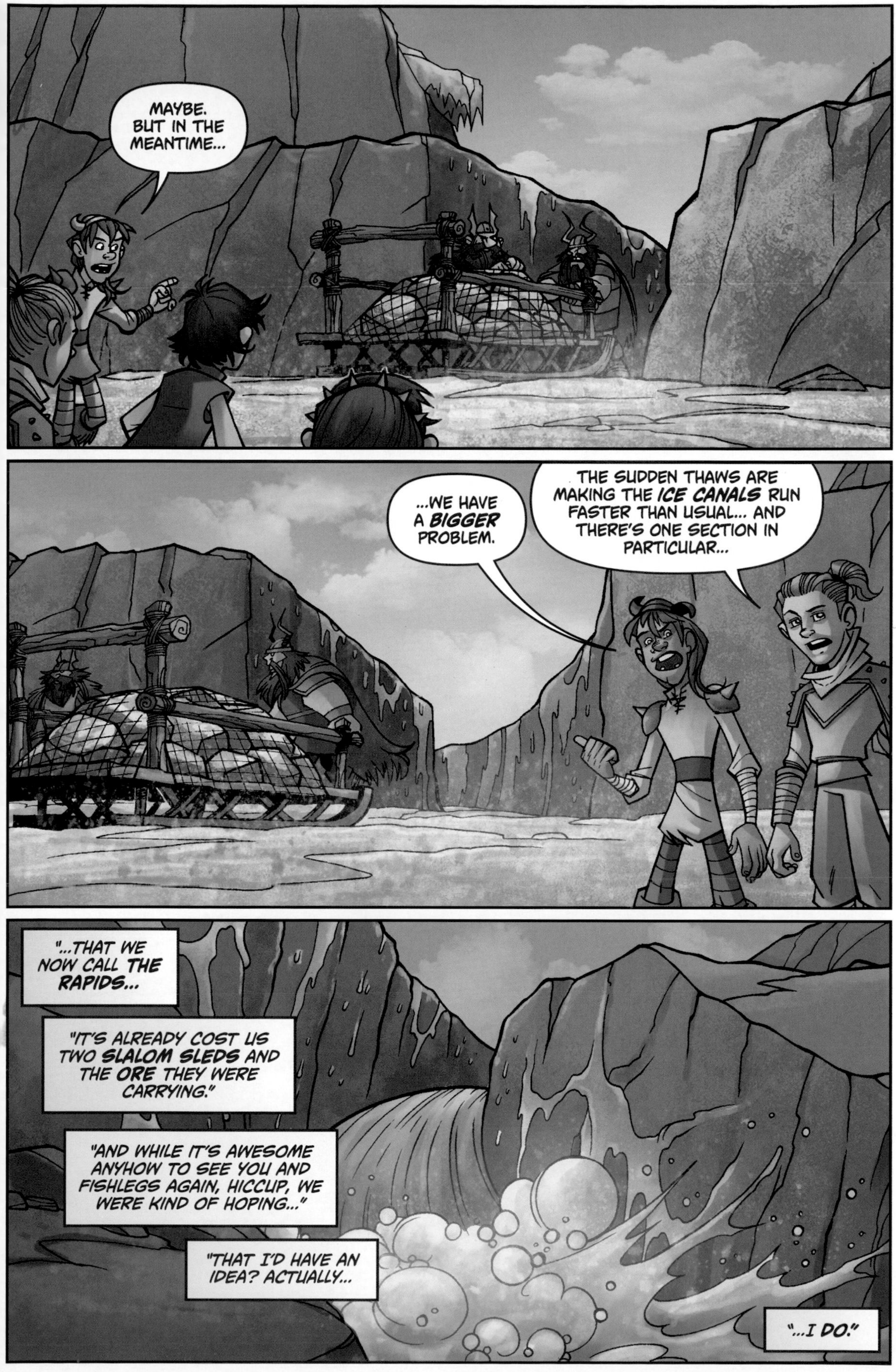
MAYBE. BUT IN THE MEANTIME...
...WE HAVE A BIGGER PROBLEM.
THE SUDDEN THAWS ARE MAKING THE ICE CANALS RUN FASTER THAN USUAL... AND THERE'S ONE SECTION IN PARTICULAR...
"...THAT WE NOW CALL THE RAPIDS...
"IT'S ALREADY COST US TWO SLALOM SLEDS AND THE ORE THEY WERE CARRYING."
"AND WHILE IT'S AWESOME ANYHOW TO SEE YOU AND FISHLEGS AGAIN, HICCUP, WE WERE KIND OF HOPING..."
"THAT I'D HAVE AN IDEA? ACTUALLY...
"...I DO."

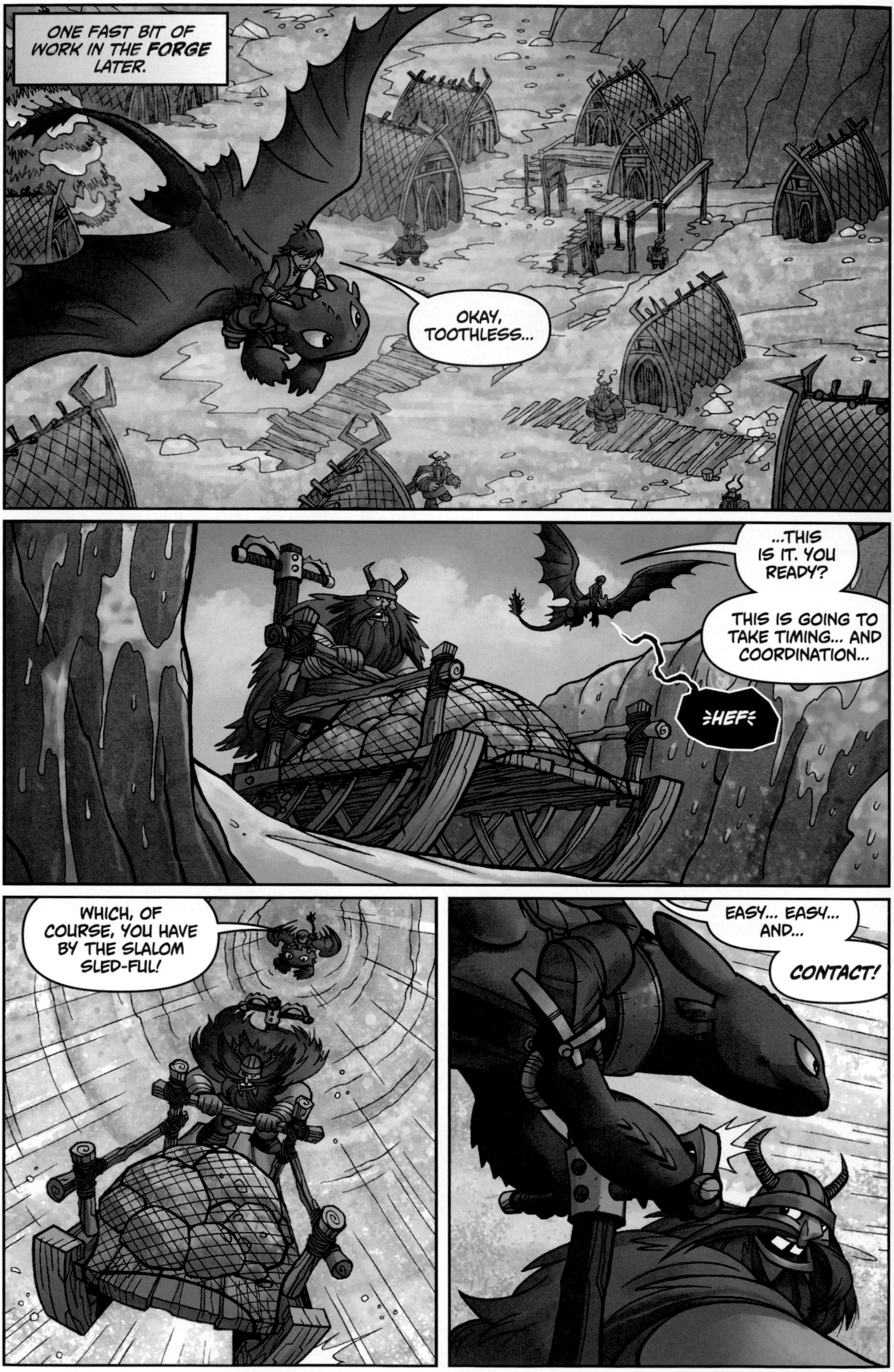
ONE FAST BIT OF WORK IN THE FORGE LATER.
OKAY, TOOTHLESS...
...THIS IS IT. YOU READY?
THIS IS GOING TO TAKE TIMING... AND COORDINATION...
HEF
WHICH, OF COURSE, YOU HAVE BY THE SLALOM SLED-FUL!
EASY... EASY... AND...
CONTACT!

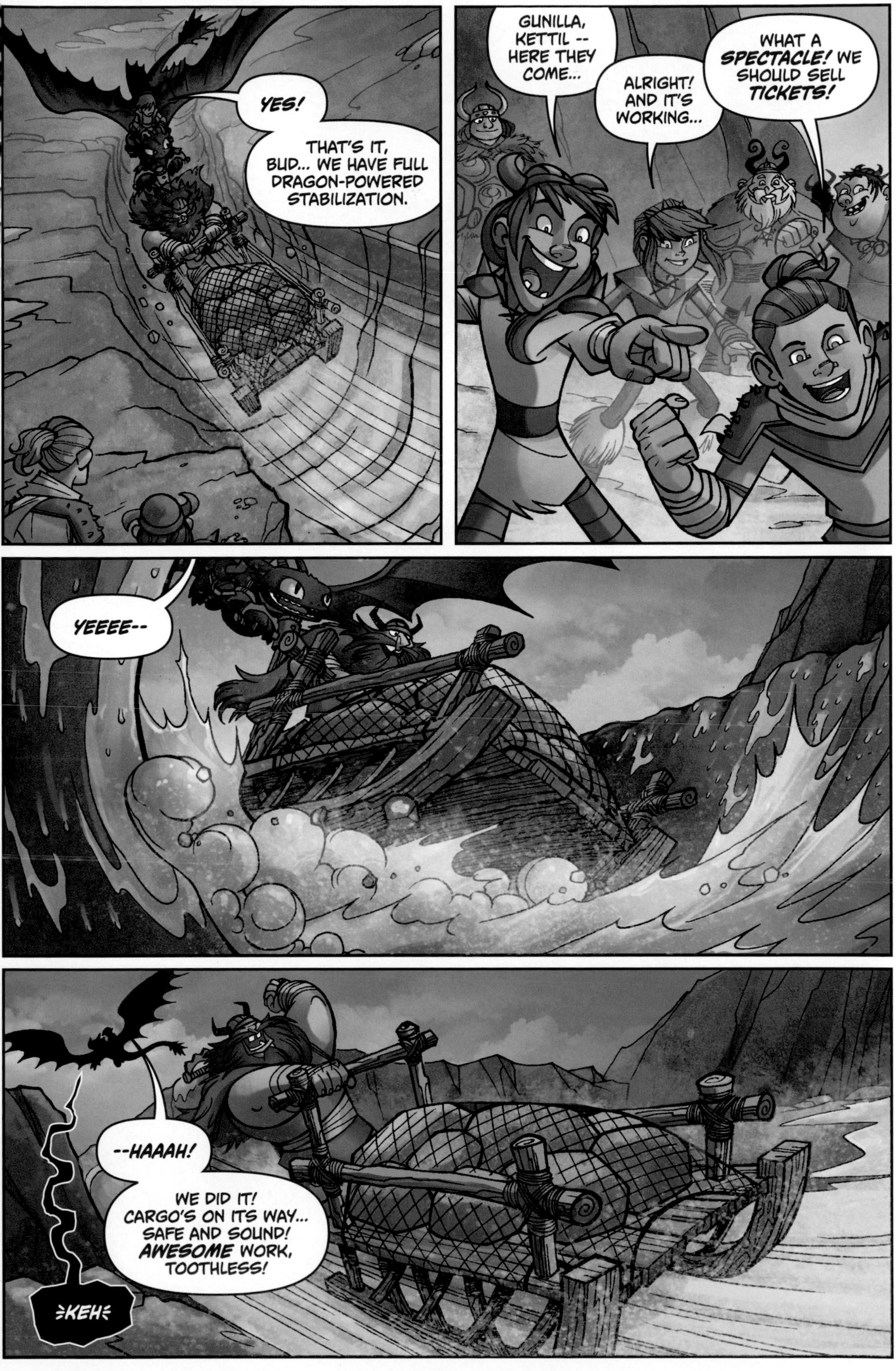
YES!
THAT'S IT, BUD... WE HAVE FULL DRAGON-POWERED STABILIZATION.
GUNILLA, KETTIL -- HERE THEY COME...
ALRIGHT! AND IT'S WORKING...
WHAT A SPECTACLE! WE SHOULD SELL TICKETS!
YEEEE--
--HAAAH!
WE DID IT! CARGO'S ON ITS WAY... SAFE AND SOUND! AWESOME WORK, TOOTHLESS!
KEH

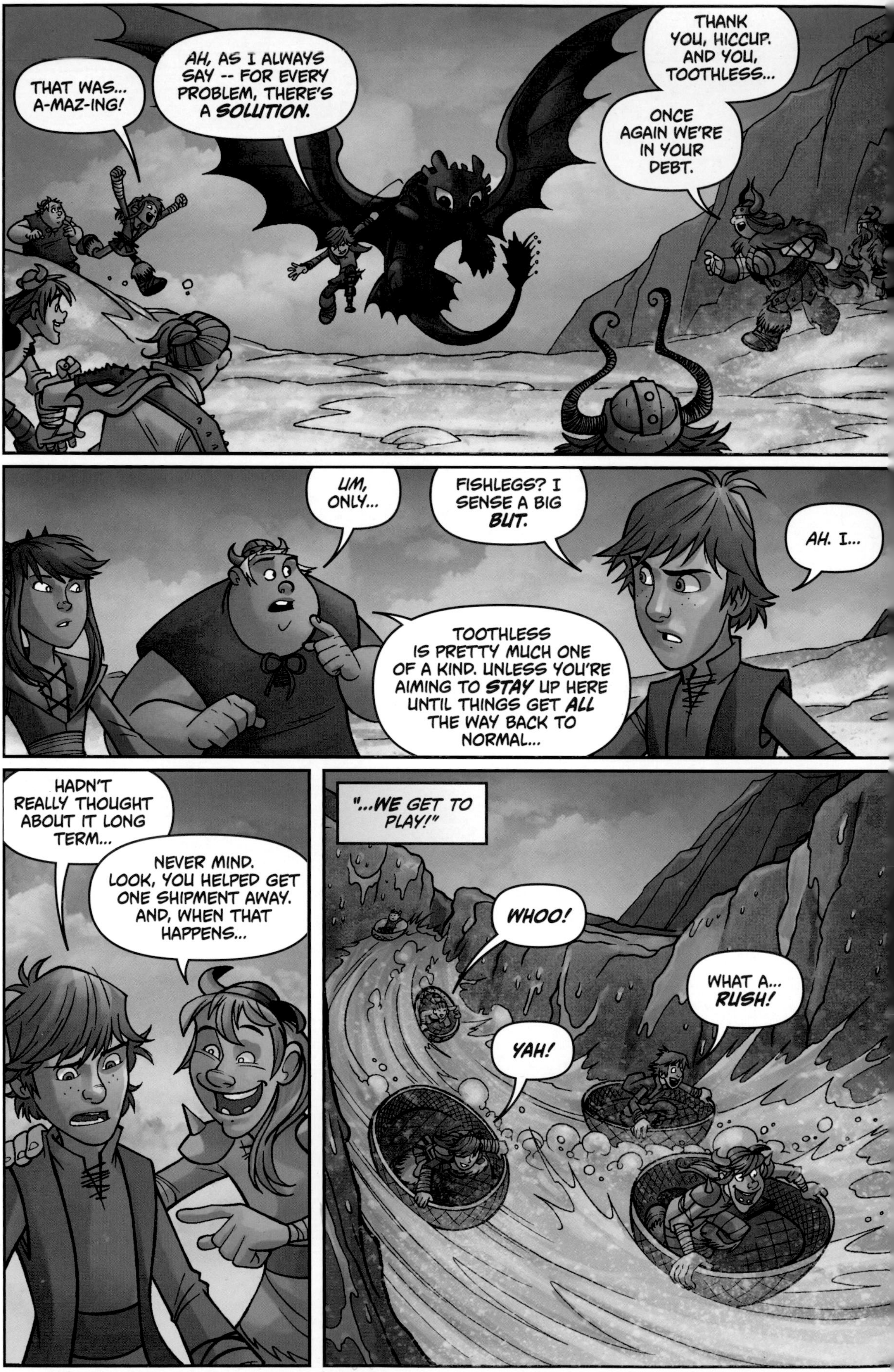
THAT WAS... A-MAZ-ING!
AH, AS I ALWAYS SAY -- FOR EVERY PROBLEM, THERE'S A SOLUTION.
THANK YOU, HICCUP. AND YOU, TOOTHLESS...
ONCE AGAIN WE'RE IN YOUR DEBT.
UM, ONLY...
FISHLEGS? I SENSE A BIG BUT.
TOOTHLESS IS PRETTY MUCH ONE OF A KIND. UNLESS YOU'RE AIMING TO STAY UP HERE UNTIL THINGS GET ALL THE WAY BACK TO NORMAL...
AH. I...
HADN'T REALLY THOUGHT ABOUT IT LONG TERM...
NEVER MIND. LOOK, YOU HELPED GET ONE SHIPMENT AWAY. AND, WHEN THAT HAPPENS...
"...WE GET TO PLAY!"
WHOO!
WHAT A... RUSH!
YAH!

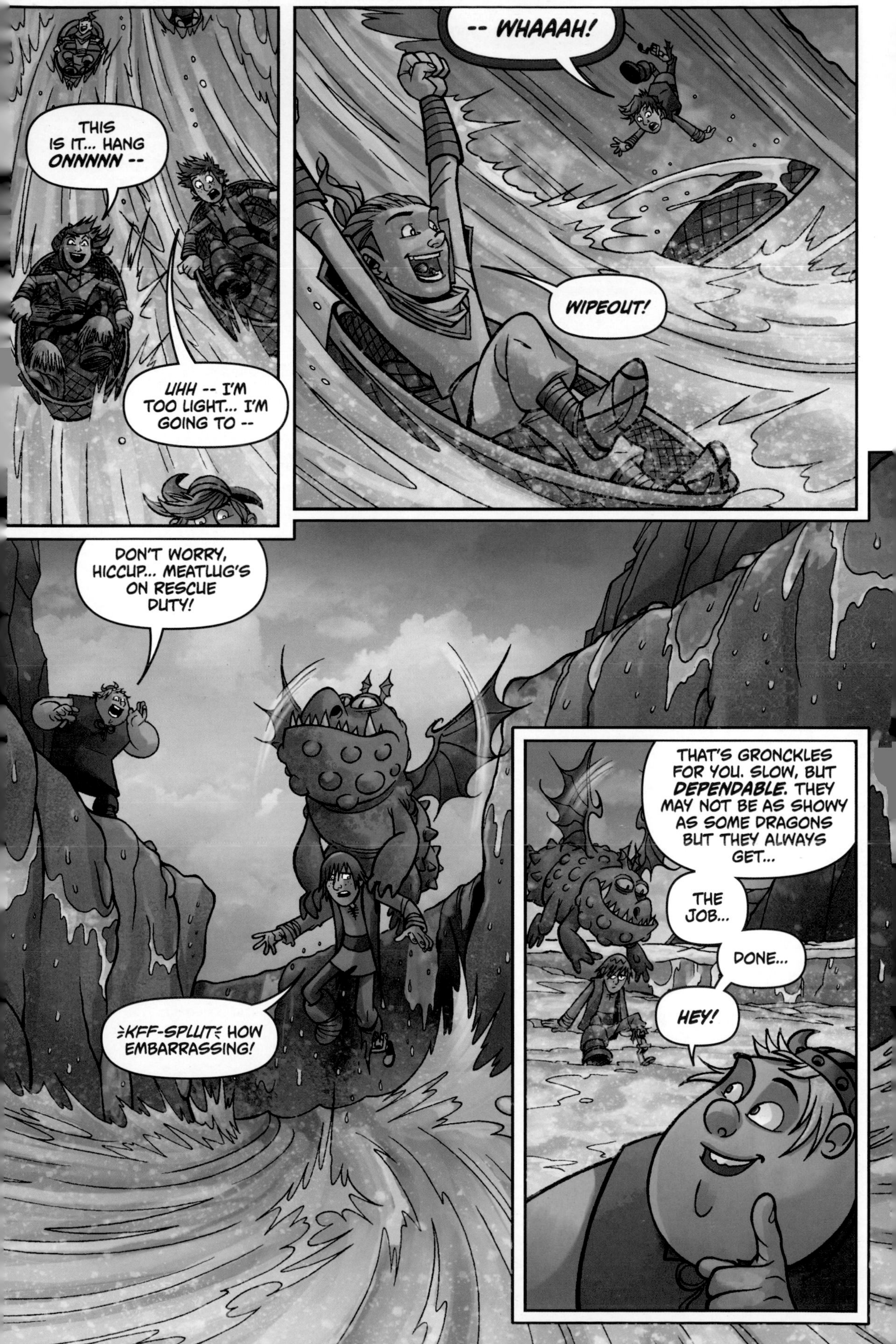
THIS IS IT... HANG ONNNNN --
UHH -- I'M TOO LIGHT... I'M GOING TO --
-- WHAAAH!
WIPEOUT!
DON'T WORRY, HICCUP... MEATLUG'S ON RESCUE DUTY!
≡KFF-SPLUT≡ HOW EMBARRASSING!
THAT'S GRONCKLES FOR YOU. SLOW, BUT DEPENDABLE. THEY MAY NOT BE AS SHOWY AS SOME DRAGONS BUT THEY ALWAYS GET...
THE JOB...
DONE...
HEY!

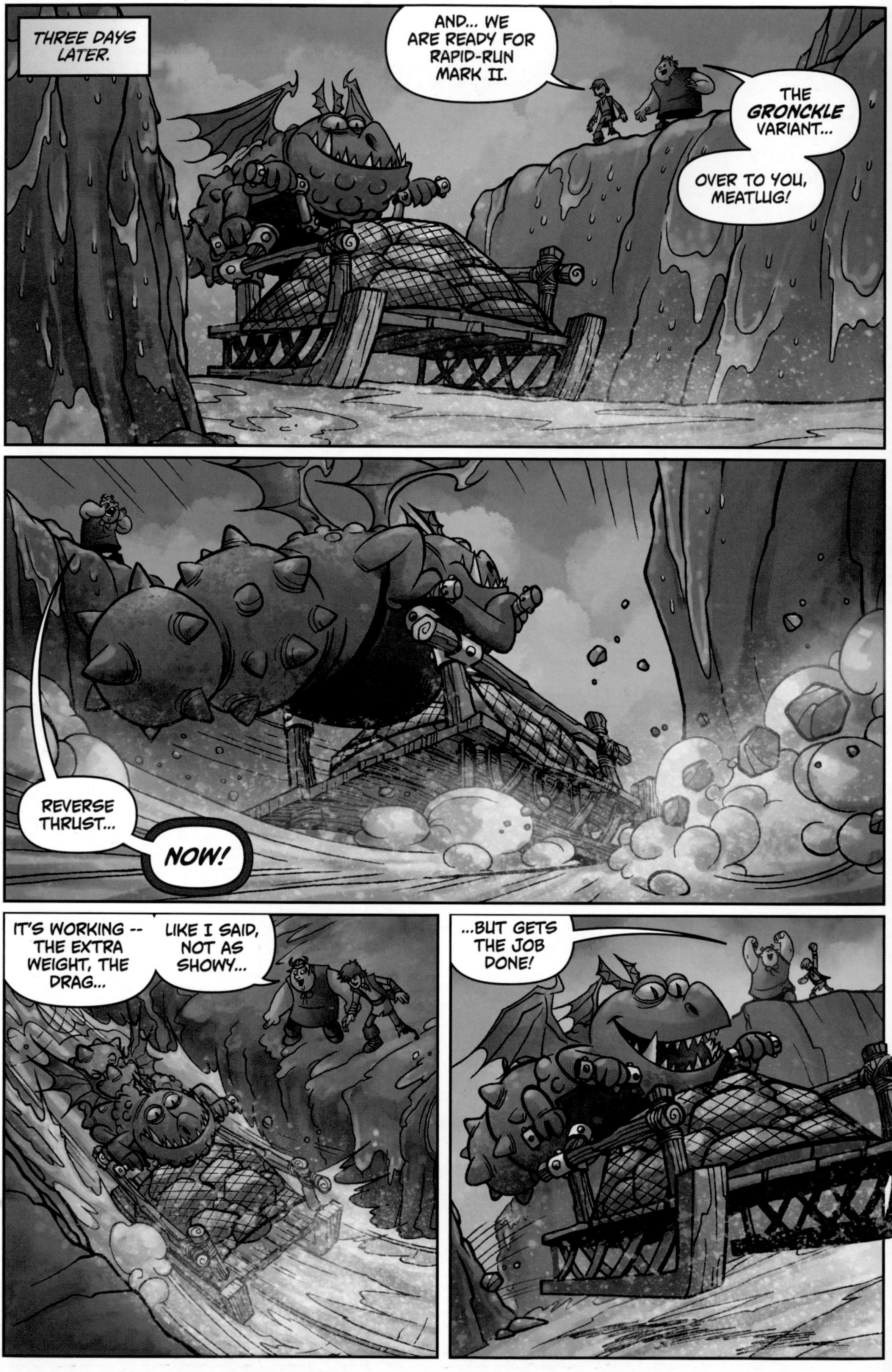
THREE DAYS LATER.
AND... WE ARE READY FOR RAPID-RUN MARK II.
THE GRONCKLE VARIANT...
OVER TO YOU, MEATLUG!
REVERSE THRUST...
NOW!
IT'S WORKING -- THE EXTRA WEIGHT, THE DRAG...
LIKE I SAID, NOT AS SHOWY...
...BUT GETS THE JOB DONE!

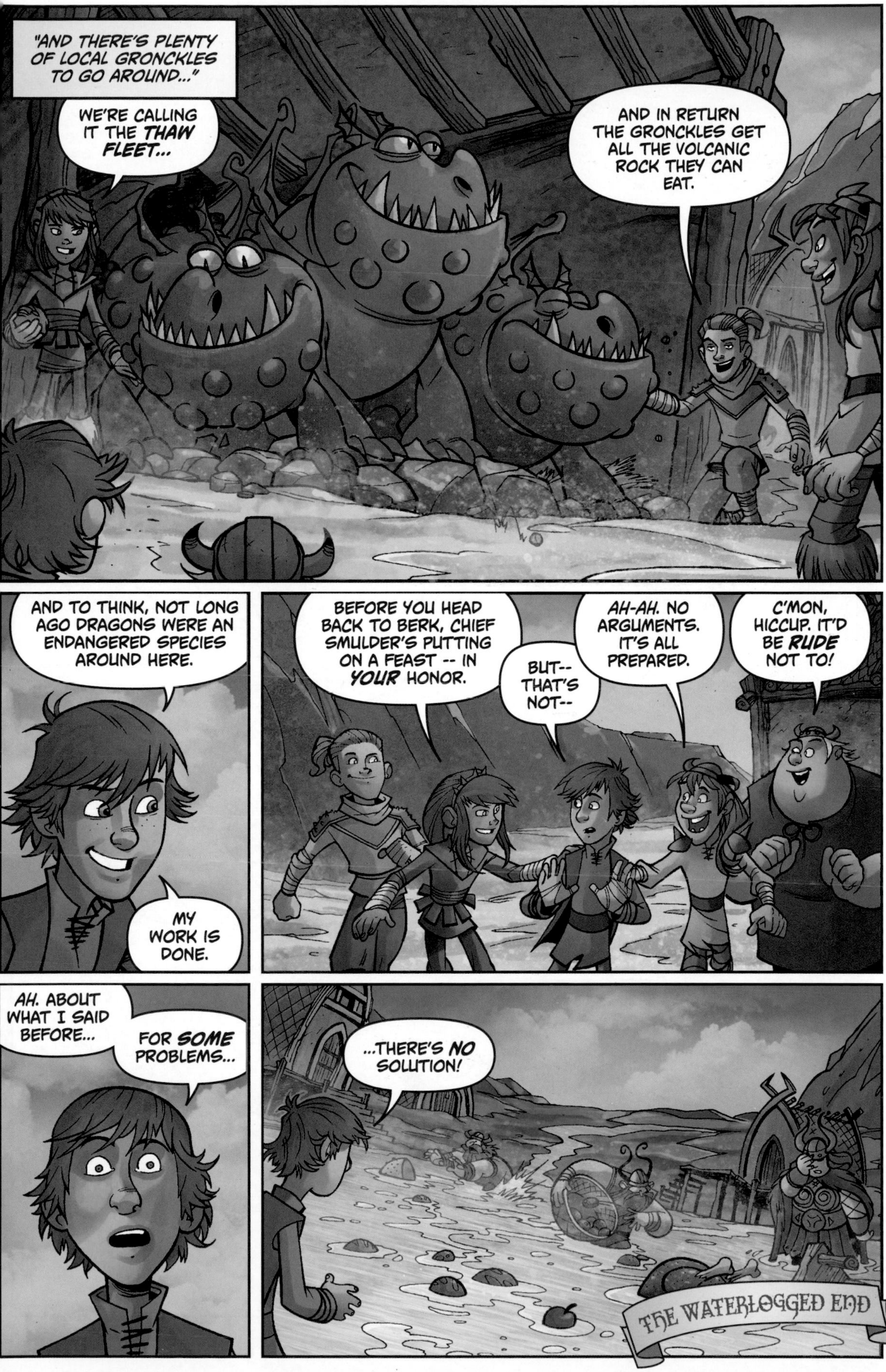
"AND THERE'S PLENTY OF LOCAL GRONCKLES TO GO AROUND..."
WE'RE CALLING IT THE *THAW FLEET*...
AND IN RETURN THE GRONCKLES GET ALL THE VOLCANIC ROCK THEY CAN EAT.
AND TO THINK, NOT LONG AGO DRAGONS WERE AN ENDANGERED SPECIES AROUND HERE.
MY WORK IS DONE.
BEFORE YOU HEAD BACK TO BERK, CHIEF SMULDER'S PUTTING ON A FEAST -- IN *YOUR* HONOR.
BUT-- THAT'S NOT--
AH-AH. NO ARGUMENTS. IT'S ALL PREPARED.
C'MON, HICCUP. IT'D BE *RUDE* NOT TO!
AH. ABOUT WHAT I SAID BEFORE...
FOR *SOME* PROBLEMS...
...THERE'S *NO* SOLUTION!
THE WATERLOGGED END

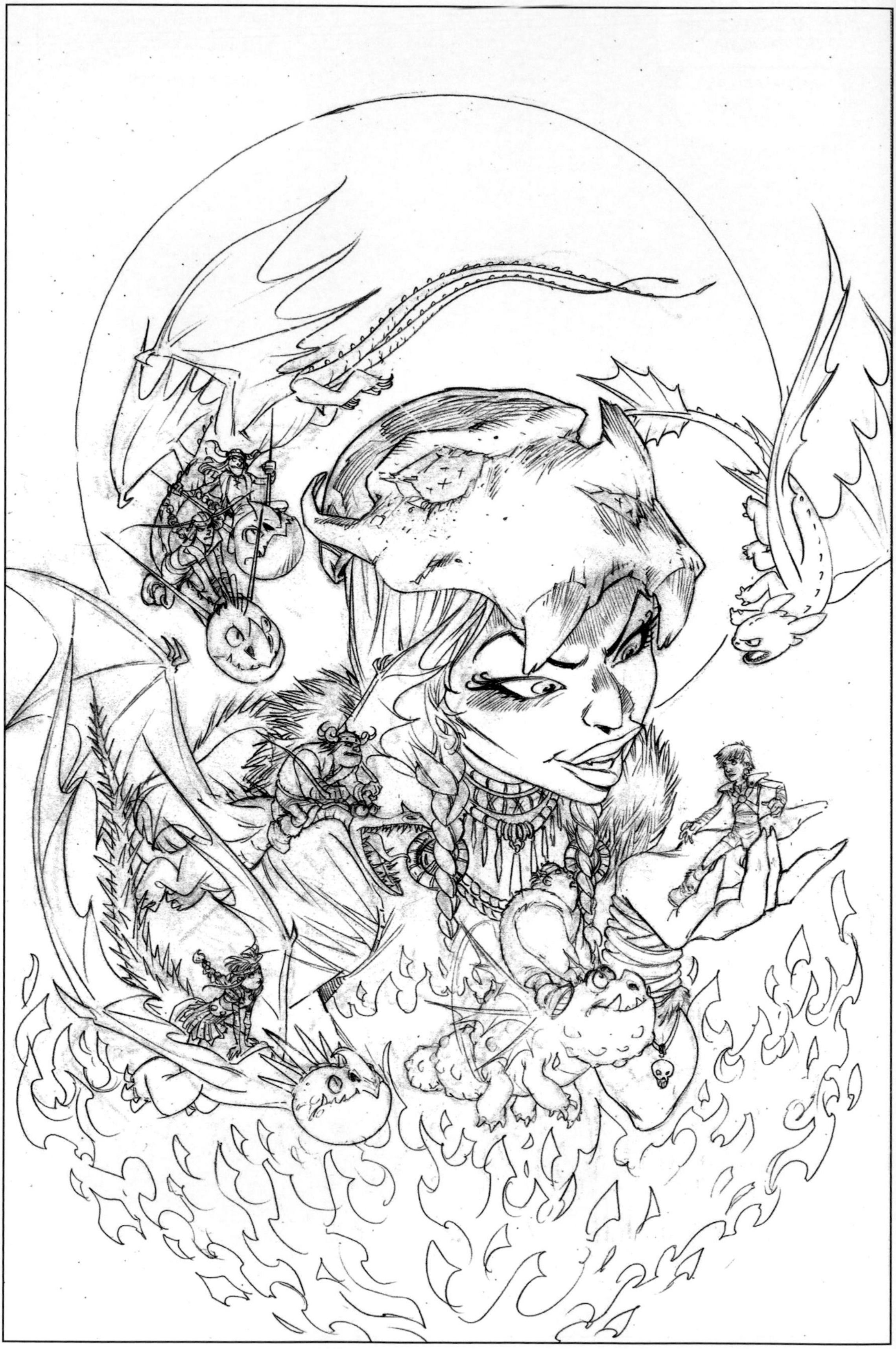

Original pencils for *The Endless Night*'s cover

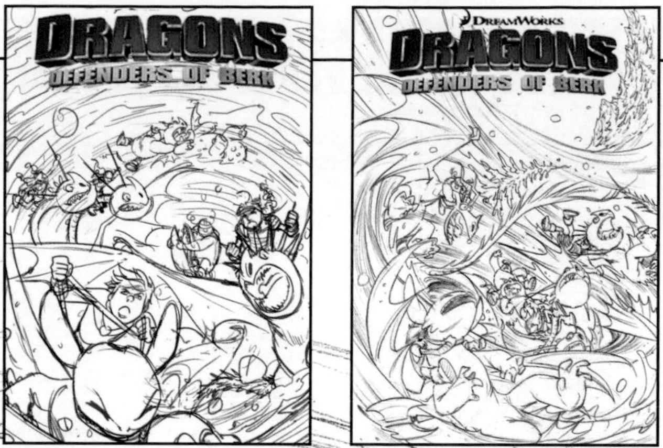
DRAGONS
DEFENDERS OF BERK
DreamWorks
DRAGONS
DEFENDERS OF BERK

Early ideas for the *Snowmageddon* cover
by artist Iwan Nazif

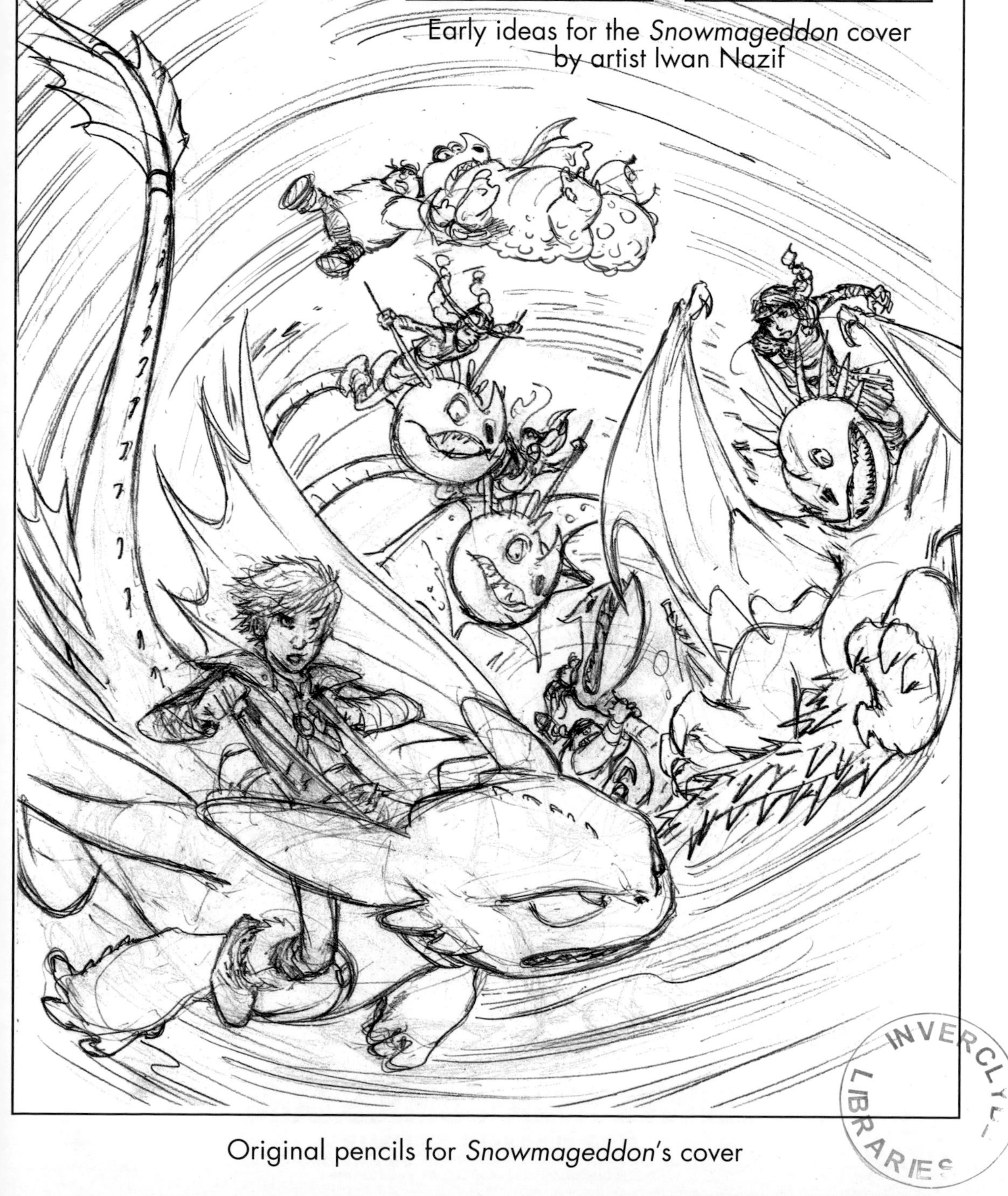

Original pencils for *Snowmageddon*'s cover

TITAN COMICS GRAPHIC NOVELS

DREAMWORKS HOME: HOME SWEET HOME

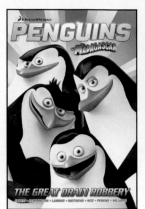

PENGUINS OF MADAGASCAR:
THE GREAT DRAIN ROBBERY

PENGUINS OF MADAGASCAR:
THE ELITE-EST OF THE ELITE

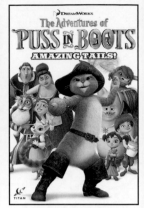

THE ADVENTURES OF PUSS IN BOOTS:
AMAZING TAILS

KUNG FU PANDA:
READY, SET, PO!

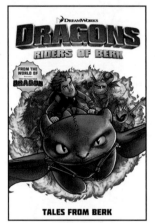

DREAMWORKS DRAGONS:
RIDERS OF BERK – TALES FROM BERK

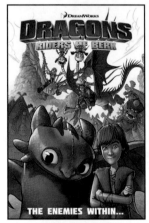

DREAMWORKS DRAGONS:
RIDERS OF BERK – THE ENEMIES WITHIN

DREAMWORKS DRAGONS: RIDERS OF BERK
COLLECTORS EDITION

DREAMWORKS DRAGONS:
MYTHS AND MYSTERIES

DREAMWORKS DRAGONS:
DEFENDERS OF BERK - ICE AND FIRE

WWW.TITAN-COMICS.COM
ALSO AVAILABLE DIGITALLY

© 2016 DreamWorks Animation LLC. All Rights Reserved

BRAND NEW FROM TITAN COMICS

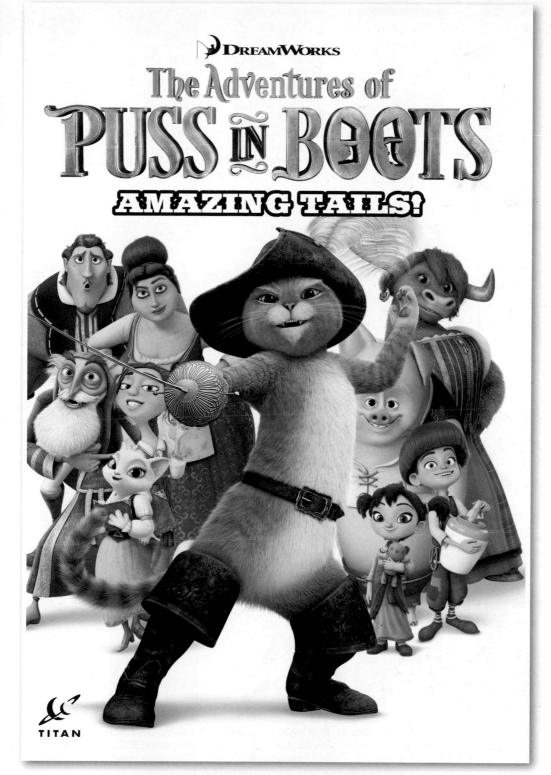

ALSO AVAILABLE DIGITALLY.

WWW.TITAN-COMICS.COM

The Adventures of Puss in Boots © 2016 DreamWorks Animation LLC. All Rights Reserved.

TITAN COMICS DIGESTS

SHREK & MADAGASCAR
HIDE & SEEK
Dreamworks Classics – 'Hide & Seek'

SHREK & KUNG FU PANDA
CONSEQUENCES
Dreamworks Classics – 'Consequences'

SHREK & MADAGASCAR
GAME ON
Dreamworks Classics – 'Game On'

HOME
Dreamworks Home – Hide & Seek & Oh

HOME
Dreamworks Home – Another Home

KUNG FU PANDA
DAZE OF THUNDER
Kung Fu Panda – Daze of Thunder

KUNG FU PANDA
SLEEP-FIGHTING
Kung Fu Panda – Sleep-Fighting

PENGUINS
WHEN IN ROME...
Penguins of Madagascar – When in Rome...

PENGUINS
OPERATION: HEIST
Penguins of Madagascar – Operation: Heist

PENGUINS
PENGUINS IN PERIL!
Penguins of Madagascar – Penguins in Peril

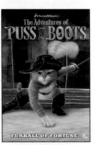

PENGUINS
SECRET PAWS
Penguins of Madagascar – Secret Paws

The Adventures of PUSS IN BOOTS
FURBALL OF FORTUNE
The Adventures of Puss In Boots – Furball of Fortune

DRAGONS RIDERS OF BERK
DRAGON DOWN
DreamWorks Dragons: Riders of Berk – Dragon Down

DRAGONS RIDERS OF BERK
DANGERS OF THE DEEP
DreamWorks Dragons: Riders of Berk – Dangers of the Deep

DRAGONS RIDERS OF BERK
THE ICE CASTLE
DreamWorks Dragons: Riders of Berk – The Ice Castle

DRAGONS RIDERS OF BERK
THE STOWAWAY
DreamWorks Dragons: Riders of Berk – The Stowaway

DRAGONS RIDERS OF BERK
THE LEGEND OF RAGNAROK
DreamWorks Dragons: Riders of Berk – The Legend of Ragnarok

DRAGONS RIDERS OF BERK
UNDERWORLD
DreamWorks Dragons: Riders of Berk – Underworld

DRAGONS DEFENDERS OF BERK
THE ENDLESS NIGHT
DreamWorks Dragons: Defenders of Berk – The Endless Night

DRAGONS DEFENDERS OF BERK
SNOWMAGEDDON
DreamWorks Dragons: Defenders of Berk – Snowmageddon

WWW.TITAN-COMICS.COM

ALSO AVAILABLE DIGITALLY

TITAN COMICS

DREAMWORKS ANIMATION SKG